Expanded Science Fiction Worlds of

Forrest J Ackerman
& Friends PLUS

Dedicated

with eternal gratitude
that they lived

to the memories of

HUGO GERNSBACK
Father of Science Fiction

BORIS KARLOFF
Father Christmas
of
Karloffilms

World Figures
&
Personal Heroes

Illustration by C. L. Moore for "Nyusa, Nymph of Darkness" (page 95).

Expanded Science Fiction Worlds of

Forrest J Ackerman
& Friends PLUS

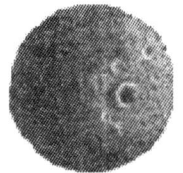

Sense of Wonder Press
JAMES A. ROCK & COMPANY, PUBLISHERS
ROCKVILLE • MARYLAND

The Expanded Science Fiction Worlds of Forrest J Ackerman and Friends PLUS
All stories selected and with notes by Forrest J Ackerman
Introduction by Forrest J Ackerman

is an imprint of *JAMES A. ROCK & CO., PUBLISHERS*

Address comments and inquiries to:
SENSE OF WONDER PRESS
James A. Rock & Company, Publishers, 113 N. Washington Street, Box 347
Rockville, MD 20850
E-mail:
jrock@rockpublishing.com   lrock@senseofwonderpress.com
Internet URL: www.SenseOfWonderPress.com
Paperbound ISBN: 0-918736-26-9
Printed in the United States of America
First Sense of Wonder Press Edition: March 2002

Cover art for this edition is from an original drawing by Neil Austin illustrating the short
story"Dhactwhu!—Remember" from the private collection of Forrest J Ackerman.

"Dwellers in the Dust", Forrest J Ackerman
"Micro-Man", by Forrest J Ackerman
"A Martian Oddity", by Forrest J Ackerman
"Confessions of a Science Fiction Addict", by Forrest J Ackerman
"The Big Sleep", by Forrest J Ackerman
"Metropolis Über Alles", by Forrest J Ackerman
"Born Witch, Burn!", by Forrest J Ackerman
"And Then the Cover Was Bare", by Forrest J Ackerman
"The Lure & Lore of 'The Blind Spot'", by Forrest J Ackerman
"Task of the Temponaut", by Norbert F. Novotny & Van Del Rio
"Yvala", by C. L. Moore and Amaryllis Ackerman
"The Cosmic Kidnappers", by Christian Vallini & S. F. Balboa
"The Girl Who Wasn't There", by Tigrina
"The Atomic Monument", Forrest J Ackerman with Theodore Sturgeon
"Nyusa", Nymph of Darkness", by Catherine L. Moore and Forrest J Ackerman
"Time To Change or Mirror Image", by Marcial Souto with Forrest J Ackerman
"Great Gog's Grave", by Forrest J Ackerman and Donald A. Wollheim
"Naughty Venusienne", by Spencer Strong and Morgan Ives
"The Time Twister", by Francis Flagg and Weaver Wright
"Dhactwhu!—Remember?", Robert A.W. Lowndes in collaboration with Forrest J Ackerman
"Tarzan and the Golden Loin", by Forrest J Ackerman
"Time of the Medusa", Forrest J Ackerman with Charles Neutzel
"Count Down to Doom", Forrest J Ackerman with Charles Nuetzel
"The Far-Out Philosopher of Science Fiction", by Forrest J Ackerman with Tigrina
"The Lady Takes A Powder", by Tigrina as told to Karlon Torgosi
"Laugh", Clone", Laugh", by Forrest J Ackerman with A. E. Van Vogt
"When Frighthood Was in Flower . . .", by Forrest J Ackerman
"The Record", Forrest J Ackerman
"The Man Who Was Thirsty", by Forrest J Ackerman
"The Radclyffe Effect", by Forrest J Ackerman
"Letter to an Angel", by Forrest J Ackerman

Contents

Contents

Contents

Introduction

The original edition of THIS VOLUME WOULD HAVE BEEN a different book had Boris Karloff not died when he did.

I had allotted myself about 10 days to meet the deadline for the preparation of this collection. I had two half-completed collaborations—"A Myth Is as Good as A Mile", with Robert Bloch, and "Laugh, Clone, Laugh" with AE van Vogt.

Then the dark tragedy struck: the world lost its favorite Frankenstein.

By that night I was deluged with requests for Karloff material. Among other triviata I had to accept the challenge of producing a 60,000-word Memorial about Boris Karloff . . . in 10 days!

The 10 days that were to be devoted to the production of this book have been decimated as though by starved ants from a disadvantaged formicary. My hours have been attacked like chopped liver at the mercy of a school of piranhas with tapeworms. Thus works the fiend of a thousand projects—one being the special Karloff Famous Monsters issue.

In other words my time has been so curtailed for this particular project that I'm clockeyed from nightly watching the little hand crawl past midnight into the wee-small.

As I said in the original introduction: NOW IT CAN be told.

This book, with slightly different contents, of course, came close to being published way back in 1948. Twenty-one years ago, in hard covers. Groff Conklin's "The Best of Science Fiction" had recently appeared; my collection was to be known as THE BUST OF SCIENCE FICTION. An ad of the time reads:

The Pirate Press, publishers of "Brains for Janes", now brings you yak-yak by Ack-Ack, the man with brains he hasn't even used yet.

Fans long acquainted with Ackerman the dealer, Ackerman the collector, Ackerman the agent, will now be nonplussed as FJA emerges on the auctorial horizon with all the stature of a newborn midget. You'll be amazed at the paucity of his writing ability, the threadbare punoramas of his plots. You will gasp as, singlehandedly, he writes himself into unparalleled cull-des-hacks. You will cheer his consummate cliches, which are even older than the hills, and alone assure him an itch in the Hill of Fame.

Write down these titles before you forget them: "Starmageddon!", "A Walk in the Moon", "No Time Like the Future", "Pre-Hysteric" and others too un-mentionable to enumerate, all in one dispensable volume of FORRY STORIES.

Unautographed at no extra cost.

In that Introduction I said: I want to especially thank Nuetzel and Powell Publications for sticking their check out to package and produce this book and I hope they don't lose their shorts because I promised them this book would make $1 million. By the time they discover I lied I'll be safe in Transylvania, playing Bram's (Stoker, that is) Lullaby for Lycanthropes with the grok-&-growl combo known as The Children of the Night.

Which is neither hither, thither nor yither.

In 1969, I wrote: My Mother, Carroll Ackerman, has waited 43 years for this book, and now that I've produced it, I don't know whether I dare show it to her. Please advise. Would you let any mother of yours read a book like this? In fact, would you read a book like this?

See you at the bankruptcy proceedings.

FORREST J ACKERMAN
Box 35252 Preuss Station
Los Angeles, CA 90035
19 Feb 69

And now, in the 21st Century edition I share again the days when great writers let the Ackermonster into the writer's pen—or is it the writer's din—and they, perhaps, forever rude the day, and night too for that matter.

Back after more than 6 lustrums, *Forrest J Ackerman and Friends PLUS*, with 31 offerings from FJA and friends, including 7 new collaborations, all back in the light of day after having rested in humble obscurity these many years. Some of my solo efforts abide alongside collabs with the likes of A. E. van Vogt, Robert A. W. Lowndes, Charles Nuetzel, William F. Nolan, Marcial Souto, Tigrina, Norbert L. Novotny, Christian Vallini, Catherine L. Moore, Big Name Female In Hiding, Charles Fritch, Donald A. Wollheim, and Theodore Sturgeon. Golden friends from a golden age!

FJA
March 2002

Our Earth was a busy place the day the aliens came from outer space, yet they found us dead—or so they thought!

Illustration for "Earth's Lucky Day" from something or other by an artist..

Earth's Lucky Day

by Francis Flagg and Forrest J Ackerman

*F RANCIS FLAGG (George Henry Weiss) was a pioneering "scientifiction" au-
thor who was running out of ideas while I was overflowing with them but
didn't have the professional standing to make a sale so we hit on the collaborating through the mail. We never met. We had one thing in common: we both lost
brothers.*

*We sold two collaborations, "Earth's Lucky Day" and "THe", and had one pub-
lished in a fanmagazine, "The Hazy Hord". Roy A. Squires, a respected fan at the
time, praised "Lucky Day" as having one of the most unusual plots ever devised.*

IT WAS HALL BROWNING of Global News who coined the phrase, and
he lived and died without ever knowing how ironical it was. In America, and
even in the staid papers of London and Paris, it screamed from front-page
headlines; and in papers everywhere, in every civilized country throughout the
world (with the exception of those still under the sway of United Forces) it
topped melodramatic articles, even if in smaller type and on inside pages.

Earth's Lucky Day, Hall Browning wrote and telecast and millions mouthed
the phrase.

It was February 19, 1973, and the TV news dispatches and the tele-lino
writers scattered the tidings to the four corners of the compass immediately
following verification of the signal triumph of science, the glorious victory of
International Armies, and hours before the world knew of the strange disappearances.

The world was in a ferment on that February day—and night.

It was day in America. Outside the fence that hemmed in the super-power
plant and the huge stratosphere globe of glassite and steel, thousands of people
milled and watched. So great was the press that at one place the fence col-
lapsed and mounted police and soldiers had to drive back the crowd. Krell and
his co-worker and fellow scientist, Maxwell Dredd, busied themselves with last
minute details. Then they entered the huge globe their genius had devised and
the door was sealed. A million eyes watched the giant globe as it rose, and a

cry of awe and wonder burst forth. It was astounding to see such an immense man-made machine rise in the air as surely and swiftly as a rocket—but without visible evidence of propulsion.

"Lord," said a stout man, mopping his brow with a handkerchief, "what if the power were to fail!" And a girl said to her boyfriend, "Think of it; they're being lifted on—what do you call it?—an energy beam."

"Yeah," he said, "something like that. It's—it's stupendous."

The huge globe rose higher and higher, glinting in the sun, dazzling the eyes that watched, every moment dwindling in size, until it was a toy balloon, a plum, a marble, "I see it," yelled a small boy. "I do, I do! Just a speck." And people with opera glasses and binoculars focused them aloft; but soon the globe had lifted beyond even their power to visualize, and disappeared into the blue immensity of space, higher than man had ever risen before without rockets. Krell and Dredd looked at their instruments and then regarded each other in triumph. Dredd regulated the flow from the oxygen tanks. Both men looked through curved glassite windows at black, star-pricked space, so black, so vacuous-looking. The globe was stationary at its maximum altitude; the rod of energy could lift it no farther. In video communication with the power station so far beneath them, Krell answered anxious inquiries.

"O.K. so far. Both of us feel fine. The air somewhat close and heavy. Colder." He signed off and busied himself noting the figures of a half-hundred delicate instruments which registered atmospheric density, temperature outside the globe, and the action of cosmic rays. The powerful new-principle telescope carried by the globe was turned upon interesting stars and planets which were viewed with a clarity never before witnessed by man. Cosmic pictures were taken.

From earth, the observers at the power station called again, anxiously. "Dredd, Krell."

Dredd answered this time. "Globe speaking." Methodically he gave certain instrument readings, certain observational data; and then, in the midst of a sentence, stopped abruptly.

When next the power station achieved communication with the globe, it was Krell speaking. "Dredd called away by momentary disturbance in the thin outside atmosphere; temperature rose a degree and a fraction; for an instant there was a blur or something like it before the telescope; we are puzzled by such phenomena happening all at once. Ah—just a moment!" His voice sounded as if he'd turned away from the mike. "What's that, Dredd? The blur again." Then suddenly: "On earth there!—on earth—my God!" His voice went up—up, then ceased with a snap.

In vain observers at the power station called frantically. "What is it? What's the matter? Krell! Dredd!" Ominous silence was the only answer; and when the power was reversed and the rod of energy lowered to earth, nothing came with it—nothing. Far above the clouds, in the thin cold regions of the stratosphere, the globe and the pioneers within it had disappeared!

On the same day that the globe rose into the stratosphere, at the same time, though not at the same hour, utilizing the self-same principle of the rod of energy generated in a compact motor as an invisible piston, functioning with tremendous speed and little friction, Lewis Drake, the black mechanical genius, demonstrated the infinite possibilities of his new type of stream-lined car and so paved the way for the obsolescence of older and slower methods of transportation.

The vehicle itself, 30 feet in length, shaped somewhat like a slim torpedo, but with oddly grooved sides and top, and with an undercarriage consisting of a single runner and imbedded in a grooved track and cushioned with compressed air, was an object of intense interest, not alone to thousands of casual spectators but to keen-eyed engineers from international countries. It was well-known that Danvers, Incorporated (which was but another name for the autonomous governments of Canada, the United States, Mexico, and the South American Republics) was financing the venture.

The single-grooved track, describing an immense circle 1200 miles in circumference and running through a half dozen central states, had taken a huge sum to build. Here too, as in the case of the stratosphere globe, police, foot and mounted, and regiments of soldiers had difficulty in controlling the crowd. For a time it seemed as though the car itself was in danger from the mob. However, the authorities had taken the precaution of placing loudspeakers at strategic points before the people gathered, and Drake himself, speaking into a microphone, pled with men and women to be quiet and orderly, to stand in their places and not to endanger their lives or his machine. This materially aided in calming the enthusiasm, the rising hysteria, and allowed the police and soldiers to control the situation.

Drake, who was not only a famous engineer but somewhat of an orator as well, spoke at length of his invention. "Not for wealth alone," he said in part, "or merely for empty honor but to bind more closely in peace and harmony the various countries and races of man, am I striving to promote more and yet more speed in methods of transportation. Anything that brings distant people within a few hours' travel of each other makes for tolerance and understanding." He reminded them of various speed records, beginning with the primitive streamlined train, *Zephyr*, in 1934 which reached a maximum of 104 miles an hour in a run from New York to Chicago; of the later *Thunderbolt* in its run from Moscow to Kiev; and how he himself, in '72, in *Lightning One*, had doubled the previous world record. All these were land records," he emphasized. Winged man, jetplanes, set records in machs and miles per second.

"Today," he said, "I hope to demonstrate in this go-devil of mine, the *Lightning Two*, speed in excess of 1000 miles an hour as a safe and feasible way of land travel." With that, he bowed his thanks to the tremendous and deafening waves of applause and entered the hermetically enclosed compartment of his car. His assistant started the secondary motor and the strangely shaped and fluted craft, *Lightning Two* looming large in gold letters on its silvery side, commenced to move. The noonday sun glinted on its body of dulled metal and silver, and reporters shouted into phones, "Drake enters his car; the door is sealed; the car moves; listen to that crowd roar! The police can't control it! It's breaking through. If the car doesn't get away—quick—But she's off!—she's off—"

And she *was* off.

Inside the car, Drake had taken the controls and started the energy rod piston. In the sealed-in gyroscopically-hung cabin neither he nor his assistant could tell they were moving. Only the instruments on the operating panel attested to the fact.

At the official starting station a hundred miles down the line, they saw a blur go by and the electronically-controlled starting bell clanged and the automatic stopwatches noted the time with an accuracy unhuman.

All along the 1200 miles of curving track spectators crowded—in the rural districts and occasional villages, knots of country-folk and farmhands—in the large cities and their environs, crowds running into the hundreds of thousands. Bells clanged officially to note the passing but no human eyes could see the speeding demon, smoothly, silently, hurtling by.

Twelve hundred miles an hour!

Even in the hermetically enclosed cabin, whose slightest sway denoted movement at all, Drake glanced at his speedometer with pale face and half-incredulous eyes. At the official starting station the observers went wild. The high-salaried scribes and famous broadcasters yelled into their phones:

"TWELVE HUNDRED MILES IN ONE HOUR!"

"DRAKE SMASHES ALL LAND SPEED RECORDS!"

"BLACK AMERICAN DESTROYS DISTANCE!"

But such super speed, once attained, cannot be braked in a league, or 20 leagues. Though Drake shut off his energy-rod piston, the car hurtled three hundred more miles before spectators glimpsed it as a blur; and it was at Eureka, a small town of 40,000 inhabitants, that the incredible incident occurred.

It must be made clear at this point that the hurtling car was seen more or less clearly by thousands of people; photographic plates attest to this, and furthermore Drake and his assistant were alive at the time. The car was equipped with a radio and, doubtless relaxing in the moment of triumph from the concentration and anxiety which must have gripped him until then, Drake chose that particular 30 seconds to broadcast a message. Hundreds of receiving sets picked it up; and there can be little doubt that it was the Black Genius talking; for there could be no mistaking his distinctive voice, with its cultured enunciation. Furthermore, the fragmentary message was preceded with the identification "*Lightning Two* speaking—*Lightning Two*;" and then: "We are safe and fine; no inconvenience from stupendous speed; transportation is . . ."

But the message was never finished. It was at that moment the weird, the uncanny thing happened. People mention feeling a wave of heat "like the breath of a furnace." Moreover, instruments in a local weather bureau showed that at that moment there was an actual increase in heat of a full degree. Then they saw the blur, the shadow. For an appreciable instant the sunlight darkened. The blur seemed to encompass the speeding car. When it lifted, the car was gone.

At first, naturally enough, it was believed that Drake had increased his speed for some unknown reason; but along that 1200 miles of circular track no bells rang to tell of his passing, no automatic watches clocked his pace. In vain thousands waited and watched. Like the stratospheric globe with Krell and Dredd, the *Lightning Two* had disappeared, and neither it nor its daring occupants were ever seen again.

The world, as had been said, was in a ferment on that 19th day of February, 1973. While scientists labored to increase the power of mankind, and humanitarians worked to increase its wisdom, blind hatred and greed strove against the spirit of progress and light. When it was 1 p.m. in New Jersey, noon in the middle west, it was night in Europe. Two great armies faced each other on a thousand-mile front. The United Forces of Balko confronted those of the International Nations. Under the stars, 5,000,000 opposing men prepared themselves for what their respective leaders believed to be the final and decisive battle of a war that had already raged for 2 years and extracted its toll of wealth and blood. In trench and dugout, in strongholds and reserve sectors, soldiers of the International Army listened to the voice of their Commanding General addressing them through loudspeakers from General Headquarters.

"BULWARK OF CIVILIZATION," he cried. "Vanguard of Freedom and Light! This very night, in a few hours at the most, you hurl your valor against the black might of reaction and greed. Remember you are fighting to bring peace and prosperity to a war-weary world, to forever strike from the limbs of yourself and children the shackles of ignorance. War must end! The philosophy that makes of blood and carnage, of suffering and hate, something high and noble, must be rooted out, forever defeated. But in the hour of victory, remember you have come to free your brothers, not to enslave them. Soldiers of the International Army, the ideals and principles of harmony, cooperation, economic well-being must prevail. The eyes of the International World are on you. Down with hate!"

ALONG THE MILES of crumbling trenches, applause burst forth like a hoarse muttering of guns, and was answered by a similar roar from the opposing trenches, for almost at the same hour and minute, the General commanding United Forces also addressed his men.

"Soldiers! Heroes!—inheritors of the glorious traditions of Alexander, Caesar, and Zelig the Great, the future of our glorious race depends on you. Yonder lies the enemy who would corrupt you and your children with the mawkish sentimentality of internationalism. He would do away with war, with military exploits that make for greatness, for martial courage and the fraternal comradeship of brothers-in-arms. War is the cathartic that purges and cleanses nations; it is the scythe ordained of God that cuts down the weak and the unfit. The strong, the brave, have no need to fear war. He who would do away with war, who would reduce all nations and races to a tame equality, is an enemy of virture, of courage, of mankind itself. Soldiers! Heroes! The eyes of history are on you. Down with Internationalism. On to victory!"

The thunderous applause of opposing armies, in answer to the two eloquent speeches, rolled and reverberated along miles of rotting trenches and dugouts. The hour for battle was at hand as masses of men made ready for the ultimate risk and sacrifice demanded of them in the name of peace and international goodwill, in the name of pride and hate. Washington spoke to London and Paris to Moscow. The Capitals of United Forces talked to one another, blond and dark, yellow and white; for such is the inevitable logic of force that arrogant theories of race and creed go down before kindred ambitions and military necessity.

Who should attack? The guns were ready, and the men behind the guns. The bio-bombs were ready and the fighting planes to carry lethal death aloft and scatter it broadcast. Soldiers with machineguns, hand-grenades, bazookas, bullets and neopalm were ready, and yet the opposing armies waited, like hounds straining on a leash.

Gen. Max of United Forces walked impatiently up and down the long staff room, his staff officers respectfully keeping out of his way. His moustaches bristled. On the tables large maps lay unrolled. On the wall, the battlefield was pricked out in relief with colored lights flashing on and off, showing the constant movement and positions of troops and batteries. He paused to study this panoramic map. He hurled orders right and left and orderlies hastened to speak into radio-phones. Suddenly an orderly said, "Sir," and held out a phone. Gen. Max snatched it. "Yes, yes. Max speaking."

The voice of the War Minister of Balko came from the capital 600 miles away. "General—it will reach you within the hour. You understand—the *weapon*—the weapon Virachov has been laboring day and night, for weeks to perfect. Within the hour, yes; do all in your power to avert giving battle until it arrives."

While this conversation was taking place, a spy, picked up in enemy territory by plane and flown to International Military Headquarters, was reporting to Gen. O. Gardner, supreme commanding officer of the International Army. Gen. Gardner regarded the spy keenly. "You are sure this is true?"

"My sources have hitherto been reliable, General."

"A new vibratory weapon, you say?"

"That the famous physicist and arms manufacturer, Nebona Virachov, has invented."

"You could get no data as to its construction?"

"None, General; the plans are too well-guarded. My informant was only able to tell of its existence and of its deadliness."

"It will be utilized in the coming battle?"

"That I cannot say. There are rumors to that effect. Its construction is being rushed. Perhaps . . ."

The General turned to his staff. "Gentlemen, we attack within the hour! It is imperative there be no delay." He turned to a vast relief map, dotted with colored lights, similar to the one on the wall of Gen. Max's headquarters. "Here, and here, pour in the reserves." He barked his orders; staff officers sprang into action; orderlies rushed back and forth. "The enemy must be given no time to bring up the new weapon. Lay down a 45-minute barrage. The aerial squadrons will support . . ."

Twenty miles back of his front line trenches, Gen. Max lifted his head with a jerk. "What is that?"

"The guns, sir."

"I know it, fool! Get the front line intelligence posts—quick!"

"Front line posts speaking. Enemy heavy guns increasing bombardment; terrific barrage being laid down along the whole front. Attack expected."

Gen. Max looked at his watch. The earth shook. The building shook. The roar of the guns increased. "Orders, sir?"

"Wait, wait."

Out there in the darkness, 20 miles away, men huddled to earth like rabbits, like half-blinded moles, and the shells rained on them and exploded, and the night was hideous with noise, with brimstone fires and smells, and the groans of the wounded and dying.

Forty-five minutes.

"It has arrived, sir."

Gen. Max exulted. "Have it taken forward and put into position at once—at the place prepared—here." He pointed to the map. And then: "Wait! I'll go with it."

The famed Virachov was in charge; the military mechanics worked like mechanical mice. "It doesn't look like much," he said, noting the high commander's disparaging look, "but you shall see, General. The ray is generated here, directed through that nozzle over there. As it travels, it spreads. Invisible, yes. Ten miles away, it covers 300 miles of front. Everything it touches vibrates—men, guns, machines. They are shaken to pieces; powder blows up, ammunition dumps. Watch!"

He deflected a lever; vacuum tubes glowed. Like a purring tiger, the grotesque mechanism awoke to life. The range finder made an adjustment and Virachov lit a cigaret. At that moment, the moon peeped over the eastern horizon, flooding the earth with silver light. Minute by minute it climbed heavenward and looked down with indifferent face on the hell of the war below.

At International HQs, Gen. O. Garner pointed to a number and spoke. The barrage lifted and the International soldiers who had advanced slowly under its cover came on in waves.

For what followed, we have the evidence of eyewitnesses: a famous war pilot overhead, two war correspondents privileged to accompany Gen. Max, but who had stood some distance from him and his staff when it happened—several orderlies and an unverifiable number of officers and men in a nearby reserve corps.

Gen. Max, in his interest in the new weapon, in his faith that victory reposed with him (hadn't the War Minister assured him of this?) made the unmilitary mistake of quitting general headquarters without issuing a single order of any vital importance. His staff accompanied him, leaving behind it only those underlings and routine clerks whose habits of military discipline and blind obedience to authority were such as to preclude the showing of any individual initiative. Such was the situation, the condition of affairs when the renowned Virachov, inhaling deeply, thoughtfully twisted a dial. "At your orders, General."

The General gave the order in a low tone as if he realized in that moment the frightfulness of the thing he was doing.

Virachov pressed a button.

An intense flame, bluish in color, hovered over the mouth of the muzzle. Virachov glanced at the illuminated dial of his wristwatch. "In exactly 30 seconds," he said—but it happened in 15.

The night was cold and clear. The wave of heat was distinctly felt. "As if a warm breath blew from the tropics," one correspondent phrased it. The light of the moon darkened, as if a shadow passed across the moon's face. It could not have been the smoke of the batteries because the wind blew westward and the moon was still climbing in the east. There were no clouds in the sky. Around Gen. Max and his staff, around Virachov and his deadly vibratory machine, the blur descended. All those who witnessed it rubbed their eyes and cried out in amazement. The lone aviator overhead, glancing downward through binoculars, muttered a startled oath. For the shadow obscuring the light of the moon, the blur enveloping the small group on the ridge, lasted but a second . . .

Ten miles distant, unaware of the miracle that saved them, of the annihilating vibration arrested in its destructive course, the International soldiers carried the enemy first line trenches, swarmed on the second, the third. There is no need to tell how the soldiers of the United Forces, after a brief but fierce resistance, demoralized without its higher command and lacking a concerted plan of action, broke and fled. How reaction and hate was forced into a sullen surrender is now a subject for history. It is enough here to note the incredible, the astounding thing which occurred atop that moonlit ridge on the night of February 19, 1973. For when the shadow lifted, the blur disappeared. Gen. Max and his staff, as well as Virachov and his weapon, had disappeared also, had vanished as if into thin air. Witnesses of the uncanny occurrence were left staring at the vacant spot on which, but a moment before, they had stood!

And what had been the cause of it all?—the cause, not alone of these mysterious disappearances but of other unaccountable happenings, such as, for instance, the vanishing of a small library in Potsdam, New York. An astounded world asked itself this question and for 25 years it asked in vain. There were those who said Drake and his car had disintegrated from excessive speed, that Gen. Max and his staff had been wiped out when the vib-ray machine backfired.

But this could scarcely be argued of Krell and Dredd in their stratospheric globe.

There was, of course, the theory that the globe had drifted off into space. But giant telescopes had scoured the skies day and night for a sight of it, all in vain. The alternate theory that it had struck a meteor seemed equally unlikely, since there was no evidence of debris. Nor could both the globe and the meteor have vaporized without leaving some trace. The contention that it had somehow broken free from the rod of forces and crashed to earth in some remote spot was the most popular—but it did not explain how it could have suddenly vanished from the sight of thousands of telescopes.

Scientists perceived, in the seemingly separate events, phenomena common to all. In each of the three major cases, mention was made of heat waves, of shadows and blurs. (It is only by inference that the Potsdam Library affair is connected up with the three others; in that case the books were reported vanished but not the building.) But beyond coming to the conclusion that the agency responsible for the mysterious disappearances was the same wherever manifested, no adequate explanation was given by science. Of course, certain superstitious sects and those who substituted religion for reason saw in it all the hand of God. It was flying in the face of Providence (despite the lunar bases and probes to Mars and Venus) to delve too deeply into the secrets of the solar system; it was daring the wrath of Divine Love to travel at such an ungodly speed upon the face of the good earth as 1200 miles per hour; and everyone knew that the people of Balko were heathens. So the hand of God had reached out over the battlefield and the devilish machines—and where were they? Where were the warlords and those who would violate His domain?

So people and institutions sought to answer their own questions, prosaically, superstitiously, and with much success.

THEN, 25 YEARS after the mysterious events, Professor Byrne and I discovered the cylinder.

We were in the Rainbow country of Northern Arizona, heading a group of scientists from the Smithsonian Institute, when we first heard of it. An Indian spoke of a huge rock that had fallen from the sky some years before. Immediately we thought of a meteor. But our first glimpse of the colossal mass, half-buried in the earth at the bottom of a wide canyon, brought us to a halt with a gasp of sheer amazement, for no meteor was ever such a peculiar color or so meticulously shaped.

Colossal. I have called it that. But you can have no concept how immense that strange cylinder loomed at first sight and how astounding it was to come upon it in such a deserted place. Though more than half its length was buried in earth, it towered over our heads like a tall building, and its girth was in proportion.

What was it? How had it come to be where we found it? These were but two of the many questions that perplexed us.

"This is not a natural mass of metal," said Dr. Tellegen, the third man of our party. "Look. You can see where it shows signs of having been worked, fashioned."

This was true; the metal was chased in spots and delicately carved.

We all stared at one another.

"In that case," said Henry Quattrocchi, the fourth member of the expedition, "it may not be solid, either,"

Not solid! Then what could it contain? With one accord we set to work with drill and hammers. Later we augmented this with much more powerful equipment parachuted to us from a plane. I shall not weary the readers with a detailed account of how we toiled to pierce the metal shell, of how we blew a section of it out and entered the interior of the cylinder. What we expected to find, I do not know; what we actually discovered ...

"My God!" gasped Tellegen, gripping my arm. Our powerful lights lit up the gloomy interior. We had drilled our way into the cylinder just above what seemed a central floor or partition. Some 20 feet back, clustered around a strange machine and supported by metal uprights, was as singular a group as one could imagine. The lights played weirdly on pale set faces and lifeless bodies. These bodies were clothed in an old-fashioned type of military uniform with helmets on their heads.

Then our eyes lifted and traveled beyond this strange tableau to remoter distances and we saw the slim, fluted craft with its silvery gleaming sides on which a name was etched. At the same moment, Professor Byrne—by accident, perhaps, focused his powerful flash-ring overhead and called our attention to what hung suspended there.

We stared, fascinated.

Through glassite walls we saw the two figures with white faces staring out. *Dead faces* ...

"What does it mean?" breathed Quattrocchi.

"It means," said Tellegen at length, "the impossible, the incredible. Can't you read the name yonder?"

"*Lightning Two*," I half whispered.

"Yes," said Tellegen, "*Lightning Two*. Drake and his machine! And above there, in their globe, Krell and Dredd. And this group—this group here..."

"Gen. Max and his staff," I stammered.

"Yes," he said. "General Max and his staff. And the Great Virachov."

We stood for a moment, staring at one another incapable of speech; then Quattrocchi gasped: "But how—when—how did they get in here? *Who sealed them in?*"

NO ONE ANSWERED. There was no answer to make. Twenty-five years ago those men with their machines had vanished; and here, two and a half decades later, we found them entombed in a strange cylinder in the heart of a wilderness.

Recovering from our first overwhelming astonishment, yes, and more than a little dread, we explored further.

The first half of the cylinder was filled with the objects we have described;

in the lower portion we found the plates. Visitors to the Smithsonian Institute II at Kennedy may see one of those plates exhibited, observe the immense letters etched on it; but the gist of the letters engraved on all the plates has never been given to the public. I shall not speculate as to the reasons for this. Suffice it to say that the discovery of the plates is fully authenticated. In addition, there is the indisputable fact that the metal of which they are composed is utterly un-known to earth. The huge cylinder, and the plates found in it, were never fashioned by earthly hands; on that science is agreed; and yet the astounding fact remains that *the printed words on the plates were in English!*

Yes, in English!—though this English was not perfect, and the letters were enormous in size, being etched into the metal with almost painful fidelity and by a process impossible to duplicate; for though the metal plates were flexible to the touch, no tempered steel point, no diamond-cutter, was able to make an impression on them.

It took 1200 of the plates—and each plate was 12 feet long and 3 in width—to contain some 500 words and characters.

The English words formed a brief document of such singular import, and was one so utterly beyond the bounds of credibility in what it implied, that were it not for the mute yet eloquent evidence of metals unknown on earth, of strange methods of etching, of certain unnatural usages and alien structures, science would have dismissed it as a preposterous hoax.

Yet there *was* the evidence of alien metals—and, too, the mysterious, ut-terly incomprehensible characters heading the document and ending it. Dili-gent attempts have been made to link these up with the hieroglyphics of an-cient Egypt, and the symbols found engraved on the ruins of Mayan temples in Mexico, but without success. Otherworldly they seem, as otherworldly as the unknown metal on which they are etched, adding to the cumulative effect of evidence which exacts a certain measure of belief from the most doubting of scientists.

With this for a foreword, we give the incredible document as copied faith-fully from the plates, with only those unavoidable conjectures inserted where meaning could only be guessed at.

***

"JDO_92_98_94. Some strange disaster evidencely hasbefallen this planette. Death's nonnoise overhangs it. Everything seemstobe in awonderful state of preservement, yet dead, without life or motion, as if when theunexpected end came its inhabitants hadbeengoing about their livingtasks.

"That these tiny beings—so sizely and structurely reductiond from ourselves—containd acertain measure of intelligence and civilizitude doesnotbedoubted.

In one of thehigher layers of thesmall planet's atmospheral envelope, aglobe was excoverd containing primitiv instruments of stelescopics and two [here an incomprehensible word was used but that it meant "man" I am certain and that is the translation given]—men whose bodys, still instinct with action, wereimobilizd by sudden death. We circumd the planet, looking for sines of life and movement but koodfownd none. Twice we were of themoment deceivedly. Believing that motion wasdetected on theplanet's surface, we downd; but some videosyncrasy of this rare atmospher musthavemisled us. We fownd evidencely a vikkle for transportation standing on agroovd track, with countless of thelittle inhabitants (stonifyd in crowds and scatterd groups) away some distance.

"Thecase next was almost alike. Conditions observd indicatd afierce killall mustongoing when themysterious malady overswept thebattlefield. Soldiers wereimmobilestruck at themoments of attack and defense. Agroup of warriors and theoddlooking killmachin which they wereroundclusterd, weretaken aboard, as previous to this were theglobe and thevikkle. These, together several other objects intresting, willbeexamind when leisurd.

"In accord to your instructions, thethought records of theplanet's inhabitant's isbeenstudyd. As we havelearnd thelanguage of reasonal beings, whatever their form or shape, follows certain basic cosmic matrixes. Thedifficulty to interpretation laynot in thelanguage selfish but in therecorded size of thethought symbols. These were extremely small; in fact, invisibly small; and calld for theusage of thepowermost of dimensionalizers. However, this difficultment becameoverwill and thepresent record will be imperishly registerd, inclosd in the [here was another strange symbol which could mean nothing else than the cylinder] and along with thelittle beings and machins pikt up for examinating, returnd to theplanet's surface. It islocated . . . [a string of symbols follows]. The present forms of life, except perhaps in bacterial shapes too infinidecimal topermit of examinating, have perisht upon theface of this little world. It now isbecome one total sepulcher.

"Unfortunately, with *our gift of eternal life and perpetual peace and plenitude* [italics mine] we havebecome here too late.

"But that thelife process willagainproduce intelligent beings on this planet, all our wisdom assures us. This reasonly, we leave behind this record of our visit. In 50,000,000 [?] we shall re-be here. Inthebetween, we shall go on to theremaining planets of this small sunar system where, hopely, reasoning lifes maybefownd—all lifely."

***

Reasoning beings . . . alive! So ended the incredible message; and it can be imagined with what utter amazement we first read it, with what mixed emotions of incredulity and belief the world of science first learned of its existence. But as I have said, there was the evidence of metals unknown to earth to convince the doubting, and the completeness with which it accounted for the mysterious disappearances of February 19, 1973.

Yet, for all that, there was something which lacked explanation, and I called it to the attention of Prof. Byrne and to Dr. Gallet of the Paris Institute. "Granted," I said, "that something mysterious visited earth and sealed the globe, the car, with their occupants, and Gen. Max and his staff, into the cylinder, how was it that no eye on earth perceived such visitors? Could they have been *invisible* men?

"And how was it such visitors could view a speeding car, a battle in progress, the excited movements of Krell and Dredd, and thousands of people, on that day which, because of the many speed and distance records simultaneously shattered we remember as Earth's Lucky Day;—how could they observe such uncommon activity and yet report it as if they believed life to be *extinct* on earth?! As if they had witnessed no movement, no action, heard no sound?"

It was Dr. Gallet who answered me at length. "It is all a profound mystery," he agreed, "and yet—aren't you mistaken in thinking no eye perceived them? Wasn't the blur, the shadow, the heat—*them*? All of them that man could see or feel."

He continued: "You have noted that the alien document implies the visitors to have been of colossal size. They evidently came from outside our solar system, from a world immensely greater than our own—both physically and scientifically—where conditions of time, even of organic structure, seemingly differ radically from earth's patterns. If we postulate beings whose day is our second or minute, whose physical structure is in accord with such conditions, then we imagine begins unable to hear us, to hear the sounds of the earth, or to perceive our motions. To them we might well appear motionless, silent, stricken with death."

We looked at one another mutely, a sense of wonder stirring once again in the corridors of the brain long disused because of a surfeit of man-made miracles stuffing them from the past decades.

"And Krell," I said, "and Dredd, and all the other poor devils, unable to make their plight known; dying, with eternal life around them!"

"Oh, I know," said Gallet, "that this explanation may not be entirely satisfactory, that it may have certain flaws; but the physical observations, the intellectual reactions of actual Brobdingnagians, beings vast beyond comprehension and existing at a time-rhythm immensely swifter than our own, would be so indescribably different from what we know that it is absurd to advance this objection or that. I can only say that my theory best fits the facts."

It did. It does. And so the world of 21st century science has decided.

And 21st century man? Our planet plundered and polluted, overcopulated (they didn't listen to José Farmer) and undernourished; psychotic, chaotic and wildly out of control; we rue the day—Earth's "Lucky" Day—that we missed our opportunity for the Millennium, the day we prided ourselves, with our limited understanding, that we had accomplished much, when in our ignorance we did not realize we had lost everything!

Everything: a brave new world—Humanhood. A dream of the ages realized: perpetual peace. Plenamins for body and mind. *Lebensraum* and *lebenstraum*. All could have been ours, a gift from the stars, from a supernal civilization Out There, from a planet of sanity . . . somewhere in the sevagram.

And our next chance at bestowed humanhood will be in—what? 50,000,000 . . . years? Our time—or theirs?

Not that it will matter, anyway. On Earth's *next* "lucky day," no matter how great the activity on our slow motion planet, we'll appear just as dead and frozen as last time to our giant would-be benefactors.

Just as dead.

If, in paralyzing point of fact, we aren't *indeed*, O God Samaritans by then a grave nude world, a cemetery planet.

Excerpt from "A Letter from Mr. Sci-Fi" in SPACEWAY SCIENCE FICTION, *June 1969:*

The Story Behind the story of "Earth's Lucky Day". One of the earliest s.f. stories I remember reading—when we still called it "scientifiction" as "The Machine Man of Ardathia" by Francis Flagg, *Amazing Stories*, November, 1927. It is regarded as a classic, at least by the likes of Donald Wollheim, Sam Moskowitz, Bill Crawford, Bob Madle and oldwave duddyfuddies like myself. "Little did I dream" that 9 years later my name wd appear with Francis Flagg as a *collaborator!* But by '34 my friend Flagg admitted to me he was running out of ideas. I was full of them but had no professional ability as a writer yet, so we hit on the happy combination of ideas/Ackerman, fictionalizing/Flagg. "Earth's Lucky Day", Apr '36 *Wonder Stories,* was the first commercial success and at 19 I was as thrilled as say you wd be today, if you're a would-be young writer, to find your name bylined with Heinlein. They liked the plot well enough in Switzerland, some years later, to dramatize it over the radio as "A Question of Time". But nearly 25 years after it was written, I reread it for reprinting. *I was appalled!* It disintegrated before my eyes. It's dreadful to have to criticize a dead idol but suddenly I realized I was older now than Flagg had been and the whole body of his works consisted of about 20 stories. With reluctant necessity I found myself editing Francis Flagg. Had I had time I might have discarded the collaboration entirely and, utilizing the idea which was mine in the first place, completely re-written it. But from 10 at night till 4 A.M., when you've been working from 10 the previous morning, is no time to write a 5700-word story against a dead-line—revising it with bloodshot eyes was bad enough. I hope I improved it; I'd be interested in the opinions of any of you who have read both versions.

Dwellers
in the Dust

by FJA

*T*HIS STORY, *in* substantially *the same form, was written by me in approximately 1934, to the best of my recollection. It was written for a contest sponsored by Wm. F. Crawford (who has published me in* Fantasy Book *in the past
and has recently asked me to do a feature for him, "A Letter from Mr. Sci-Fi", for
his revived* Spaceway *magazine)—it was written with Crawford's* Marvel Tales *in
mind when I was about 18 years old and I think it tied for a 4th place prize. Had*
Marvel Tales *continued beyond its 5th issue the story would have been printed
"way back when".*

Fifteen years later on, when Crawford was publishing Fantasy Book, *I got out
the yellowing manuscript, rewrote it slightly and sold it to him.* Science Fiction
Digest *liked the story sufficiently well, when it started up in 1954, to reprint it in
its first issue. I believe I updated it a bit at that time and put in the prophetic part
about breaking the Anglo-Sexon language barrier in 1960 and the sartorial revolution to come which would result in the "pneumonia neckline" for women.*

This time 'round you are reading it virtually as it stood in 1954.

*Incidentally, altho my dearly beloved maternal grandparents certainly did, I
personally put no stock in the notion of a soul, an ego entity that can exist separate from the body. Just so you don't get any ideas. Just for the record.*

"NONSENSE; THEY'RE DEAD; what you say is the same as that there's an
eternity of every moment."

"As there surely is, John; as there surely is!" George Romani had trapped
me into arguing with him again about his pet hobby: Chronportation. Talking
time-travel with George was practically tantamount to creating perpetual motion of the jaw, and I should have known better. But, no; I plunged in where
angels would have feared to tread with all the saints in heaven rooting for
them.

"An eternity of every moment," George continued. "As Dunne put it: Nothing dies. The people of the past are alive and living now. The men and women
of all ages—cavemen to our brave new world—are loving and hating, working

19

and playing, fighting and dying. Every great battle is being fought right now—back in time past. Columbus is sailing, Jeanne d'Arc is burning, and—"

"Pasteur is pasteurizing, I suppose! So, these long-departed—these corpses—these dwellers in the dust are doing all that!" I snorted. There is a certain exasperating quality to my snort that always has a telling effect on George: He starts telling me what a fool I am, in language which the law of 1954 does not allow in print. Now the Anglo-Saxon renaissance of 1960—but I am anticipating my story.

"Exactly!" George flamed like a Bunsen burner. "Just as you and I. To the people of the future, we are the dwellers in the dust, as you put it."

This was too much. "So now there are people of the future! And I suppose they are dust, too, even though they aren't born yet?"

"Yes!" hissed George. "And everything isn't so funny to me, you dusty devil. Come along!" And he grasped my shoulder and dragged me protesting from my chair and amber cheer toward his laboratory.

Romani's experimental lab was clean and white and ordered. No sloppy sinks, no chemical stinks. The lady from Good Housekeeping would certainly have given him her Gold Medal seal of approval. On the broad translucite table in the center of the lab reposed a contraption I had not seen before. Like nothing so much, it was, as a stereopticon—the "magic lantern" predecessor of the moving picture.

"My time machine," George explained succinctly, continuing facetiously, "You've heard of the concept, I presume. The original story was reprinted widely shortly after the demise of Wells, its conceptor. John, this is it—what I've been working on to prove my theories. Father Time permitting, you are looking at the first 'temport'."

I made no comment for the moment; walked over to the table and stared at the device. Small and ineffectual-looking in appearance, it scarcely seemed creditable that it could contain the magic capable of transporting a person across the mysterious gap of Time.

I glanced at my curvex. "George," I said, "according to my wrist model time-machine, it's time to retire if this tinker toy is all you've dragged me in here to see. Really, your sense of humor is about as funny as a malignant tumor!"

"And your simile is as inelegant as an elephant," he chided me. "But I am completely serious. That's a time-machine. Only, we don't ride it—we turn it on us. A ray."

"A ray. Hoo-ray. As for turning it on us . . ."

"Look here! I've already experimented with the chron-ray on myself, John. It really works. I've gone into the past. It occurred to me you might like to accompany me. That sis of yours—the tragedy that makes you drink so much . . ."

Lorie! Instantly I was sobered. Little sister Lorie: I thought of her crumpled body once vibrant with life; her blue face, blue as her eyes from which the light had gone. If only there had been some way I could have prevented her—How many times I had longed to turn back the clock. Now—what was this George was saying could be done?

A trip into the past?

"George! You would take me back? That thing really could send me back two years? You could do that—now? There's no danger, no possibility of injury from the ray? And I—we—would come back?" I was clutching at a wild hope, an opportunity to change the past.

For answer my friend silently drew up two chairs before the ray-projector.

"Sit down, John. I can and will take you back. Now if you like. Back two years. There will be no danger"—I did not catch the import of his emphasis, then—"no possibility of injury. And we will come back."

I sank onto the chair, my mind a maelstrom. The alcoholic fog had cleared but fear of the unknown clouded my brain.

George sat beside me. "Back 26 months, isn't it? What location?"

"You can adjust that too? Then make it just outside the York Hotel. Where the Jolson Theater is today."

George's artistic hand reached out to the table and a firm finger clicked a toggle on the instrument that faced us—the machine of destiny that was to erase 800 days since the death of my sister Lorie.

"That would be about 19 February 1954, right? In front of the York." And a brilliant orange ray leapt squarely at us.

THERE WAS ABSOLUTELY no period of transition. No sickening sensation, no wrenching, no mad mélange of night melting into day in reverse. George and I simply stood before the hotel, which had not yet been destroyed by the block-square conflagration.

We stood on a crowded sidewalk; automatically, I moved back out of the way of pedestrians. George followed.

"Well?" His enthusiasm was as boyish as a teenager, for all his 38 years.

I simply stared dumbly, another thing I do well. The people's clothing, I noted dully as men and women swarmed by, was just beginning to reflect the sartorial revolution to come in the summer of '54. A few pioneering "Roemons" (after Cherilyn Roemon, cinemactress who blazed the trail in the Torch film SATELLITE STOWAWAY) beneath their cello-furs were wearing the "pneumonia neckline," the sartorial nova of the summer which died a-borning after a smidge of sensationalistic publicity in the press but came back like a boomerang two years later. Another season, I knew, would see men emancipated from those traditional tyrants of the throat, neckties.

A mauve-cravat emerged from the York, expertly tied at the soft throat of the suavest blackguard that ever took a girl off guard. Krebs! Tony Krebs. Anthony C. B. Krebs, the 3d.

George did not know this carrion by sight: Krebs had vanished on a round-the-world tour after what had happened to my sister and I had not met George until after Lorie was dead. But I had told him the whole sordid story, and cursed in several languages—this millionaire Machiavelli who had swept poor Lorie, first off her feet then into the trash-heap. George seemed instinctively to recognize him.

When I saw Krebs, I lost my head. Hate fueled me, lent jets to my feet. I leaped for this throat like an unleashed Mercury. To seize that throat, batter that self-satisfied face beyond recognition, choke—

But my hand closed on empty air! Off balance, I lunged into the revolving door, went teetering through, tripped and sprawled dizzily on the floor.

No one noticed me. Gradually it dawned on me that this was but a dream. George and his theories, or my heavy drinking, or a combination of both, had put me to sleep. Presently I should wake from this.

George was tugging at my shoulder. "Get up, John."

I rose unsteadily. "Pour me another—" But wait! I was still in the lobby of the York—a hotel which hadn't existed for two years. Did the dream still persist?

"George—?"

"It means this, John: We are here in—essence—only. The ray dissociates our egos from our bodies and we have but to think of the time and place we wish to explore and with the speed of thought we are there. But we can play only the role of inactive observers. We cannot mingle with the dwellers in the dust, else become dust ourselves. In other words, the past is immutable: We cannot change it."

I saw now what he had meant by "no possible danger."

I WAS COMPLETELY depressed. Sharing neither his zeal for science nor taste for adventure, time-travel meant little to me as a revolutionary achievement. Perhaps I lacked a romantic nature. But what my ordinary reactions would have been cannot fairly be judged, for in a trip to the past I had seen nothing but a chance to undo what had befallen my sister.

"Let's go back," I said.

"Back?" George was startled. "But doesn't this interest you here? Wouldn't you like to look around in the past? See your sister again?"

"No! God, George, don't you understand—I couldn't bear to see Lorie as she was, once; happy, alive but fore-damned, and I unable to influence her. It would be a mockery too horrible to bear. Come on, George; let's go back!"

I STARED UNBELIEVING at the hordes of men, women and children flowing through him as though he were a sieve, and waited for his answer. Then a thought—imperative, terrifying—struck me.

"George! What is happening to our bodies back there in the laboratory? Suppose there should be a fire?"

"There's nothing in the lab combustible," he assured me. "You know that."

"Our bodies are in a state of suspended animation," he continued.

"But mightn't someone come in, see us and think we were dead? Embalm us or cremate us or something?" I quailed at the thought of remaining a naked ego, isolated in eternity.

"Unlikely!" George laughed. "You're imagining things. Who would be coming in my place this time of night? Anyway, with the ray on they should be able to see it's an experiment. Say," he attempted to divert my mind from its morbid visions, "if nothing interests you in the past, how about a flip to the future?"

"The future?" The future. The term seemed a semantic blank at the moment, empty of meaning. Passage into the past I could vaguely rationalize, revisiting what had once been. But the future—a thing inchoate, as yet uncreated. The concept dazed me. Probably that was why I offered no resistance when George said, "Come on, link your mind with mine and let's take a look at what 1975 holds in store. Ready? Hup, tup, thrip, forp—Onward Christian Soldiers!"

CORUSCATING STAR-SHELLS burst above me—in eerie silence. I realized for the first time that sight seemed the only sense retained in the ego state.

I turned to question George when the stratoscraper to my right burst out its sides with a noiselessness that was unnerving. If an invisible entity can have gooseflesh, I had enough for a whole gander.

Chunks of concrete, splinters of plastic and ragged girder fragments enveloped me. Instinctively I cringed. Day blacked out before me, though I felt nothing. I must be pinned—crushed, squashed flat, utterly buried beneath multitons of girder and glass—yet I felt nothing of pain or awful weight.

Only terror.

I looked for George. There, lying ahead of me, incased in ruin, I saw him. Alive! And not only alive but alive and smiling. Laughing! He got up and walked through the black mass, a searchlight held in his hand.

"Get up!" he commanded, chuckling. "Don't you realize you can't get hurt? You're just a dweller in the dust. In this world, smoke can't even get in your eyes—unless you imagine it. Remember, I told you only your ego is here.

"Oh, and about the searchlight," he went on, while I sat silent and perplexed. "I forgot to tell you: You can have all kinds of luxuries on your time-trip. Things which are only thoughts in your mind when you're in your body are realities—or realities for all practical purposes—when in the temport form. I dreamed up this flash to see my way around. All we have to do to get out of this Black Hole of Calcutta is believe we're up topside again."

And then he sobered, "There's war up there, isn't there? Gotham's getting hell blown out of it. But not atomic. That was a superexplosive, alright, but still chemical, I'd say."

"God, is this what we've got to look forward to—really—a generation from our time?"

George preferred not to answer. "Let's go up," he said. "Look around."

I demurred, contemplating the horror we were certain to witness. "Uh-uh. I don't think so. My God—it's pretty far-fetched, I know, but I might see myself getting killed! Well, it could happen, couldn't it? I'd be haunted from here on in, George."

"Haunted by your own ghost, huh?" George shrugged. "Ready to return, then? I can come ahead again any time, without you. Might even figure out a way to beat what's happening, somehow. You want to—"

On the verge of returning to the present, an inspiration hit me. "Wait a minute. What did you say—how does it work, again, about imagining things, and being places, and all that? Could I connect up with a certain party, do you think?" George saw what I was driving at. "You mean, if you consciously willed to be where Krebs is now, would you be transported there? Hm; well, I honestly don't know, John. But if you want to try, I'm with you."

Want to try? Yes! The risk of running into "myself" was a minor one compared with the possible satisfaction of seeing Krebs suffer in that holocaust above.

I looked squarely at George. "Okay." Then I addressed myself to a greater entity. "If there is a God," I said, "take me to Krebs!"

I DID NOT recognize the thing at my feet at first. It looked like a life-sized man, made of rubber and hollow, blown bigger than normal so that it had burst its clothes . . . burst even its skin.

The purple face was worst.

The eyes bulged, Lorre-like; the tongue protruded like a tapeworm grown fat.

This, then, was the unlovely end product of BW: Biological Warfare. This bloated, contorted, plum-faced horror.

My ego felt a nausea that I was physically unable to relieve.

I felt great compassion for the thing at my feet that had once been a man. Till my attention focused on a scar on the throat. What Krebs had been so careful to keep concealed by a muffler, the mark of the goiter operation.

Then, fallen at the corpse's side, I spied the monogrammed cigarette case: ACBK-III. Anthony C. B. Krebs, the 3d.

Anthony Krebs the last!

His evil had come to an end. "Satisfied, John?"

"Let's go, George."

SOMETHING WAS STINGING my cheeks. I opened my eyes as George slapped me again. "Quit playing possum," he bantered, lifting me gently out of the chair by my hair-roots.

I grimaced, started to yelp, "Well, don't snatch me bald!"—but sneezed violently instead. Some particles had settled in my quiescent nostrils during the absence of my ego. So I groaned, "Dwellers in the dust, indeed!"

George said: "Gesundheit!"

Micro-Man

by FJA

SHAKA TABULO!
This mighty oath in Esperanto sounds ferocious but actually all it means is a very innocuous "chess table".

But I am upset because now, when I need it, where is the copy of the fanzine Specula *containing the first publication of "Micro Man"? Suddenly it isn't in alphabetical order in my file of published works.*

Specula *was a particularly neat package of amateur s.f. & fantasy fiction and articles published in 1941 and this story of mine first appeared there under the title "Me and the Mite" under the pseudonym, Carl F. Burk. I don't remember the origin of the Burk nom-de-plume—used only once—but I have a feeling that I picked one unlike the usual run of Weaver Wright and Allis Villette, etc., so that I wouldn't be suspected of writing the story. I no longer remember why I wanted it to be a secret at first; I think it may have had something to do with having a little fun with my friend the publisher (Arthur Louis Joquel II), that he wouldn't know till after the story appeared that I had written it; or perhaps I was interested to know what readers thot of it without the FJA byline.*

It was first professionally published in the second issue of Ted Carnell's New Worlds *in England in 1946 and I was pleased but upset because they failed to italicize the final paragraph as intended. In its second incarnation it was called "The Micro Man" and attributed to Alden Lorraine, a tribute to the memory of my only brother, Alden Lorraine Ackerman, who was killed shortly before his 21st birthday on 1 Jan 45 in the Battle of the Bulge . . .*

Attributed to Weaver Wright, "Micro-Man" was published next year in America in Fantasy Book #1. *The next year Atlantis Distributors published it south of the border in* Los Cuentos Fantasticos: *"Micro-Hombre"! The last time it saw print was sometime in the 50s in the Sunday fiction section of the* New York Post.

AE van Vogt once commented to me about the story in 1947 that he had read it with considerable surprise, that he had not realized I was that much of an author and that he found it "a very enjoyable little story".

From that day to this I don't believe anyone has mentioned it.

THE EARLY MORNING streetcar, swaying and rattling along its tracks, did as much to divert my attention from the book I was reading as the contents of

26

the book itself. I did not like Plato. Comfortable though the seat was, I was as uncomfortable as any collegiate could be whose mind would rather dwell upon tomorrow's football game than the immediate task in hand—the morning session with Professor Russell and the book on my lap.

My gaze wandered from the book and drifted out the distorted window, then fell to the car-sill as I thought over Plato's conclusions. Something moving on the ledge attracted my attention: it was a scurrying black ant. If I had thought about it, I might have wondered how it came there. But the next moment a more curious object on the sill caught my eye. I bent over.

I couldn't make out what it was at first. A bug, perhaps. Maybe it was too small for a bug. Just a little dancing dust, no doubt.

Then I discerned—and gasped. On the sill, there—it was a man! A man on the streetcar's window sill—a *little* man! He was so tiny I would never have seen him if it hadn't been for his white attire, which made him visible against the brown grain of the shellacked wood. I watched, amazed as his microscopic figure moved over perhaps half an inch.

He wore a blouse and shorts, it seemed, and sandals. Something might have been hanging at his side but it was too small for me to make out plainly. His head, I thought, was silver-colored, and I think the headgear had some sort of knobs on it.

All this, of course, I didn't catch at the time, because my heart was hammering away excitedly and making my fingers shake as I fumbled for a matchbox in my pocket. I pushed it open and let the matches scatter out.

Then, as gently as my excitement would allow, I pushed the tiny man from the ledge into the box; for I had suddenly realized the greatness of this amazing discovery.

The car was barely half-filled and no attention had been directed my way. I slid quickly out of the empty seat and hurriedly alighted at the next stop.

In a daze, I stood where I had alighted waiting for the next No. 10 that would return me home, the match-box held tightly in my hand. They'd put that box in a museum one day!

I collect stamps—I've heard about getting rare ones with inverted centers, or some minor deviation that made them immensely valuable. I'd imagined getting one by mistake sometime that would make me rich. But this! They'd billed King Kong as "The Eighth Wonder of the World," but that was only imaginary—a film . . .

A terrifying thought crossed my mind.

I pushed open the box hastily: maybe *I* had been dreaming. But there it was—the unbelievable; the Little Man!

A car was before me, just leaving. Its polished surface had not reflected through the haze and the new design made so little noise that I hadn't seen it. I jumped for it, my mind in such a turmoil that the conductor had to ask three times for my fare. Ordinarily, I would have been embarrassed, but a young man with his mind on millions doesn't worry about little things like that. At least, not this young man.

How I acted on the streetcar, or traversed the five blocks from the end of the line, I couldn't say. If I may imagine myself, though, I must have strode along the street like a determined machine. I reached the house and let myself into the basement room. Inside, I pulled the shades together and closed the door, the matchbox still in my hand. No one was at home this time of day, which pleased me particularly, for I wanted to figure out how I was going to present this wonder to the world.

I flung myself down on the bed and opened the matchbox. The little man lay very still on the bottom.

"Little Man!" I cried, and turned him out on the quilt. Maybe he had suffocated in the box. Irrational thought! Small though it might be to me, the little box was as big as all outdoors to him. It was the bumping about he'd endured; I hadn't been very thoughtful of him.

He was reviving now and raised himself on one arm. I pushed myself off the bed and stepped quickly to my table to procure something with which I could control him. Not that he could get away but he was so tiny I thought I might lose sight of him.

Pen, pencil, paper, stamps, scissors, clips—none of them were what I wanted. I had nothing definite in mind but then remembered my stamp outfit and rushed to secure it. Evidently college work had cramped my style along the collecting line for the tweezers and magnifier appeared with a mild coating of dust. But they were what I needed and I blew on them and returned to the bed.

The little man had made his way half an inch or so from his former prison; was crawling over what I suppose were, to him, great uneven blocks of red and green and black moss.

He crossed from a red into a black patch as I watched his movements through the glass and I could see him more plainly against the darker background. He stopped and picked at the substance of his strange surroundings, then straightened to examine a tuft of the cloth. The magnifier enlarged him to a seeming half inch or so and I could see better, now, this strange tiny creature.

It *was* a metal cap he wore and it did have protruding knobs—two of them—slanting at 45° angles from his temples like horns. I wondered at their use but it was impossible for me to imagine. Perhaps they covered some actual growth; he might have had real horns for all I knew. Nothing would have been too strange to expect.

His clothing showed up as a simple, white, one-piece garment, like a shirt and gym shorts. The shorts ended at the knee and from there down he was bare except for a covering on his feet which appeared more like gloves than shoes. Whatever he wore to protect his feet, it allowed free movement of his toes.

It struck me that this little man's native habitat must have been very warm. His attire suggested this. For a moment I considered plugging in my small heater; my room certainly had no tropical or sub-tropical temperature at that time of the morning—and how was I to know whether he shivered when he felt chill. Maybe he blew his horns. Anyway, I figured a living Eighth Wonder would be more valuable than a dead one; and I didn't think he could be stuffed. But somehow I forgot it in my interest in examining this unusual personage.

The little man had dropped the cloth now, and was staring in my direction. Of course, "my direction" was very general to him; but he seemed to be conscious of me. He certainly impressed me as being awfully different but what his reactions were I didn't know.

But someone else knew.

IN A WORLD deep down in Smallness, in an electron of a dead cell of a piece of wood, five scientists were grouped before a complicated instrument with a horn like the early radios. Two sat and three stood, but their attention upon the apparatus was unanimous. From small hollowed cups, worn on their fingers like rings, came a smoke from burning incense. These cups they held to their noses frequently and their eyes shone as they inhaled.

The scientists of infra-smallness were smoking!

With the exception of a recent prolonged silence, which was causing them great anxiety, sounds had been issuing from the instrument for days. There had been breaks before but this silence had been long-enduring.

Now the voice was speaking again; a voice that was a telepathic communication made audible. The scientists brightened.

"There is much that I cannot understand," it said. The words were hesitant, filled with awe. "I seem to have been in many worlds. At the completion of my experiment, I stood on a land which was brown and black and very rough of surface. With startling suddenness, I was propelled across this harsh country and, terrifyingly, I was falling. I must have dropped 75 feet but the strange buoyant atmosphere of this strange world saved me from harm.

"My new surroundings were gray and gloomy and the earth trembled as a giant cloud passed over the sky. I do not know what it meant but with the suddenness characteristic of this place it became very dark and an inexplicable violence shook me into insensibility.

"I am conscious, now, of some giant form before me but it is so colossal that my eyes cannot focus it. And it changes. Now I seem confronted by great orange mountains with curving ledges cut into their sides. Atop them are great, grayish slabs of protecting opaque rock—a covering like that above our Temples of Aerat—'on which the rain may never fall.' I wish that you might communicate with me, good men of my world. How go the Gods?

"But now! These mountains are lifting, vanishing from my sight. A great *thing* which I cannot comprehend hovers before me. It has many colors but mostly there is the orange of the mountains. It hangs in the air and from the portion nearest me grow dark trees as round as myself and as tall. There is a great redness above that opens like the Katus flower, exposing the ivory white from which puffs the Tongue of Death. Beyond this I cannot see well but ever so high are two gigantic caverns from which the Winds of the Legends blow— and suck. As dangerous as the Katus, by Dal! Alternately they crush me to the ground, then threaten to tear me from it and hurl me away."

My nose was the cavern from which issued the horrifying wind. I noticed that my breath distressed the little man as I leaned over to stare at him, so drew back.

Upstairs, the visor buzzed. Before answering, so that I would not lose the little man, I very gingerly pinched his shirt with the tongs and lifted him to the table.

"My breath! I am shot into the heavens like Milo and his rocket! I traverse a frightful distance! Everything changes constantly. A million miles below is chaos. This world is mad! A giant landscape passes beneath me, so weird I cannot describe it. I—I cannot understand. Only my heart trembles within me. Neither Science nor the Gods can help or comfort in this awful world of Greatness!

"We stop. I hang motionless in the air. The ground beneath is utterly insane. But I see vast uncovered veins of rare metal—and crystal, precious crystal, enough to cover the mightiest Temple we could build! Oh, that Mortia were so blessed! In all this terrifying world, the richness of the crystal and the marvelous metal do redeem.

"Men!—I see . . . I believe it is a temple! It is incredibly tall, of black foundation and red spire, but it is weathered, leaning as if to fall and very bare. The people cannot love their Gods as we—or else there is the Hunger . . . But the Gods may enlighten this world, too, and if lowered, I will make for it. A sacred Temple should be a haven—

"Friends! I descend."

The little man's eye had caught my scissors and a glass ruler as I suspended him above my desk. They were his exposed vein of metal and the precious crystal. I was searching for something to secure him. In the last second before I lowered him, his heart swelled at the sight of the "Temple"—my red and black pen slanting upward from the desk holder.

A stamp lying on my desk was an inspiration. I licked it, turned it gum side up and cautiously pressed the little man against it feet first. With the thought, "That ought to hold him," I dashed upstairs to answer the call.

But it didn't hold him. There was quite a bit of strength in that tiny body.

"Miserable fate! I flounder in a horrid marsh," the upset thought-waves came to the men of Mortia. "The viscous mire seeks to entrap me but I think I can escape it. Then I will make for the Temple. The Gods may recognize and protect me there."

I MISSED THE call—I had delayed too long—but the momentary diversion had cleared my mind and allowed new thoughts to enter. I now knew what my first step would be in presenting the little man to the world.

I'd write a newspaper account myself—exclusive! Give the scoop to Earl. Would that be a sensation for *his* paper! Then I'd be made. A friend of the family, this prominent publisher had often promised he would give me a break when I was ready. Well, I *was* ready!

Excited, dashing downstairs, I half-formulated the idea. The headlines—the little man under a microscope—a world afire to see him. Fame . . .pictures . . .speeches . . .movies . . .TV . . .money . . .

But here I was at my desk and I grabbed for a piece of typing paper. They'd put that in a museum, too!

The stamp and the little man lay just at the edge of the sheet and he clutched at a "great orange mountain" covered by a "vast slab of curving, opaque glass" like the "Temples of Aerat." It was my thumb but I did not see him there.

I thrust the paper into the typewriter and twirled it through.

"I have fallen from the mountain and hang perpendicularly, perilously, on a limitless white plain. I tremble, on the verge of falling, but the slime from the marsh holds me fast."

I struck the first key.

"A metal meteor is roaring down upon me. Or is it something I have never before witnessed? It has a tail that streams off beyond sight. It comes at terrific speed.

"I know. The Gods are angry with me for leaving Mortia land. Yes! 'Tis only

They who kill by iron. Their hands clutch the rod in mighty tower Baviat and thrust it here to stamp me out."

And a shaking little figure cried: "Baviat tertia! . . . Mortia mea . . ." as the Gods struck wrathfully at a small one daring to explore their domain. For little man Jeko had contrived to see Infinity—and Infinity was only for the eyes of the Immortals, and those of the Experience who dwelt there by the Gods' grace. He had intruded into the realm of the rulers, the world of the After Life and the Gods Omnipotent!

A mortal—in the land of All!

IN A WORLD deep down in Smallness, in an electron of a cell of dead wood, five scientists were grouped before the complicated instrument so reminiscent of early radios. But now they all were standing. Strained, perspiring, frightened, they trembled, aghast at the dimensions the experiment had assumed; they were paralyzed with terror and awe as they heard of the wrath of the affronted Gods. And the spirit of science froze within them and would die in Mortia land. "Seek the skies only by hallowed Death" was what they knew. And they destroyed the machine of the man who had found Venquil land—and thought to live and fled as Jeko's last thoughts came through.

For many years five frightened little men of an electron world would live in deadly fear for their lives and for their souls after death; and would pray, and become great disciples, spreading the gospels of the Gods. True, Jeko had described a monstrous world; but how could a mere mortal experience its true meaning? It was really ethereal and beautiful, was Venquil land, and they would spend the rest of their days insuring themselves for the day of the Experience—when they would assume their comforted place in the world of the After Life.

As I struck the first letter, a strange sensation swept over me. Something compelled me to stop and look at the typing paper. I was using a black ribbon, but when, the key fell away, there was a tiny spot of red . . .

A Martian Oddity

by FJA

L ITTLE TO SAY about this shorty.
Its one and only previous appearance was as "Behind the Ate Ball" in Marvel
Science Stories *for Nov '50. It bore no byline and wasn't included on the Table
of Contents so it could truly be called a "lost story".*

Bea Mahaffey, the Beautiful Editor of Other Worlds, *once told me she had
read it and enjoyed it. I am not aware that anyone else in the world has, all these
years, been aware of its existence.*

I hope you consider the resurrection worthwhile.

THE WIFE OF the Mayor of Eastern Canalopolis, Mars, was very nervous.
She hopped about like a zand-flea. It was all because of that *man* who was
coming to dinner.

It was not every night that the Mayor's wife entertained an Earthman for
supper; this was the firstime in Zumbarian (Martian) history that a Karterian
(Earthman) was to dine on Mars. Gray Leybury was the first rocketeer to reach
our neighbor planet.

Shona* Aardvark (whose name purely by cosmic coincidence coincided
with that of a popular terrestrial crossword puzzle pet) was quite upset at the
progress of her preparations. Her ten tentacles twitched and she wished she
had as many hands as she tried to manage her pots and pans with only three
pairs. Mrs. Aardvark was world-famous (Mars-world, that is) for the excellence
of her cuisine (a French word which did not exist on Mars, which made her feat
all the more remarkable) and her husband had impressed upon her that on this
historic occasion she must reach a culinary pinnacle.

A new high in heartburn (the Martian sign of a successful meal).

By divine providence, Leybury had landed on the left bank of Canalopolis,
ancient home of the green Martians, who were traditional enemies of the purple
Martians of the right bank, who were now green with envy. Mayor Aardvark
was extremely anxious to make a resounding hit with the hero from Earth by
having a meal prepared for him that would, as the Earthmen were fond of
saying, "melt in his mouth." Aardvark, as in fact were all Martians, was fairly
familiar with Earthian sayings, for interplanetary radio had been operating on

Mars for several years now. Every cultured green Martian was acquainted with Karterese (or English) in addition to Vrest Zumbarian (high Martian) as opposed to the Kanyon Zumbarian or low Martian mumbled on the wrong side of the Grand Canal.

Mayor Aardvark had heard it said that, on the Camel Soup commercial, "the way to a man's heart is through his stomach." Certain physiologists, never having seen an Earthman, argued that this meant Earthmen's hearts were located behind their stomachs but Mayor Aardvark interpreted this saying on a poetic rather than a biological basis.

AT LAST KLIRO and Dezdra, the double moons of Mars, rose in the evening sky and Mr. Leybury, the man from the planet which was only mono-satellitic, sat at the dinner table of Mrs. Aardvark.

Mrs. Aardvark, as women the worlds over will, mentally appraised Mr. Leybury; and while she found him wanting in certain Zumbarian qualities, she liked him at once because he looked her straight in the eye. Let us be charitable to Mrs. Aardvark's mentality and say that she was unusually ill at ease, otherwise she would have realized Mr. Leybury had no choice: It was rather disconcerting that he should have two eyes rather than the normal *one.*

Then, too, Mrs. Aardvark noticed, the Earthman suffered a lack of a full complement of arms and had no tentacles at all, which paucity of manly charms made Mrs. Aardvark feel very sorry for Mr. Leybury's shonakanatonawana-tok. (See footnote.) This was a sympathy she might well have spared the rocketeer as he was in fact a misogynistic bachelor who had fled Earth to escape the tentacles—purely figurative, of course—of a neurotic nymphomaniac!

Finally, Mr. Leybury was so small (only 6'3") that he had to be accommodated in the baby's high-chair.

But aside from his midget proportions and unaesthetic pink color, he looked almost Martian. The household pets—all 17 of them—were fed first, of course, according to Zumbarian custom; and then the guest was invited to eat.

As an appetizer Mrs. Aardvark served baloney and applesauce á la banana oil, a classic combination from recipes of the Raring Twenties that she had once heard of. As Mr. Leybury consumed her delicacy (deliciously served lukewarm) Mrs. Aardvark noted with satisfaction that he lost some of his pallor and began to turn a healthy Martian green.

Then came the entree.

With a sense of total triumph Mrs. Aardvark nudged Mr. Aardvark underneath the table with her third leg as she served the roast horse. That is to say, not strictly roast horse but the Zumbarian equivalent, an animal famous for its tough meat. Mrs. Aardvark was familiar with the Earth saying, "I'm so hungry I could eat a horse," and she felt certain Mr. Leybury had not had a satisfying meal since he left Earth.

AFTER THE MEAL was over the Mayor, excusing himself, rose from the table and hopped on his polite leg to the potted yuccaktis plant. Amidst the leaves he belched twice. Mrs. Aardvark simultaneously raised one of her six hands to her eating mouth (her talking mouth was immaculately free of food) and pointedly coughed. Perhaps radio reception from Earth was not all that it could be in clarity but she was not about to be outdone in the after dinner amenities by her husband, and she was sure she had heard it said that among Earthmen a burp in the hand was considered to be worth two in the bush.

THE LAST SENSATION Mr. Leybury had before he died was one of consuming thirst. While the food he had been served had been edible, if teddible, oddly no beverage had accompanied the repast.

He could not intuit it but his hosts themselves were parched for thirst; however, in deference to the known custom of their guest they had considerately refrained from drinking, for the Aardvarks were conscious of the etiquette of Earth that prohibited the imbibing of liquids with food. A Karterian fictionizer by the name of Rudwar Khiplikh had summed it up this:

"Eats is eats and wets is wets and never the twins shall meat."

The Aardvarks had heard it on a broadcast from Earth one night.

Mrs. Aardvark, at the behest of her husband, had done her best to make an impression on the famous gastronaut from Earth and she had succeeded beyond her fondest expectations.

Mrs. Aardvark's dramatic dinner made an undying impression on Mr. Leybury when he dropped dead.

It had been an aard night's vark as Shona. A. had put her awl into an old Earthian proverb:

One man's meat is another man's poison.

*Equivalent of Mrs., abbreviation for Sitonakanatonauana-tok.

Confessions of a Science Fiction Addict

by FJA

*A*FTER HOURS *was a poor man's* PLAYBOY *magazine published in 1957 by the man who in 1958 was to bring* FAMOUS MONSTERS OF FILMLAND *to the noosestands from Maime to Karloffornia.*

The 4th issue was science-fantasy oriented and Forry Ackerman-dominated, with the piece reprinted herewith plus "Screamoscope is Here!" (genesis of the famous/infamous FAMOUS MONSTERS *style) and "The Great Male Robbery", a scientale of 1980 with a twist in its tale; plus a kind of Lovecraftale of horror by Arthur Porges, "I Meet My Love Again", and numerous out-of-this-world girl fotos leaving little to the imagination.*

In a less sophisticated era—say the 30s—I suppose this article would have been called "breezy" or "spicy".

I GOT THE habit when I was 9. For 31 years I been trying to kick it but it always kicks back. Yeah, man, that's the story of my life: I get a kick out of science fiction.

It could happen to you.

I got my first fix in '26, a blast in the arm that was a mixture of amazing adventure and romanticized science from a trio of pen-men named Julie, Ed and "HG." Jules was French, the oldest of the three, and an egghead like H.G. His last name, as I recall, was Verne; Herb's was Wells. Ed, short for Edgar—his last name was Burroughs and he had a funny middle one, Race or Rice—Ed was an egg-layer, leastwise a lot of his gals were. He told tall tales about Princesses of Mars, which planet he called Barsoom, and you won't believe this, but his babes were real chicks in the sense of the word that when they had babies they actually laid 'em neatly wrapped up in shells! Crazy! I been tryin' to remember all day (1926 is a long time away) whether they came wrapped in blue for boys and pink for girls... And I often wondered whatever became of Ed; last I heard he was soothing his jungled nerves in Africa with some Jane named Tarzan.

I'll bet to most of you readers 1926 is just an ancient date in a history book but (and sometimes I wonder how this was possible) I was *alive* then! If you could call it living. Oh, we had movies—"flickers"—but they didn't talk, and you couldn't see Lollobrigida's bust in 140 feet of Skinemascope and blushing Sexicolor. We didn't even have double features yet, like Sophia Loren. There was no TV, no Eve Meyer, no calypso, no Anita Ekberg, no jukeboxes, no Jayne Mansfield, no dream car designs, no *$64,000 Question*, no Lili St. Cyr, no ballpoint pens, no Marilyn Monroe, no Art Students' Ball, no rock 'n' roll, no Pogo, no bikinis, no—well, there were lots of things that there weren't. Worst of all, probably, was the fact that *there wasn't any AFTER HOURS!* Lucky science fiction came along just at that time to make life bearable.

IT ALL BEGAN with *Amazing Stories*, this thing that a generation later we call "sci-fi." *Amazing* was the first science fiction magazine and in April 1926 you could have bought its nearly 200 large-size pages for a quarter—a first edition collector's item that today catalogs for around $50. The magazine is still being published and its current editor recently sold one of his own stories from its pages to the movies: "The Cosmic Frame," which will be marqueed as THE ATTACK OF THE SAUCER MEN.

There were some pretty hot contributors to those early years of *Amazing*: Jules Verne with his "Trip to the Center of the Earth" and "Robur the Conqueror," H. G. Wells with "The Time Machine" and "The War of the Worlds" and "When the Sleeper Wakes," and other names well known today such as Edgar Allan Poe, Curt Siodmak, Ray Cummings and Edgar Rice Burroughs.

Incidentally, for the records, Buck Rogers was born in the pages of *Amazing* in August 1928. He was known as Anthony Rogers at the time, in the story "Armageddon—2419 A.D." His creator, Phil Nowlan, is now dead but Nowlan's character lives on. In introducing the story, the editor enthused: "We have rarely printed a story in this magazine that for scientific interest, as well as suspense, could hold its own with this particular story. We prophesy that this story will become more valuable as the years go by. It certainly holds a number of interesting prophecies, of which no doubt, many will come true." In World War II, G. I. Joe fought with one of the "crazy Buck Rogers" inventions: the not-so-crazy rocketgun known as the *bazooka*...

TIME ROCKETED ON and new titles came to join the lone spacewolf at the newsstands. *Amazing* had a double-thick companion every 3 months in *Amazing Quarterly*, and rivals in *Science Wonder, Air Wonder, Amazing (Scientific) Detective, Astounding* and (tho short-lived) *Miracle. Weird Tales* too printed pseudo-science fiction. Radio ran serials about "Ooomamarooloo," the mysterious woman from Mars, and Poppa Poppavitch, bad mad scientist.

As the 20s drew to a close, the silver screen had pictures of a prehistoric monster running amok in London (THE LOST WORLD by Conan Doyle), a melodrama of a marvelous robot in a 21st century Cosmopolis with skyscrapers a mile high (METROPOLIS), a subsea civilization in Jules Verne's MYSTERIOUS ISLAND, and a trip to Earth's satellite in the German import, WOMAN IN THE MOON.

In 1930 the first British All-Talking Picture was a prophecy of the world of 1940. The same year, Fox Studios (which was yet to become 20th Century-Fox and eventually 21st Century) made a memorable musicomedy of a flight to Mars in 1980, JUST IMAGINE. In the latter, J-21 and LN-18, a boy and girl of 1980, were showing Single-0, a survivor from 1930 who had been unconscious for 50 years, the technological advances of their scientific era. Inserting a coin in a device that looked like a combination between a jukebox and a pinball machine, they pressed a button and a couple of pills popped out. One, they explained to him, was steak, the other apple pie. After he had swallowed both, they asked him how he enjoyed his meal. "The steak was a little tough," he reported ruefully. "Give me the good old days." Another button was pressed, another miracle of speed and compaction wrought before the eyes of the visitor from the past, who only shook his head and repeated, "Give me the good old days." Finally, the couple demonstrated the modern method of producing children. Preselecting the infant's sex, they pulled a lever and down a slide slid a freshly-diapered brand-new "bundle of joy." The man from the past looked aghast and with a newfound and heartfelt expression said for the third time what he had said originally: "GIVE ME THE GOOD OLD DAYS!" This was daring and risqué dialog a quarter of a century ago and it fractured the audiences.

Several years later when the word went out that a film was to be made of Philip Wylie's *Gladiator*, science fiction fans familiar with its very virile superman-hero and his sexy performances everywhere from canoes to bedroom closets wondered how the picture'd get past the Hays Office—the cinema censorship bureau of the time. The answer was simple: instead of a serious scientifilm they made a slapstick scientifarce, a not-so-wily treatment of the Wylie novel that bore little resemblance to the original. "The Last Man On Earth" fared better when it was made as a musicomedy called IT'S GREAT TO BE ALIVE, with the world's sole male survivor of the man destroying *masculitis* becoming a premium priority piece of beefcake on the female market. The most beautiful women in all the world came before Mr. Lucky, as slaves before a Sultan, to bid for his favor. And when you've got about a billion women to pick from, this can become a problem.

SCIENCE FICTION IS maybe too dry for your taste? All equations and formulas and no sex? Whoever told you that! And don't you believe it. Take *The*

Black Flame, for instance, a novel by Stan Weinbaum, from another of whose works the recent SHE-DEVIL was filmed. Margaret of Urbs—called Black Margot—invincible and ruthless ruler of the world some centuries hence. Poets sing of her: "Glorious? Superb? None of these can name the splendor of the ebon flame." Exotic, erotic; a princess of passion: "A black flame blowing cold across the world," kindling cauldrons of lava in the hearts of men, feared and hated by women of lesser beauty, ageless and immortal, demon-driven and riding roughshod across dangerous hills and perilous plains toward the unknown horizons of tomorrow.

Or take the strange case of *The Four-Sided Triangle*. The 4-sided *what*—? Yes, you read right. The age-old dilemma of two men in love with the same girl. But does one man shoot his rival, wait for the honeymoon to run its course to divorce; does the girl commit suicide or go off with a *third* guy? No, none of these ordinary fiction solutions, for remember, this is *science* fiction, where the magician pulls a *rocketship* rather than a rabbit out of the hat. The sci-fi answer to the knotty naughty problem is a kind of have-your-coke-and-drink-it-too solution, where the girl gets made twice. Or, rather, perhaps it better be explained another way: she is duplicated. An extra is made of the girl. Like two kewpie dolls can be made from one mold, well, a second real live doll is made. It's an invention. Money can be duplicated, everything. Only if you think that's the end of the story and the quartet walk happily into the sunset, you've got no idea of the surprises in store for you if you get ahold of the pocketbook. It's a Galaxy novel.

Remember the song, "I'm My Own Grandma?" Once upon a time there was an s.f. story about a crazy mixed-up kid who became her own daughter! This weird state of affairs came about in approximately the following manner: A time machine is an imaginary device that, instead of transporting you like an auto, train or plane from one place to another, moves you from one *time* to another. Like say ahead to 1984 or back to 1492. In this case this woman went back from the present times to about 25 years before, married a man, had a daughter, died, and the daughter grew up to become the woman who went back into the past, married a man, had a daughter...etc. If anybody understands how his could be, send your explanation to the editor and win a free Trip to the Year 2000—but don't expect to come back, this offer is for a Limited *Time* Only.

Then there was this Venusian dish named Nyusa, and a spaceman met up with her when she bumped into him in the dark in a big hurry to escape a crowd of ruffians who were after her for some reason or other. The spaceman is quite startled in the black of night (Venus has no moon) to feel that the girl who has run into his arms is quite naked. He is even more startled when he gets her safely to a room and turns on the light, to find he's rescued a beautiful bundle of—nothing! This was a yarn I collaborated on myself some years ago called "Nymph of Darkness." More recently I did one called "The Naughty Venusienne" in which once again the heroine, this time named N'yvonnaise, is invisible. Science fiction is full of fascinating women, so much so in fact that I am presently putting together an anthology about out-of-this-world wenches called *Women of Wonder*. There is plenty to wonder about at the women of science fiction. For one thing, for the first 20 years or so of their existence they must have had kidneys of concrete because it wasn't till about 10 years ago that one finally broke down for the firstime and had to go to the Little Girls' Powder Room (on a spaceship yet!) But, mundane matters aside, in sci-fi you'll meet some of the most sighful sirens imaginable: Sharane, Yvala, Norhala, Aerita, Aladoree. These glamorous females from other worlds and other times may have such added attractions as wings, fins, tails or even an additional mammary gland (that's a breast, buster, in case you're the kind who doesn't like to call a spade a shovel); but whatever that certain something extra is that distinguishes them from everyday women, you may depend upon it that their enchanting faces and flawless figures would send Kim Novak, Ava Gardner, Mitzi Gaynor, Betty Brosmer, Lily Christine and all the movie stars and pinup girls scampering to their masseusses and make-up men. Outside of the hey-boy men's mags, there is more pulchritudinous epidermis per square inch displayed in the action-adventure brand of science fiction than any other category of story. Just watch out for the women who can read men's minds, altho with the kind of cuties in their birthday suities that many authors (myself included) write about, they don't have to be telepathic to tell what's on the villain's mind—or the hero's either, for that matter.

Not that I am saying science fiction is the sexiest reading matter on the stands today or that sci-fi stories are just an excuse (so who needs an excuse?) to introduce a scantily-clad girl in the plot. Plenty of women keep their clothes on in these imaginative tales and yet manage to be fascinating: In the pages of today's sci-fi magazines you'll find lots of serious, solid, literary, thought-provoking stories. The kind I, personally, like most and would recommend to anyone looking for the best in science fiction. Aldous Huxley, George Orwell, Ray Bradbury, Robert Heinlein, Gore Vidal and Philip Wylie are among the respected names in science fiction. From shorts to serialized novels, s.f. works have been featured in *Saturday Evening Post, Bluebook, Esquire*, in fact all of the topnotch national magazines. Several years ago *Life* devoted 8 pages to saying good things about science fiction. Hard cover books have been devoted to the topic. NBC has given it an hour-long accolade over the air lanes. Walt Disney—but there is no need to list the long line of acceptances science fiction has had in latter years. The apprentice years of apology for the subject are long in the past.

THERE ARE "Shanes" in western films that stand gun and holster above the common breed just as there are SLANS in science fiction that soar beyond the stars. You'll find full measure of treasure on the asteroids, flying saucers from Sirious, invasions from Arcturus, prison riots on Pluto, wars of the sexes, Frankensteinian monsters, the rape of the Solar System, Queens of Atlantis, the center of the Earth, Mars and the Year One Million; heroes and heroines by the hundreds, of incredible adventures from here to—Infinity.

Did you know that a sci-fi yarn bylined by Mickey Spillane sold out one of the largest editions of an s.f. mag ever published? (Tale was called "The Veiled Woman"). John Steinbeck has just brought out a kind of science fiction book, a short novel about the near future called "The Short Reign of Pippin IV."

What about the people who *read* science fiction? Are they screwballs, eightballs, rebels without a cause? Tongue-tied, wall-eyed wall-flowers? Four-eyed 97 lb. weaklings who couldn't woo a 3-dimensional girl if they knew one? Or professors with brains sticking out their ears?

Well, John Payne—you may have caught a few of this star's movies—has been a science fiction fan for many years.

Rita Hayworth is a regular reader.

John Barrymore Jr. is about as great an enthusiast about the field as his dad was an actor. And of course there's Orson Welles and Fritz Lang.

[Today, in 1969, we number Alan Arkin, Shirley MacLaine, Christopher Lee, Sammy Davis Jr.]

Marla English, but for a fluke of fate, would have been crowned Miss Sci-Fi of the Pacificoast in '52.

Out in LA there's an s.f. club that's held weekly meetings nonstop for 22 years, racking up the impressive total of over 1000 meetings, and the member-ship (which incidentally has got a clean bill of health from the FBI) consists of Deanagers to Jack Benny-agers of many nationalities, including many couples with children—and grandchildren. Doctors, lawyers, merchants, chiefs, teach-ers, students, artists, businessman and busboys...everybody enjoys science fic-tion. Hi-fi fans, sports car to custom car enthusiasts, opera-goers to soap opera lovers. In short, PEOPLE of all sorts dig science fiction the most.

If you are a people, you too may do the sci-fi flip. It's wilder, much wilder. If you like stories that are really out-of-this-world, try mixing some sci-fi in with your *AFTER HOURS* reading!

The
Big Sleep

by FJA

ANY INTRODUCTION TO this little "what-is-it?" could turn out to be longer than the item itself.
So, without further ado...

ONE PREHISTORIC NIGHT a frog, tired no doubt from leaping out from under the feet of multi-ton dinosaurs all day, lay down on his cozy caliche mineral bed. This took place in Artesia, New Mexico in the days when it was probably described, if at all, as something like Ug-Ug Wah.

Approximately 2,000,000 years later, a workman, digging a cellar for a new home, unearthed the same frog. He (the buried batrachian) was still sawing a log. That the greenback had survived in a state of suspended animation for 2000 milleniums was the only conclusion that Chas. Ashton, consulting petroleum geologist, could come to, tho he shook his head in disbelief.

Frère frog had been buried in a mineral bog, 7 feet underground. Because there was no crevice or opening, it would have been manifestly impossible for the grownup tadpole to have entered the bed after its formation.

The ludicrous Lazarus lived for two days after his miraculous resurrection. Then he croaked.

Metropolis
Über Alles

by FJA

*O*NE OF THE *most gratifying achievements of my life, "talking" the novel Me-tropolis into paperback for those who had never previously had the opportunity to read the book. I received all kinds of "thank you" letters after the Ace edition went on sale in '63. (And I'm delighted to report that I've once again brought* Metropolis *to life, this time—in the 75th Anniversary Edition with graphics and stillustrations—from Sense of Wonder Press.)*

Recently I had the extreme thrill to sit in front of a TV with the man who made METROPOLIS, Fritz Lang, and in his own home see once again Rotwang, the robotrix and the Ultra City as included in the 21st Century special, "Stranger Than Science Fiction".

If you don't get the message from the following wordage that I consider it sage advice to see and/or read Metropolis *at your earliest opportunity, then I had better turn in my alphabet.*

Welcome to Metropolis, My Home Town.

Population—estimated by my slan-friend A. E. van Vogt—approximately 40 million.

I've lived here since I was 10 years old. It's the most exciting, fabulous city on the face of the earth—and under it. London, Los Angeles, New York, Paris, Berlin, Tokyo ... all rolled and roiled into one.

Just imagine!

When I say the magic name—*Metropolis*—it is as tho I combine the skyscraping dominance of the Empire State Building with the elegance of the Taj Mahal, the fame of the Eiffel Tower and the eternal mystery of the Sphinx of Egypt. *Metropolis*—The New Babel, architectural masterpiece of monolithic magnificence. The skyscrapers of the 20th century dwarfed by the towering stratoscrapers of the 21st.

And far beneath, in man-made caverns below, the monster-machines of Moloch: the incredible, inhuman Geyser Machine, the Heart Machine, that must be forever tended by the Human Clocks, the subterranean sub-humans, the helpless workers of the mole-world who slave their hopeless lives away, serfs for the surface people, blind puppets to the will of the Master of Metropolis.

The Master of Metropolis: *Joh Fredersen*, a man forged of ten-point steel, cold as the surface of Pluto—and as distant. A ruler as ruthless and imperious as ancient Caesar.

Hidden somewhere amidst the futuristic superstructures of Metropolis is an anachronistic dwelling, a baroque and gothic survival housing a laboratory wherein alchemical marvels are performed. With the Seal of Solomon on its door, the legendary Golem might have been born here hundreds of years before. Today a wild-eyed white-haired albino spider spins within, a sinister genius who has sacrificed one hand to his supramundane science. It is the eerie abode of *Rotwang*, the evil Ralph 124C41+ of his day.

And Rotwang has created *Futura*—sometimes also called *Parody*—a simulucrum in sentient metal of artificial female flesh. A robotrix of which Rossum might have dreamt.

Metropolis—the book—has been compared to Karel Capek's play *RUR*, to Samuel Butler's Utopian novel *Erewhon*, "of a future period when machinery would develop a soul and become man's master", to *The Time Machine*, in which "the restless far-seeing mind of H.G.Wells conceived an unforgettable picture of the development of social and economic conditions under his Eloi, the epicurean and effete aristocrats of the future world, and their underground and uncanny slaves, the Morlocks." *When the Sleeper Wakes* (Wells), *Land Under England* (O'Neill*), Looking Backward* (Bellamy) and *Summer in 3000* (Martin)—two of which came later—are reminiscent in some respects of the book.

When I speak of *Metropolis* the film there is nothing with which to compare it: it remains the science-fantasy classic incomparable, the single greatest scientifilm I ever saw.

This masterpiece originally sold in book form in the late 20's in a chain of Ten Cent Stores! A wretched piece of book-making, the first edition nevertheless has become a cornerstone item in the collections of film adaptation collectors and a work particularly coveted by aficionados of fantasy filmdom. The lastime I had a spare copy it was snapped up for $25. It is undoubtedly going for more now.

Today, in its 75th year and at the birth of the new Millenium is hightime, and over time, that a new edition of this unique book be made available. Thea von Harbou, its gifted authoress, now dead, in her lifetime exhibited a literary mind that leapt ahead of reality. When rocketry was in its infancy, long before it was in its launching cradle, she authored the world-famous *Woman in the Moon*, both book and screenplay. "The Indian Tomb", "The Isle of the Immortals", "Destiny", "Spies"; "Siegfried" in film form and a cinemadaptation of "Dr. Mabuse"; were among Frau von Harbou's literary and motion picture legacy. She was married to the celebrated director Fritz Lang, who so masterfully materialized her masterpiece *Metropolis* on the screen.

"*Metropolis* is unlike any other novel as yet written," enthused an observer at the time. "It is distinct, unique and original. It has a tremendous drama of conflicting forces and an idyllic love theme."

The language of the novel is sometimes as thesauric as Shiel, as kaleidoscopic as Merritt in "The Metal Emperor", as bone-spare as Bradbury in "The Skeleton", as poetic as Poe, as macabre as Machen. The title belongs on your Hugo Award shelf along with *The World Below, The House on the Borderland, The Demolished Man, The Forever War, Childhood's End, Last Men in London, Stranger In A Strange Land, 1984*.

Science and Fantasy, Horror and Beauty; Mystery, Menace, Madness, Magnificence, Significance—Once in a Lifetime all the Elements were Magically Combined to Create the Imaginative Classic, the Filmasterpiece Supreme:

METROPOLIS!

This is the book on which the film was based.

The book has been called a work of genius.

I agree. In the next few hours you will have an experience in reading that will last you all the rest of your life.

> —FORREST J ACKERMAN
> Apt. 4sJ, Rotwang Towers
> Lang Level and Harbou Skyway
> METROPOLIS
> 24 Novembro 2027

6 April 2027

I've lost track (remember, I'm 111 years old), I think I've now seen METROPOLIS 119 times. And MEGALOPOLIS, the scientifilm first projected in 2001, numerous times. I remember 1918's World War was described as "the war to end war." Then I devoted 3 years 4 months and 29 days to WW2 and my brother lost his life. H. G. Wells said, "If we don't end war, war will end us." I never thought I'd live to see WW3—The Terrorist War—but it pearlharbored us, a surprise attack, alas.

A quarter century ago in 2001, Anne Hardin was proofreading this 75th Anniversary Edition of *METROPOLIS* during the 2 weeks following September 11. She's my collaborator on *RAINBOW FANTASIA, MARTIANTHOLOGY* and many other Sense of Wonder Press publications of the last 5 lustrums. Her reaction: "I think in many ways I could have inserted the text on the destruction of Metropolis into the *NY Times* any day of the past 2 weeks and the vivid picture of a city's destruction would have been the same: the images of fire, heat and being trapped by water, the trains crashing in and preventing Maria's escape with the children—all too real. The resemblance between Manhattan and the Metropolis of the film is chilling; the imagination of the set builders was remarkably prescient." She continues: "There are stories and there are STO-RIES. Only once in a blue moon does someone's mind create a novel concept. Just think of all the books that Shelley's book influenced. Seems to me the same incredible creativeness that you see in *Frankenstein* is present in *Metropolis*. And the translation has a rhythm to it that is hypnotic. I also wonder if von Harbou was influenced by Meyrink's *Der Golem*: I think bringing Futura to life as Maria is a bit akin to the infusion of life in the man of clay, eh?"

Judge for yourself!

In the meantime, on a happier note, in my original introduction I noted that A. E. van Vogt, whom we lost 27 years ago, estimated the population of Metropolis to be 40 million; for purists I have since learned that the correct figure is 60 million.

Read, now, Thea von Harbou's coruscating classic; it will give you a rush like an evening in Yoshiwara!

> —4sJ Ackerman
> Frank Paul Penthouse
> Helms Estate
> 124C41 Gernsback Gardens
> 451 Bradbury Way &
> Siodmak Strasse
> Marlene Memorial Circle
> METROPOLIS

Born Witch, Burn!

by FJA

*P*UBLISHED IN THE last issue of Sex & Censorship *in 1958.*
We've come a long way in 11 ever-improving years toward the ultimate goal:
the Denmark Ideal of no official insistence that portrayed sexuality is a government's
concern, the end of the wearisome war between the obscenophiles and the
pornophobes, with the recognition that "a little lubricity now & then is relished
by the beast in men"—Barbarella.

*In the 20s they destroyed the art of Wallace Smith (*Fantazius Mallare*) and*
broke his heart—too late for Smith, the same work now sells as posters in psyche-
delic shops.

Burning witches has always produced a bad odor and there's too much smog
in the mental atmosphere already clouding men's minds.

Young people!—pleasure me this: an utter end to Puritan madness, a brave
nude world of Pan set free.

We're next door to 1970. I hope in the Censor-free Seventies Born Witch,
Burn! *will read like an incomprehensible horror-fantasy.*

ROSALEEN NORTON HAS been branded a freak, a 20th century witch, a
depraved mad-woman and a vehement variety of other slanderous epithets by
her contemporary critics and—peers? She is an artist of the supramundane.

The Art of Rosaleen Norton is a handsome accomplishment in bookmaking.
The oversize 10"x13" pages are printed on rag content paper, hand-bound in
gold-embossed crimson leather. There are 32 extraordinary grease-pencil re-
productions of the Luciferian people, places and *things* that dwell darkly in the
weird Louvrecraftian world of Rosaleen Norton. The work is metaphysical in
nature; but there is a matterphysical side to it, so very vermilion in its inextrica-
bly sexual delineation that YOU *CAN'T* SEE IT NOW.

Come back in, maybe, 1970. If the Anti-Sex League of 1984 doesn't get us
first.

The 80-page volume (with illustrated flyleaves) of Norton art was published
in Australia in 1952 in an edition limited to 1000 copies, 350 being bound in

leather, and the first 20 numbered collector's items featuring a bonus of an original color work signed by the artist. The majority of copies were liquidated in the land of their origin. Half a dozen may have reached America. Two found haven in Hollywood.

I once saw a copy in the pale vampiric hands of the late Bela Lugosi. It was fitting that the aged Dracula should be admiring the volume, vocally and volubly, for the original intention had been to bind the book in batskin. It came close to not being bound at all, for in the land of the Southern Cross bookbinding is traditionally women's work, and the ladies of the bindery took one look at what they were expected to bind and revolted in righteous indignation.

The phallic, the pubic, the graphically hermaphroditic and sapphic were a bit too thick for their thin skin.

The *Sydney Sunday Sun*'s review of the volume explained: "Sex symbolism is portrayed with such stark abandon in a strictly limited edition of an art work just published here that an all-male staff of book-binders was engaged to bind the work. The artist—a woman—has steeped her drawings in medieval demonology and witchcraft."

According to a report in the *New Australian Post*, in 1952 Rosaleen Norton was "an attractive brunet with massive, arched eyebrows and somewhat prominent teeth who effected loose-fitting black silk slacks, a brown Chinese-style jacket, golden earrings, painted toenails, and sandals, and smoked cigarettes in a long holder." A short time later I met an Australian teleplaywright, a bibliophile of the baroque who claimed to know "Roey" Norton personally, and he commented *en passant* that the somewhat protruding teeth were permanently dyed green from breathing ether and she was a Daughter of Bilitis.

She was certainly not a typical housewife.

One journalist of the day characterized her as "one of the few real uninhibited, completely, unselfconscious Bohemians in modern Australia." Three years before the publication of *The Art of Rosaleen Norton*, the controversial artist was acquitted of an obscenity charge over an exhibition of her unpunch-pulling paintings at Melbourne University. Her offtrail art has been passionately praised and furiously condemned in Sydney, Melbourne and Adelaide.

New Zealand born (1917), she began drawing at the age of 3; ran away from home to become an artists' model in her teens; and worked at odd times elsewhere at such prosaic jobs as newspaper artist, waitress, nightclub assistant and telegraph messenger. Who knew they were receiving a wire from Rosaleen Norton, who would one day electric-defy the art world?

Walter Glover, hot water publisher of *The Art of Rosaleen Norton*, in perfacing the volcanic volume, stated: "Although the subject matter of her work has frequently raised storms of disapproval and on one occasion led to the banning of an exhibition of her paintings, no one has denied her power to draw. Opinions have never been fair to her either as an artist or a person. Miss Norton is a highly intellectual human with a keen sense of feeling, generous to extremes. Due to her arrogance and individuality she has never attempted to defend herself against personal slanders."

Six years ago *The Art* of Roey sold for $50 a copy before the court trial in Australia officially outlawed it. Miss Norton, her poetic collaborator Gavin Greenlees and the publisher all narrowly escaped stiff sentences when it was agreed that the remaining unsold copies of the edition would be destroyed. Before that a very few copies were flown into the USA (first class, at a cost of $8 apiece airmail) in order to avoid confiscation by Customs. $1000 has been estimated as a conservative purchase price today for a copy of this *esoterica rararbilia* but who but a connoisseur could afford it? A far cry from the purpose of the publisher, who stated: "In publishing this book I have attempted to present in the most appropriate manner possible the work of two talented people whose art might otherwise have been lost to the public."

Publisher Walter Glover reported: "During the long period in which we worked as a trio on the preparation of this book I had ample opportunity to become well acquainted with the authors and their way of life. I, too, experienced similar difficulties that they had encountered from prurient society in achieving recognition for their work."

Of Greenlees, whose poetry accompanies the artwork, it is related that, "In common with Shelley and Shaw, I was hated and miserable at school." At the age of twelve Greenlees won 3 successive poetry competitions sponsored by the Australian Broadcasting Commission. The next 3 years were spent experimenting with Surrealism and the Freudian dream world, studying Lantreamont, Rimbaud, Joyce and other Moderns. In Sydney in 1949 he began a course of psychological study, taking Jung, Ouspensky and Dostoyevsky as guides. He met Miss Norton in 1949, thereafter devoting himself to a study of the Occult. When last heard of he was evolving a system based on Alchemy as a means of self-knowledge.

In the fascinating pages of Norton's Banned Book lie encounters with Lilith, Binah, Geburah, Qlipha, Gargos, Ourobouros, Anubine, Eloi, Ermulie and all manner of phantasms, principles, spirits, voodoo priestesses, dynamic energies of cosmic ideation, elementals, sex forces, archangels and imaginary creatures.

It is dedicated to *The King in Yellow* (occult ruler of a demesne created by novelist Robert W. Chambers shortly before the turn of the century) "with grateful acknowledgements to The Familiars, and the Very Peculiar People, who helped in various ways to make it possible, and to those heavily disguised angels, the two demons."

In the art appear kaleidoscopic pyrotechnical burgeonings of the bodies of birds, beasts, fish and human begins amalgamated with hands, faces, snakes, suns. Gargoyles and gryphons leer and jeer. Cannibalism, lesbianism, bestialism burst birth-naked from the pregnant pages.

A naked wanton were-woman hotly embraces a powerful black jungle cat. Verboten relation. *Cry Censor!*

Here are diableries drawn from the secret diary of Dorian Gray, diaboliques from a lost sketchbook by Heinrich Kley.

Echoes of Seabrook, Aleister Crowley, Madame Blavatsky, Gustav Meyrink, Machen, Blackwood, Lovecraft, "Dr. Lao," Poe, Robert Bloch, Richard Matheson and the Ray Bradbury of *Dark Carnival* reverberate from stalactite to stalagmite in the picturesque grottoesque Merrittesque abysses of Rosaleen Norton's macabre acolyte-of-night mind.

Her illuminating wand with its four-dimensional rays has dipped deep into the Reservoir of Revelations known to Blake, Beardsley, Lindsay, Finlay, Wallace Smith, G. N. Fish, Hannes Bok, Burt Shonberg, Ron Cobb and (an artist for whom she is known to have expressed a preference "even above Mortensson") Morris Scott Dollens.

Such few copies of *The Art of Rosaleen Norton* as have escaped the authorized arsonists of Australia and the import impounders of the USA now exist in Limbo. Phoenixlike, in a more enlightened era, they may arise from the ashes of the book burners to take their place with the great art of the esoteric.

Charms around you, Rosaleen Norton, wherever, whatever, witchever you are.

And Then the Cover Was Bare

by FJA

I'VE REVISED THIS one so many times I've lost track. It was written originally to enter in a contest based on an Ellery Queen *cover. Don't remember who, exactly, but I was probably beaten out by John MacDonald or Gerald Heard or Cornell Woolrich or some such clod.*

Original form was full of current in-jokes, such as the editor's name being McBoucher. At a later date Tod Blanche (get it?—Ted White) got into the act as an editor.

In the last revision before this, at a time when 1968 was still a few years in the future, I had selected it as the date the epidermis dam broke. And I wasn't so far wrong, not by (you should pardon the Blochism) a damsite.

ONE DAY IN 1972 the transformation was complete. Jok Strap's eyes roved over the magazine rack and marveled.

On *Turf* a beauteous blond was perched, a la Lady Godiva, on a Black Beauty.

Life's cover pictured 99.44% of Vanity Chere, the hottest model since Eve introduced the fig leaf, in a "z'string": the penultimate reduction of the Bikini bathing suit.

Authors' Digest featured an authoress, "stripped for action," illustrating an article with a nude twist called "Get the Feel of Your Subject." Jok grinned as the entendre doubled in his mind.

"Looking for any title in particular?" the vendor's voice interrupted Strap's reverie.

"Oh, er, uh, *Fantasex Stories.*" The editor made a feeble motion toward the crazy quilt of carnality. "They all look alike to me."

It was true. The time had come—the inevitable end of the Sex Sells Everything syndrome—when every last magazine bid for the buyer's attention with an unclad torso . . . and not a falsie in a carload. *Carnal, Sex Shooters, Raunch Romances, Lust, True Torture Tales, Spiritual Guidance, Astron-Erotology, Sex It To Me, Astounding GALaxies, Sci-Fi, Spy-Fi, Laddies' Homo Companion,*

51

Nudiscoveries, Fiendish Tales, Tales of Dracula, Marquis de Sade Monthly, Grue Book, Rod & Scream, Free Love (now $5, due to inflation)—all, all flaunted a tall, medium, small, blond, brunet, redheaded, reclining, dancing, diving, running, jumping, singing, kneeling, sleeping, climbing, dressing undressed doll!

1975, and there was no longer a magazine or pocketbook that didn't feature bare flesh on the cover. You could close your eyes, stab your finger and pull out a plum—a plum of feminine pulchritude, a pulchri*nude*, to quote Bloch's mintiest coinage.

"A beauty, ain't she?" Strap shuddered as the newsboy, a white-haired old lecher of 70, handed him the mid-April issue of *Fantasex*. On the scarlet cover shrieked an earthy nude, illustrating Tod Salmon's "The Vampire Who Hated Blood." Strap gave a $3 bill, pocketed the magazine and stepped back onto the branch ride-walk for Mad Ave.

In the office of the Managing Ed. of *Allergy King*, Strap found a very worried Patrick de Graw. "Why the melancholia?" Strap queried.

"Aw, it's the rockey-jockeys," Pat complained. "They're off their rockets."

"The King kids?"

"Who else?"

"What's clogging their jets now?"

"The usual."

"The covers?"

"Yeah, the covers. They're so blonked on the subject they can't crink. Believe me, Jok! They wish they'd never followed the mob. 'Nude dames,' they been muttering all morning; 'a quarter hundred of 'em in the past 2 years, all the time getting nuder on our covers. The nuder gender! Ha! How nude can you get? We used to display some originality but now all we display is sex. What's original about a nude? A nude hasn't been original since Adam's old lady stuck a figleaf on her figure. But when we started spicing up our covers with sex, who cared how many eyebrows shot up—as long as sales shot up, too? The conservatives followed our lead and look what it's led to: an epidemic of epidermis! Damn all dames and their lily-white frames'!

"Then they phoned Bill Rotsler to have Vanity Chere 'cop over to his Studio and flew out of here for there themselves."

"Gok," said Strap, ran his hand through his hairs and pulled out his pipe. "This is serious! Pat, I'm off to Rotsler's nudio."

HE WAS TOO late.

He found Rotsler in a state of shock, eyes staring, Lorre-like, at the corpse.

It was gorgeous, even in death.

Vanity's golden body half sat, half reclined: her world-famous dimpled derriere was protected from the chill blue lamination of the floor by a rose-pink negligee which had once endorsed her luscious torso. Her rhapsodisical limbs lay in limpid abandon; her head lolled back, a cascade of amber hair almost caressing her crossed wrists behind. She had met her end by strangulation and the murder sash still was drawn taut about the throat that had been the chalice of a thousand kisses. Supporting her, the cloth stretched to either side behind a pair of curtains.

Something struck Strap as terribly, unnaturally familiar about this scene—that Dunne-for, "I-have-been-here-before" feeling. There lay lovely Vanity Chere, posed with Death, poised in death, reminding him frighteningly of something similar he had seen in the half-remembered past.

And when, like the snap of a camera shutter, it clicked in his mind where he knew that tableau, he knew the motive for the murder—and who had killed the word's choicest piece of chizkak.

Vanity Chere was posed in an exact duplication of a scene on an *Allergy King* cover of some years before. Strap remembered it well, now . . . His own name had appeared on the cover in conjunction with his annual selection of the best mystery books of the preceding year. The cover had been a contest cover—a contest *un*cover—a beautiful nudachrome by Rotsler. The nude had rocketed sales; the publisher had been happy with the financial report; Rotsler had been happy (it had resulted in an increased demand for his services); Sylvius Agricola, the contest winner, had been happy when his yarn, "It Began With Bikini," had been awarded the $2000 prize.

But *everybody* hadn't been ecdysiastically ecstatic.

Strap remembered the bitter correspondence from New York, the brooding conversations when he was in Gotham. Sure, flesh was selling the book, but if you took a pride in your reputation, your ability to discover choice detectival hit-bits, if your nose-for-clues was no longer as important an attraction as a cutie with no clothes on . . . well.

Yes, Strap recalled the rankling recriminations, the burgeoning guilt complex as other periodicals followed suit, the incipient paranoia.

He found his voice. "Come out, boys," he choked.

With a simulacrum of life, the enchanted corpse lowered her perfect back till her fair head touched the floor. The straining sash on either side relaxed and Vanity Chere's body lay supine.

Their knuckles as bone-white as the sash they clutched, out from either side of the portico stepped the collaborators known as *Allergy King*.

The Lure & Lore
of "The Blind Spot"

by FJA

*T*HIS WAS THE *Introduction I wrote for the First Edition hardcover volume of* THE BLIND SPOT *published by Prime Press in 1951. Cover & illustrations by the late Hannes Bok. The Sequel,* THE SPOT OF LIFE, *was scheduled, and I was to have introduced it as well with further forgotten facts and new information but the untimely death of the publisher cut down the press in its . . . prime.*

The night of the Planchette Adventure, which you are about to read about, I swear my host told me of stepping on an 18" ant ("an experience you don't soon forget") somewhere in northern California and that he was going back and get pictures and I would be among the first to see them.

Then he fell out of communication with me.

I kept looking for a gi-ant on the cover of LIFE.

Finally I forgot the man's name.

Late in '68, out of the blue, he phoned me. Practically the first question out of my mouth was, "What about that super ant?"

He doesn't remember anything about a super ant.

Am I manufacturing memories?

It is difficult to type with this silly constricting white coat they have put on me. I swear they have fastened it backwards!

THE BLIND SPOT opens with the words: "Perhaps it were just as well to start at the beginning. A mere matter of news." Suppose I use them in the same sense:

A mere matter of news: The first installment of this fabulous novel was featured in *Argosy All-Story Weekly* for 14 May 1921. Described as a "different" serial, it was introduced by a cover by Modest Stein. In the foreground was the profile of a girl of another dimension—ethereal, sensuous, the eternal femi-nine—the Nervina of the story. Filmy crystalline earrings swept back over her bare shoulders. Dominating the background was a huge flaming yellow ball, like our Sun as seen from the hypothetical Vulcan—splotched with murky, mys-terious *globii vitonae*. There was an ancient quay, and emerging from the ultra-marine waters about it a silhouetted metropolis of shires, domes and minarets.

It was 1921, and that generation thus received its first glimpse of the alien landscape of *The Blind Spot* and the baroque beauty of an immortal woman of fantasy fiction.

The authors? Homer Eon Flint was already a reigning favorite with post-World War I enthusiasts of imaginative literature, who had eagerly devoured his *Lord of Death* and *Queen of Life*, his "King of Conserve Island" and "The Planeteer." Austin Hall was well known and popular for his *Almost Immortal*, "Rebel Soul," and "Into the Infinite."

Then came this epoch-making collaboration. When Mary Gnaedinger launched *Famous Fantastic Mysteries* magazine she early presented *The Blind Spot*, and printed it again in that magazine's companion *Fantastic Novels*. These reprints are now collectors' items, almost unobtainable, and otherwise the story has long been out of print. Rumor has it an unauthorized German version of *The Blind Spot* has been published in book form. There is another book called *The Blind Spot*, and also a magazine story, and a major movie studio was to produce a film of the same title. However, here is presented the only hard-cover version of the only *Blind Spot* of consequence to lovers of fantasy.

Who wrote the story? When I first looked into the question, as a 15-year-old boy, Homer Eon Flint (he originally spelled his name with a "d") was already dead of a fall into a canyon. In 1949 his widow told me: "I think Homer's father contributed that middle name"—the same name (with slightly different spelling) that the Irish poet George Russell took as his pen-name, which became known by its abbreviation AE. Mrs. Flindt said of Flint's father: "He was a very deep thinker and enjoyed reading heavy material." Like father, like son. "Homer always talked over his ideas with me and although I couldn't always follow his thoughts it seemed to help him to express them to another—it made some things come more clearly to him."

Flint was a great admirer of H. G. Wells (this little grandmother-school-teacher told me) and had probably read all his works up to the time when he (Flint) died in 1924. He had read Doyle and Haggard, but: "Wells was his favorite—the real thinker."

Flint found a fellow-thinker in Austin Hall, whom he met in San José, California, while working at a shop where shoes were repaired electrically—"a rather new concept at the time." Hall, learning that Flint lived in the same city, sought him out, and they became fast friends. Each stimulated the other. As Hall told me 20 years ago of the origin of *The Blind Spot*:

"One day after we had lunched together, I held my finger up in front of one of my eyes and said: 'Homer, couldn't a story be written about that blind spot in the eye?' Not much was said about it at the time but four days later, again at lunch, I outlined the whole story to him. I wrote the first 18 chapters;

Homer took up the tale as 'Hobart Fenton' and wrote the chapters about the House of Miracles, the Living Death, the rousing of Aradna's mind, and so forth, up to The Man from Space, where once again I took over."

To *The Blind Spot* Hall contributed a great knowledge of history and anthropology, while Flint's *fortes* were physics and medicine. Both had a great fund of philosophy at their command.

When I met Hall (about four years older than Flint) he was in his 50s: a devil-may-care old codger (old to a 15-year-old, that is) full of good humor and indulgence for a youthful admirer who had journeyed far to meet him. He casually referred to his 600 published stories and I carried away the impression of one who resembled both in output and looks that other fiction-factory of the time, Edgar Wallace.

Finally: Several years ago, before I knew anything about the present volume, I had an unusual experience. (At that time I had no reason to think *The Blind Spot* would ever become available as a book, for the location of the heirs proved a Herculean task by itself; publishers had long wanted to present this amazing novel but could not do so until I located Mrs. Mae Hall and Mrs. Mabel Flindt.) While, unfortunately, I did not take careful notes at the time, the gist of the occurrence was this:

I visited a friend whose hobby (besides reading fantasy) was the occult, who volunteered to entertain me with automatic writing and the ouija-board. Now, I share Lovecraft's skepticism towards the supernatural, regarding it as at best a means of amusement. When the question arose of what spirits we should try to lure to our planchette, the names of Lovecraft, Merritt, Hall and Flint popped into my pixilated mind. So I set my fingers on the wooden heart and, since my host was also a Flint admirer, we asked about Flint's fatal accident. The occult communicator spelled out:

N O A C C I D E N T — R O B B E R Y.

There followed something about being held up by a hitchhiker. Then Hall (or at least some energy-source other than my own conscious mind) came through too, and when I asked if he had left any work behind he replied:

Y E S — T H E L A S T G O D L I N G.

Later I asked his son about this (without revealing the title) and Javen Hall told me of the story his father had been plotting when he died: "The Hidden Empire" or "The Child of the Southwind." Whatever was pushing the planchette failed to inform me that when I found Austin Hall's son and widow, they would put into my hands an unknown, unpublished fantasy novel by Hall: *The House of Dawn*! Some day it may appear in print.

Meanwhile you are getting understandably impatient to explore that unknown realm of the Blind Spot. Be on your way and—*bon voyage!*

Task of
the Temponaut

by Norbert F. Novotny & Van Del Rio
(Authors of *The Eagle Has Landed*)

*I*f *looks could kill,
this is a hair-raising story.*

THE TEMPONAUT CHECKED the space-time coordinates of his panchronicon. The sight thru the transparent dome of the time machine coincided with the site he had expected to see: the place where "She" lived.

The chrono-killer reached for his weapons, then disembarked from the vehicle that had materialized him in this strange sector of the past. As he set out for his task, he felt slightly sorry for the poor reptilian creatures that would soon get in his way, attempting to stop him, this invader of their twilight zone.

The battlefield was dark but lit with occasional flashes of artificial light. The rugged terrain teemed with half-human, half-reptile creatures which surrounded a beleaguered man whose electric sword and flaming disintegrators cut deep into the writhing mass of repellent flesh. The serpent-men, armed with weird weapons, charged in impotent rage, their primitive methods of attack useless against the invader's glittering armor.

The newly arrived human reached the top of the hill just in time to observe the other temponaut, who looked exactly like him in his protective suit of metal. Temponaut #2 saw that temponaut #1 was somewhat ahead of him, cutting a swath toward the Lady of the Snakes who was chained to a rock, whilst hell-spawned figures stood guard. It was a nightmarish scene.

Two identical shining time travelers stood out in the darkness as they moved in boldly, blasting and crackling their way toward the woman with the thousand snakes on her head. They got close enough to observe her female figure, their faces protected by the mirror-reflecting eye-shields but not wishing to risk looking the Gorgon in the face. So the two futurians moved in from the flanks, avoiding the face of death.

Suddenly the temponaut who had arrived first, as if irresistibly attracted by the fascinating female's figure, lowered his gaze and stared for a moment at her unclad feet. They were undeniably beautiful. He stared enraptured while the other chrono-killer tended to the business for which he had been sent.

Armored temponaut #2 continued to kill while #1's gaze slowly ascended the curving column of the deadly female's figure.

The storm worsened.

The gaze rose to the knees.

Lightning flashed.

Eyes were fastened on a trim waist.

Thunder crashed.

Suddenly, as if by an invisible order, the reptilians stopped in their tracks, observing the spot where the Gorgon once more was about to petrify a human being. The second invader of the past from time's future also stopped. He stood but a few feet removed from he who had arrived first.

The first temponaut continued to gaze thru his metallic helmet, a one-way mirror shielding his eyes. His gaze rested, now, on Her throat . . . but in a moment his reckless eyes rose higher.

For that last, lethal look. But then—

Time stood still . . . and in that frozen moment the second warrior from Earth-to-be realized a staggering truth. Before him his twin figure was swiftly raising his sword—but not fast enough. While the storm stopped as if to take a breath, the second temponaut, who had been late in arriving on the scene, calmly blasted the head of the swordsman to oblivion.

Instead of blood and brains, wires sprang from the half-melted helmet of the destroyed Earthling. It was evident, now, why he could not be seduced by the Gorgon: he was a robot.

And the second man-at-arms was human enough to leave the domain of the serpent woman with all the haste of a water-snake escaping a piranha. In this Godforsaken place beyond reason, in the realm of meta-history, his mission was to prevent the destruction of the Gorgon.

Because the war of 2022 A.D., against the androids, was a war to preserve a segment of the human psyche peculiarly precious to humans.

Their ancient myths.

Yvala

by C. L. Moore and Amaryllis Ackerman

*A*MARYLLIS? I confess: 'tis I, FJA. Had I been born a girl, that is the name my parents had selected for me. So what is my byline doing on this strange interplanetary story from the pages of Weird Tales in 1936? Because I have just waked up to the realization, 66 years later, that I was as much a collaborator on this story as on "Nyusa, Nymph of Darkness"! I contacted Catherine, under the spell of the Russian screen siren Anna Sten, and outlined the plot and named the character. Some years later when I met a Mr. & Mrs. G. Gordon Dewey, I recognized the name of one of their daughters, Julhi, as being a CLMoore name, but the middle name of Sharane (Merritt's The Ship of Ishtar heroine) baffled me. "Eve-uh-lah? How do you spell that?" "Y-v-a-l-a." "Ee-vah- la!" I exclaimed. "Why, I made up that name!" Today Sharane Yvala Dewey is nicknamed Syd and is a grandmother living in the Hawaiian Islands. Yvala's inspirator, glamorous Anna Stem (whose first husband was an Esperanto korespondanto of mine in Kiev)— ascended to angelhood several years ago—but not before being on all-fours in my living room playing with our cat Meetzi.

NORTHWEST SMITH LEANED against a pile of hemp-wrapped bales from the Martian drylands and stared with expressionless eyes, paler than pale steel, over the confusion of the Lakkdarol space-port before him. In the clear Martian day the tatters of his leather spaceman's garb were pitilessly plain, the ray-burns and the rents of a hundred casual brawls. It was evident at a glance that Smith had fallen upon evil days. One might have guessed by the shabbiness of his clothing that his pockets were empty, the charge in his ray-gun low.

Squatting on his heels beside the lounging Earthman, Yarol the Venusian bent his yellow head absently over the thin-bladed dagger which he was juggling in one of the queer, interminable Venusian games so pointless to outsiders. Upon him too the weight of ill fortune seemed to have pressed heavily. It was eloquent in his own shabby garments, his empty holster. But the insouciant face he lifted to Smith was as careless as ever, and no more of weariness and wisdom and pure cat-savagery looked out from his sidelong black eyes than Smith was accustomed to see there. Yarol's face was the face of a seraph, as so many Venusian faces are likely to be, but the set of his mouth told a tale of dissoluteness and reckless violence which belied his features' racial good looks.

"Another half-hour and we eat," he grinned up at his tall companion.

Smith glanced at the tri-time watch on his wrist.

"If you haven't been having another dope dream," he grunted. "Luck's been against us so long I can't quite believe in a change now."

"By Pharol I swear it," smiled Yarol. "The man came up to me in the New Chicago last night and told me in so many words how much money was waiting if we'd meet him here at noon."

Smith grunted again and deliberately took up another notch in the belt that circled his lean waist. Yarol laughed softly, a murmur of true Venusian sweetness, as he bent again to the juggling of his knife. Above his bent blond head Smith looked out again across the busy port.

Lakkdarol is an Earthman's town upon Martian soil, blending all the more violent elements of both worlds in its lawless heart, and the scene he watched had under-currents that only a ranger of the spaceways could fully appreciate. A semblance of discipline is maintained there, but only the space-rangers know how superficial that likeness is. Smith grinned a little to himself, knowing that the bales being trundled down the gangplank from the Martian liner Inghti carried a core of that precious Martian "lamb's-wool" on which the duties ran so high. And a whisper had run through the New Chicago last night as they sat over their segir-whisky glasses that the shipment of grain from Denver expected in at noon on the Friedland would have a copious leavening of opium in its heart. By devious ways, in whispers running from mouth to mouth covertly through the spacemen's rendezvous, the outlaws of the spaceways glean more knowledge than the Patrol ever knows.

Smith watched a little air-freight vessel, scarcely a quarter the size of the monstrous ships of the Lines, rolling sluggishly out from the municipal hangar far across the square, and a little frown puckered his brows. The ship bore only the non-committal numerals which are all the freighters carry by way of identification, but that particular sequence was notorious among the initiate. The ship was a slaver.

This dealing in human freight had received a great impetus at the stimulation of space-travel, when the temptation presented by the savage tribes on alien planets was too great to be ignored by unscrupulous Earthmen who saw vast fields opening up before them. For even upon Earth slaving has never died entirely, and Mars and Venus knew a small and legitimate traffic in it before John Willard and his gang of outlaws made the very word "slaving" anathema on three worlds. The Willards still ran their pirate convoys along the spaceways three generations later, and Smith knew he was looking at one now, smuggling a cargo of misery out of Lakkdarol for distribution among the secret markets of Mars.

FURTHER MEDITATIONS ON the subject were cut short by Yarol's abrupt rise to his feet. Smith turned his head slowly and saw a little man at their elbow, his rotundity cloaked in a long mantle like those affected by the lower class of Martian shopkeepers in their walks abroad. But the face that peered up into his was frankly Celtic. Smith's expressionless features broke reluctantly into a grin as he met the irrepressible good-humor on that fat Irish face from home. He had not set foot upon Earth's soil for over a year now—the price on his liberty was too high in his native land—and curious pricks of homesickness came over him at the oddest moments. Even the toughest of space-rangers know them sometimes. The ties with the home planet are strong.

"You Smith?" demanded the little man in a rich Celtic voice.

Smith looked down at him a moment in cold-eyed silence. There was much more in that query than met the ear. Northwest Smith's name was one too well known in the annals of the Patrol for him to acknowledge it incautiously. The little Irishman's direct question implied what he had been expecting—if he acknowledged the name he met the man on the grounds of outlawry, which would mean that the employment in prospect was to be as illegal as he had thought it would be.

The merry blue eyes twinkled up at him. The man was laughing to himself at the Celtic subtlety with which he had introduced his subject. And again, involuntarily, Smith's straight mouth relaxed into a reluctant grin.

"I am," he said recklessly.

"I've been looking for you. There's a job to be done that'll pay you well, if you want to risk it."

Smith's pale eyes glanced about them warily. No one was within earshot. The place seemed as good as any other for the discussion of extra-legal bargains.

"What is it?" he demanded.

The little man glanced down at Yarol, who had dropped to one knee again and was flicking his knife tirelessly in the intricacies of his queer game. He had apparently lost interest in the whole proceeding.

"It'll take both of you," said the Irishman in his merry, rich voice. "Do you see that air freighter loading over there?" and he nodded toward the slaver.

Smith's head jerked in mute acknowledgment.

"It's a Willard ship, as I suppose you know. But the business is running pretty low these days. Cargoes too hot to ship. The Patrol is shutting down hard, and receipts have slackened like the devil in the last year. I suppose you've heard that too."

Smith nodded again without words. He had.

"Well, what we lose in quantity we have to make up in quality. Remember the prices the Minga girls used to bring?"

Smith's face was expressionless. He remembered very well indeed, but he said nothing.

"Along toward the last, kings could hardly pay the price they were asking for those girls. That's really the best market, if you want to get into the 'ivory' trade. Women. And there you come in. Did you ever hear of Cembre?"

Blank-eyed, Smith shook his head. For once he had run across a name whose rumors he had never encountered before in all the tavern gossip.

"Well, on one of Jupiter's moons—which one I'll tell you later, if you decide to accept—a Venusian named Cembre was wrecked years ago. By a miracle he survived and managed to escape; but hardships he'd undergone unsettled his mind, and he couldn't do much but rave about the beautiful sirens he'd seen while he was wandering through the jungles there. No-body paid any attention to him until the same thing happened again, this time only about a month ago. Another man came back half-cracked from struggling through the jungles, babbling about women so beautiful a man could go mad just from looking at them.

"Well, the Willards heard of it. The whole thing may sound like a pipe-dream, but they've got the idea it's worth investigating. And they can afford to indulge their whims, you know. So they're outfitting a small expedition to see what basis there may be for the myth of Cembre's sirens. If you want to try it, you're hired."

Smith slanted a non-committal glance downward into Yarol's uplifted black gaze. Neither spoke.

"You'll want to talk it over," said the little Irishman comprehendingly. "Suppose you meet me in the *New Chicago* at sundown and tell me what you've decided."

"Good enough," grunted Smith. The fat Celt grinned again and was gone in a swirl of black cloak and a flash of Irish merriment.

"Cold-blooded little devil," murmured Smith, looking after the departing Earthman. "It's a dirty business, Yarol."

"Money's clean," observed Yarol lightly. "And I'm not a man to let my scruples stand in the way of my means. I say take it. Someone'll go, and it might as well be us."

Smith shrugged.

"We've got to eat," he admitted.

"THIS," MURMURED YAROL, staring downward on hands and knees at the edge of the space-ship's floor-port, "is the prettiest little hell I ever expect to see."

The vessel was arching in a long curve around the Jovian moon as its pilot braked slowly for descent, and a panorama of ravening jungle slipped by in an unchanging wilderness below the floorport.

Their presence here, skimming through the upper atmosphere of the wild little satellite, was the end of a long series of the smoothest journeying either had ever known. The Willard network was perfect over the three planets and the colonized satellites beyond, and over the ships that ply the spaceways. This neat little exploring vessel, with its crew of three coarse-faced, sullen slavers, had awaited them at the end of their journey outward from Lakkdarol, fully fitted with supplies and every accessory the most modern adventurer could desire. It even had a silken prison room for the hypothetical sirens whom they were to carry back for the Willard approval and the Willard markets if the journey proved successful.

"It's been easy so far," observed Smith, squinting downward over the little Venusian's shoulder. "Can't expect everything, you know. But that *is* a bad-looking place."

The dull-faced pilot at the controls grunted in fervent agreement as he craned his neck to watch the little world spinning below them.

"Damn' glad I'm not goin' out with you," he articulated thickly over a mouthful of tobacco.

Yarol flung him a cheerful Venusian anathema in reply, but Smith did not speak. He had little liking and less trust in this sullen and silent crew. If he was not mistaken—and he rarely made mistakes in his appraisal of men—there was going to be trouble with the three before they completed their journey back into civilization. Now he turned his broad back to the pilot and stared downward.

From above, the moon seemed covered with the worst type of semi-animate, ravenous super-tropical jungle, reeking with fertility and sudden death, hot under lurid Jupiter's blaze. They saw no signs of human life anywhere below as their ship swept in its long curve over the jungle. The tree-tops spread in an unbroken blanket over the whole sphere of the satellite. Yarol, peering downward, murmured:

"No water. Somehow I always expect sirens to have fish-tails."

Out of his queer, heterogeneous past Smith dragged a fragment of ancient verse, "—gulfs enchanted, where the sirens sing . . ." and said aloud, "They're supposed to sing, too. Oh, it'll probably turn out to be a pack of black-faced savages, if there's anything but delirium behind the story."

The ship was spiraling down now, and the jungle rushed up to meet them at express-train speed. Once again the little moon spun under their searching eyes, flower-garlanded, green with fertile life, massed solid in tangles of ravening growth. Then the pilot's hands closed hard on the controls and with a shriek of protesting atmosphere the little spaceship slid in a long dive toward the unbroken jungle below.

In a great crashing and crackling they sank groundward through smothers of foliage that masked the ports and plunged the interior of the ship into a green twilight. With scarcely an impact the jungle floor received them. The pilot leaned back in his seat and heaved a tobacco-redolent sigh. His work was done. Incuriously he glanced at the forward port.

Yarol was scrambling up from the floor-glass that now showed nothing but crushed vines and branches and the reeking mud of the moon's surface. He joined Smith and the pilot at the forward port.

They were submerged in jungle. Great serpentine branches and vines like cables looped downward in broken lengths from the shattered trees which had given way at their entrance. It was an animate jungle, full of hungry, reaching things that sprang in one wild, prolific tangle from the rich mud. Raw-colored flowers, yards across, turned sucking mouths blindly against the glass here and there, trickles of green juice slavering down the clear surface from their insensate hunger. A thorn-fanged vine lashed out as they stood staring and slid harmlessly along the glass, lashed again and again blindly until the prongs were dulled and green juice bled from its bruised surfaces.

"Well, we'll have some blasting to do after all," murmured Smith as he looked out into the ravenous jungle. "No wonder those poor devils came back a little cracked. I don't see how they got through at all. It's—"

"Well—Pharol take me!" breathed Yarol in so reverent a whisper that Smith's voice broke off in mid-sentence and he spun around with a hand dropping to his gun to front the little Venusian, who had sought the stern port in his exploration.

"It's a road!" gasped Yarol. "Black Pharol can have me for dinner if there isn't a road just outside here!"

THE PILOT REACHED for a noxious Martian cigarette and stretched luxuriously, quite uninterested. But Smith had reached the Venusian's side before he finished speaking, and in silence the two stared out upon the surprising scene the stern port framed. A broad roadway stretched arrow-straight into the dimness of the jungle. At its edges the hungry green things ceased abruptly, no encroaching by so much as a tendril or a leaf into the clearness of the path. Even overhead the branches had been forbidden to intrude, their vine-looped greenery forming an arch above the road. It was as if a destroying beam had played through the jungle, killing all life in its path. Even the oozing mud was firmed here into a smooth pavement. Empty, enigmatic, the clear way slanted across their line of vision and on into the writhing jungle.

"Well," Yarol broke the silence at last, "here's a good start. All we've got to do is follow the road. It's a safe bet there won't be any lovely ladies wandering around through this jungle. From the looks of the road there must be some civilized people on the moon after all."

"I'd be happier if I knew what made it," said Smith. "There are some damned queer things on some of the moons and asteroids."

Yarol's cat-eyes were shining.

"That's what I like about this life," he grinned. "You don't get bored. Well, what do the readings say?"

From his seat at the control panel the pilot glanced at the gages which gave automatic report on air and gravity outside.

"O.K." he grunted. "Better take blast-guns."

Smith shrugged off his sudden uneasiness and turned to the weapon rack.

"Plenty of charges, too," he said. "No telling what we'll run into."

The pilot rolled his poisonous cigarette between thick lips and said, "Luck. You'll need it," as the two turned to the outer lock. He had all the indifference of his class to anything but his own comfort and the completion of his allotted tasks with a minimum of effort, and he scarcely troubled to turn his head as the lock swung open upon an almost overwhelming gush of thick, hot air, redolent of green growing things and the stench of swift decay.

A vine-tip lashed violently into the opened door as Smith and Yarol stood staring. Yarol snapped a Venusian oath and dodged back, drawing his blast-gun. An instant later the eye-destroying blaze of it sheered a path of destruction through the lush vegetable carnivora straight toward the slanting roadway a dozen feet away. There was an immense hissing and sizzling of annihilated green stuff, and an empty path stretched before them across the little space which parted the ship's outer lock from the road. Yarol stepped down into reeking mud that bubbled up around his boots with a stench of fertility and decay. He swore again as he sank knee-deep into its blackness. Smith, grinning, joined him. Side by side they floundered through the ooze toward the road.

Short though the distance was, it took them all of ten minutes to cover it. Green things whipped out toward them from the walls of sheared forest where the blast-gun had burned, and both were bleeding from a dozen small scratches and thorn-flicks, breathless and angry and very muddy indeed before they reached their goal and dragged themselves into the firmness of the roadway.

"Whew!" gasped Yarol, stamping the mud from his caked boots. "Pharol can have me if I stir a step off this road after this. There isn't a siren alive who could lure me back into that hell again. Poor Cembre!"

"Come on," said Smith, "Which way?"

Yarol slatted sweat from his forehead and drew a deep breath, his nostrils wrinkled distastefully.

"Into the breeze, if you ask me. Did you ever smell such a stench? And hot! God! I'm soaked through already."

Without words Smith nodded and turned to the right, from where a faint breeze stirred the heavy, moisture-laden air. His own lean body was impervious to a great variation in climate, but even Yarol, native of the Hot Planet, dripped with sweat already and Smith's own leather-tanned face glistened and his shirt clung in wet patches to his shoulders.

The cool breeze struck gratefully upon their faces as they turned into the wind. In a gasping silence they plodded muddily up the road, their wonder deepening as they advanced. What had made the roadway became more of a mystery at every step. No vehicle tracks marked the firm ground, no footprints. And nowhere by so much as a hair's breadth did the forest encroach upon the path.

On both sides, beyond the rigid limits of the road, the lush and cannibalistic life of the vegetation went on. Vines dangled great sucking disks and thorn-toothed creepers in the thick air, ready for a deadly cast at anything that wandered within reach. Small reptilian things scuttling through the reeking swamp mud squeaked now and then in the toils of some thorny trap, and twice they heard the hollow bellowing of some invisible monster. It was raw primeval life booming and thrashing and devouring all about them, a planet in the first throes of animate life.

But here on the roadway that could have been made by nothing less than a well-advanced civilization the ravening jungle seemed very far away, like some unreal world enacting its primitive dramas upon a stage. Before they had gone far they were paying little heed to it, and the bellowing and the lashing, hungry vines and the ravenous forest growths faded into half-heard oblivion. Nothing out of that world entered upon the roadway.

As they advanced the sweltering heat abated in the steady breeze that was blowing down the road. There was a faint perfume upon it, sweet and light and utterly alien to the fetor of the reeking swamps which bordered their way. The scented gusts of it fanned their hot faces gently.

Smith was glancing over his shoulder at regular intervals, and a pucker of uneasiness drew his brows together.

"If we don't have trouble with that crew of our before we're through," he said, "I'll buy you a case of *segir*."

"It's a bet," agreed Yarol cheerfully, turning up to Smith his sidelong cat-eyes as insouciantly savage as the raving jungle around them. "Though they were a pretty tough trio, at that."

"They may have the idea they can leave us here and collect our share of the money back home," said Smith. "Or once we get the girls they may want to dump us and take them on alone. And if they haven't thought of anything yet, they will."

"Up to no good, the whole bunch of 'em," grinned Yarol. "They—they—"

His voice faltered and faded into silence. There was a sound upon the breeze. Smith had stopped dead-still, his ears straining to recapture the echo of that murmur which had come blowing toward them on the breeze. Such a sound as that might had come drifting over the walls of Paradise.

In the silence as they stood with caught breath it came again—a lilt of the loveliest, most exquisitely elusive laughter. From very far away it came floating to their ears, the lovely ghost of a woman's laughing. There was in it a caress of kissing sweetness. It brushed over Smith's nerves like the brush of lingering fingers and died away into throbbing silence that seemed reluctant to let the exquisite sound of it fade into echoes and cease.

THE TWO MEN faced each other in rapt bewilderment. Finally Yarol found his voice.

"Sirens!" he breathed. "They don't have to sing if they can laugh like that! Come on!"

At a swifter pace they went on up the road. The breeze blew fragrantly against their faces. After a while its perfumed breath carried to their ears another faint, far-away echo of that heavenly laughter, sweeter than honey, drifting on the wind in fading cadences that died away by imperceptible degrees until they could no longer be sure if it was the lovely laughter they heard or the quickened beating of their own hearts.

Yet before them the road stretched emptily, very still in the green twilight under the low-arching trees. There seemed to be a sort of haze here, so that though the road ran straight the green dimness veiled what lay ahead and they walked in a queer silence along the roadway through ravening jungles whose sights and sounds might almost have been on another world for all the heed they paid them. Their ears were straining for a repetition of that low and lovely laughter, and the expectation of it gripped them in an unheeding spell which wiped out all other things but its own delicious echoes.

When they first became aware of a pale glimmer in the twilight greenness ahead, neither could have told. But somehow they were not surprised that a girl was pacing slowly down the roadway toward them, half veiled in the jungle dimness under the trees.

To Smith she was a figure walking straight out of a dream. Even at that distance her beauty had a still enchantment that swallowed up all his wondering in a strange and magical peace. Beauty flowed along the long, curved lines of her body, alternately cloaked and revealed by the drifting garment of her hair, and the slow, swinging grace of her as she walked was a potent enchantment that gripped him helpless in its spell.

Then another glimmer in the dimness caught his eyes away from the bewitchment that approached, and in bewilderment he saw that another girl was pacing forward under the low-hanging trees, her hair swinging about her in slow drifts that veiled and unveiled the loveliness of a body as exquisite as the first. That first was nearer now, so that he could see the enchantment of her face, pale golden and lovelier than a dram with its subtly molded smoothness and delicately tilted planes of cheek-bone and cheek smoothing deliciously upward into a broad, low forehead whence the richly colored hair sprang back in tendrils like licking flames. There was a subtle Slavic tilting to those honey-colored features, hinted in the breadth of the cheeks and the sweet straightness with which their planes slanted downward to a mouth colored like hot embers, curving now in a smile that promised—heaven.

She was very near. He could see the peach-like bloom upon her pale gold limbs and the very throb of the pulse beating in her round throat, and the veiled eyes sought his. But behind her that second girl was nearing, every whit as lovely as the first, and her beauty drew his gaze magnet-like to its own delicate flow and ripple of enchantment. And beyond her—yes, another was coming, and beyond her a fourth; and in the green twilight behind these first, pale blurs bespoke the presence of yet more.

And they were identical. Smith's bewildered eyes flew from face to face, seeking and finding what his brain could still not quite believe. Feature by feature, curve by curve, they were identical. Five, six, seven honey-colored bodies, half veiled in richly tinted hair, swayed toward him. Seven, eight, nine exquisite faces smiled their promise of ecstasy. Dizzy and incredulous, he felt a hand grip his shoulder. Yarol's voice, bemused, half whispered, murmured:

"Is this Paradise—or are we both mad?"

The sound of it brought Smith out of his tranced bewitchment. He shook his head sharply, like a man half-awake and striving for clarity, and said, "Do they all look alike to you?"

"Every one. Exquisite—exquisite—did you ever see such satin-black hair?"

"Black—black?" Smith muttered that over stupidly, wondering what was so wrong with the word. When realization broke upon him at last, the shock of it was strong enough to jerk his eyes away from the enchantment before him and turn them sharply around to the little Venusian's rapt face.

Its stainless clarity was set in a mask of almost holy wonder. Even the wisdom and weariness and savagery of its black eyes were lost in the glamor of what they gazed on. His voice murmured, almost to itself, "And white—so white—like lilies, aren't they? —blacker and whiter than—"

"Are you crazy?" Smith's voice broke harshly upon the Venusian's rapture. That trance-like mask broke before the impact of his exclamation. Like a man awaking from a dream, Yarol turned blinking to his friend.

"Crazy? Why—why—aren't we both? How else could we be seeing a sight like this?"

"One of us is," said Smith grimly. "I'm looking at red-haired girls colored like—like peaches."

Yarol blinked again. His eyes sought the bevy of bewildering loveliness in the roadway. He said, "It's you, then. They've got black hair, every one of them, shiny and smooth and black as so many lengths of satin, and nothing in creation is whiter than their bodies."

SMITH'S PALE EYES turned again to the road. Again they met honey-pale curves and planes of velvet flesh half veiled in hair like drifting flames. He shook his head once more, dazedly.

The girls hovered before him in the green dimness, moving with little restive steps back and forth on the hard-beaten road, their feet like the drift of flower-petals for lightness, their hair rippling away from the smoothly swelling curves of their bodies and furling about them again in ceaseless motion. They turned lingering eyes to the two men, but they did not speak.

Then down the wind again came drifting the far echo of that exquisite, lilting laugh. The sweetness of it made the very breeze brush light against their faces. It was a caress and a promise and a summoning almost irresistible, floating past them and drifting away into the distance in low, far-off cadences that lingered in their ears long after its audible music had ceased.

The sound of it woke Smith out of his daze, and he turned to the nearest girl, blurting, "Who are you?"

Among the fluttering throng a little shiver of excitement ran. Lovely, identical faces turned to him from all over the whole group, and the one addressed smiled bewilderingly.

"I am Yvala," she said in a voice smoother than silk, pitched to caress the ear and ripple along the very nerve fibers with a slow and soothing sweetness. And she had spoken in English! It was long since Smith had heard his mother tongue. The sound of it plucked at some hidden heart-string with intolerable poignancy, the home language spoken in a voice of enchanted sweetness. For a moment he could not speak.

The silence broke to Yarol's low whistle of surprise.

"I know now we're crazy," he murmured. "No other way to explain her speaking in High Venusian. Why, she can't ever have—"

"High Venusian!" exclaimed Smith, startled out of his moment of silence. "She spoke English!"

They stared at each other, wild suspicions rising in their eyes. In desperation Smith turned and hurled the question again at another of the lovely throng, waiting breathless for her answer to be sure his ears had not deceived him.

"Yvala—I am Yvala," she answered in just that silken voice with which the first had answered. It was English unmistakably, and sweet with memories of home.

Behind her among the bevy of curved, peach-colored bodies and veils of richly tinted hair other full red lips moved and other velvety voices murmured, "Yvala, Yvala, I am Yvala," like dying echoes drifting from mouth to mouth until the last syllable of the strange and lovely name faded into silence.

Across the stunned quiet that fell as their murmurs died the breeze blew again, and once more that sweet, low laughter rang from far away in their ears, rising and falling on the wind until their pulses beat in answer, and falling, fading, dying away reluctantly on the fragrant breeze.

"What—who was that?" demanded Smith softly of the fluttering girls, as the last of it faded into silence.

"It was Yvala," they chorused in caressing voices like multiple echoes of the same rich, lingering tones. "Yvala laughs—Yvala calls . . . Come with us to Yvala . . ."

Yarol said in a sudden ripple of musical speech.

"Geth norri a'Yvali?" at the same moment that Smith's query broke out.

"Who is Yvala, then?" in his own seldom-used mother tongue.

But they got no reply to that, only beckonings and murmurous repetitions of the name, "Yvala, Yvala, Yvala—" and smiles that set their pulses beating faster. Yarol reached out a tentative hand toward the nearest, but she melted like smoke out of his grasp so that he no more than grazed the velvety flesh of her shoulder with a touch that left his fingers tingling delightfully. She smiled over her shoulder ardently, and Yarol gripped Smith's arm.

"Come on," he said urgently.

IN A PLEASANT dream of low voices and lovely warm bodies circling just out of reach they went slowly on down the road in the midst of that hovering group, walking up-wind whence that tantalizing laughter had rung, and all about them the golden girls circled on restless, drifting feet, their hair floating and furling about the loveliness of their half-seen bodies, the echoes of that single name rising and falling in cadences as rich and smooth as cream. Yvala—Yvala—Yvala—a magical spell to urge them on their way.

How long they walked they never knew. The changeless jungle slid away behind them unnoticed; the broad, enigmatic pavement stretched ahead, a mysterious, green gloom shadowing the whole length of that laughter-haunted roadway. Nothing had any meaning to them outside the circle the murmurous girls were weaving with their swaying bodies and swinging hair and voices like the echoes of a dream. All the wonder and incredulity and bewilderment in the minds of the two men had sunk away into nothingness, drowned and swallowed up in the flagrant magic of their enchantresses.

After a long, rapt while they came to the roadway's end. Smith lifted dreaming pale eyes and saw as if through a veil, so remotely that the scene had little meaning to him, the great park-like clearing stretching away before them as the jungle walls fell away on either side. Here the primeval swamplands and animate green life ceased abruptly to make way for a scene that might have been lifted straight over a million years. The clearing was columned with great patriarchal trees ages removed in evolution from the snake things which grew in the hungry jungle. Their leaves roofed the place in swaying greenery though which the light sifted with twilight softness upon a carpet of flower-starred moss. With one step they spanned ages of evolution and entered into the lovely dim clearing that might have been lifted out of a world a million years older than the jungle that raved impotently around its borders.

The moss was velvety under their pacing feet. With eyes that but half comprehended what they saw, Smith gazed out across the twilight vistas through the green gloom brooding beneath the trees. It was a hushed place, mystical, very quiet. He thought sometimes he saw the flash of life through the leaves overhead, the stir of it among the trees as small wild things crossed their path and birds fluttered in the foliage, but he could not be sure. Once or twice it seemed to him that he had caught an echo of bird-song, somehow as if the melody had rung in his ears a moment before, and only now, when the sound was fading, did he realize it. But not once did he hear an actual song note or see any animate life, though the presence of it was rife in the green twilight beneath the leaves.

They went on slowly. Once he could have sworn he saw a dappled fawn staring at him with wide, unhappy eyes from a covert of branches, but when he looked closer there was nothing but leaves swaying emptily. And once upon his inner ear, as if with the echo of a just-past sound, he thought he heard a stallion's high whinny. But after all it did not greatly matter. The girls were shepherding them on over the flowery moss, circling like hollow-throated doves whose only music was "Yvala—Yvala—Yvala . . ." in unending harmony of rising and falling notes.

They paced on dreamily, the trees and mossy vistas of park sliding smoothly away behind them in unchanging quiet. And more and more strongly that impression of life among the trees nagged at Smith's mind. He wondered if he might not be developing hallucinations, for no arrangement of branches and shadows could explain the wild boar's head that he could have sworn thrust out among the leaves to stare at him for an instant with small, shamed eyes before it melted into patterned shadow under his direct gaze.

HE BLINKED AND rubbed his eyes in momentary terror lest his own brain was betraying him, and an instant later was peering uncertainly at the avenue between two low-hanging trees where from the corner of his eye he thought he had seen a magnificent white stallion hesitating with startled head upflung and the queerest, urgent look in its eyes, somehow warning and afraid—and ashamed. But it faded into mere leaf-cast shadows when he turned.

And once he started and stumbled over what was nothing more than a leafy branch lying across their path, yet which an instant before had looked bewildering like a low-slung cast-beast slinking across the moss with sullen, hot eyes upturned in hate and warning and distress to him.

There was something about these animals that roused a vague unrest in his mind when he looked at them—something in their eyes that was warning and agonized and more hotly aware than are the eyes of beasts—something queerly dreadful and hauntingly familiar about the set of their heads upon their shoulders—hinting horribly at another gait than the four-footed.

At last, just after a graceful doe had bounded out of the leaves, hesitated an instant and flashed away with a fleetness that did not look like the fleetness of a quadruped, turning upon him as she vanished a great-eyed agony that was warning as a cry, Smith halted in his tracks. Uneasiness too deep to be magicked away by the crooning girls urged him of danger. He paused and looked uncertainly around. The doe had melted into leaf-shadows flickering on the moss, but he could not forget the haunting shame and the warning of her eyes.

He stared about the dim greenness of the tree-roofed clearing. Was all this a lotus-dream, an illusion of jungle fever, or a suddenly unstable mind? Could he have imagined those beasts with their anguished eyes and their terribly familiar outlines of head and neck upon four-footed bodies? Was any of it real at all?

More for reassurance than for any other reason he reached out suddenly and seized the nearest honey-colored girl in a quick grip. Yes, she was tangible. His fingers closed about a firm and rounded arm, smoothly soft with the feel of peach-bloom velvet over its curving surface. The girl did not pull away. She stopped dead-still at his touch, slowly turning her head, lifting her face to his with a dream-like easiness, tilting her chin high until the long, full curve of her throat was arched taut and he could see the pulse beating hard under her velvet flesh. Her lips parted softly, her lids drooped low.

His other arm went out of its own accord, drawing her against him. Then her hands were in his hair, pulling his head down to hers, and all his uneasiness and distress and latent terror spun away at the kiss of her parted lips.

The next thing he realized was that he was strolling on under the trees, a girl's lithe body moving in the bend of his arm. Her very nearness was a delight that sent his senses reeling, so that the green woodland was vague as a dream and the only reality dwelt in the honey-color loveliness in the circle of his arm.

Dimly he was aware that Yarol strolled parallel with them a little distance away through the leaves, a bright head on his shoulder, another golden girl leaning against his encircling arm. She was so perfectly the counterpart of his own lovely captive that she might have been a reflection in a mirror. Uneasily, a remembrance swam up in Smith's mind. Did it seem to Yarol that a snow-white maiden walked with him, a black head leaned upon his shoulder? Was the little Venusian's mind yielding to the spell of the place, or was it his own? What tongue could it be that the girls spoke which fell upon his ears in English phrases and upon Yarol's in the musical lilt of High Venusian? Were they both mad?

Then in his arm the supple golden body stirred, the softly shadowed face turned up to his. The woodland vanished like smoke from about him in the magic of her lips.

THERE WERE DIM glades among the trees where piles of white ruins met Smith's unseeing eyes sometimes without leaving more than the merest trace of conscious remembrance. Vague wonders swam through his mind of what they might once have been, what vanished race had wrested this clearing from the jungle and died without leaving any trace save these. But he did not care. It had no significance. Even the half-seen beasts, who now turned eyes of sorrow and despair rather than warning, had lost all meaning to his enchanted brain. In a lotus dream he wandered on in the direction he was urged, unthinking, unalarmed. It was very sweet to stroll so through the dim green gloom, with purest magic in the bend of his arm. He was content.

They strolled past the white ruins of scattered buildings, past great bending trees that dappled them with shadow. The moss yielded underfoot as softly as thick-piled carpets. Unseen beasts slunk by them now and then, so that the tail<trail?> of Smith's eye was continually catching the—almost—hint of human-ity in the lines of their bodies, the set of a head upon bestial shoulders, the clarity of urgent eyes. But he did not really see them.

Sweetly—intolerably sweetly—and softly, laughter rang through the woods.

Smith's head flung up like a startled stallion's. It was a stronger laughter now, from near, very near among the leaves. It seemed to him that the voice indeed must come from some lovely, ardent houri leaning over the wall of Paradise—that he had come a long way in search of her and now trembled on the very brink of his journey's end. The low and lovely sound echoed through the trees, ringing down the green twilight aisles, shivering the leaves together. It was everywhere at once, a little world of music superimposed upon the world of matter, enclosing everything within its scope in a magical spell that left no room for any other thing but its lovely presence. And its command rang through Smith's mind with the sharpness of a sword in his flesh, calling, calling unbearably through the woods.

Then they came out of the trees into a little space of mossy clearing in whose center a small white temple rose. Somehow Yarol was there too—and somehow they were alone. These exquisite girls had melted like smoke into oblivion. The two men stood quite still, their eyes dazed as they stared. This building was the only one they had seen whose columns still stood upright, and only here could they tell that the architecture of those fallen walls whose ruins had dotted the wooded glades had been one at variance to anything on any world they knew. But upon the mystery of that they had no desire to dwell. For the woman those slim columns housed drove every other thought out of their dazzled minds.

She stood at the center of the tiny temple. She was pale golden, half veiled in the long cloak of her curls. And if the siren girls had been lovely, then here stood loveliness incarnate. Those girls had worn her form and face. Here was that same exquisitely molded body, colored like honey, half revealed among the drifts of hair that clung to it like tendrils of bright flames. But those bewildering girls had been mere echoes of the beauty that faced them now. Smith stared with a kindling of colorless eyes.

Here was Lilith—here was Helen—here was Circe—here before him stood all the beauty of all the legends of mankind; here on this marble floor, facing them gravely, with unsmiling eyes. For the first time he looked into the eyes that lighted that sweet, tilt-planed face, and his very soul gasped from the sudden plunge into their poignant blueness. It was not a vivid blue, not a blazing one, but its intensity far transcended anything he had words to name. In that business a man's soul could sink forever, reaching no bottom, stirred by no tides, drowned and steeped through and through with an infinity of absolute light.

When the blue, blue gaze released him he gasped once, like a drowning man, and then stared with new amazement upon a reality whose truth had escaped him until this moment. That instant of submerged ecstasy in the blue deeps of her eyes must have opened a door in his brain to new knowledge, for he saw as he stared a very strange quality in the loveliness he faced.

Tangible beauty dwelt here, an indwelling thing that could root itself in human flesh and clothe a body in loveliness as with a garment. Here was more than fleshly beauty, more than symmetry of face and body. A quality like a flame glowed all but visibly—no, more than visibly—along the peach-bloomy lines and smoothly swelling curves of her, giving a glory to the high tilt of her bosom and the long, subtly curved thigh and the exquisite line of shoulder gliding down into fuller beauty half veiled in drifting hair.

In that dazed, revealing moment her loveliness shimmed before him, too intensely for his human senses to perceive save as a dazzle of intolerable beauty before his half-comprehending eyes. He flung up his hands to shut the glory out and stood for a moment with hidden eyes in a self-imposed darkness though which beauty blazed with an intensity that transcended the visible and beat unbearably on every fiber of his being until he stood bathed in light that permeated the ultimate atoms of his soul.

THEN THE BLAZE DIED. He lowered shaking hands and saw that lovely, pale-gold face melting slowly into a smile of such heavenly promise that for an instant his senses failed him again and the world spun dizzily around a focus of honey-pale features breaking into arcs and softly shadowed curves, as the velvety mouth curled slowly into a smile.

"All strangers are very welcome here," crooned a voice like a vibration of sheerest silk, sweeter than honey, caressing as the brush of a kissing mouth. And she had spoken in the purest of earthly English. Smith found his voice.

"Who—who are you?" he asked in a queer gasp, as if his very breath were stopped by the magic he faced.

Before she could answer, Yarol's voice broke in, a little unsteady with sudden, savage anger.

"Can't you answer in the language you're addressed in?" he demanded in a violent undertone. "The least you could do is ask her name in High Venusian. How do you know she speaks English?"

QUITE SPEECHLESS, SMITH turned a blank gray gaze upon his companion. He saw the blaze of hot Venusian temper fade like mist from Yarol's black eyes as he turned to the glory in the temple. And in the lovely, liquid cadences of his native tongue, that brims so exquisitely with hyperbole and symbolism, he said:

"Oh, lovely and night-dark lady, what name is laid upon you to tell how whiter than sea-foam is your loveliness?"

For the moment, listening to the beauty of phrase and sound that dwells in the High Venusian tongue, Smith doubted his own ears. For though she had spoken in English, yet the loveliness of Yarol's speech seemed infinitely more suited to have fallen from the lyric curving of her velvet-red mouth. Such lips, he thought, could never utter less than pure music, and English is not a musical tongue.

But explain Yarol's visual illusion he could not, for his own steel-pale eyes were steadfast upon richly colored hair and pale gold flesh, and no stretch of imagination could transform them into the black and snow-whiteness his companion claimed to see.

A hint of mirth crept into the smile that curled up the softness of her mouth as Yarol spoke. She answered them both in one speech that to Smith was pure English, though he guessed that it fell upon Yarol's ears in the music of High Venusian cadences.

"I am Beauty," she told them serenely. "I am incarnate Beauty. But Yvala is my name. Let there be no quarrel between you, for each man hears me in the tongue his heart speaks, and sees me in the image which spells beauty to his own soul. For I am all men's desire incarnate in one being, and there is no beauty but Me."

"But—those others?"

"I am the only dweller here—but you have known the shadows of myself, leading you through devious ways into the presence of Yvala. Had you not gazed first upon the reflections of my beauty, its fullness which you see now would have blinded and destroyed you utterly. And later, perhaps, you shall see me even more clearly . . ..

"But no, Yvala alone dwells here. Save for yourselves there is in this park of mine no living creature. Everything is illusion but myself. And am I not enough? Can you desire anything more of life or death than you gaze on now?"

The query trembled into a music-ridden silence, and they knew that they could not. The heaven-sweet murmur of that voice was speaking sheerest magic, and in the sound of it neither of them was capable of any emotion but worship of the loveliness they faced. It beat out in waves like heat from that incarnate perfection, wrapping them about so that nothing in the universe had existence but Yvala.

Before the glory that blazed in their faces Smith felt adoration pouring out of him as blood gushes from a severed artery. Like life-blood it poured, and like life-blood draining it left him queerly weaker and weaker, as if some essential part of him were gushing away in great floods of intensest worship.

But somewhere, down under the lowest depths of Smith's subconsciousness, a faint disquiet was stirring. He fought it, for it broke the mirror surfaces of his tranced adoration, but he could not subdue it, and by degrees that un-ease struggled up through layer upon layer of rapt enchantment until it burst through into his conscious mind and the little quiver of it ran disturbingly through the exquisite calm of his trance. It was not an articulate disquiet, but it was somehow bound up with the scarcely seen beasts he had glimpsed—or had he glimpsed?—in the wood. That, and the memory of an old Earth legend which, try as he would, he could not quite exorcize: the legend of a lovely woman—and men turned into beasts . . . He could not grasp it, but the elusive memory pricked at him with little pinpoint goads, crying danger so insistently that with infinite reluctance his mind took up the business of thinking once more.

Yvala sensed it. She sensed the lessening in that life-blood gush of rapt adoration poured out upon her loveliness. Her fathomless eyes turned upon his in a blaze of transcendent blueness, and the woods reeled about him at the impact of their light. But somewhere in Smith, under the ultimate layer of con-scious thought, under the last quiver of instinct and reflex and animal cravings, lay a bedrock of savage strength which no power he had ever met could wholly overcome, not even this—not even Yvala. Rooted deep in that immovable solid-ity the little uneasy murmur persisted. "There is something wrong here. I mustn't let her swallow me up again—I must know what it is . . ."

That much he was aware of. Then Yvala turned. With both velvety arms she swept back the curtain of her hair, and all about her in a glory of tangible loveliness blazed out the radiance that dwelt in such terrible intensity here. Smith's whole consciousness snuffed out before it like a blown candle-flame.

REMOTELY, AFTER EONS it seemed, awareness overtook him again. It was not consciousness, but a sort of dumb, blind knowledge of processes going on around him, in him, through him. So an animal might be aware, without any hint of real self-consciousness. But hot above everything else the tranced ado-ration of sheer beauty was blazing now in the center of his universe, and it was devouring him as a flame devours fuel, sucking out his worship, draining him utterly. Helpless, unbodied, he poured forth adoration into the ravenous blaze that held him; and as he poured it out he felt himself fading, somehow sinking below the level of a human being. In his dumb awareness he made no attempt to understand, but he felt himself—degenerating.

It was as if the insatiable appetite for admiration which consumed Yvala and was consuming him sucked him dry of all humanity. Even his thoughts were sinking now as she drained him, so that he no longer fitted words to his sensations, and his mind ran into figures and pictures below the level of human minds . . .

He was not tangible. He was a dark, inarticulate memory, bodiless, mindless, full of queer, hungry sensations . . . He remembered running. He remembered the dark earth flowing backward under his flying feet, wind keen in his nostrils and rife with the odors of a thousand luscious things. He remembered the pack baying around him to the frosty stars, his own voice lifting in exultant, throat-filling clamor with the rest. He remembered the sweetness of flesh yielding under fangs, the hot gush of blood over a hungry tongue. Little more than this he remembered. The ravenous craving, the exultation of the chase, the satisfying reek of hot flesh under ripping fangs—all these circled through his memory round and round, leaving room for little else.

But gradually, in dim, disquieting echoes, another realization strengthened beyond the circle of hunger and feeding. It was an intangible thing, nothing but the faint knowledge that somehow, somewhere, in some remote existence, he had been—different. He was little more than a recollection now, a mind that circled memories of hunting and killing and feeding which some lost body in long-ago distances had performed. But even so—he had once been different. He had—

Sharply through that memory-circle broke the knowledge of presences. With no physical sense was he aware of them, for he possessed no physical senses at all. But his awareness, his dumb, numb mind, knew that they had come—knew what they were. In memory he smelled the rank, blood-stirring scent of man, felt a tongue lolling out over suddenly dripping fangs; remembered hunger gushed up through his sensations.

Now he was blind and formless in a formless void, recognizing these presences only as they impinged upon his. But from the man-presences realization reached out and touched him, knowing his presence, realizing his nearness. They sensed him, lurking hungrily so close. And because they sensed him so vividly, their minds receiving the ravenous impact of his, their brains must have translated that hungry nearness into sight for just an instant; for from somewhere outside the gray void where he existed a voice said clearly:

"Look! Look—no, it's gone now, but for a minute I thought I saw a wolf . . ."

The words burst upon his consciousness with all the violence of a gun-blast; for in that instant, he *knew*. He understood the speech the man used, remembered that once it had been his speech—realized what he had become. He knew too that the men, whoever they were, walked into just such danger as had conquered him, and the urgency to warn them surged up in his dumbness. Not until then did he know clearly, with a man's word-thoughts, that he had no being. He was not real—he was only a wolf-memory drifting through the dark. He had been a man. Now he was pure wolf—beast—his soul shorn of its humanity down to the very core of savagery that dwells in every man. Shame flooded over him. He forgot the men, the speech they used, the remembered hunger. He dissolved into a nothingness of wolf-memory and man-shame.

Through the dizziness of that a stronger urge began to beat. Somewhere in the void sounded a call that reached out to him irresistibly. It called him so strongly that his whole being whirled headlong in response along currents that swept him helpless into the presence of the summoner.

A blaze was burning. In the midst of the universal emptiness it flamed, calling, commanding, luring him so sweetly that with all his entity he replied, for there was in that burning an element that wrenched at his innermost, deepest-rooted desire. He remembered food—the hot gush of blood, the crunch of teeth on bone, the satisfying solidarity of flesh under his sinking fangs. Desire for it gushed out of him like life itself, draining him—draining him . . . He was sinking lower, past the wolf level, down and down . . .

Through the coming oblivion terror stabbed. It was a lightning-flash of realization from his long-long humanity, one last throb that brightened the dark into which he sank. And out of that bed-rock of unshakable strength which was the core of his being, even below the wolf level, even below the oblivion into which he was being sucked—the spark of rebellion flashed.

Before now he had floundered helplessly with no firmness anywhere to give him foothold to fight; but now, in his uttermost extremity, while the last dregs of conscious life drained out of him, the bed-rock lay bare from which the well-springs of his strength and savagery spring, and at that last stronghold of the *self* called Smith he leaped into instant rebellion, fighting with all the wolf-nature that had been the soil from which his man-soul rooted. Wolfishly he fought, with a beast's savagery and a man's strength, backed by the bed-rock firmness that was the base for both. Space whirled about him, flaming with hungry fires, black with flashes of oblivion, furious and ravenous in the hot presence of Yvala.

But he was winning. He knew it, and fought harder, and abruptly felt the snap of yielding opposition and was blindingly aware again, blindingly human. He lay on soft moss as a dead man lies, terribly relaxed in every limb and muscle. But life was flowing back into him, and humanity was gushing like a river in spate back into the drained hollows of his soul. For a while he lay quiet, gathering himself into one body again. His hold on it was so feeble that sometimes he thought he was floating clear and had to struggle hard to force re-entrance. Finally, with infinite effort, he tugged his eyelids open and lay there in a deathly quiet, watching.

Before him stood the white marble shrine which housed Beauty. But it was not Yvala's delirious loveliness he gazed on now. He had been through the fire of her deepest peril, and he saw her now as she really was—not in the form which spelled pure loveliness to him, and, as he guessed, to every being that gazed upon her, whether it be man or beast—not in any form at all, but as a blaze of avid light flaming inside the shrine. The light was alive, quivering and trembling and animate, but it bore no human form. It was not human. It was a life so alien that he wondered weakly how his eyes could ever have twisted it into the incarnate loveliness of Yvala. And even in the depths of his peril he found time to regret the passing of that beauty—that exquisite illusion which had never existed save in his own brain. He knew that as long as life burned in him he could never forget her smile.

IT WAS A thing of some terribly remote origin that blazed here. He guessed that the power of it had fastened on his brain as soon as he came within its scope, commanding him to see it in that lovely form which meant heart's-desire to him alone. It must have done the same thing to countless other beings—he remembered the beast wraiths that had brushed his brain in the forest with the faint, shamed contact of theirs. Well, he had been one of them—he knew, now. He understood the warning and the anguish in their eyes. He remembered too the ruins he had seen in the woods. What race had dwelt here once, imposing its civilization and its stamp of quiet glades and trees upon the ravenous forest? A human race, perhaps, dwelling in seclusion under the leaves until Yvala the Destroyer came. Or perhaps not a human race, for he knew now that to every living creature she wore a different form, the incarnation of each individual's highest desire.

Then he heard voices, and after an infinity of effort twisted his head on the moss until he could see whence they came. At what he saw he would have risen if he could, but a deathly weariness lay like the weight of worlds upon him and he could not stir. Those man-presences he had felt in his beast-form stood here—the three slavers from the little ship. They must have followed them not far behind, with what dark motives would never be known now, for Yvala's magic had seized them and there would be no more of humanity for them after the next few moments were past. They stood in a row there before the shrine with an ecstasy almost holy on their faces. Plainly he saw reflected there the incarnate glory of Yvala, though to his eyes the thing they faced was only a formless flame.

He knew then why Yvala had let him go so suddenly in that desperate struggle. Here was fresh fodder for her avidity, new worship to drink in. She had turned away from his outworn well-springs to drain new prey of its human-ity. He watched them standing there, drunk with loveliness before what to them must be a beautiful woman veiled in drifting hair, glowing with more than mortal ardency where, to him, only a clear flame burned.

But he could see more. Cloudy about those three figures, rapt before the shrine, he could see—was it some queer reflection of themselves dancing in the air? The misty outlines wavered as, with eyes that in the light of what he had just passed through had won momentarily a sight which penetrated beyond the flesh, he looked upon that dancing shimmer which clearly must be the reflection of some vital part of those three men, visible now in some strange way at the evocation of Yvala's calling.

They were man-shaped reflections. They strained toward Yvala from their anchorage in the bodies that housed them, yearning, pulling as if they would forsake their fleshly roots and merge with the incarnate beauty that called them so irresistibly. The three stood rigid, faces blank with rapture, unconscious of that perilous tugging at what must be in their very souls.

Then Smith saw the nearest man sag at the knees, quiver, topple to the moss. He lay still for a moment while from his fallen body that tenuous reflection of himself tugged and pulled and then in one last great effort jerked free and floated like a smoke-wreath into the white-hot intensity at the shrine. The blaze engulfed it, flaring brighter as if at the kindling of new fuel.

WHEN THAT SUDDEN brightness died again the smoke-wreath drifted out, trailing through the pillars in a form that even to Smith's dimmed eyes wore a strange distortion. It was no longer man-formed. All of humanity had burned out from it to feed the blaze that was Yvala. And that beast foundation which lies so close under the veneer of civilization and humanity in every human creature was bared and free. Cold with understanding, Smith watched the core of beast instinct which was all that remained now that the layer of man-veneer had been stripped away, a core of animal memories rooted eons deep in that far-away past when all man's ancestors ran on four paws.

It was a cunning beast that remained, instinct with foxy slyness. He saw the misty thing slink away into the green gloom of the woods, and he realized afresh why it was he had seen fleeting glimpses of animals in the park as he came here, wearing that terrible familiarity in the set of their heads, the line of shoulder and neck that hinted at other gaits than four-footed. They must have been just such wraiths as this, drifting through the woods, beast-wraiths that wore still the tatters and rags of their doffed humanity, brushing his mind with the impact of theirs until their vividness evoked actual sight of the reality of fur and flesh, just for a glimpse, just for a hint, before the wraith blew past. And he was cold with horror at the thought of how many men must have gone to feed the flame, stripping off humanity like a garment and running now in the nakedness of their beast natures through the enchanted woods.

Here was Circe. He realized it with a quiver of horror and awe. Circe the

Enchantress, who turned the men of Greek legend into beasts. And what tremendous backgrounds of reality and myth loomed smokily behind what happened here before his very eyes! Circe the Enchantress—ancient Earthly legend incarnate now on a Jovian moon far away through the void. The awe of it shook him to the depths. Circe—Yvala—alien entity that must, then, rove through the universe and the ages, leaving the dim whispers behind her down the centuries. Lovely Circe on her blue Aegean isle—Yvala on her haunted moon under Jupiter's blaze—past and present merged into a blazing whole.

The wonder of it held him so rapt that when the reality of the scene before him finally bore itself in upon his consciousness again, both of the remaining slavers lay prone upon the moss, forsaken bodies from which the vitality had been sucked like blood into Yvala's flame. That flame burned more rosily now, and out of its pulsing he saw the last dim wraith of the three who had fed her come hurrying, a swinish brute of a wraith whose grunts and snorts were almost audible, tusks and bristles all but visible as it scurried off into the wood.

Then the flame burned clear again, flushed with hot rose, pulsing with regular beats like the pulse of a heart, satiate and ecstatic in its shrine. And he was aware of a withdrawal, as if the consciousness of the entity that burned here were turned inward upon itself, leaving the world it dominated untouched as Yvala drowsed and digested the sustenance her vampire-craving for worship had devoured.

SMITH STIRRED A little on the moss. Now, if ever, he must make some effort to escape, while the thing in the shrine was replete and uninterested in its surroundings. He lay there, shaken with exhaustion, forcing strength back into his body, willing himself to be strong, to rise, to find Yarol, to make his way somehow back to the deserted ship. And by slow degrees he succeeded. It took a long while, but in the end he had dragged himself up against a tree and stood swaying, his pale eyes alternately clouding with exhaustion and blinking awake again as he scanned the space under the trees for Yarol.

The little Venusian lay a few steps away, one cheek pressing the ground and his yellow curls gay against the moss. With closed eyes he looked like a seraph asleep, all the lines of hard living and hard fighting relaxed and the savageness of his gaze hidden. Even in his deadly peril Smith could not suppress a little grin of appreciation as he staggered the half-dozen steps that parted them and fell to his knees beside his friend's body.

The sudden motion dazed him, but in a moment his head cleared and he laid an urgent hand on Yarol's shoulder, shaking it hard. He dared not speak, but he shook the little Venusian heavily, and in his brain a silent call went out to whatever drifting wraith among the trees housed Yarol's naked soul. He bent over the quiet yellow head and called and called, turning the force of his determination in all its intensity to that summoning, while weakness washed over him in great slow waves.

After a long time he thought he felt a dim response, somewhere from far off. He called harder, eyes turned apprehensively toward the rosily pulsing flame in the shrine, wondering if this voiceless summoning might not impinge upon the entity there as tangibly as speech. But Yvala's satiety must have been deep, and there was no changing in the blaze.

The answer came clearer from the woods. He felt it pulling in toward him along the strong compulsion of his call as a fisherman feels a game fish yielding at last to the tug of his line. And presently among the leafy solitudes of the trees a little mist-wraith came gliding. It was a slinking thing, feline, savage, fearless. He could have sworn that for the briefest instant he saw the outlines of a panther stealing across the moss, misty, low-slung, turning upon him the wise black gaze of Yarol—exactly his friend's black eyes, with no lessening in them of lost humanity. And something in that familiar gaze sent a little chill down his back. Could it be—could it possibly be that in Yarol the veneer of humanity was so thin over his savage cat-nature that even when it had been stripped away the look in his eyes was the same?

Then the smoke-beast was hovering over the prone Venusian figure. It curled round Yarol's shoulders for an instant; it faded and sank, and Yarol stirred on the moss. Smith turned him over with a shaking hand. The long Venusian lashes quivered, lifted. Black, sidelong eyes looked up into Smith's pale gaze. And Smith, in a gush of chilly uncertainty, did not know if humanity had returned into his friend's body or not, if it was a panther's gaze looking up into his or if that thin layer of man-soul veiled it, for Yarol's eyes had always looked like this.

"Are—are you all right?" he choked in a breathless whisper.

Yarol blinked dizzily once or twice, then grinned. A twinkle lighted up his black cat gaze. He nodded and made a little effort to rise. Smith helped him sit up. The Venusian was not a fraction so weak as the Earthman had been. After a little interval of hard breathing he struggled to his feet and helped Smith up, apprehension in his whole demeanor as he eyed the flame that pulsed in its white shrine. He jerked his head urgently.

"Let's get out of here!" his silent lips mouthed. And Smith in fervent agreement turned in the direction he indicated, hoping the Yarol knew where he was going. His own exhaustion was still too strong to permit him anything but acquiescence.

They made their way through the woods, Yarol heading unerringly in a swerveless course toward the roadway they had left such a long time ago. After a while, when the flame-housing shrine had vanished among the trees behind them, the Venusian's soft voice murmured, half to itself.

"—wish, almost, you hadn't called me back. Woods were so cool and still—remembering such splendid things—killing and killing—taste of hot blood—I wish—"

The voice fell quiet again. But Smith, stumbling on beside his friend, understood. He knew why the woods seemed familiar to Yarol, so that he could head for the roadway unerringly. He knew why Yvala in her satiety had not even wakened at the withdrawal of Yarol's humanity—it was so small a thing that the loss of it meant nothing. He gained a new insight in that moment into Venusian nature that he remembered until the day he died.

Then there was a gap in the trees ahead, and Yarol's shoulder was under his supportingly, and the road to safety shimmered in its tree-arched green gloom ahead.

The Cosmic Kidnappers

by Christian Vallini & S. F. Balboa

*P*olish job.

"WHAT ABOUT THE RESEARCH, AIQUY?"

"I was thinking of introducing you to the Hunters."

They entered the large living room and there they were, a hundred of them, the Hunters. And there was the Teacher, too. He was shouting at his pupils.

"What's the matter?" Aiquy asked the Teacher.

"They're the best Hunters we've got. And if they foul up, well—how can we depend on to do things right?"

"They've fouled up?"

"They don't seem to understand! They've 10 ears and they turn all of them deaf to me. You know they must take the greatest care in capturing those creatures, you know the captives cannot be taken back to their planet."

"So what's the trouble?" Aiquy asked nervously through that throat reserved for alarm.

"We've got a strategic plan to follow. The individuals we snatch must be insignificant, unknown. They have to be. The disappearance of high authorities, famous figures, would be noticed. Trouble would ensue. And today Kaiaich has captured one of their race that was well known."

"Who?" Aiquy swallowed through his 12th, his throat which functioned exclusively for apprehension.

"His name is pronounced Ambroce Beerce."

The Girl
Who Wasn't There

minorly by me, mainly by TIGRINA

*W*HEN BILL NOLAN was soliciting the contents for the first issue of Gamma—asking for contributions by Bradbury, Beaumont, van Vogt, Rod Serling, Tennessee Williams, Fritz Leiber—he also contacted me. He said he wanted contributions by Big Name Authors.

Hey, ma—looka me: a BNA! The only way I could be a bigger name author would be to be Clinton Constantinescu or Epaminondas Thucydides Snooks.

Anyway, I dug up a semi-pro story from Inside, a fanzine that paid contributors in 1953, and submitted "The Lady Takes A Powder". This was a fantasyarn which had been written by a friend of mine, the mono-named and tiger-maned Tigrina, and revised by myself. The entire ending, about the suicide bridge and the witch, was purely my own. But basically it was Tigrina's story.

Originally, in '53, the story had inadvertently been published with a single byline—and wouldn't you know, it was mine; Tigrina who got left off.

So the second time 'round on the merry-go-round I wanted to make sure Tigrina got her credit.

How did it come out in Gamma?

Of course.

To make matters worse, here was the story solely credited to me, and hardly a word I had contributed to it was left!

It is my understanding that Bill Nolan excised the first 1000 words, dropped the protagonist's age down 3 years, eliminated her name (Roxona) and changed the sex from feminine to masculine of the person who gets involved with her.

After the Invisible Girl gets off the bus, my ending vanished and a new one was substituted by Charles Fritch.

So the story you are about to read is about 75% Tigrina, 15% Fritch, 9% Nolan and 1% Ackerman. For the 50-50 collaboration, read "The Lady Takes A Powder", directly following, and if you are not old enough to remember the expression "take a powder", it means "scram . . . vamoose . . . beat it . . . vanish."

In other words, split.

Obviously the expressions "hippy", "that was his bag", "go-go" and the refer- ence to Dark Shadows *did not appear in the original 1953 version.*

Any questions?

(And if Tigrina's name gets omitted this time and only mine appears, I am going to shoot one of my pseudonyms!)

THE INVISIBLE GIRL continued: "The day the little woman selling cosmet- ics came to the door I never would have let her in, except—well, it was my 18th birthday and I was feeling very grownup and self-assured. You see, my parents were dead and I lived with my aunt and uncle. They were very strict—never allowed me to use lipstick or nail polish. But my aunt had given me $10 and told me I could spend it for anything I wanted. I suppose she thought I'd buy books with it. I had a marvelous collection of fiction and nonfiction on witch- craft, sorcery . . . oh, everything that was rather off-trail or unusual."

I wondered what she looked like, as I held her hand, very reassuring in its solidity.

"Anyway," she went on, "when this weird little old woman came to the door with her array of cosmetics, it seemed to me like a wonderful opportunity to do what I pleased. My aunt and uncle happened to be out so I invited the little old lady inside.

"You know the old witch in *Hansel and Gretel?* Well, this woman looked like a modern version of her, only she had a pleasant, mischievous twinkle in her slanted green eyes. Any misgivings I might have had about her were quickly banished when she opened her case and laid out the most enticing rainbow display of bottles, jars and flasks.

"She winked at me. 'This is the firstime you've ever bought cosmetics, isn't it?'

"I had the strange feeling she could gaze deep inside my miserable little soul.

"I finally ended up by buying a box of face powder, an odd little bottle of perfume, a lipstick and a jar of face cream. The funny thing was, she insisted on presenting me with an extra large size jar of cream, said it was a gift from her for my 18th birthday. I didn't remember until afterward that I hadn't told her it *was* my birthday.

"When my aunt and uncle returned, they were furious. My aunt immedi- ately took the cosmetics and threw them in the trash barrel. I rushed to my room and locked myself in. Then I cried and cried. It was too utterly humiliat- ing. A girl my age being denied the use of a few harmless cosmetics.

"I must have fallen asleep. I awoke about a quarter of twelve. The house was silent. I got out of bed and cautiously crept downstairs in the dark.

"At the trash barrel the spicy fragrance made me weep again. It was hopeless to salvage the face powder. I couldn't find the lipstick in the dark but my hands closed on the jar of facial cream—miraculously unbroken. I put it in my pocket and stole back upstairs.

"In my room I turned on the desk lamp and began to rub the contents of the jar on my face. I was in that sort of unreasonable, irrational mood when you make all sorts of crazy, impractical resolutions. With every motion of my hand I thought 'I'll show them! They can't boss me!'

"In the distance I heard a town clock boom out midnight—the witching hour. My facial completed, I walked to the mirror to satisfy my vanity. But the sight that met my eyes left me limp with fright. I had no face! My hair was visible and the rest of my body but my face and neck—well, they just weren't there!

"I reached up—and discovered I could feel my face but I couldn't see it. Then I noticed a portion of my hand was invisible, too, the parts that touched the cream.

"Suddenly I felt very adventurous and my spirits soared, for I realized that at last I'd found a way to escape. I undressed and rubbed myself from head to toe with the magic cream. When I returned to the mirror I was not disappointed: I was totally invisible!

"I was free! Free to roam where I willed, unseen. The whole city was mine!

"But I was tired and decided to wait until morning. I put on my nightgown, expecting to see the garment apparently floating in air. But it was now invisible. I discovered later that any object that comes into contact with me automatically vanishes.

"Well, I left early the next morning. I didn't have much money but I knew that I could raid the kitchen of some swank hotel or cafe. They served scrumptious meals, too, I found out!"

I heard her invisible lips smack in reminiscence. They were probably full rich red lips, I decided, and very kissable.

"At night I stayed at the best hotels, sleeping in unrented rooms. It was risky, of course. Once I was surprised by a room being rented during the night." She laughed. "When I jumped out of bed, the sheets waved around like a ghost, and the poor guest nearly had heart failure.

"As for clothing or anything else I need, I just appropriate them. I hope you're not too shocked."

"Not at all. I can understand your problem. I wish I could help you."

"You have already," she said, "by just letting me talk to you. It's been so long since I've been able to talk with someone so understanding."

"You could go see a doctor," I suggested.

"I thought of that," she said with a sigh, "but is this invisibility of mine science or sorcery? Besides, I couldn't stand being a guinea pig with doctors pawing over me and making examinations, and stories in the newspapers, and notoriety, and—and my aunt and uncle finding me again . . ."

I felt her invisible hand grip my arm desperately. "Oh, you can't imagine how lonely I've been! You might imagine it would be a great lark. It was, at first, but not any more. I try to make friends with people but when I speak to them, they're afraid and think they are having hallucinations. I—just don't know what to do."

She began to cry invisible tears and I put my arm around her comfortingly.

"I'm sorry," she said, suddenly irritated. "It isn't *your* problem." She stood up, pulling her hand from my grasp.

"Wait," I said, but she was already beyond reach.

The bell sounded as she invisibly pulled the stop cord. The doors snapped open and I could sense the girl's invisible body going into the dark street outside.

The doors snapped shut again before I could gather my wits. She was going out of my life just as suddenly as she came in. I couldn't lose her.

"Wait!" I cried, leaping into the aisle.

"Make up your mind, buddy," the bus driver said wearily.

I almost leaped from the bus in my haste. The bus whooshed off and I stood there listening for a moment.

"Where are you?" I whispered into the darkness. Then louder: "Speak to me. Please!"

There was no answer. She had gone.

HOW DO YOU find an invisible girl? Do you put an ad in the paper? I thought of notifying the police but I knew they'd only laugh at me.

But I *must* find her. I don't even know her name but I do know that I love her and need her. I understand her problem—because I'm almost 20 and I live with very strict parents—and they never let me do *anything*.

It's lonely now without my invisible girlfriend. I roam the streets at night calling out to her, begging her to answer me. I confided in a few friends but they said it was only hallucination.

I didn't imagine it. I couldn't have. I need her too much for that. She was there, she *was*, I know it.

I've got proof.

My hand—that lucky one once held delightfully imprisoned in her soft feminine grasp—is starting to turn invisible!

The Lady
Takes A Powder

by Tigrina as told to Karlon Torgosi

*T*HE FEATURE PICTURE set the stage for my weird adventure. It was DARKER THAN YOU DREAMED, and certainly superior to the run-of-the-thrill, boy-meets-ghoul type of thing that Hollywood shamelessly, repetitiously and profitably, my husband tells me, produces.

I had been seduced into the theater by the combination of Gregory Decker and the supernatural theme. I felt sure I had just witnessed an Academy Award performance in Laurel Leigh's superbly lupine portrayal of the lycanthrope who committed suicide with a silver bullet. Now I prepared to relax with the Nellie Pan cartoon.

As my mind gradually unfroze from the chilling climax, I became aware of the aroma of buttered popcorn. Probably a hippy sitting next to me, I thought, and that was his bag.

The interior of the show had seemed stygian to my nyctalopic eyes when I first entered, and my attention had been raptly centered on the screen during the werewolf film. As I glanced surreptitiously to either side of me for the first time, I was surprised to see that no one was sitting within three seats of me but a bag appeared to be resting on the left arm of the seat to my left.

Out of the corner of my eye I glimpsed Nellie on the screen pulling a top hat out of a rabbit's ear and the next moment was too absorbed in the deviltry of the minx to wonder over the minor mystery of the missing popcorn muncher. It was not till the prevues came on that I again became aware of an aroma emanating from immediately to my left, this time the richness of bittersweet chocolate. And, although I distinctly heard the sound of sharp teeth crunching a candy bar, I saw no one at my side. A quick look about only served to confuse me further for nowhere nearby could I see anyone eating anything.

As I slipped on my coat and began to slide toward the aisle, giving a good imitation of a go-go dancer, I had a queer sensation that I was being followed. Did I imagine an invisible hip nudged mine? And then I heard a silvery, tinkly laugh close to my ear!

"It's time for me to leave, too," a girl's voice volunteered in a whisper.

"Wasn't Greg wonderful?"

"He surely—" I started to agree, then the aisle tilted up at a 45° angle and grew a mile long and my legs went as rubbery as bubble gum.

There was no one at my side. No one could possibly have spoken to me.

I made the exit but only because it was wide. I knew that I was staggering.

The way my teeth were chattering while waiting for the bus, they could have been used for castanets. Still shaking, I boarded the streamlined behemoth when it eventually pulled up to the curb.

The bus was not crowded. I sat by myself in the back. Color began to return to my cheeks as I contemplated the normalcy, the safety of the bus. The bus, monarch of the boulevard, lord of the lesser cars.

The familiar, light interior of the bus. The inevitable carcards. Then . . .

An invisible blotter drank the moisture from my tongue. An unseen pixie fizzed a bottle of seltzer on my scalp. And I failed the B.O. Test as sweat made my armpits soggy; I saw the leatherette cushions of the seat next to me flatten out and I realized, as Everett later indelicately phrased it, that "somebody's derriére sat there!"

With my ten thumbs I fumbled for my compact. I hardly recognized my own face, chalk-white, as, under the pretext of applying my lipstick, I whispered to the air: "Is someone there?"

Then any hopes I had entertained that this was a delusion ripped like a pair of poor quality nylons when the bodiless voice replied, "You really don't mind my following you, do you? One gets so terribly lonely when one is invisible."

"Lonely...? Invisible...?" I suppose I gasped in the accepted manner of a *Dark Shadows* actress. "You mean you're really invisible—not a ghost?"

Then curiosity overcame by basic fear, and I continued in a lowered tone, so that I would not be overheard, "How did it ever happen? Did you get mixed up with H. G. Wells, or are you a scientist's daughter?"

"Neither! My name is Roxana, I'm 22, and quite as ordinary as anyone else. Except, of course, I'm invisible."

"You weren't born that way, surely? It would have been in the papers."

"No, I was visible till last year. It all began on my 21st birthday..."

I closed my eyes, rested my head against the window and pretended to sleep as this amazing story was whispered into my ear. Hear it out. I promise I won't betray you in the end and say, "And I woke from my dream with the bus driver tapping my shoulder and saying `Lady, this is as far as I go.' "

Roxana continued

"You know the old witch in *Hansel and Gretel*? Well, she looked like a popular conception of her, only she had a pleasant, mischievous twinkle in her oddly slanted green eyes. Any misgivings I might have had about her were quickly banished when she opened her case and laid out the most enticing rainbow display of bottles, jars and flasks.

"It all looked like such fun, so I bought a box of face powder, an odd little bottle of perfume, a lipstick and a jar of face cream. The funny thing was, she insisted on presenting me with an extra large size jar of cream, said it was a gift from her for my 21st birthday. I remembered afterward that I hadn't told her it *was* my birthday.

"When my aunt and uncle returned, they were furious. My aunt immediately took the cosmetics and threw them in the trash barrel. I rushed to my room and locked myself in. Then I cried and cried. It was too utterly humiliating. A girl my age being denied the use of a few harmless cosmetics.

"I must have fallen asleep in utter exhaustion. I remember awakening about quarter to twelve. The house was silent. My aunt and uncle always retired punctually at 9:00.

"I was in a defiant mood. Cautiously I crept downstairs in the dark.

"At the trash barrel the spicy fragrance of the spilled perfume made me weep again at its loss as I groped among the broken bits of glass. It was hopeless to salvage the face powder; the box had burst and its contents would now be indistinguishable from the roach powder on the basement floor. I couldn't find the lipstick in the dark but my hands closed on a jar—the unspilled facial cream. Hastily I put it in my pocket and stole back upstairs.

"In my room I cautiously locked my door, turned on the desk lamp and by its low light began to rub the contents of the jar methodically on my face. I was in that sort of unreasonable, irrational mood when you make all sorts of crazy, impractical resolutions. With every motion of my hand I thought, 'I'll show them! They can't boss me!' In fact, I firmly resolved to run away the very next day.

"In the distance I heard a town clock boom out the hour of midnight—the witching hour. My facial completed, I walked to the mirror to satisfy my vanity visually. But the sight that met my eyes when I gazed into the looking glass left me limp with terror: I had no face! My hair was visible, and the rest of my body, but my face and neck—they just weren't there!

"I put my hand up to my face to feel the invisible part of me. It was still there. I could feel it, but I couldn't see it. And yet, I knew I wasn't partially blinded, because I could see the other objects in the room quite clearly.

"Then I noticed a portion of my hands was invisible too—just the fingertips—the part that touched the cream.

"The corny old witch! She'd said the use of cosmetics would surprise me and change my life. Vanishing cream! I was totally invisible!

"Free! Free to roam where I willed, unseen. Free, 21 and invisible!

"Then I looked at things from a more practical viewpoint. Even if I couldn't be seen, I didn't want to go around undressed. There was the weather, for one thing; and for another, I had no way of knowing just how long the effect of the mysterious cream might last. And besides, defiant though I was, I didn't want to start on my new adventures at midnight. After my childish emotional outburst I was very tired and craved a good night's rest.

"But I couldn't go to bed with the greasy cream, so I decided to take a shower and cleanse it off. But it wouldn't come off!

"When I put on my nightgown, I expected to see a ludicrous sight in my mirror. I thought I'd see my nightgown apparently standing there in mid-air, all by itself. But it, too, cast no reflection!

"It was an inexplicable phenomenon, one of many. I eventually found that any inanimate object that comes into contact with me automatically vanishes. Clothing, food, and so on.

"Well, I left early the next morning. I didn't take much with me. As for clothes or anything else I need, I just appropriate them. I hope you aren't too shocked."

Her astonishing recital seemed momentarily at an end. Pretending to awaken, I yawned, covering my mouth and commenting, "No, I imagine many a girl in your predicament would have a ball 'appropriating' beautiful clothes, jewelry, furs, expensive cosmetics..."

I felt a pressure on my arm. "I can see you don't understand," said Roxana. "It may sound like fun—but what good are fine clothing and precious jewels when they become invisible upon contact with me? And, anyway, I don't take anything unless I absolutely need it. I'm not light-fingered by nature."

"Why haven't you called your case to the attention of some scientist?" I queried cautiously.

"But that's just it! Is this in the realm of science or sorcery? Besides, I couldn't stand being a guinea pig.

"If you've seen any movies about invisible people, or read any books, or even just thought about it sometime, you might imagine it would be a great lark. But it isn't. You wouldn't believe how difficult it is, how many problems confront and perturb you, things that never occur in tailor-made stories.

"I used to try to make friends with people but when I spoke to them they'd be afraid and think I played practical jokes on drunks who'd lost their weekend but I soon got tired of playing a female Shadow. In fact...I'm very tired of every-thing."

The driver called 5th Street. "Look," I said, "I get off at the next stop, but I'd like to—"

I felt her move away from me. "I'm going to the end of the line." A tone of finality adumbrated her words like the closing of a coffin lid, causing me to shudder.

"Well... Goodbye and good luck!" And with that banality I parted company with Roxana, the Invisible Girl.

THAT NIGHT I missed my compact. I was very upset; it was the one Everett gave me on our 5th wedding anniversary. Where could I possibly have lost it? The last I recalled seeing it was on the bus. Roxana?

I found the same bus driver next day and asked him if a compact answering the description of mine had been found and reported. None had.

I put an ad in the paper. I got a phone call the first day. An elderly lady had found it and could not deliver it to me but she would be glad to return it to me if I would call. Out of curiosity I asked her where it had been found. The impact of her answer struck me like an obstetrician's slap on a newborn babe: By the bridge at the end of the bus line. The bridge that had been baptized by the blood of a suicide the day it opened to the public! And how many despairing souls had flung themselves to destruction from it in the intervening years? A score or more, enough to damn it with the name, Suicide Bridge.

Suicide Bridge! My compact found there could mean only one thing: The desolation of her invisible state had driven Roxana to this final desperate act. What impulse had caused her to take my compact I would never know but I would retrieve Everett's gift.

THE FINDER ANSWERED the doorbell on the third ring. She extended my compact in her wrinkled hand. There was a jolly twinkle in her eyes.

In her oddly slanted eyes. In her green eyes.

It shouldn't have happened to Hansel and Gretel!

The Atomic Age has dawned but the devil is still in the market for souls! Even innocent souls that can be duped to sin.

Roxana, poor soul, took a powder. I sacrificed my vanity case for my sanity. Yes, I fled empty-handed. Nobody is going to write a tragic comedy about me called "A Compact With the Devil"!

The Atomic Monument

FJA . . . with Theodore Sturgeon

M *ORE ACCURATELY, BY Theodore Sturgeon; adaptation by FJA.*
In the April 1946 Astounding Science Fiction *Sturgeon had a memorable short story "Memorial". It has not been reprinted in 9 of his collections; it may have been in a 10th, if there is a 10th, but I don't believe so. I believe I have them all on my pocketbook shelves, and I have not found the story included in any of the 9.*

It would be worth your while to hunt up the back issue and read the story in its entirety.

The little 400-word version here is just the heart of the matter. After the full story's publication I asked for and received permission from Sturgeon to translate the essence of the story into Esperanto for publication in Glom, *short for* Fantasticonglomeration, *an amateur mimeographed magazine I was publishing at the time for the members of the Fantasy Amateur Press Association.*

Later I translated my Esperanto back into English and the version was published in Mexico in the professional S.F. periodical Los Cuentos Fantasticos.

The present publication of this tiny version, nearly a quarter century after its origination, will come, I trust, as a pleasant surprise to "mia amiko Tecjo" (my friend Ted).

Don't forget to read the original, in Sturgeon's own stirring words.

ANTONIO VASQUEZ, THE philosophical physicist, believed that if he should create, by an atomic bomb, a gigantic radioactive crater in a deserted spot in Mexico, it would stand as a warning to the world for centuries to come. That such a terrible living reminder of the tremendous power of the A-bomb would act as a bridle on the arms of beast-men, anxious to loose their destructive devilworks on the Earth.

He exploded his superbomb in secret.

These things immediately happened as a consequence:

Mexico became hysterical. Nothing could be confirmed. It was simpler to announce: WE ARE ATTACKED! Then the panicked people demanded revenge, and the government agreed, because in that way certain officials could command uncustomary powers.

And so the First Atomic War began.

And the Second.

After that there were no more atomic wars. The War of the Monsters was a barbaric affair, and the biologically altered mutants conquered the ragged remainder of mankind—now for the most part sterile—because the radioactively altered quasi-humans were very strong.

Then the Mutants died off, because they were alien to nature.

Some men remained—but the rats multiplied in fantastic quantities, and the hunted humans fell beneath savage, rending teeth.

And there scourged the world three plagues.

After that, there wandered over the face of the world crouching, unclothed half-humans, whose heredity was rooted in homo sapiens; but they could be frightened both individually and as a race, so they could not progress.

THE CRATER, IN the year 5000, had changed little during the centuries. It still was an angry memento of the misuse of a great force; and because of it, organized warfare was a forgotten thing. Because of the dream of humanitarian Vasquez, the world was free of the useless smoke and filth of "defense" industries. The crack and cry of bombs, and the soporific beat of marching feet, no longer was heard; and finally the Earth knew peace.

To venture near the Crater meant slow and certain death, and every living thing felt respect for it and fear of it. Really it gleamed at night, and a pale, deadly aura surrounded it. A broken region extended from it, beyond the horizon.

Nothing lived there. Nothing could.

Because of that monument, peace was a necessity. The planet could never forget the horror that war could liberate.

Noble dream; ironic realization!

Nyusa, Nymph of Darkness

by Catherine L. Moore and FJA

*A*T LAST, 66 years after she was born, Nyusa takes first place in the title of this *collaboration, as it was alway intended she should. She received the honor in the year of her inception of being voted third place among best fantasies of the year in a prestigious Australian poll.*

THE THICK VENUSIAN dark of the Ednes waterfront in the hours before dawn is breathless and tense with a nameless awareness, a crouching danger. The shapes that move murkily thru its blackness are not daylight shapes. Sun has never shone upon some of those misshapen figures, and what happens in the dark is better left untold. Not even the Patrol ventures there after the lights are out, and the hours between midnight and dawn are outside the law. If dark things happen there the Patrol never knows of them, or desires to know. Powers move thru the darkness along the waterfront to which even the Patrol bows low.

Thru that breathless blackness, along a street beneath which the breathing waters whispered, Northwest Smith strolled slowly. No prudent man ventures out after midnight along the waterfront of Ednes unless he has urgent business abroad, but from the leisurely gait that carried Smith soundlessly thru the dark he might have been some casual sightseer. He was no stranger to the Ednes waterfront. He knew the danger thru which he strolled so slowly, and under narrowed lids his colorless eyes were like keen steel probes that searched the dark. Now and then he passed a shapeless shadow that dodged aside to give him way. It might have been no more than a shadow. His no-colored eyes did not waver. He went on, alert and wary.

He was passing between two high warehouses that shut out even the faint reflection of light from the city beyond when he first heard that sound of bare, running feet which so surprised him. The patter of frantically fleeing steps is not uncommon along the waterfront, but these were—he listened closer—yes, certainly the feet of a woman or a young boy. Light and quick and desperate. His ears were keen enough to be sure of that. They were coming nearer swiftly. In the blackness even his pale eyes could see nothing, and he drew back against the wall, one hand dropping to the ray gun that hung low on his thigh. He had no desire to meet whatever it was which pursued this fugitive.

But his brows knit as the footsteps turned into the street that led between the warehouses. No woman, of whatever class or kind, ventures into this quarter by night. And he became certain as he listened that those feet were a woman's. There was a measured rhythm about them that suggested the Venusian woman's lovely, swaying gait. He pressed flat against the wall, holding his breath. He wanted no sound to indicate his own presence to the terror from which the woman fled. Ten years before he might have dashed out to her—but ten years along the spaceways teaches a man prudence. Gallantry can be foolhardy sometimes, particularly along the waterfront, where any of a score of things might be in close pursuit. At the thought of what some of those things might be the hair prickled faintly along his neck.

The frantic footsteps came storming down the dark street. He heard the rush of breath thru unseen nostrils, the gasp of laboring lungs. Then those desperate feet stumbled a bit, faltered, turned aside. Out of the dark a hurtling figure plunged full-tilt against him. His startled arms closed about a woman—a girl—a young girl, beautifully made, muscular and firmly curved under his startled hands—and quite naked.

He released her rather quickly.

"Earthman!" she gasped in an agony of breathlessness. "Oh, hide me, hide me! Quick!"

There was no time to wonder how she knew his origin or to ask from what she fled, for before the words had left her lips a queer, greenish glow appeared around the corner of the warehouse. It revealed a pile of barrels at Smith's elbow, and he shoved the exhausted girl behind them in one quick motion, drawing his gun and flattening himself still further against the wall.

Yet it was no nameless monster which appeared around the corner of the building. A man's dark shape came into view. A squat figure, broad and misshapen. The light radiated from a flash-tube in his hand, and it was an oddly diffused and indirect light, not like an ordinary flash's clear beam, for it lighted the man behind it as well as what lay before the tube, as if a greenish, luminous fog were spreading sluggishly from the lens.

The man came forward with a queer, shuffling gait. Something about him made Smith's flesh crawl unaccountably. What it was he could not be sure, for the green glow of the tube did not give a clear light, and the man was little more than a squat shadow moving unevenly behind the light tube's luminance.

He must have seen Smith almost immediately, for he came straight across the street to where the Earthman stood against the wall, gun in hand. Behind the glowing tube-mouth Smith could make out a pale blur of face with two dark

splotches for eyes. It was a fat face, unseemly in its puffy pallor, like some grub
that has fed too long upon corruption. No expression crossed it at the sight of
the tall spaceman in his leather garb, leaning against the wall and fingering a
ready gun. Indeed, there was nothing to arouse surprise in the Earthman's atti-
tude against the wall, or in his drawn gun. It was what any nightfarer along the
waterfront would have done at the appearance of such a green, unearthly glow
in the perilous dark.

Neither spoke. After a single long glance at the silent Smith, the newcomer
began to switch his diffused light to and fro about the street in obvious search.
Smith listened, but the girl had stilled her sobbing breath and no sound be-
trayed her hiding place. The sluggish searcher went on slowly down the street,
casting his foggy light before him. Its luminance faded by degrees as he re-
ceded from view, a black, misshapen shadow haloed in unholy radiance.

WHEN UTTER DARK had descended once more Smith holstered his gun
and called to the girl in a low voice. The all but soundless murmur of bare feet
on the pavement heralded her approach, the hurrying of still unruly breath.

"Thank you," she said softly. "I—I hope you need never know what horror
you have saved me from."

"Who are you?" he demanded. "How did you know me?"

"They call me Nyusa. I did not know you, save that I think you are of Earth,
and perhaps—trustworthy. Great Shar must have guided my flight along the
streets tonight, for I think your kind is rare by the sea edge, after dark."

"But—can you see me?"

"No. But a Martian, or one of my own countrymen, would not so quickly
have released a girl who dashed into his arms by night—as I am." In the dark
Smith grinned. It had been purely reflexive, that release of her when his hand
realized her nudity. But he might as well take credit for it. "You had better go
quickly now," she went on, "there is such danger here that—"

Abruptly the low voice broke off. Smith could hear nothing, but he sensed
a tensing of the girl by his side, a strained listening. And presently he caught a
faraway sound, a curious muffled wheezing, as if something short-winded and
heavy were making laborious haste. It was growing nearer. The girl's caught
breath was loud in the stillness at his elbow.

"Quick!" she gasped. "Oh, hurry!"

Her hand on his arm tugged him on in the direction the squat black searcher
had taken. "Faster!" And her anxious hands pulled him into a run. Feeling a little
ridiculous, he loped thru the dark beside her with long, easy strides, hearing
nothing but the soft fall of his own boots and the scurrying of the girl's bare
feet, and far behind the distant wheezing breath, growing fainter.

Twice she turned him with a gentle push into some new byway. Then they paused while she tugged at an unseen door, and after that they ran down an alley so narrow that Smith's broad shoulders brushed its walls. The place smelled of fish and decayed wood and the salt of the seas. The pavement rose in broad, shallow steps, and they went thru another door, and the girl pulled at his arm with a breathed,

"We're safe now. Wait."

He heard the door close behind them, and light feet pattered on boards.

"Lift me," she said after a moment. "I can't reach the light."

Cool, firm fingers touched his neck. Gingerly in the dark he found her waist and swung her aloft at arm's length. Between his hands that waist was supple and smoothly muscled and slim as a reed. He heard the fumble of uncertain fingers overhead. Then in an abrupt dazzle light sprang up about him.

He swore in a choked undertone and sprang back, dropping his hands. For he had looked to see a girl's body close to his face, and he saw nothing. His hands had gripped—nothing. He had been holding aloft a smooth and supple—nothingness.

He heard the fall of a material body on the floor, and a gasp and cry of pain, but still he could see nothing, and he fell back another step, lifting an uncertain hand to his eyes and muttering a dazed Martian oath. For look tho he would, he could see no one but himself in the little bare room the light had revealed. Yet the girl's voice was speaking from empty air. "What— why did— Oh, I see!" and a little ripple of laughter. "You have never heard of Nyusa?"

THE REPETITION OF the name struck a chord of remote memory in the Earthman's mind. Somewhere lately he had heard that word spoken. Where and by whom he could not recall, but it aroused in his memory a nebulous chord of night peril and the unknown. He was suddenly glad of the gun at his side, and a keener awareness was in the pale gaze he sent around the tiny room.

"No," he said. "I have never heard the name before now."

"I am Nyusa."

"But where are you?"

She laughed again, a soft ripple of mirth honey sweet with the Venusian woman's traditionally lovely voice.

"Here. I am not visible to men's eyes. I was born so. I was born—" Here the rippling voice sobered, and a tinge of solemnity crept in. "—I was born of a strange mating, Earthman. My mother was a Venusian, but my father my father was Darkness. I can't explain . . . But because of that strain of Dark in me, I am invisible. And because of it I—I am not free."

"Why? Who holds you captive? How could anyone imprison an invisibility?"

"The—Nov." Her voice was the faintest breath of sound, and again, at the strange word, a prickle of nameless unease ran thru Smith's memory. Somewhere he had heard that name before, and the remembrance it roused was too nebulous to put into words, but it was ominous. Nyusa's breathing whisper went on very softly at his shoulder. It was a queer, unreal feeling, that, to be standing alone in a bare room and a girl's sweet, muted murmur in his ears from empty air.

"The Nov—they dwell underground. They are the last remnant of a very old race. And they are the priests who worship That which was my father. The Darkness. They prison me for purposes of their own.

"You see, my heritage from the lady who bore me was her own lovely human shape, but the Thing which was my father bequeathed to his child stranger things than invisibility. I am of a color outside the range of human eyes. And I have entry into—into other lands than this. Strange lands, lovely and far—Oh, but so damnably near! If I could only pass by the bars the Nov have set to shut me away. For they need me in their dark worship, and here I must stay, prisoned in the hot, muddy world which is all they themselves can ever know. They have a light—you saw it, the green glow in the hands of the Nov who pursued me thru the dark tonight—which makes me visible to human eyes. Something in its color combines with that strange color which is mine to produce a hue that falls within man's range of vision. If he had found me I would have been—punished—severely, because I fled tonight. And the Nov's punishments are—not nice.

"To make sure that I shall not escape them, they have set a guardian to dog my footsteps—the thing that wheezed on my track tonight—Dolf. He sprang from some frightful union of material and immaterial. He is partly elemental, partly animal. I can't tell you fully. And he is cloudy, nebulous—but very real, as you would have discovered had he caught us just now. He has a taste for human blood which makes him invaluable, tho I am safe, for I am only half human, and the Nov—well, they are not wholly human either. They—"

She broke off suddenly. Outside the door Smith's keen ears had caught a shuffle of vague feet upon the ground, and thru the cracks came very clearly the snuffle of wheezing breath. Nyusa's bare feet pattered swiftly across the boards, and from near the door came a series of low, sibilant hissings and whistlings in a clearer tone than the sounds the great Dolf made. The queer noise crescendoed to a sharp command, and he heard a subdued snuffling and shuffling outside and the sound of great, shapeless feet moving off over flagstones. At his shoulder Nyusa sighed.

"It worked that time," she said. "Sometimes I can command him, by virtue of my father's strength in me. The Nov do not know that. Queer, isn't it—they never seem to remember that I might have inherited more from their god than my invisibility and my access to other worlds. They punish me and prison me and command me to their service like some temple dancing girl—me, the half divine! I think—yes, I think that someday the doors will open at my own command, and I shall go out into those other worlds. I wonder—could I do it now?"

The voice faded into a murmurous undertone. Smith realized that she had all but forgotten his presence at the realization of her own potentialities. And again that prickle of unease went over him. She was half human, but half only. Who could say what strange qualities were rooted in her, springing from no human seed? Qualities that might someday blossom into—into—well, he had no words for what he was thinking of, but he hoped not to be there on the day the Nov tried her too far.

HESITANT FOOTSTEPS BESIDE him called back his attention sharply. She was moving away, a step at a time. He could hear the sound of her bare feet on the boards. They had almost reached the opposite wall now, one slow step after another. And then suddenly those hesitating footfalls were running, faster, faster, diminishing in distance. No door opened, no aperture in the walls, but Nyusa's bare feet pattered eagerly away. He was aware briefly of the vastnesses of dimensions beyond our paltry three, distances down which a girl's bare feet could go storming in scornful violation of the laws that held him fast. From far away he heard those steps falter. He thought he heard the sound of fists beating against resistance, the very remote echo of a sob. Then slowly the patter of bare feet returned. Almost he could see a dragging head and hopelessly slumped shoulders as the reluctant footfalls drew nearer, nearer, entered the room again. At his shoulder she said in a subdued voice,

"Not yet. I have never gone so far before, but the way is still barred. The Nov are too strong—for a while. But I know, now. I know! I am a god's daughter, and strong too. Not again shall I flee before the Nov's pursuit, or fear because Dolf follows. I am the child of Darkness, and they shall know it! They—"

Sharply into her exultant voice broke a moment of blackness that cut off her words with the abruptness of a knife stroke. It was of an instant's duration only, and as the light came on again a queer wash of rosy luminance spread thru the room and faded again, as if a ripple of color had flowed past. Nyusa sighed.

'That's what I fled," she confided. "I am not afraid now—but I do not like it. You had best go—or no, for Dolf still watches the door I entered by. Wait—let me think."

Silence for a moment, while the last flush of rose faded from the air, to be followed by a ripple of fresh color that faded in turn. Three times Smith saw the tide of red flow thru the room and die away before Nyusa's hand fell upon his arm and her voice murmured from emptiness,

"Come. I must hide you somewhere while I perform my ritual. That color is the signal that the rites are to begin—the Nov's command for my presence. There is no escape for you until they call Dolf away, for I could not guide you to a door without having him sense my presence there and follow. No, you must hide—hide and watch me dance. Would you like that? A sight which no eyes that are wholly human have ever seen before! Come."

Invisible hands pushed open the door in the opposite wall and pulled him thru. Stumbling a little at the newness of being guided by an unseen creature, Smith followed down a corridor thru which waves of rosy light flowed and faded. The way twisted many times, but no doors opened from it nor did they meet anyone in the five minutes or so that elapsed as they went down the hallway thru the pulsing color of the air.

At the end a great barred door blocked their passage. Nyusa released him for an instant, and he heard her feet whisper on the floor, her unseen hands fumble with something metallic. Then a section of the floor sank. He was looking down a shaft around which narrow stairs spiraled, very steeply. It was typically a Venusian structure, and very ancient. He had descended other spiraled shafts before now, to strange destinations. Wondering what lay in store for him at the foot of this, he yielded to the girl's clinging hands and went down slowly, gripping the rail.

He had gone a long way before the small, invisible hands plucked at his arm again and drew him thru an opening in the rock thru which the shaft sank. A short corridor led into darkness. At its end they paused, Smith blinking in the queer, pale darkness which veiled the great cavern that lay before them.

"Wait here," whispered Nyusa. "You should be safe enough in the dark. No one ever uses this passage but myself. I will return after the ceremony." Hands brushed his briefly, and she was gone. Smith pressed back against the wall and drew his gun, flicking the catch experimentally to be sure it would answer any sudden need. Then he settled back to watch.

BEFORE HIM A vast domed chamber stretched. He could see only a little of it in the strange dark pallor of the place. The floor shone with the deep sheen of marble, black as quiet water underground. And as the minutes passed he became aware of motion and life in the pale dark. Voices murmured, feet shuffled softly, forms moved thru the distance. The Nov were taking their places for the ceremony. He could see the dim outlines of their mass, far off in the dark.

After a while, a deep, sonorous chanting began from nowhere and every-where, swelling and filling the cavern and echoing from the domed ceiling in reverberant monotones. There were other sounds whose meaning he could not fathom, queer pipings and whistlings like the voice in which Nyusa had commanded Dolf, but invested with a solemnity that gave them depth and power. He could feel fervor building up around the dome of the cavern, the queer, wild fervor and ecstasy of an unknown cult for a nameless god. He gripped his gun and waited.

Now, distantly and very vaguely, a luminance was forming in the center of the arched roof. It strengthened and deepened and began to rain downward toward the darkly shining floor in long streamers like webs of tangible light. In the mirrored floor replicas of light reached upward, mistily reflecting. It was a sight of such weird and enchanting loveliness that Smith held his breath, watch-ing. And now green began to flush the streaming webs, a strange, foggy green like the light the Nov had flashed thru the waterfront streets in pursuit of Nyusa. Recognizing the color, he was not surprised when a shape began to dawn in the midst of that raining light. A girl's shape, half transparent, slim and lovely and unreal.

In the dark pallor of the cavern, under the green luminance of the circling light, she lifted her arms in a long, slow, sweeping motion, lighter than smoke, and moved on tiptoe, very delicately. Then the light shimmered, and she was dancing. Smith leaned forward breathlessly, gun hanging forgotten in his hand, watching her dance. It was so lovely that afterward he could never be sure he had not dreamed.

She was so nebulous in the streaming radiance of the light, so utterly un-real, so fragile, so exquisitely colored in the strangest tints of violet and blue and frosty silver, and queerly translucent, like a moonstone. She was more unreal now, when she was visible, than she had ever seemed before his eyes beheld her. Then his hands had told him of her firm and slender roundness—now she was a wraith, transparent, dream-like, dancing soundlessly in a rain of lunar color.

She wove magic with her dancing body as she moved, and the dance was more intricate and symbolic and sinuous than any wholly human creature could have trod. She scarcely touched the floor, moving above her reflection in the polished stone like a lovely moonlight ghost floating in mid-darkness while green moon-fire rained all about her.

With difficulty Smith wrenched his eyes away from that nebulous creature treading her own reflection as she danced. He was searching for the sources of those voices he had heard, and in the green, revealing light he saw them ring-ing the cavern in numbers greater than he had dreamed. The Nov, intent as one man upon the shimmering figure before them. And at what he saw he was glad he could not see them clearly. He remembered Nyusa's words, "—the Nov are not wholly human either." Veiled tho they were in the misty radiance and the pallor of the dark, he could see that it was so. He had seen it, unrealizing, in the face of that squat pursuer who had passed him in the street.

They were all thick, shapeless, all darkly robed and white-faced as slugs are white. Their formless features, intent and emotionless, had a soft, unstable quality, not shaped with any human certainty. He did not stare too long at any one face, for fear he might make out its queer lack of contour, or understand the portent of that slug-white instability of feature.

Nyusa's dance ended in a long, floating whirl of unhuman lightness. She sank to the floor in deep obeisance, prostrate upon her own reflection. From the front ranks of the assembled Nov a dark figure stepped with upraised arms. Obediently Nyusa rose. From that dark form, from the sluglike, unfeatured face, a twittering whistle broke, and Nyusa's voice echoed the sounds unerringly, her voice blending with the other's in a chant without words.

SMITH WAS SO intent upon watching that he was not aware of the soft shuffling in the dark behind him until the wheeze of labored breath sounded almost upon his neck. The thing was all but on him before that sixth sense which had saved him so often before now shrieked a warning and he whirled with a choked oath of surprise and shock, swinging up his gun and confronting a dim, shapeless immensity out of which a dull glow of greenish light stared at him. His gun spat blue flame, and from the imponderable thing a whistling scream rang quaveringly, echoing across the cavern and cutting short that wordless chant between the Nov and the girl.

Then the dark bulk of Dolf lurched forward and fell smotheringly upon Smith. It bore him to the floor under an engulfing weight which was only half real, but chokingly thick in his nostrils. He seemed almost to be breathing Dolf's substance, like heavy mist. Blinded and gasping, he fought the curiously nebulous thing that was smothering him, knowing he must win free in a few seconds' time, for Dolf's scream must bring the Nov upon him at any moment now. But for all his efforts he could not break away, and something indescribable and nauseous was fumbling for his throat. When he felt its blind searching his struggles redoubled convulsively, and after a frantic moment he staggered free, gulping in clean air and staring out into the dark with wide eyes, trying to make out what manner of horror he had grappled with. He could see nothing but that dull flare, as of a single eye, glowing upon him from an imponderable bulk which blended with the dark.

Dolf was coming at him again. He heard great feet shuffling, and the wheezing breath came fast. From behind the shouts of the Nov rose loud, and the noise of running men, and above all the high, clear call of Nyusa, screaming something in a language without words. Dolf was upon him. That revolting, unseen member fumbled again at his throat. He thrust hard against the yielding bulk and his gun flared again, blue-hot in the dark, full into the midst of Dolf's unstable blackness.

He felt the mass of the half-seen monster jerk convulsively. A high, whistling scream rang out, shrill and agonized, and the sucking organ dropped from his throat. The dim glow of vision dulled in the shape's cloudy midst. Then it flickered, went out. Somehow there was a puff of blackness that dissolved into misty nothing all about him, and the dark shape that had been Dolf was gone. Half elemental, he had gone back into nothingness as he died.

Smith drew a deep breath and swung round to front the first of the oncoming Nov. They were almost upon him, and their numbers were overwhelming, but his flame-gun swung its long arc of destruction as they swarmed in and almost a dozen of the squat, dark figures must have fallen to that deadly scythe before he went down under the weight of them. Pudgily soft fingers wrenched the gun from his hand, and he did not fight hard to retain it, for he remembered the blunt-nosed little flame-thrower in its holder under his arm and was not minded that they should discover it in any body-to-body fight.

Then he was jerked to his feet and thrust forward toward the pale radiance that still held Nyusa in its heart, like a translucent prisoner in a cage of light. A little dazed by the swiftness of events, Smith went on unsteadily in their midst. He towered head and shoulders above them, and his eyes were averted. He tried not to flinch from the soft, fish white hands urging him forward, not to look too closely into the faces of the squat things swarming so near. No, they were not men. He knew that more surely than ever from this close sight of the puffy, featureless faces ringing him round.

At the brink of the raining light which housed Nyusa the Nov who had led the chanting stood apart, watching impassively as the tall prisoner came forward in his swarm of captors. There was command about this Nov, an air of regality and calm, and he was white as death, luminous as a corpse in the lunar reflections of the light.

They halted Smith before him. After one glance into that moveless, unfeatured face, slug pale, the Earthman did not look again. His eyes strayed to Nyusa, beyond the Nov who fronted him, and at what he saw took faint hope again. There was no trace of fear in her poise. She stood straight and quiet, watching, and he sensed a powerful reserve about her. She looked the god's daughter she was, standing there in the showering luminance, translucent as some immortal.

SAID THE LEADER Nov, in a voice that came deeply from somewhere within him, tho his unfeatured face did not stir.

"How came you here?"

"I brought him," Nyusa's voice sounded steadily across the space that parted them.

The Nov swung round, amazement in every line of his squatness.

"You?" he exclaimed. "You brought an alien to witness the worship of the god I serve? How dared—"

"I brought one who had befriended me to witness my dance before my father," said Nyusa in so ominously gentle a tone that the Nov did not realize for a moment the significance of her words. He spluttered Venusian blasphemy in a choked voice.

"You shall die!" he yelled thickly. "Both of you shall die by such torment—"

"S-s-s-zt!"

Nyusa's whistling hiss was only a sibilance to Smith, but it cut the Nov's furious flow abruptly short. He went dead quiet, and Smith thought he saw a sicker pallor than before spreading over the slug face turned to Nyusa.

"Had you forgotten?" she queried gently. "Forgotten that my father is That which you worship? Dare you raise your voice to threaten Its daughter? Dare you, little worm-man?"

A gasp ran over the throng behind Smith. Greenish anger suffused the pallid face of the priest. He spluttered wordlessly and surged forward, short arms clawing toward the taunting girl. Smith's hand, darting inside his coat, was quicker than the clutch of his captors. The blue flare of his flamethrower leaped out in a tongue of dazzling heat to lick at the plunging Nov. He spun round dizzily and screamed once, high and shrill, and sank in a dark, puddly heap to the floor.

There was a moment of the deepest quiet. The shapeless faces of the Nov were turned in one stricken stare to that oddly fluid lump upon the floor which had been their leader. Then in the pack behind Smith a low rumble began to rise, the mutter of many voices. He had heard that sound before—the dawning roar of a fanatic mob. He knew that it meant death. Setting his teeth, he spun to face them, hand closing firmer about the butt of his flame-thrower.

The mutter grew deeper, louder. Someone yelled, "Kill! Kill!" and a forward surge in the thick crowd of faces swayed the mass toward him. Then above that rising clamor Nyusa's voice rang clear.

"Stop!" she called. In sheer surprise the murderous mob paused, eyes turning toward the unreal figure in her cage of radiance. Even Smith darted a glance over his shoulder, flame gun poised in mid-air, his finger hesitating upon the catch. And at what they saw the crowd fell silent, the Earthman froze into stunned immobility as he watched what was happening under the rain of light.

Nyusa's translucent arms were lifted, her head thrown back. Like a figure of triumph carved out of moonstone she stood poised, while all about her in the misty, lunar colors of the light a darkness was forming like fog that clung to her outstretched arms and swathed her half-real body. And it was darkness not like any night that Smith had ever seen before. No words in any tongue could describe it, for it was not a darkness made for any vocal creature to see. It was a blasphemy and an outrage against the eyes, against all that man hopes and believes and is. The darkness of the incredible, the utterly alien and opposed.

SMITH'S GUN FELL from shaking fingers. He pressed both hands to his eyes to shut out that indescribably awful sight, and all about him heard a long, soft sighing as the Nov sank to their faces upon the shining floor. In that deathly hush Nyusa spoke again, vibrant with conscious godhood and underrun with a queer, tingling ripple of inhumanity. It was the voice of one to whom the unknown lies open, to whom that utterly alien and dreadful blackness is akin.

"By the Darkness I command you," she said coldly. "Let this man go free. I leave you now, and I shall never return. Give thanks that a worse punishment than this is not visited upon you who paid no homage to the daughter of Darkness."

Then for a swift instant something indescribable happened. Remotely Smith was aware that the Blackness which had shrouded Nyusa was spreading thru him, permeating him with the chill of that blasphemous dark, a hideous pervasion of his innermost being. For that instant he was drowned in a darkness which made his very atoms shudder to its touch. And if it was dreadful to him, the voiceless shriek that rose simultaneously from all about him gave evidence how much more dreadfully their god's touch fell upon the Nov. Not with his ears, but with some nameless sense quickened by that moment of alien blackness, he was aware of the scream of intolerable anguish, the writhing of extra human torment which the Nov underwent in that one timeless moment.

Out of his tense awareness, out of the spreading black, he was roused by a touch that startled him into forgetfulness of that dreadful dark. The touch of a girl's mouth upon his, a tingling pressure of sweet parted lips that stirred delicately against his own. He stood tense, not moving a muscle, while Nyusa's mouth clung to his in a long, close kiss like no kiss he had ever taken before. There was a coldness in it, a chill as alien as the dark that had gathered about her translucency under the light, a shuddering cold that struck thru him in one long, deep-rooted shock of frigid revulsion. And there was warmth in it, headily stirring the pulse which that cold had congealed.

In that instant while those clinging lips melted to his mouth, he was a battleground for emotions as alien as light and dark. The cold touch of Darkness, the hot touch of love. Alienity's shuddering, frozen stab, and humanity's blood-stirring throb of answer to the warm mouth's challenge. It was a mingling of such utter opposites that for an instant he was racked by forces that sent his senses reeling. There was danger in the conflict, the threat of madness in such irreconcilable forces that his brain blurred with the effort of compassing them.

Just in time the clinging lips dropped away. He stood alone in the reeling dark, that perilous kiss burning upon his memory as the world steadied about him. In that dizzy instant he heard what the rest, in their oblivious agony, could not have realized. He heard a girl's bare feet pattering softly along some incline, up and up, faster and faster. Now they were above his head. He did not look up. He knew he would have seen nothing. He knew Nyusa walked a way that no sense of his could perceive. He heard her feet break into an eager little run. He heard her laugh once, lightly, and the laugh cut off by the sound of a closing door. Then quiet.

Without warning, on the heels of that sound, he felt a tremendous release all about him. The darkness had lifted. He opened his eyes upon a dimly lighted cavern from which that rain of light had vanished. The Nov lay in quivering windrows, about his feet, their shapeless faces hidden. Otherwise the whole vast place was empty as far as his eyes could pierce the dark. Smith bent and picked up his fallen gun. He kicked the nearest Nov ungently.

"Show me the way out of this place," he ordered, sheathing the flamethrower under his arm.

Obediently the sluggish creature stumbled to his feet.

THE GENESIS OF AN INVISIBLE VENUSIENNE
Afterword to Nymph of Darkness
by Forrest J Ackerman

THERE IS AN apocryphal story that the California town of Azusa was so named because when a nomenclature for it was sought it seemed that everything had already been appropriated from A to Z in the USA.

There is no truth to the rumor that Nyusa was initially known as NY, USA; like Wendayne (my wife's naturalized citizen name when she came to Earth from somewhere beyond Infinity), Nyusa burgeoned in my brain in the same manner as Tarzan in Edgar Rice Burroughs': the result of many mental gymnastics with quixotic sound combinations till the satisfactory amalgamation materialized. En passant, it is a virtually forgotten fact—except by Sharane Yvala Dewey, a woman I knew as a little girl, who was so named by her science fiction author father G. Gordon Dewey, who was captivated by the name of A. Merritt's heroine in *The Ship of Ishtar* and the Yvala of Catherine Moore's Northwest Smith adventure of the same name—it is a practically unknown fact that I created the character (pronounced Ee-vah-lah). I hope it's not unchivalrous to suggest it, with dear Catherine so mentally decimated by Alzheimer's disease that she has not known me or herself or what she wrote for two years or more (1987), but reflecting on the origin of the story it occurs to me I might retroactively be entitled to a byline on "Yvala" because in retrospect I feel I contributed about as much inspiration and plot gimmick to it as I did to "Nymph." I will not belabor the point, however, since Catherine's memory is a blank book and she is in no position to agree or disagree with my observation. (Incidentally, Gordon Dewey gave his other daughter a Catherine character name: Judai.)

The January-February 1948 club organ of the Los Angeles Science Fantasy Society *Shangri-LA*, featured the following article by me on the story behind the story on *Nymph of Darkness*.

THE "NYMPH" O' MANIACK
by Forrest J Ackerman

THIS IS THE story behind the story of a collaboration in which I was honored to have my name linked some years ago with the lovely and talented Catherine Moore, now the wife of an old friend—sensational Henry Kuttner. As I am composing this article a few hours before midnite, New Year's Eve, I believe it would be apropos to preface it with a quotation from a New Year letter from Catherine which I ran across in searching for the material for the following.

1936: "Dear Forrie: Happy New Year. And by the way, if you heard a new year's horn blowing extra loudly just at midnight, your time, and couldn't locate it—that was me. I blew a special blast for you at about 2:00 a.m. or thereabouts, as nearly as I can remember now—of New Year's morning just as the radio announced that it was at that moment midnight in Los Angeles. I never quite believe things like that—different times, I mean. Of course, know that you lose a day going round the world, and all that—but somehow can't quite believe it anyway. I read a story somewhere once in which someone in New York phoned someone in London, and over the wire 'the late afternoon New York traffic vibrated weirdly in the stillness of the London night.' It seems impossible, if you see what I mean."

Catherine Moore—puzzled by geo-chronological paradoxes!

But about *Nymph of Darkness* by C.L. Moore and F. J Ackerman, whose chief claim to fame was that it was among the titles which vied for third place as best fantasy of the year in a poll taken among the "Auslanders"—the Australian fans, down under. (Also, it was one of the earliest stories illustrated by Hannes Bok, a new artist whom a young fan named Ray Bradbury had personally persuaded the late Farnsworth Wright to try.)

Here is the original outline I sent to Catherine when she was living in Indianapolis and working in a bank vault:

THE NYUSA NYMPH—One short and exciting experience in the adventure-filled life of Northwest Smith . . . Of a fleeing figure in the nite that bumped into NW at the Venusian waterfront— an unseen form—that of Nyusa, the girl who was born invisible! Further details: The business of the squat creature who came swiftly slinking thru the street, short on the heels of the figure in NW's arms, with the strange lite-tube in its hands flashing from side to side (it would have caused Nyusa to become visible, you know—the lite from the tube) . . . and of Nyusa, whose abnormally high body-temperature kept her comfortable free from clothing; so that invisible she remained, as born—And from what she fled, and how NW was of service to her, etc.—I will leave to you.

MOORE to Ackerman: I think I know why the pursuer's flash made Nyusa visible. Did you ever notice the peculiar colors one's skin turns under different lights? A violet ray machine turns lips and nails—as I remember—a sickly green, and the blue lights they use in photographers shops, sometimes, make you purple. I once figured out why, but can't remember and haven't time now to go into it. Something about complementary colors and mixing yellow and blue, and whatnot. Well, you remember in Bierce's *The Damned Thing* his invisible monster was a color outside our range of perception. Couldn't this flash-light be of some shade which, combined with Nyusa's peculiar skin-tone, produced a visible color? And Venus is the Hot Planet anyhow, so no need to increase her body temperature above normal to make it possible for her to run about in the altogether. Smith had met her in the absolutely black dark of the starless Venusian night. She came tearing down the street and bumped into him, and, tho considerably astonished to find his arms full of scared and quite unadorned girl, he of course didn't realize her invisibility then. Afterward came this squat, dark pursuer, flashing his greenishly glowing ray to and fro. When he'd gone by she heard another sound—origin yet unknown, to me or anyone else—which so alarmed her that she pulled Smith into a run and guided him at top speed thru [the spellings "thru" & "tho" are Catherine's] devious byways and into an un-lighted room. "Lift me up," said she, "so I can reach the light." And when it goes on he realizes that he is holding in midair a beautifully muscular, firmly curved armful of nothingness. He had just dropped her onto the floor and staggered back, doubting his sanity. What happens next I don't know. If you have any more ideas, they'll be welcome. This is the stage of a story when I usually sweat blood for several days, racking an absolutely sterile brain for ideas. Then something takes fire and the whole story just gallops, with me flying along behind trying to keep up with it. Very strenuous. Think hard and see if you can find any possible reasons, sane or insane, as to what the noise was she had heard, why it alarmed her so, whether she is invisible just by a freak of nature or whether by some mysterious mastermind's intent. I suspect she is in the power of some insidious villain, but I don't know yet. All thru the preface of the story I've made such veiled hints about the nameless horrors which stalk by night along the waterfront of Ednes, that said villain might be almost anything—some horror out of the ages before man, or some super-brain of the far advanced races we know nothing of, or an unhappy medium like the Alendar. (That reminds me—Vaudir is the infinitive of—as I remember my col-lege days—the French verb wish. I presume Nyusa is purely original with you, so you deserve more credit than I, for it's a grand name.) ["Thank you kindly, ma'am," said the 18-year-old lad. "There is no truth to the rumor that I made it up from the initials of our major metropolis, N.Y, U.S.A."]

ACKERMAN to Moore: [This is the point where I was supposed to come in for my big hunk of egoboo, quoting my share in the development of the plot, but I can't find the vital letter! What I wrote must be imagined from the mirror of Catherine's reply.]

MOORE to Ackerman: Thanks for the further suggestions. I had already gone on past my stopping point when I wrote you, so can't use all your ideas, but have incorporated Dolf and the dancing-girl idea. It seems Nyusa is—sorry—really innately invisible, being the daughter of a Venusian woman and a Dark-ness which is worshipped by a queer race of slug-like, half-human beings which dwell under the Venusian city of Ednes. (Incidentally, Ednes, the city where in the Minga stood, is simply lifted bodily out of the middle of Wednesday.) Any-how, Nyusa is forced by the priests to dance in their ritual worship under a peculiar light which renders her visible in a dim, translucent way. And because of her mixed breed she has access into other worlds from which her masters bar her out by their own strange mental powers because she'd never return to dance for them if she once got away. Dolf guards her for the same reason. I think now that Nyusa's captors drive her too far sometime, and she realizes that after all she is half divine, and calls upon the strain of Darkness within her to burst the bonds they have imposed. Smith, attacked by Dolf as he hides in their temple watching the ritual dance, fights with the worshippers and kills the high priest, whereupon their power over Nyusa is weakened and she exerts her demi-divinity to escape. Thus, tho Smith doesn't get the fortune you suggested, he at least is spared the expense of buying her any clothes, which was a very practical idea on your part.

ACKERMAN to Moore: I have a suggestion about the ending. Shambleau stunned Smith; to this day he had probably not forgotten "it." Sweet, was the girl of the Scarlet Dream. While in the Black Thirst, he gazed upon beauty incredible. But Shambleau was to be shunned; and the girl of the Dream . . . Vaudir dissolved. So, let the Nymph—Nyusa—just before she escapes . . . couldn't she—kiss Smith? A kiss never to be forgotten: a kiss . . . so cool, with a depth drawn out of Darkness. And yet, a kiss of fire—from her Venusian strain—hot, alive, searing Northwest's lips. A kiss, of delicious demi-divinity . . . a fond caress of frozen flame. Making it, under your care, Catherine, a kiss smothering with extra-mundane emotion, leaving the readers gasping. Smith's reward, the kiss, becomes famous and concludes the story.

MOORE to Ackerman: I do wish I had had your suggestion about the parting kiss before I finished. I wasn't able to expand the idea as fully as I'd have liked to, both because of the space-saving necessity and because to give it the attention it deserved I'd have had to write the story toward it from the beginning. It was a grand idea and would have given the story just the punch it needed at the end. Oh well, no story of mine is complete unless I leave out some major point until too late. I meant to make Shambleau's eyes shine in the dark, and to play up the idea of the Guardians in *Black Thirst*.

"Nymph of Darkness" was first published in the printed fan magazine *Fantasy Magazine*, in the April 1935 issue, and professionally published, in an expurgated form, in the December 1939 *Weird Tales*.

Time To Change
or
Mirror Image

by Marcial Souto with FJA

*M*ARCIAL SOUTO OF Montevideo/Uruguay is the Shibano Yano of Japan, *the Cozzi of Italy, the Grabnar of Yugoslavia, the Nesvadba of Czechoslova-kia, Gallet of France, Ernsting of Austria/Germany, Carnell of England.*

That is to say, the necessary monomaniac of his particular sector of the Imagi-Nation.

His short story, "Time to Change", in its original language was an instant hit and was adapted to TV as a several minute long (I believe he said six) fantasy feature.

Late in '68 when he was my houseguest, he translated his story into English. 358 words. I rephrased it—and it grew exactly 50 words in the English version, 50 words that, obviously, I felt increased its impact—and Marcial agreed. How much of a collaborator that makes me, I leave to your own judgment.

Certainly the strange idea was 100% Souto.

Perhaps he will become the Dunsany of Uruguay? Or one day they may say that Dunsany was the Souto of England.

A DESERTED HOUSE.

Old.

Dark.

The window shades are torn and the window panes have fallen from their frames.

Inside, all is silent. Occasionally, a leaf wafted in by the wind is imitated by the Mirror. (Yes, imitated.) Then it falls and lies quiescent, waiting for companions.

The Mirror of simulucrums hangs in the center of a wall . . . and this creator of doppelgangers is the only thing of livingness in the house. It is large and has almost forgotten what men look like. The rusting wire from which it hangs is growing weaker and weaker . . .

There was a time when men and women used to stand in front of Mirror. Then it would copy them with rapacious need and, by night, when everyone was asleep, would descend to the floor to try the shapes of those who had stood before it. It would walk about the room testing its imitation legs and, sometimes, putting its man or woman head out the window, it would see the trees and the houses beyond.

But it never dared go out.

And any little noise would make it run to the wall to hang again from the nail, inert, unsuspected.

But now it could not do that any more. Its memory was blurring and it could not reproduce living things correctly. The lastime it tried, its legs and the shape of the body were so defective that the ersatz fell to the floor. Mirror had to look in its memory for the vague shape of a cat so that, aided by its four legs, it might reach the wall.

Men . . . Men . . . I have forgotten you . . . I won't be able to copy you . . . any more. I am forgetting everything . . . everything . . . forgetting . . .

Who am I?

THE WIRE BROKE.
One turn in the air.
Twenty-three fragments.
Face up.

SPRING CAME, STRONG winds blowing, drying damp places and stirring green whispers from brown tree limbs.

One day, the sun took a butterfly to the window of the old, dark, deserted house.

The fragile airborne sentient beauty-shape circled 'round several times, slowly, hovering at last o'er the splintered shards of quicksilvered and reflective glass: the disastered Mirror.

From it, one—three—eight—twenty—twenty-three unusual butterflies arose.

Diamond brooches with tinkling crystal wings. Rainbows of light, they fluttered to the window without panes and out into the open air, the bright day.

Free.

Without shadows, without fear.

Reflecting glory as they soared into the sky.

Great Gog's Grave

by Forrest J Ackerman and Donald A. Wollheim

*O*nly collab twixt Wollheim and myself and I can't for the life of me recall how it came about.

Naturally, when my girlfriend Dora asked me to help her hunt for Gog's grave, my first impulse was to argue with her. I'm a natural-born skeptic. I'm told—I don't believe it—that my first words were, "There ain't no Santy Claus." But I fought the impulse and said yes, figuring it would turn out to be a lark in the bone park that would result in nothing more serious than skinned shins and maybe a few feelcops.

Gog was a legend, nothing more. It seems that before the first white settlers had come to Center City, the Indians had told stories about a huge man-monster who lived nearby. This creature was humanoid—only three times as big as a man—hairy, fanged like a wild animal, and pretty near immortal. The Indian legend had it that Gog had always been here—that he'd haunted the locality even before the redskins had arrived. Still, when it came right down to it, nobody had ever claimed to have seen Gog, so the founding fathers had located the first colonial graveyard just about where Gog's grave, or cave, or fave spot was supposed to be—which shows what little regard Europeans had for the native folktales.

For a while, everything was all right. Then there was a series of midnight mysteries. Something kidnapped a number of colonists, and their bodies were never found. Something broke into some houses . . . from the roof. Something left impossibly big footprints along the roads.

The colonists suspected the Indians, but they couldn't prove it. Anyway, the disturbances stopped after a while. About fifty years later, another outbreak occurred—people missing, big footprints, the whole carbon copy. Then another fifty years, and another, and now, just recently, again. The whole city had had a recent recurrence of stories about Gog. There'd been some mighty mysterious footprints found in mud on rainy mornings at the city edge where the old cemetery's located. I'd seen them myself. They were pretty big, I'll admit—

much too big for any bear or circus giant's foot. The foot had to have been maybe twenty inches long, with awfully long claws. Personally, I thought it was a gag.

But the newspaper people picked up on it, dug up all the old legends of Gog, and rewrote them for the Sunday specials. From the records and old newspaper accounts, the reporters figured out that Gog evidently slept for about fifty years, then came out from wherever he was hiding, satisfied his hunger with a few peopleburgers, and went back to his pad. This, they said, must have been going on for centuries, and it was now just about fifty years since his last visitation. The native, they concluded, was evidently getting restless.

The stories sounded like fodder for *Fate* magazine. Being a skeptic, I don't believe in that sort of thing. Old wives' tales and fairy stories, that's all they are to me. But my girl Dora's got a hyperactive imagination. She decided she'd find out for herself, and maybe sell the account of the adventure to the papers. So when she asked me to join her at the old underground dormitory that night, I said, "Anything you dig, baby, I dig, too. I'm all a-Gog over you!"

Around midnight, we drove my old heap out to the edge of the city, parked it by the ghouly gates, and, lugging a shovel and pick that Dora had picked up from somewhere, we hoofed it into the cemetery. The place was abandoned. There wasn't any watchman because nobody had been buried there in over seventy years. The colonists had used it, and now it was sort of a public park, only the city had never quite gotten around to fixing it up. It was all overrun with weeds, and the limestone tombstones from a hundred or two hundred years back were mostly fallen over or unreadable with age.

Dora figured Gog's grave would be somewhere near the center. She was going to turn over the old tombstones and see if any of them mentioned it. Could be the original settlers had marked the spot the Indians had thought was Gog's underground tepee.

Anyway, it was a hard night's work for sure. I figured maybe I could make out a bit with Dora during the rest breaks. She might even be so grateful for my help she'd say yes the next time I asked her to marry me. We turned over a number of tombstones, but didn't find anything helpful. We read a lot of funny old inscriptions and found some graves that were as old as the city. We came finally to one big old slab set in the ground—the kind of headstone that usually marks the resting place of some bigwig—and sat down on it for a while. My hand started wandering, and Dora, meaning to kick me, kicked the stone instead.

It rocked.

"Hey!" she yelped. "What's this?"

We got up and looked. Sure enough, the headstone was loose. It looked like it had only just fallen over. I pushed the pick under one end and levered it. The stone moved slowly aside. An opening was revealed. The slab covered a hole in the ground—an opening like an open grave.

No, not a grave. More like an entrance. There were old stone stairs going down into total darkness beneath the ground. We looked at each other, wondering what to do. If it weren't for the fact that I didn't want my girl to think I was curiously yellow, I'd have set a new Olympic record getting out of there. I was scared witless.

But Dora wasn't. She was only excited. She said, "Let's go down and see where they lead us!"

Like a zombie I nodded. I carried the pick, she carried the lantern, and we carried on together down those spooky stairs. They were awful old and worn. Down we went into the black hole beneath that slab in the center of the city's haunted graveyard. It was dampish, and the moldy dirt of the wall around us had a morgue-like smell. We were descending a sort of sloping shaft and getting deep, far below burying level. We went down about thirty steps and around a little curve, then came out into a sort of cave-like room. Not exactly my idea of an underground theater.

We looked around. It was a stone-enclosed place, maybe half a hundred feet long. There was no other exit, just the old stairs leading in. I breathed easier when I saw there was nothing moving down there, not even a rat or a beetle. I suppose, going down those stairs, I hadn't quite known what to expect. Maybe Gog. But all there was in that old cave were skeletons.

Lots of skeletons.

We walked around among the bones. They were all bare and white and old. There were maybe a couple of hundred of them. They had to have been lying there for years on end.

"I guess maybe this was a mass grave back in colonial days," I said at last. "Maybe even earlier. That has to be where the Gog story came from. 'Gog' was really an epidemic, or a massacre, and they buried all the bodies here in 'Great Gog's Grave.' That's where the story came from!"

"Y-yes," Dora said uneasily. It seemed a logical explanation. She bent over, fumbling amid the dirt and scraps on the floor, and picked up something. It was a coin. A copper cent. The light from the lantern lit the date on the penny. We looked at it: 1931.

We looked at each other wordlessly.

There had been no epidemic—nothing—in 1931 . . . just the last time there had been so many mysterious disappearances.

We turned around and started on the double back up those stairs. Halfway up, I started trying to talk myself out of it. "Jesus," I said, "we're acting like a couple of fools to run out without checking out the cave further. I bet the cops know all about those bodies. I bet we'll just look like a couple of kids when we tell them about this. There just can't be anything like this Gog thing."

"No," said Dora as we were nearing the top, "there must be some perfectly simple explanation. I don't really believe in that foolish old fable." We reached the surface level and panted up the last two or three steps. "There is no such thing as Gog."

"Oh, yes there is, my pretty," said a deep voice.

We turned in tandem and saw bloodrust on the talons of the monster reaching for us as it crouched by the entrance to its hidden grave, its huge hungry eyes feverish with bloodlust as its slavering tusks opened cavernously for its first meal in fifty years.

Tomorrow the papers and radio and TV will report the first of a new series of mysterious disappearances.

But if Gog was expecting a warm meal in Dora and me, he was disappointed. Our blood was running as cold as ice.

The Naughty Venusienne

by Otis Kaye and Morgan Ives (Big Name Female In Hiding)

My plot, polished by a professional female writer, now dead, who preferred anonimity.

HAVE YOU EVER tried to spank an invisible girl?

At some time in your life, *sans doute*, it is to be presumed that—according to your sex and station—you have: (A) spanked your *cherie* because she rolled those so beautiful eyes at some *ami* other than you; (B) taken the hairbrush to your *femme* because she bought a bathing suit *trop Bikini*; or, (C) been placed face-downward across the knees of *Papá* for the bite of the belt because you came home at an hour too late and with the *brassiére* torn from your shoulder.

You are familiar with the manner in which the skirts of the struggling captive must be raised well above the waist, so, and how—in spite of blushes, squeals and the frantic protests of outraged or pretended modesty, the little silken panties must be pulled off, by force if necessary, so that no protection, however slight, remains for the exposed place of punishment.

But—*mon Dieu!* How does one remove the dress of a girl who habitually wears no dress?

How does one pull panties from a little bottom which has never worn panties?

Above all, how does one spank *le derriére* which is not there?

Ah, you ask me, how do I get into a predicament so ridiculous? Patience, and I will explain all.

I am Georges Gallant, of the *Astronef*, the first French space ship to explore the planet Venus. As I descend toward this planet sacred to the goddess of Love, I have the misfortune to crash, and I am knocked unconscious.

When I regain my senses, it is only to believe that I have once again lost them; I discover myself lying on my back, near a cool pool of water, and although there is no person to be seen, I have the curious impression that someone is bending over me. Simultaneously, I realize that I must have injured my head in the crash, for there is pain, and I feel a trickle of blood above my eyes.

120

As I become aware of this, I feel a cooling hand brush my brow, a hand with moist fingers, although there is still no one to be seen. Instinctively, I reach up my hand and I encounter—

Are they pears? Oranges? Melons? *Mais non*, these fruitful descriptions are but poetic terms for the indescribable. No man who has ever loved could mistake their feel. Smooth as velvet, soft and pliant as two kittens they are, these twin mounds of fleshy delight encountered by my happy hands; two pliable, pendent, splendid, *invisible* breasts!

But no sooner have my amazed fingers clasped and identified these heavenly delights, than the sample is withdrawn from my touch, and a stinging slap is instantly and smartly delivered to my face! I lie stunned for a moment, then, painfully and dazed, I crawl to the pool's edge and dip my whirling head into the water to clear it of these hallucinations.

You are dreaming, Georges, I tell me. A blow from nowhere? Invisible breasts? *Non*, it is the thing incredible, you are dreaming or delirious. I lie there, bathing my face and resting, when there is a sudden splash in the water. Painfully, I raise my head, but see nothing at first—then, *nom d'un nom*, beneath the surface of the water, I see two gorgeous, creamy, pink-tipped breasts, the very breasts of my hallucination!

Now, however, they are attached to a charming torso, quite nude, tapering down to a trim little waist, hips deliciously formed, and a pair of shapely legs ending in dainty little feet.

But I see that the beautiful body has no head!

Quel horreur! The body, it begins to swim. As it slides gracefully forward, the hips are first elevated, then disappear, one leg after another vanishes as they approach the surface of the water, first one arm, then the other, cleaves the surface, appearing and vanishing in a supple subtle rhythm. And as the lovely swimming body rolls lissomly on its back to float, it loses its beautiful breasts. And then I understand. I am no fool, me.

So this is a native of Venus! In the atmosphere, it is her natural state to be invisible, but through some strange chemical property of her body, it becomes opaque when submerged in water, so that whatever portion of her pretty flesh is immersed in the pool can be clearly seen.

As if to oblige me, and prove my theory, she sinks completely beneath the surface, and for a moment I am treated to the vision of a face the most captivating, *ravissant!*

So I met N'yvonnaise, the exquisite (if invisible) Venusienne N'yvonnaise, who later returned to Earth with me, my bride.

Even before the *Astronef* lifted from the surface of Venus for the return trip to Earth, I became aware of the terrible temper of my lovely Venusienne.

The girls of Venus, I learned, are independent, headstrong little creatures, and whenever I gave N'yvonnaise an order which she had no intention of obeying, she would simply slip out of the homemade *brassiére* and panties which—anticipating a promised expedition to the *Rue de la Paix*, she had fashioned herself from scraps of my clothing, and dance away invisible, taunting and teasing me, until I gave in and implored the naughty witch to return.

However, as soon as we had left her native world behind, and embarked on the long return voyage to Earth, I knew that I must gain the upper hand. A man, after all, must be the master in his house. Enchanting as the willfulness of my lovely *fiancée* might be for a little time, married life was quite another matter, and my naughty bride must learn that soon.

"My little N'yvonnaise," I say to her, "we must have a child. But this child, will he be visible, like me? Or invisible, like his Mama? Or will he be translucent? Come to bed with me, so that next *Avril* we may know the answer."

Although I cannot see her face, I can see that she is pouting.

"*Non!*" she cries to me, "You will not see me, you cannot show me how much you love me in your bed! If we make the love, it must be in the bathtub, and the bathtub must be full to overflowing, so that you can see all of me and tell me how I am lovely!"

"*Mon Dieu*, it shall not be so, naughty one," I storm. "What! Can we fill to overflowing a bathtub in an *Astronef*, where there is not the gravity?"

"Then, *cherie*, you shall not have me at all," she taunts, and I know the moment has come to take a stand with my little mischievous one.

"N'yvonnaise," I order, "this has gone too far. Such willfulness, I will not have it! Come, turn yourself across my knee, and you shall learn that a man of Earth is master, even of the woman he loves!"

"*Non!*" and N'yvonnaise tears off her *brassiére* and quickly wiggles her lovely (if invisible) legs out of her panties. Weightless in the ship's free fall, they float in the air, and N'yvonnaise, she has vanished into invisibility again. I swim toward the floating lingerie, trying to catch N'yvonnaise, but like an invisible eel she eludes me, playing with me, teasingly, touching me naughtily with light, invisible fingers, then darting away from one corner of the cabin to another.

I abandon my blind search and hang very quietly in midair. I hear her breathing nearby, and I turn my back, as to pretend I have given up the fight—as always before when we quarrel.

"Georges, *mon ami*—" I hear her soft cajoling voice, and her little fingers flicker across my cheek. I spring quickly in the direction of the sound, and ah! I have collided with her in midair!

"Now, my little wicked one," I tell her, "there will be an end to this much nonsense!"

I pull her to a chair, and I bend her warm and flexible body, by touch, across my knees and prepare to lay on.

But *hélas!* There my problem was only beginning! For without the little panties, I could not see my goal! N'yvonnaise writhed and wriggled, squirming like a fish under my imprisoning arm, and when my other hand came down to spank her, as often as not I would strike myself!

By Venus, I vow, but there must be a way out of even this dilemma! I reach for a can of talcum powder which I use after shaving, and, still holding my squirming and naked N'yvonnaise across my lap, I twist off the lid of the tin, and I sprinkle . . . I sprinkle the white powder down upon the *derriére!* I smooth it softly across her fleshy mounds, until the two fine, white powdered cheeks are clearly visible.

"Now, my naughty bottom," I cry, "I go to work on you with a vengeance!"

But do you know! N'yvonnaise neither wept, nor cried, nor begged for mercy, nor even promised to be a good girl. I have forgotten—but with the *Astronef* in interplanetary space, moving at free fall—*my blows have no weight!*

Sapristi!

The Time Twister

by Francis Flagg and Weaver Wright

*M*y title, my plot,
Flagg's professional touch.

WHILE LEARNED IN many and abstruse problems, Franklyn Streiff's title of Professor was an honorary one, bestowed on him by a sometimes impressed if not always admiring public. The eccentric inventor had for many years lived on his Kansas farm with a spinster sister who did not always appreciate the colossal erudition, not to say genius, of her brother. Kate keenly resented the time and money he "squandered on foolish experiments." And for twenty years he had not done a lick of farm work.

"I am a scientist, not a tiller of the soil," the Professor had told his sister with proper pride. "Hire a man, if you will. Run the farm, if you want to. As for me, I ask but to be left in peace."

So Kate had hired Hank Weston, a thoughtful individual who during his years of servitude had listened to the Professor with commendable attention.

It little became Hank, who had a vast respect for learning, to contradict the Professor's findings on any subject. But when the latter began to speculate on the unity of time and space, pointing out that it was just as possible to travel in the one as the other, Hank felt called upon to remonstrate.

"You mean to say," he questioned incredulously, "that I could go back a hundred years?"

"If you had the proper machine in which to travel, yes."

"But that'd take me back to before I was born."

The Professor smiled tolerantly.

"Look at this diagram, Hank. This line is the time continuum. It incorporates space, too. This dot is you. It doesn't matter when you were born, or when you will die: You exist right now, that's the fact. Traveling into the past or future wouldn't make you grow any younger or older. Such a thought is naive. Let me demonstrate the mechanics of it for you. If NU equals TS, and we calculate with non-Euclidean mathematics . . ."

The Professor busily sketched and Hank stared owlishly. Finally Streiff had a blackboard that could have been submitted in a surrealists' art exhibit and Hank had an expression of incomprehension. "It don't sound reasonable," the farmhand objected. "If I went back—"

"I know," interjected the Professor, "if you went back you might meet your own father as a young man and you'd be older than he, or maybe he and your mother would be kids going to school."

"Haw, haw! That'd be funny, that would."

"Considered superficially," gritted Professor Streiff, "such would seem to be the case; but it is impossible to say so for certain. The unpredictable action of electrons in the atom, the riddle of the nebulae and stars and human life in an exploding universe, hint that we may expect to be surprised by the vagaries of time.

"Wishing to live forever, for instance, may be as absurd as desiring to grow in size forever. That is an interesting speculation—I must make a note of it. However, the paradoxes of which you prate may exist nowhere but in your imagination. That," he declared didactically, "is what I propose to discover beyond peradventure."

Streiff became confidential in manner.

"This machine with which you have sometimes given me a helping hand through the years, Hank, and often inquired the nature of"—he pointed to a curious contrivance occupying the center of his laboratory and workshop—"is nothing less than a panchronicon. A time-machine!"

Hank's face fell into the pattern employed by the people who were skeptical of the Wright Bros., of Columbus, and, a bit further back, in the unrecorded days of pre-history, the quasi-humans who questioned the pantomine of Brut, the caveman, when he indicated that the flint he would strike on rock would make a wood-eating flower blossom.

"You're joking, Professor," he suggested.

"Joking! I was never more serious in my life. Another week and it will be ready. Then, Hank, then"—his long face took on a look of triumph—"I shall prove that which will make me greater than Newton and Einstein, a more marvelous explorer than Columbus or Byrd. Why, they won't be in it with me at all. And you, my friend, can say you knew me intimately, can boast of my acquaintance. Ah, Hank, how proud of me you will be then. How this flouting countryside will honor its famous citizen!"

NOW HANK WESTON was not a complete fool. But after all, despite his sagelike reflections and desultory readings (mostly in magazine sections of Sunday papers where marvelous feats of science are often set forth with dramatic illustrations), he was a simple sort who had lived his days in rural surroundings. He knew enough to suspect that there were thousands of strange things he didn't know. Therefore the Professor found him a receptive audience.

As Hank watched the queer machine take shape, as he even helped give the finishing touches to its construction, the sight of the machinery, the monologues of the enthusiastic Streiff, the dynamic dream of time-travel, exerted over him a mesmeric influence. Kate Streiff was caustic about his absentmindedness.

"Don't forget you're hired to do farm work," she said bitingly, "and not to listen to that crazy brother of mine. Hank Weston, if I catch you sneaking into his workshop again, when you oughtta be hoeing corn, offa this farm you go!"

"Yes," said Hank, meekly, but the Professor's laboratory and oratory were twin magnets that drew his iron will and melted it down. So one windy summer's afternoon he crept away from the heat and his haying to visit the forbidden barn.

HE FOUND THE Professor in a fever of elation.

"Hank, you are just in time! Look—it's finished!"

Hank eyed "it" doubtfully. It was the strangest contraption he had ever seen. Not even the Sunday supplements had ever dished up an odder illustration. Partly it resembled a top, and then again one could trace a corkscrew likeness in its shaft. Two cushioned seats set astride brief horsebacks, saddle-wise.

"Will it work?" Hank asked hoarsely,

"Work?" barked the Professor. "Of course it will work!"

"How do you know?"

"Because I've experimented with the cat. I'll show you."

He picked up a spitting feline and secured it to one of the seats.

"I deflect this lever, so," he said, standing back.

Hank's eyes nearly parted company with their sockets as he watched the result. The toplike contrivance spun, and as it spun the corkscrew shaft wove in and out in a most bewildering fashion. As the speed increased, the machine became a blur in which nothing substantial was discernible. Indeed, whether owing to the camouflaged lines and angles of its construction or otherwise, one might well be forgiven for imagining that cat and machine had disappeared.

After a minute, the Professor once more manipulated the lever and the bizarre mechanism with its load gradually came back into visibility and ceased rotating. An unhappy cat hung limply on the seat, mewing melancholically.

"You see!" said Streiff triumphantly.

"Huh?" grunted his undecided acolyte. "She went over all right," crowed the Professor.

"Over where?"

"Into the future, of course!"

"You mean—the cat—went ahead-in time?"

"Didn't you see what happened with your own eyes?" the Professor snapped.

"Yeah," faltered the farm-hand, "but are you sure?"

"Certain! Where else could it have gone? And now," he added excitedly, "it only remains for us to undertake the trip."

"Us!" Hank's head resembled a revolving door. "Nossir, not me, Professor! I'm not risking my life in no contraption like that. It ain't safe."

"Safe? Why of course it's safe!"

"How do you know?"

"Didn't the cat come back all right?"

"Well, I'm no cat."

Professor Streiff regarded Hank severely.

"Hank, it can't be that you're afraid. My dear friend, what cowardly weakness is this? Consider Columbus, Magellan, Perry, Byrd. Did they feel fear? Perhaps, but they conquered such unmanly symptoms. In that lay their greatness. Strength of character, Hank. They had strength of character, and their names are immortal. Your name too can be immortal!

"Think of it, Hank: Posterity will inscribe it in its annals along with those of Pasteur, Darwin, Koch, Madame Curie. 'Hank Weston, copilot with Professor Franklyn Leonard Streiff, of the first time-machine ever invented'! That's the way it'll read under your portrait in the pantheon of fame. Can you forego such a chance? No! Opportunity knocks but once."

The Professor produced from a locker a flask of amber fluid.

"Here, drink of this." He poured out two generous tumblers full. "A toast to our coming flight! Down it, man! Ah, that puts the sparkle in the eyes and the stout courage in the heart. Have another. Hank, this day will go ringing down the corridors of time. Finish the bottle, my friend. Now take your seat there. Yes, there—your feet in the stirrups. I seat myself beside you. What's that?"

A shrill feminine voice was heard calling loudly,

"Franklyn! Franklyn!"

"Ssh-sh," admonished the Professor. "Keep still, it's Kate—always sticking her nose in where it isn't wanted."

A rush of steps came along the passageway, fists banged at the bolted door.

"Frank! Hank! Are you there?"

"Don't speak on your life," breathed the Professor.

Hank had no intention of speaking.

"Oh," cried Kate frustratedly, "where can they be!"

They heard, in rhythm with their pumping hearts, her feet pound down the stairs. From a distance the sound of her voice came back, still shouting, "Franklyn! Hank!"

The Professor shook his head.

"She is, I should judge, vastly excited over something. Quite unseemly of her. Ah me, how many times I've tried to reason with that woman. Poise, Hank, poise. Cultivate it as a flower, my friend. And now, we are ready at last—ready to flee the petty irritations of the moment. Your feet are secure, your hands are gripping the bars? O, glorious moment!" And he knifed the lever.

THE TIME-MACHINE gave a wild lurch—like a merry-go-round gone mad it spun. What the Professor expected is hard to say, but whatever it was, crystallized reality surpassed it. With a sudden roar of thunder the whole world turned black, existence split asunder.

He and Hank were pathetic straws that a mighty wind buffeted, beat. There was a rending and a tearing; a howling fury of tortured air surrounded and sought to destroy them. They and the machine seemed whirling down the everlasting vistas of space.

Then with a sickening swoop and a terrible jolt, their journey ceased. Consciousness, too, came to an end . . .

"Professor! Oh, Professor!"

To the thin wail of Hank's voice Streiff came back to life and reason. His mouth was full of dust, his body full of aches, his head a throbbing pain. Yet miraculously he was alive.

From a clear sky the sun shone torridly. The Professor blinked painfully, sat up, regarded the scene about him ruefully. He groaned.

The garret was gone; the farmhouse and farm buildings had also disappeared. Some twenty feet away lay what was left of the time-machine, a twisted mass of metal and plastic. A row of young cotton trees was missing. Not far off an old foundation showed where a house once might have stood. Change, change—everything was unmistakably changed. Despite his aches and bruises, Franklyn Leonard Streiff, first time-traveler, surged to his feet. There could be no doubt about it—this was the future!

"Victory, Hank! Victory!" he cried. "My machine was a perfect success. We have traveled in time!"

Hank stared at him without enthusiasm.

"I think," he said woefully, "that my neck is broken."

"Nonsense, nothing of the sort. Stand up and let me look you over. How could your neck be broken when you can twist it so? Ah, Hank, I'm afraid you lack the spirit of a true explorer and scientist. Forget your minor aches, man, and realize the stupendousness of the thing we have done. As far as I can calculate, we have journeyed some hundred odd years into the future."

"And how," demanded Hank practically, "are we going to get back?"

The Professor stared perplexedly at the scrapped machine, strewn unceremoniously on the sands of time.

"By heaven," he confessed, "I hadn't thought of that!" After a moment he brightened. "But we may not *want* to return, had you thought of that? But everything in its place. The people of the 21st Century are undoubtedly skilled mechanics, and could reconstruct the panchronicon from my instructions. Ah, Hank, what marvelous advances science and invention must have made in a century! Time enough for mankind to have united peacefully into a Wellsian Egalitarian World. *Kredeble, la mondo paca parolas Esperanton—semantike korektita.*"

"Huh?" Hank ejaculated at the latter. "Is that Spanish or Latin, Professor?"

"Neither, Hank. You remember the artificial language I learned in my youth. Esperanto. I said it is credible that the peaceful world will now be speaking the scientifically synthesized auxiliary tongue, the symbology of its vocabulary having been corrected semantically, of course."

"Oh. And atomic power and rocket ships to—" Hank started to speculate, but interrupted himself with a yell.

"My God, look! What's that?"

The Professor stared.

Loping across country with prodigious leaps, spindle legs flashing, small head set at the end of an enormously long and thin neck which raised it some fifteen feet from the ground, was the most bizarre-looking creature imaginable. It passed, and in seeming pursuit lumbered a colossus of a beast bearing on its leathery back a dark-skinned man in a breech-clout. The rider brandished a long spear and shouted wild and unintelligible words.

The two wrecked time-travelers goggled. A giraffe in Kansas! And being hunted by a barbarian on an elephant! The combination was too utterly fantastic and incredible.

"Oh," moaned Hank, "I wish I was safe back home."

They made themselves as inconspicuous as possible. Conspicuity under the circumstances would have been inviting catastrophe, they felt.

A dozen zebras whirled by; and after them, on gaily caparisoned horses, came a band of copper-colored hunters, stripped to the waist, long hair floating loose, wearing fringed trousers and leggings.

The hunters yelled, and urged their mounts to greater speed.

"Really," said Professor Streiff, scratching his nose, "really, the people of the future appear to have odd habits! I wonder if I didn't deflect the switch a trifle too hard and go into the past? Or perhaps the Asiatics have somehow overthrown

America. Elephants and giraffes on Kansas plains might be explained by—"

The growl which interrupted his theorizing was explained by a huge Numidian lion which he turned to find regarding him with a meditative look from a scant ten yards' distance. Hank saw the king of beasts a second later.

AS THE PAIR stared, horror-stricken, the tawny cat opened its cavernous mouth and again there issued from it a rumbling roar. It is only fair to record that the Professor's foot slipped, otherwise he would have beaten Hank on the getaway by three seconds flat. As it was, despite his wrenched knee, he was neck and neck with his copilot when they dived over a section of the foundation on which a house had once stood. Had either glanced back they would have seen the lion, like a big puzzled Persian, squatting on its haunches and following their flight with inquisitive eyes. But they had no time to glance back. All energies and faculties were concentrated on finding a two-man hole with no room for a lion.

And miraculously enough the hole presented itself for their accommodation. A section of cellar wall swung outward disclosing a dark burrow into which they unanimously flung themselves, almost bowling over as they did so the person who had opened the door.

"Shut it quick!" screamed the Professor, "there's a savage lion outside!"

The door shut with a bang.

"Land's sakes," complained a woman's high-pitched querulous voice, a voice inexplicably familiar to both their ears, "so here you are at last."

On his hands and knees in the gloom, breathless from his headlong flight, Kate Streiff's bewildered brother babbled, "What year is this?"

"What year! Well, I always said, Franklyn, you weren't quite right, and now I know it! What's more, you're making as big a dumb idiot outta Hank Weston.

"When I heard the radio warning about the tornado and saw we was right in the path of that twister, I tried to warn you two to git in the storm-cellar. Hammered on your door, I did, but I guess you were gallivantin' round, or," with a suspicious sniff, "out boozing. Pity you weren't killed, the both of you!"

With a groan of disillusionment the Professor buried his head in his arms. They hadn't traveled in time after all. He and Hank were still in 1947, and—a cyclone had devastated the farm! Oh, it couldn't be true, all his high hopes dashed like this. In one last feeble attempt to save the situation he pleaded, "But the lion, the elephant, the giraffe and zebras—where did they all come from?"

"I guess," said Kate, "the twister must have struck Lao Bros. Circus that was showing over at Edgeville, and some of the animals got loose."

The strangling noises from his throat that Professor Streiff tried to suppress in the darkness were despairingly animalistic in nature.

Illustration for "The Time Twister" from something or other by an artist..

Dhactwhu!— Remember?

Robert A.W. Lowndes in collaboration with FJA

*T*HIS IS MAINLY Bob Lowndes' story, the same "Doc" Lowndes who edits all those great nostalgia mags such as The Magazine of Horror, Startling Mystery and Famous Science Fiction; the "Doc" Lowndes who once called himself by the Esperanto pen name of Rovelo and edited a science fiction "fanzine" in the artificial Universalanguage; the "Doc" Lowndes honored as Guest of Honor at the 3-day sci-fi convention known as the Lunacon in New York 1969.

My contribution was mainly in the language. Phrases like "shards of sleep", "ebon metropolis", "Abaddon black" (black as hell), "resistant ray" (after the story of the same name by the pioneer stf Francis Flagg); "my brain was a wilted brown lettuce-head", "lambent flames", "robotaxis" and—ah, yes—lustrum!

Somebody used the word "lustrum" (half a decade) somewhere in print many years ago, I was "ensorcelled" by it and have been using it at every opportunity since. Along with "burgeon" and a few other fancy words that flip me.

"Dhactwhu" per se was kind of an in-joke. World War II was in progress (that was progress?) when I worked on the story—or at least it hadn't been so long over that its special terminology had been forgotten. Britains, at last tiring of acrimoniously replying "Don't you know there's a war on?" when asked some insane question such as "Where can I get a steak?" or "a gallon of petrol?" took to using the acronym, "Dyktawo?" I picked it up for a time as the publishing name for my fanzines—Dyktawo Pubblications—and eventually, in alienly altered form, it served in the title of the tale following. When the story originally appeared in the Apr '49 issue of Super Science Stories it bore the exotic pair of nom-de-plumes Wilfred Owen Morley & Jacques Deforest Erman.

You get one-half guess which was me.

CHAPTER I
Don't You Know?

DHACTWHU!
Remember?

If that word means anything to you, it means a lot to us all. Maybe I can awaken some latent memory in you. Your mind may hold the Rosetta Stone destined to recapture a lost secret of time and space . . .

We were three lone men and an obsessing dream, pushing our way into the heart of a well-nigh unexplored wilderness, somewhere in South America. Perhaps we were fools, too. But I'm thinking of Andrew Milton; he'd been known for over 20 years to his students at that mid-west university as a hide-bound conservative. So I don't think you'd call him the fool. Then, Fletcher Amsbury. At one time or another he'd been in the service of nearly all of the allied nations, during the second world war. So you can't say he was a fool; fools don't last in his game. As for me, Stanley Denning—well, maybe . . .

Three lone men, lost in the jungle, with only a dream to guide us. Plodding stubbornly on, after our guides and bearers had deserted us. Leaving a trail behind us which we knew would soon be obliterated. Hacking our way ahead, when what maps there were warned us we could expect nothing here but fever and slow or sudden death.

What drew us to this lost world? I can't answer that for certain even now. All I know is that as long as I can remember, Amsbury and I had dreamed of finding a colossal black city, hidden in this jungle. It was the most persistent dream I've ever heard of. We grew up together, Amsbury and I, and we used to tell each other stories of the city, and try to guess its meaning.

But from the very first we knew we must never tell anyone else unless they gave the sign first.

Then one day Amsbury came in and said simply: "Get ready. I think I know where it is."

I hadn't heard him enter my apartment; I hadn't seen him since the beginning of the war. But I got right up and started packing.

I knew what Amsbury knew, without asking.

And while we were checking out of the hotel, Amsbury mentioned the word of which you may have a hazy recollection. "Dhactwhu." He didn't say it loudly, and put no more emphasis upon it than if he were noting the time. But a tall, gray-haired man put down the paper he was reading.

"My name is Andrew Milton," he said. "I overheard."

And before either Amsbury or I could say anything, he added: "I will go with you."

After that it was the roll of tires, the rumble of trains and the throb of ships' motors. Heat, and the soft dipping of canoe paddles in green river waters. Silent parading along beaten trails, then struggling into untrodden territory. The desertion of our guides and porters.

But on the third night after the men who had accompanied us broke and would go no farther, we came upon the great black city alone. Three madmen, and an impossible dream made real.

We stood in silent awe on the outskirts of the ebon metropolis. I couldn't even whisper to communicate my emotion to the others. But there was no need.

I wasn't afraid, simply wonder-struck before the bigness and beauty of it. I was ashamed to break the silence.

Finally Amsbury swallowed, choked: "This is as I have dreamed of it."

We stood on the fringe of the jungle in the moonlight, staring across a strangely clear expanse at sheer, jet-black walls that must have climbed a full 50 feet into the air. And they stretched in either direction as far as we could see.

There was no break in those barriers. And they were Abaddon black.

Three acolytes of an ancient mystery, worshipping before their dream. We couldn't see much of the wonder city itself, yet; only its spires and colonnades peered down on us from behind those walls.

Milton said: "I don't remember how to get in. There's nothing that looks like a gateway, arch or any other means of entrance. Do you remember, Armsbury, you, Denning?"

I roused myself from contemplation of the jet wall before us. "No, I can't remember how to get in."

"There was a path," Amsbury whispered, "a path as white as that wall is black, and almost blinding against the barrier. It led up to an opening in one of the spires. The path was resistant, yet it seemed to have no thickness whatsoever. I was afraid to step on it, yet I did . . ."

"And walked into the tower?" I asked.

He shook his head. "There's a break in my dreams, then. The next thing I remember is being inside the city—alone."

Milton stretched. "I'm for shut-eye right now. Maybe you'll dream the missing link tonight. Let's continue tomorrow. You'd better turn in too, Denning— it's your turn to stand second watch."

"I'll come soon," I answered. "The moon isn't very high now, and I want to wait until it's over the far tower. Maybe something will happen then. I have a hunch—"

Milton started, his hand fumbling awkwardly at his hip. "Over there," he breathed tensely, his eyes flaring to indicate the direction. We crouched instinctively, our eyes straining in the dim lights, hearts hammering.

"Some animal?" whispered Amsbury.

"Probably just my nerves," muttered Milton as we drew back, "but we can't be too careful." He was silent a moment, then he murmured, "Dhactwhu!"

And something like a chill shot through me, yet it wasn't terror. It was a kind of secret joy but there was sadness mixed up with it and the melancholy lent a desperate quality to the joy . . .

"Now you know?" I asked him anxiously.

He looked pained. "I ought to," he sighed. "I thought that when we found this place, just the sight of it would open something that's been locked up inside me. Locked up inside all three of us. But I still don't know any more than I did yesterday."

"I wonder if we came too late?" I said gloomily.

We prepared our sleeping bags and crawled into them without saying good night.

SOMEONE WAS SHAKING me awake. For a moment I wasn't quite sure where I was. Then it was all clear in my mind. "Sorry, Fletch," I mumbled. "I'll be right up."

"It's me, Milton," came a voice. "Amsbury is gone."

I sat upright, then, and all the shards of sleep fell off. "That's what I wanted to tell him!" I gasped. "I wanted to warn him to wait for the moon—"

"What are you talking about?"

I shook my head. "I'm—I'm not entirely sure, but there's one thing I seem to remember—

"Amsbury told us about a sort of white road leading down from the tallest tower. But it isn't safe to walk on it until the moonlight is full on the spire. And you have to hurry, even then, because there's just enough time for a man to walk it quickly."

"Have you any idea what this road is?"

I shook my head. "But maybe we'll find out when we see it."

We followed Amsbury's trail up to the blank space between the walls of the city and the jungle surrounding it. Amsbury had passed this way; his prints led off to the right.

They led to a point, then broke off, as if Amsbury had dissolved into thin air.

I looked up at the forbidding black walls and rested my hand on their glassy surface. "There's no use looking," I said. "We won't find Amsbury tonight."

Milton nodded. "For some reason, I believe you."

"And," I added, "I think there's only one way we can get into this city. Tomorrow night, when the moon is high—when the moonlight touches that tower. Then we will be able to see exactly what—"

Milton's eyes swept across the star-studded sky. "Why not?" he whispered. "Why not mechanisms activated by lunar rays? We know there are elements in the light reflected from the moon which are not found in ordinary sunlight."

I'll never know how we managed to endure that next day, waiting for night to come.

We were crouching by the great wall, watching Luna lift herself into the sky, and every faint stirring of air seemed to whisper, "Dhactwhu !" And with every breath we echoed that whisper.

If only we could remember! It seemed then as if the fate of worlds rested somewhere in the inner meaning of that alien word. And, in the end, we came to know that we were right.

Finally the vigil was over: the moonlight glowed upon the great wall.

Milton grasped my arm. "Look—the tower!"

The lunar rays hadn't touched that great spire yet but something else was happening and I felt fear race up and down my spine. For something was emerging from the windowless tower, something that looked partly like a two-dimensional snake, and partly like a wafer-thin river of light, flowing down to meet us.

White, it was, this languorous, writhing wonder—a blinking albinism that contrasted perfectly with the abysmal black of the city.

"The white path!" breathed Milton. "Amsbury's enchanted entrance into the city!" He started forward, as if to leap upon it.

"Wait!" I warned. "Wait for the moon!"

Milton looked up into the heavens. The rays from the full moon were not yet directly on the tower.

I reached down, picked up a branch from the ground and flung it upon the blinding highway. It seemed to melt into the pure white of it, then disappear.

"That must be what happened to Amsbury!"

Milton's voice was a hoarse whisper. "Gone—vanished. Disintegrated."

THE MOON HAD climbed higher, now. I threw another branch onto the path; it bounded off, a little piece of it breaking loose and lingering near the edge—unharmed. "It's safe," I said, an unaccountable calmness controlling my voice.

I took a deep breath and hesitantly stepped up onto the white road.

It was solid, substantial as any concrete highway I'd ever put my foot on. I took a few more steps, trying not to look down. I kept on climbing, Milton right behind me. As we drew near I could see what looked like a doorway in the dark. Milton paused. "Don't stop," I warned him. "There's no telling how long this thing will be safe."

Ironic time to talk of safety, when we were about to step deliberately into what might well be a death-trap. I tried not to think about the diabolic welcoming devices with which some ancient cities were strewn, as I went through that door. An instant later, Milton was beside me.

"Why did you stop?" I asked him.

He grinned. "Just dropped something. My watch. See?" He pointed to it, resting on the white ramp a short way back.

"Don't go after it—" I started to say, then the watch melted into the whiteness, and was gone.

We couldn't see from here but it was plain enough that the moonlight no longer bathed the tower. Below us, the highway was retreating, coming back to its source.

"Fantastic!" breathed Milton. "Utterly and completely fantastic!"

"But real," I added.

He nodded. "Quite real. And when fantasy becomes stark, objective fact, it's no use going into philosophical discussion about it. We have to find out why, now."

As if to punctuate that thought, the doorway through which we'd come seemed to fill in, becoming the same ultimate black as the walls around us. For a moment we were in total darkness and I knew how a trapped animal feels.

Were we trapped? I fumbled around my belt for the hand lamps we carried, unfastened mine.

But before I could snap it on, the room began to brighten, as if someone behind the scenes were working a rheostat, until the entire chamber was bathed in a sourceless glow.

"It's bare," Milton murmured, "and no sign of an exit—"

"Back against the wall!" I whispered. "There's something—"

Over at the far end of the room, the wall was parting; our hands fell instinctively to the heavy service pistols we carried. What manner of being would come through that portal? A giant spider? A monster bat?

It was a man—or, at least, it looked human. The man was tall, with a face like a wooden dummy. There was a grace and suppleness in his movements which made me think of seals sporting in the sea. He was simply clad: a cossack skirt, ski-jumper's trousers and sandals.

Strangely, it was the colors of his costume which affected one most strongly. Purple and black! The colors that had always had a strange effect upon me—almost as strong as that of the single word the being uttered as it stood looking at us.

"Dhacthwu!"

CHAPTER II
The Purple Man

FOR A SECOND my entire being surged with exaltation. I started forward, eager to return his greeting, as if I'd found a long-lost brother. But something tugged at my subconscious, warned me to wait. I clutched Milton's arm. "Don't answer," I murmured. "I've a hunch . . ."

Milton nodded shortly. "Hello," I called out in as genial tones as I could muster. "We come as friends." I held out both hands, and repeated the word. "Friends."

The purple one strode forward, no trace of expression on his face. His eyes were fathomless.

"Habla usted Español?" I asked him. No reply. Milton the professor tried French, German, Latin, Russian and that mixture of Romantic languages, Esperanto. "Cu vi komprenas Esperonton?" The figure shook its head, and repeated the word which still sent shivers of anticipation up and down my spine.

"Dhactwhu!"

Could it be a test? Was he repeating the word in the hope of some betraying response from us?

Milton turned to me gloomily. "Unless he has some way of reading minds—which I doubt—we'll have to resort to the old-fashioned system—"

He broke off suddenly, his eyes fixed on the doorway behind the figure. I followed his gaze and started at the sight of the creature there.

It was vaguely like a dog but not a canine one would choose for a pet. It might have been the inspiration for those legends of the hounds of Hades. A huge creature, eyes glowing phosphorescently, long fangs gleaming, body streamlined, it crouched there. Crouched, and—

"Look out!" cried Milton, seizing the purple man's arm and pulling him to one side. It was too late; the impact of that hurtling mass of killerflesh hurled him to the floor.

I grabbed my gun but the purple man was already grappling with the monster. He thrust a fist into that hellish throat, while the hound clawed and coughed and struggled, trying to rend its way free.

I dared not fire for fear of hitting the man but in an instant I saw a break and slammed the gun-butt down hard on the creature's head. There was a sound of bone cracking and it went limp.

I whirled 'round to the sharp report of Milton's pistol, to see a second hound twisting in midair from the impact of a heavy slug. It fell heavily, to the floor, kicking.

The purple being rose, apparently unhurt. He motioned us to follow him, and walked toward the wall on another side of the room. A section slid aside and we hurried after the purple man, our pistols ready as we kept an eye out for any more of the devil dogs.

Our guide was up ahead in the passage. The faint glow seemed to be following us. We could see a short distance ahead but already the section through which we had come was dark.

We followed the solitary figure to a small room, containing only a wide couch and a small table. On the latter a large flagon stood, filled with some fluid I didn't recognize.

Without a word or gesture our guide left us.

Milton went up to the wall where we had entered. Nothing happened. Carefully he went around the entire wall-surface of the cubicle, his hands running along the smooth face of it. No doors appeared.

"It seems we're invited to stay," I said.

Milton dropped on the bed.

I followed suit.

"Call me if any food appears," he yawned.

"Have you any idea what the composition of this place might be? Or about that resistant ray we walked on?"

"Your guess is as good as mine."

"And Amsbury, is he dead?"

"You saw what happened to my watch—and to that branch."

"I saw it," I admitted. "But they didn't disintegrate; they disappeared." Amsbury might still be alive . . .

WHETHER THE DREAMS preceded reality or were inspired by it I shall never be sure. I cannot recall the precise order of events yet I know this came first: I awoke to find myself paralyzed. It was as if I had no corporeal structure whatsoever, but were sheer, matterless entity.

I saw the purple man departing from our room bearing the body of a man under his arm. It was Milton. Through the section of wall went the purple man, then I was alone in the night and the timelessness of that room. I couldn't think, I couldn't move.

Presently the alien returned and bent over me. I could still feel nothing, but the shifting vista told me that I, too, had been lifted and was now being borne away.

Down limitless corridors the purple man bore me, until at last we stepped out into daylight. A clear, bright day where the azure of the sky above was a painted thing, hardly to be believed. I saw now that the solid masses within the city were also of that same jet material that composed the magnificent walls.

A bird was circling over us; it swooped down toward the wall—and suddenly it was a bloody, headless thing, wings beating frantically to sustain its dying body.

The purple man bore me to a large platform, circular in shape, slightly raised above the ground level, where he joined a similar figure. I could not see at first, then the other figure moved so that I could see that it, too, bore a man slung carelessly under one arm. Milton.

I saw the second figure raise his arm, pointing to the sky.

And suddenly the ground was slipping away from under me.

There was no consciousness of motion, no dizziness. I could see the spread of terra firma, apparently curving up around me, see it gradually flattening out until at last it was the outer surface of a spheroid. Around me the azure had become a deeper blue and now and then we would plunge into titanic banks of clouds.

How fast were we going? There was no sense of motion or time, nor could I feel the friction of my ascent. It seems that we could not have been rising at any great speed, otherwise my clothing might well have ignited like a meteor.

Below us, I could see Earth diminishing into a compact mass, luminous and blue. The medium through which we were traveling became dark and we must have been well beyond the stratosphere.

There was a brightness emanating from the figure carrying Milton, a coruscating brightness that looked for all the world like the fiery train made by Fourth-of-July sparklers hurled into the air. And around me I could see the glowing lights of stars, more stars than I had ever seen on earth.

I realize now that I could not have seen them in their true light, those celestial bonfires, glowing incandescently against the utter night of interplanetary space; had their real brilliance struck me, my eyes would have been burned-out cinders, my brain a wilted brown lettuce-head.

No longer could I see the Earth. We might have been floating still in space. We had long passed the point where motion could be judged by the appearance of other objects.

I am not an astronomer so I cannot tell what course we took through the lanes of space to our destination. Even when it has been explained to me again and again, I do not understand. They have tried to clarify it by likening gravitational forces to winds and currents upon our own terrestrial oceans.

For all I know, lustrums, decades, might have passed—years and years of Earth time—while we flashed through the void to a distant world. At last I saw a spheroid approaching us and gradually it swelled until it filled my vision. And the black of space grew lighter until it became a deep green. And we plunged into cloud-like masses, the verdant hue of lightning, until at last the face of this world rose up and engulfed us.

One more thing I cannot explain. At one point in that interminable journey across the void I saw that we were surrounded by a host of beings like the ones bearing Milton and myself. In their arms they carried lovely dark girls, motionless as we were.

They were a vast troop of purple-faced beings, their arms raised rigidly above their heads, and a trail of coruscations emanating, seemingly, from their very fingertips. For a time we were all in this stellar company, then they moved away from us and soon were out of my limited line of vision.

But that was before the green world came out of space.

We landed on a raised circular platform, mate to that on earth save that it was located on an open plain. The beings that bore us stood unmoving until the seeming "earth" before us slid aside and we were taken down into an airlock and the door to the surface slid shut above us. But not before I had seen that the tall grass that grew on the plain was yellow, that a small orange sun hung in a sky in which other stars were visible and that the ground of this weird planet was a steelish gray.

I RECALL BEING carried again through corridors, of being placed upon something that looked like an operating table; then all impressions drifted away as true sleep overcame me. And my dreams were all of the journey recently done, except that I was swimming in luminous ether, from world to world, in pursuit of dark-haired sirens.

And out of space came the purple ones to snatch my prizes away from me; from behind dead, dark satellites they would rush, lambent flames spurting from their extended hands, swooping down upon our party like hawks and bearing away the fairest of the maids.

I would fly in pursuit but they would wheel and fling a word which wrung all power out of me, so that I fell helplessly in the illimitable abyss. And as I fell, the word would echo in my ears with thunder of doom unguessable.

"Dhactwhu!"

And I knew that if I could but remember the meaning of the word, the overhanging doom would be averted, the dark-haired girls no more tormented, and the evil purple ones would depart.

So finally, despair haunting my heart, I screamed the word aloud, hoping the potent sound of it would shatter the mechanism by which the purple ones flashed through space.

"Dhactwhu!"

And the timbres of the word sped faster than a bullet of light. Arrowing through the ether, they overtook those who scintillated in the distance, so that they fell like lightning-blasted branches, toppling into the abyss where I floated helplessly.

But one of the purple beings reached out and grasped my shoulder and became—

Milton!

I was sitting up in a comfortable bed. "Milton! Where are we?"

He smiled and shrugged his shoulders. "We're—here. Just precisely at what point in the known universe 'here' is, I'm not yet sure. But we arrived safely, and we've been in this place for several—days.

"They performed an operation on us back in the black city so we could endure the space-voyage; they reversed it here. Only it took you longer to come out of the anesthetic than I."

"Then my impressions that we were carried here by the purple-faced brutes, were just dreams? We came in a spaceship?"

He shook his head. "Your impressions were the same as mine, judging by what you were mumbling in your sleep. I've been up and around all day but haven't seen much. They didn't want to start language instruction until you were awake."

I sighed. "No thought helmets?"

"No thought helmets, no hypnotic teachings, no telepathy. It appears there's no royal road, we'll have to learn the hard way. But chances are they've organized the technique of teaching language so we can be on primitive speaking terms in a few days."

It took us only three weeks.

They let us out into the underground city. But I could not enjoy such freedom, exploring this baby world within the parent planet. In the back of my mind something was stirring constantly, making me ever more impatient to discover the crux of this whole affair. Before it was too late, an inaudible voice warned me.

Why did those thoughts come to me then? I don't know. I thought them as Milton and I strode about among strange sights. I tried desperately to remember something as we gazed upon lush growths of yellow plant-life, watching the odd-shaped birds twittering in the yellow trees, felt the steel-gray "earth" beneath our feet and let our eyes follow the pink clouds in the greenish "sky." Had I known, I don't think I would have guessed we were not upon the surface of the planet, particularly after we were caught in a shower one day—a shower that spattered us greenly, like ink spots!

And I missed the smell of earth after that rain. And green grass, brown earth, blue water. Purple color here, but blue was seldom seen.

Even now, I dream of blue skies . . .

It is hard to tell of the city for we were like men moving through a dream. There were moving ways as well as footpaths; there were three-wheeled vehicles corresponding to taxis—only without drivers, and we rode those moving ways, trod those paths and amused ourselves by being driven around in the robotaxis—without seeing a sign of human habitation.

We learned exactly one answer to the countless questions we fired at our alien mentor: his name.

ALTHANN-5, AS we had come to know the single plum-colored being who had been our instructor, guide and sole companion since our arrival on the green world, did not seem surprised when one morning we faced him with a demand for straight answers to the myriad inquiries he had been evading.

"We are unhappy," said Milton. "Curiosity is a prime factor with us, Althann-5, and every time you refuse us an answer we feel disturbed and uneasy. Now we have reached the breaking point.

"We cannot help being lonely for the world we have left but we could endure it if our attentions were occupied with delving into the mysteries here. But when that is forbidden us, what is there for us to do but pine away?

"Only Earthmen do not pine away peacefully, Althann-5," I added. "They take action."

We waited anxiously as the purple man considered our ultimatum, his face as inscrutable as ever. The closest we had ever known him to approach an emotion was an occasional expression of approval about our progress with language or our deductions from what little we had been able to see. He had seemed to understand that such bits of praise spurred us on and made us content.

"I am not sure you are as yet entirely ready," he replied, "in spite of your remarkable progress but this unbalanced condition of which you speak makes the step advisable. Very well, then, we shall go to Althann now."

"Althann?"

"The original. Althann is as you; I and Althann-1, 2, 3 and 4 are but duplicates—machines."

Milton, I think, was more amazed than I. "Why didn't I realize that?" he gasped. "It explains innumerable things about you. But you didn't seem to act like a metal being; you seemed to require food and rest just as we—"

"I am not composed of metal," he interrupted. "Nor am I a machine in the sense that I have wheels, wires, springs, levers or other artificial, tooled parts within me. I am—what you might call a chemical copy."

He cut further conversation short. We went out of the room, out of the building into one of the automatic taxis, heard him give the instructions into the address-port.

A short trip, then we disembarked at one of the few taller buildings, rode a spiraling escalator to its top floor. The tension was such that I didn't retain much of what I saw. We followed Althann-5, entering at last what might easily have been an attractive apartment in uptown New York, allowing for the oddities of furniture design and appliances.

The android addressed the stranger who stood, his back to us, before what appeared to be a screen with a typewriter keyboard below it.

"They are here, Althann."

The man turned.

Milton stuttered first, "Am-Amsbury!"

"There's no time for detailed explanations now," said Amsbury after hand-clasps and the first shock of seeing our friend again had worn off. "Except to tell you that the white path broadcast me here—disintegration then re-integration."

"But you—Althann!" I gasped.

He smiled. "Only by adoption. The original Althann made me his heir. Come into the next room and look at some films. The entire history of these people is recorded on microfilm. The reason we've kept you waiting so long is that Thanya and I have been going over the historical library, carefully selecting the material we have to show you."

A door opened and a purple-skinned woman entered. There was something regal and incredibly ancient about her. She extended a patrician hand—warm, slim, as lovely as could be offered by the loveliest woman of our own people. "Dhactwhu," she whispered.

Amsbury-Althann shook his head. "They don't know either, Thanya." He nodded to us. "Let's go."

EVEN IF I had the space to describe in detail what Milton and I saw in that projection room (what we've seen many times over since) such a description would be impossible. There exist no words in any of the 3000 Terrestrial tongues; no experience in the general memory of the human race as referent for the unfamiliar terms. Just one example will suffice: I have said that the skins of these people were purple, that purple was the most common color on this world. To us, but not to them. The color-perceptions of these people are more complex than our own; to them there exist four primary colors: red, yellow, blue and indigo, all with permutations and combinations which we cannot sense.

On the screen we saw the golden age of the Elders, the builders of the black city of the jungle and of countless others, some of which are known either in their ruined forms, or in legends. The remains on Easter Island, the fantastic Zimbabwe, the better-known legendary Atlantis . . .

We saw them, in colossal factories, produce great mirrors which were perfect reflectors, saw these flawless mirrors placed in exact alignment, watched wide-eyed as light itself was captured between these polished surfaces and reflected between them indefinitely until its cosmic speed was tamed, its composition altered, until it metamorphosed into a solid mass; became, in fact, the elusive material of which the city in the jungle was constructed. Matter had gone beyond imagining, blacker than total blackness, durable to the end of time.

And, in a less solid form, we saw them thus produce the resistant ray—actually not a two-dimensional beam, but a super-flexible "tape" which appeared to have no thickness.

And we saw the playgrounds of these people, vast areas where nature was permitted to run its course unchecked—where they went to lead the primitive lives of savages, fashioning their own weapons and tools, choosing caves for homes. During the winters in these playgrounds they decorated these caves with drawings of the plants and animals about them, using crude paints.

I remember ejaculating to Milton as I saw this: "The Cro-Magnards!" And Amsbury nodded, "Quite right. Many were killed or suffered death through natural causes in the playgrounds; it is their remains which puzzle our paleontologists and make them wonder what happened to the Cro-Magnards.

"No remains of the Elders, other than these, have been found because in the cities their dead were always disintegrated."

"Then what happened to them?" whispered Milton.

"Watch," the lovely Thanya replied.

I sank back, my attention again focused on the screen, wondering if scenes of terrific warfare or natural catastrophe would appear. But I hadn't begun to understand.

We saw the Elders constructing rocketships bound first for the moon, then the planets; saw them reach Earth's satellite successfully, then land on Mars.

On the red planet they found a strange form of semi-vegetable life, living symbiotically with crustacean sand-dwelling mammals. The Elders made contact with this stapledonian creature, found it to be by far their superior in intelligence.

Then came the fateful expedition which marked the final step in the existence of the Elders. A slight defect in the mechanism of an exploring ship, a forced landing wherein several members were mortally hurt and the ship damaged beyond hope of repair. And the Martian intelligence made the Elders a proposition. It was hopelessly bound to Mars as long as it existed side by side with the crustacean-creature; it had progressed there as far as it could possibly go.

But if it were to establish symbiosis with Earthmen, new vistas would be opened. With them, it could explore the entire universe; it could bring to them senses and perceptions they themselves could not hope to develop for many centuries; it could make them nearly immortal.

Some of the party, fatally injured, would soon die. Why not, asked the intelligence, try an experiment; perform operations upon these members, which the Martian supermind would direct. Unless their brains had been damaged, it could save their lives by taking direct command of their bodies.

I do not think I have ever seen so dramatic and intense a scene as this episode, as the expedition discussed and argued the question. Would not this symbiosis rob man of his individuality—make him little more than a physical servant of the Martian? Dying members of the expedition finally settled the dispute by insisting that the operation be performed—with the understanding that they would be put to death by their fellows should their actions indicate that their identities had been submerged.

As breathless as if we were in the wrecked rocket, Milton and I watched the intricate operation, beheld the actions of the first New Men.

There was a difference—but even the most skeptical of the expedition had to admit that the marriage of Mars' mind to earthmen did not seem to make the earthmen less human.

The reel ended with a way of communication with Earth being found, so that the entire party was rescued.

Amsbury turned to us and said, "Can you guess now what happened to the Elders?"

"The human race on Earth became New Men!" I said.

Thanya nodded. "Yes, with the exception of a small colony. But why did they leave Earth?" "It must be that there was something about Earth which the Martian could not endure. So they simply packed up and moved."

The purple patrician nodded. "You are right," she said. "You will see the exodus in the next film."

MY BRAIN WAS a carousel for hours after we had seen the culmination of the flight from Earth to Ygrinat.

"Amsbury, you still haven't explained one of the prime mysteries. Why are the New Men living in an underground city here—and where are they? What became of Althann? Where are Thanya's people?

"And what is Dhactwhu?"

"You remember my saying that some of the Elders chose not to become New Men and to remain on Earth. They did so and in time became the progenitors of the human race of today."

Thanya said, "We kept in close touch with Earth and it is all recorded. You may see later. Changing conditions, disease and survival of the most fit changed them. But the human brain, even in the stunted primitives, remained. And part of the brain contains ancestral memories.

"But we are satisfied there are some humans alive today who still remember the Elders!" "You mean," said Milton, "that 'Dhactwhu' refers to 'memory of the Elders'?"

"You are very near right," she said. " 'Dhachtwhu' is the beginning of a phrase—a proverb which the Elders knew. It refers specifically to the treatment of a certain sickness—one which we had conquered long before the first flight to Mars."

Her eyes went wide. "But that was thousands of years ago—tens of thousands! We had forgotten about such things because when we became what we are today the control our brains now had over our bodies was such that no sickness could touch us we thought. No accident could harm us for long unless the brain were hopelessly damaged. We could replace lost members as crustaceans do.

"But now—for over a century—our entire race has been sick. We have been dying and are helpless to combat the illness. We do not know what it is; we haven't been able to find out."

"Then," whispered Milton, "your hope is to find some person on Earth who has the knowledge you seek in his hidden memories!"

"Yes. Somewhere on Earth there must be a man or woman—perhaps several persons—who remember. Who when they hear the word 'Dhactwhu,' will be able, without thinking, to repeat the entire phrase.

"We know this is so because there are a number who are stirred by the syllables. You three, for example.

"There must be someone who remembers completely!"

"But how can such a person or persons be found, Thanya'?"

"That's where we come in," Amsbury answered for her. "One of us must go back and try to find some way of getting the message before the world. And that is going to be a job.

"Althann-5 will take one of us back and remain in the city with Anthann-4. There are always some duplicates there to keep undesired attention away and to transport anyone who might be able to help the people of Ygrinat."

"Which of us shall go back?" asked Milton.

"We'll settle that later," replied Amsbury. "First we must plan a campaign—figure out as many practical ways as possible of spreading the message to the people of Earth without attracting attention to what we're doing."

I turned to Thanya. "Are there—many of your people now?"

The purple of her skin became very faint. She shook her head wordlessly, and arose.

The chamber to which Thanya took us looked like a mausoleum. We gazed upon an even dozen little coffins, each containing a charming child. "They are all," whispered Thanya. "Five boys and seven girls—the last 12 children born. We decided to put them in suspended animation as soon as they were old enough, in hopes that Dhactwhu might be found and they would have a chance to live."

My mouth was dry. "These are—all—?'

She nodded mutely as she lingered over the form of a little girl, lying amidst masses of soft, violet hair. "This is Thanala," she said.

I DO NOT know how long we slept for we were exhausted; all I remember is being shaken and arising sleepily to see Amsbury fully dressed. His throat was husky as he spoke.

"It's happened, Stan. Sooner than I expected."

"What?"

"Thanya—during the night."

"Thanya! Oh, no! Then—then only those children—?"

"All who are left of the New Men."

I dressed absentmindedly. I was choking as I asked, "What can we do, Fletch? Thanya gone, and we know nothing of this city, really."

"The city will run itself for a thousand years to come; the duplicates—there are a good many of them left—will help us. Thanya gave them orders some time ago to cooperate with us."

I looked out the oval window at the rising orange sun, then remembered it was artificial. "But why was this city built beneath the surface?"

"They originally thought the sickness was due to something in the atmosphere—something that came from outside. They spent years in removing, sterilizing everything below and sealing it off —but it didn't help. They are almost all gone, now, unless—Dhactwhu . . ."

Milton joined us later. "Two of us must stay here and wait. How shall we decide?"

"I'll go back," declared Amsbury. "Unless one of you feels he can't bear staying here indefinitely. It really isn't essential, I suppose, if you feel you must go back to Earth. The androids can keep things going . . ."

"I'll stay," I said.

"Likewise," said Milton.

Amsbury nodded approvingly. "Very well, then. Stan—you're the writer; you're to write up the general outline of what has happened to us. I'll try to get it published back on Earth. It may take a long time because care is essential—we must not attract attention to the city in the jungle or to what we are doing. Not yet.

"Just how I am going to go about spreading the word Dhactwhu without letting on the why and wherefore, I haven't figured out. Can't do it here. But I'll find a way when I get back."

"But why the secrecy'?"

Milton chewed the ends of his mustache. "Lord, look at the mess they're making of atomics! This is too much for the human race to get all at once. If these people can be revived, then they can help us—and perhaps we can help them. But to have the super-civilization of a race thousands of years in advance of us dumped suddenly in our laps—!

"I think I know what is on your mind, Amsbury. You plan not only to awaken Dhactwhu but also quietly to kidnap a small group of people who can be trusted and bring them here—to form a colony?"

"Right! Stan, you thought you saw some of the duplicates carrying girls in their arms on your way here, eh? Well, I can't promise anything in the way of beauties, but you'll see some Earth people coming here soon; and if I can find any likely ladies with adventurous spirits, your vision will come true to a certain extent."

Althann-5 is taking Amsbury back to Earth with this manuscript. If you've Martian heritage, surely you will not fail to speak!

Whoever are you . . . wherever you are . . . speak the full phrase in the language of the Elders and you will be heard.

Dhactwhu!

Remember?

READER'S NOTE: The cover illustration (by Neil Austin) for this edition of Expanded Worlds of FJA & Friends PLUS was commissioned for this story.

Tarzan and the Golden Loin

by FJA

I GUESS YOU could call this an indiscretion of my youth except I was 30 at the time. Well, when you're 52, 30 seems pretty young.

The sober fact is (guilty! guilty!) I don't believe this alleged interview with Edgar Rice Burroughs ever took place! It's a bald-faced lie and everybody knows that's the worst kind.

As I read this back to myself after 22 years, I began to be more and more suspicious. "Sure, I visited ERB three times that I remember, but I don't remember ever discussing Tarzan & Love so intimately with him."

When I hit his so-called reference to Igrinat the Devil-Cat I was positive of my perfidy; for Igrinat, as any cool cat can no doubt figure out easily enough, is simply Tigrina spelled sidewise! (Tigrina: one of my life-time femme friends.)

Oh, the description of his home, his den, is true, and any quotes directly attributed to his works; but the rest is pretty much a tissue of lies.

It was never meant for American eyes but just an excuse for some breast shots and beefcake in the French girly mag V.

Frankly, I did it for the francs.

Forgive me, ERB, wherever you are—and I hope it's looking over the shoulders of your sons and daughter, Bob Hodes, Vern Coriell, Cox Cazedessus, Gabe Essoe and other of your fans, whispering in their ears, "May my autograph fade from all of Ackerman's collection of my works! May Hista the Snake hiss upon him! Tarzan, good; Efjay, bad!"

Here they come with the sackcloth; I've already made an ash of myself.

WHO IS THE world's greatest lover? Would you name Don Juan, Rudolph Valentino, Romeo, Errol Flynn, Clark Gable, Cary Grant, Jim Warren or Brad Pitt? Each of these dashing gentlemen will undoubtedly have his enthusiastic supporters—but many a modern girl would leave them all at the call of the incomparable Adonis of the jungle, TARZAN! Yes, in any poll of the most popular lovers in history, real or fictional, Tarzan would certainly rate one of the top positions.

What woman, seeing this strong bronzed giant on the screen, has not secretly longed to be his mate, has not imagined the immense power of his arms, has not dreamed of the intense thrill of his savage kiss, his lips searing and bruising hers? Tarzan, the masterful beast-man, who could tame any woman as he tames the wild lions, leopards, panthers and other she-cats of the jungles!

Tarzan was "born" about 35 years ago. [Which dates this as 1947.] Recently I drove to Tarzana, a suburb of Los Angeles, California, to meet his creator, genial Edgar Rice Burroughs. I learned much from him about this fabulous character who women (and men) find so fascinating.

Burroughs lives in semi-seclusion near the end of a country lane. His 6-room home is surrounded by a colorful garden and lush green lawn. A family orchard and servants' quarters are located at the rear.

Sunshine streamed through the windows as we sat in his "den," drinking coca-cola and discussing Tarzan. The room was ornately decorated. Among the unusual furnishings was a golden-brown "tapa cloth" of palm fibre from the Hawaiian Islands, a colorfully woven American Indian Chief's blanket of wool, a painted tiger slinking across a Japanese silk screen, a huge vermilion jar decorated with ebony elephants, monkeys and other jungle creatures, and a pair of oriental statuettes on horseback, resting on twin tables on either side of the room.

"Tarzan and love?" he repeated my question. "As I put it in my first book, 'With him near, who could entertain fear? The girl wondered if there was another man on earth with whom a girl could feel so safe.' The feeling of safety is a great factor in the psychology of love."

"But not the only ingredient," I interjected. "There is a certain amount of latent masochism in most women that makes a fearful pleasure of their master's displeasure."

"Yes," he agreed, "the woman who taunted Tarzan too far might find herself confronted by a veritable cave-man, ready to swing her by the hair and beat her. But ordinarily he is very well behaved."

"How do you visualize Tarzan?" I asked.

He reflected a moment, then answered: "He is a perfect type of the strongly masculine. Though a killer of men and of beasts, he kills dispassionately, except on those rare occasions when he kills for hate—though not the brooding, malevolent hate which disfigures the features with hideous lines. His are fine features, with frank, brave eyes proclaiming a chivalrous soul." And that is just what Jane Porter, heroine of the series, thought when first she saw Tarzan: What a perfect creature! There could be no baseness beneath that god-like exterior. Never had such a man strode the earth since the beginning of time!

"Do you remember how you wrote Tarzan's first love scene?" I asked.

"Just a minute," the author replied, and stepped to a shelf containing rows of his titles. He picked out a well-worn copy of *Tarzan of the Apes*, thumbed through it till he found the passage he sought, and read aloud:

"Finally Tarzan drew her to him very gently and stooped to kiss her, but first he looked into her eyes and waited to learn if she were pleased, or if she would repulse him.

"Just an instant the girl hesitated, and then she realized the truth, and throwing her arms about his neck she drew his face to hers and kissed him—unashamed.

" 'I love you—I love you,' she murmured."

Tarzan, in his 25 or more adventures, has been tempted by many a beauteous woman, including several Queens. In *The Forbidden City* he met alluring Queen Mentheb, and on no less than 4 occasions he has been exposed to the charms of Queen La of the jeweled city of Opar. In *The City of Gold* he befriended a nymph named Nemone; and, when he left his mate behind on the earth's surface and descended into Pellucidar, the strange prehistoric world of our earth's interior, he discovered the lovely Jana, known as the Red Flower of Zoram.

"But despite all the beautiful women he has met," said Burroughs, "this man, who could have the women of the world at his feet and be master of a harem if he so desired, has remained true to his one love. It is this quality of faithfulness, I believe, that makes him appeal so to women."

Tarzan's latest book-adventure, filled with romance and intrigue, is titled *Tarzan and the Foreign Legion*.

Turning from the Tarzan of fiction, I asked Mr. Burroughs about Tarzan in the films. "Is it true that he was the first hero ever to make a million dollars for a movie maker?"

"Yes," Mr. Burroughs replied, "and we were all astonished—and delighted."

Of the many actors who have portrayed Tarzan on the screen since the original Elmo Lincoln, Herman Brix was Burroughs' favorite. He made the serial also released as a feature, THE NEW ADVENTURES OF TARZAN. This was actually shot in Guatamala.

But despite the author's preference for Mr. Brix (who, by the way, is now starring in Warner Bros. pictures under the name of Bruce Bennett) by far the most popular Tarzan ever to appear on the screen has been Johnny Weissmuller. Together with the Irish colleen, Maureen O'Sullivan, the public considered him the ideal lord of the jungle.

When I mentioned the name of Maureen O'Sullivan, it reminded Mr. Burroughs of one of her early successes. "I think," he chuckled, "that we at the MGM Studios pioneered the abbreviated type of garment which the French now call a bathing suit. This was when we made the film called TARZAN AND

HIS MATE. In fact, in looking through copies of V, I frequently see costumes which consist of no more than Miss O'Sullivan wore in that picture."

I smiled too, for I have a long memory for long white legs and lovely rounded hips and full firm breasts burgeoning forth from a peek-a-boo bodice. "Isn't that the picture—?" I began, and Burroughs, anticipating me, laughed, "Yes, that was one of the rare films that ever got by the censors, where a woman's breasts were shown on the American screen.

"Was, er, it really Maureen O'Sullivan?" I ventured. After all, who paid any attention to her face during the sensual moments when one had the opportunity to enjoy her uncovered breasts?

"No," he explained. "If you remember the sequence—and I judge from the gleam in your eye that you do—Miss O'Sullivan, in the part of Jane, was playing by a river's bank with Tarzan. She was teasing her lover and in retribution Tarzan playfully pushed her into the water. As she fell, a branch of a nearby tree ripped off her brassiere. It was a long shot, and actually it was Maureen's double who was pushed into the water—especially since the scene had to be shot a number of times to satisfy the director. Loosely as the brassiere was fastened, the prop-man had difficulty in getting the tree to cooperate and catch just right to remove the garment from the girl's bosom."

"And once in the water?" I asked.

"Once in the water, a professional swimmer substituted for Miss O'Sullivan. She was a charming creature, chosen not only for her ability to swim gracefully under water but for the beauty of her breasts. Believe me, it was an extremely popular set for several days while this daring 'mermaid' was disporting herself!"

The latest Tarzan film being produced, this time on the RKO lot, is titled TARZAN AND THE MERMAIDS, but cinegoers will be disappointed to discover that the mythical sirens must now conform to Hollywood standards of morality and hide their charms in filmy brassieres.

In English we have a saying, "Imitation is the sincerest form of flattery," and certainly no character has ever been so widely imitated—in books, magazines, newspapers, on the radio and on the screen—as Tarzan. In America we have seen books and magazines devoted to such Tarzan-like characters as "Jan of the Jungle," "Ka-Zar, King of Fang & Claw," "Ki-Gor, Lord of the Jungle," "Kwa, King of Beasts," and many others.

"And all of these imitations have not been confined to the male sex, either!" laughed Mr. Burroughs. "In fact, I myself introduced the character of 'The Jungle Girl,' and Dorothy Lamour and many others have played her on the screen, and there are now magazines on the market featuring the exploits of Nyoka, Queen of the Jungle; Camilla, the Blond Goddess of Africa; Igrinat, the Devil-Cat; to name but a few."

These beauteous Amazons, briefly clad in the skins of ferocious animals they themselves have killed with bow and arrow, spear or other primitive weapon, fight and suffer but never die in the pages of American "pulps" and "comic" books. Many are the horrible fates that confront them: They may be tied to a stake and menaced by fire by a ring of dancing, shouting, brown-skin cannibals; they may be bound hand and foot and thrown into crocodile-infested waters, or flung bare-handed and defenseless into an arena of hungry lions; or they may be tied by their wrists to the limb of a tree, to hang unprotected in the air at the mercy of a rival. But do not cringe so—she will be saved by the counterpart of Tarzan, if Tarzan himself is busy off in another part of the limitless jungle!

And admirers of Tarzan, the Eternal Lover, need never fear that this dauntless hero will ever die, for there are plans afoot to make him immortal in his next film, which will be titled TARZAN AND THE FOUNTAIN OF YOUTH. [I guess this became TARZAN'S MAGIC FOUNTAIN.]

Count Down
to Doom

FJA . . . with Charles Nuetzel

*T*HIS ONE WAS *written because some "things" simply must be brought to the attention of the reader. It was done for "fun" for* Famous Monsters of Filmland *[#15, January 1962]; and I ran it through the typewriter to slant it for this magazine. I offer it here to politically make the original author CN happy, and hopefully give the reader a little pun . . .*

THE SHADOWY BEING glided thru the darkness like the memory of an echo of a whisper.

It was virtually invisible as it slithered along the wall, an evil horror from the underworld. It was intently seeking something it wanted more than anything in the world—blood! This unnatural craving was greater than mere want, it was necessity: the creature *needed* blood to survive.

Its quarry? What was its nature?

The thing that it followed was, too, a shadow within a shadow. It moved under protective mantle of midnight, afraid to be caught unaware.

The War had done this to the world. The Third World War and its horror-filled aftermath, the unholy chaos following the cloudburst of citybusters on civilization.

Now, after what seemed like weeks to the famished first creature, it was on the trail of "food." This being of blackness and blasphemy feared nothing living or dead for it was itself—undead. Human in form, it had once had a title recognized among men. The thirsty Count—they called him Dracula—felt fear only of daylight. When the sun's lethal rays lightened the sky his bat-wings took him to a debris-filled sanctuary beneath a ruined mausoleum. There, in the final resting place of the dead, he slept his restless sleep in the preservative Transylvanian soil of his centuries-old coffin.

A radioactive cloud parted briefly and the moon's scarred face peered down in shock at the leprous planet Earth below. In the far distance of the near-deserted land Dracula heard the howling of a dying dog.

Stealthily the desperate vampire inched forward across the fused blob of what had once been an automobile. A wan ray from the moon washed across Dracula's hollow cheeks, reflected from the bone-whiteness of two sharp teeth. The vampire's eyes were sunken pools of unfathomable depth.

Then the moon was hidden again by the low black cloud bank which hovered over the skeletal city. Now was the time to move faster, quicken the pace, strike! Now was the time to drink blood, suck in the thick red liquid, feast on its life-giving warmth, gorge the hungry gnawing in the pit of the stomach.

Almost a-wing in his eagerness, Dracula swooped. The figure ahead whirled at the sound of the flying footsteps and—

Dracula stopped dead-still at the sight of the mysterious thing he had been about to attack. Shock vibrated thru his frail frame, horror shook his undernourished, blood-famined body. He opened his mouth and a high-pitched shriek of ultimate despair escaped his pale vampire lips. He staggered backwards.

In an instant Dracula realized what the thing he had been stalking was. Earlier he had thought it a human being, even tho he knew how few were left. But one look at that potato-white face, that onion-bald head, and he recognized the thing as—THE *Thing from another world!*

A *real* monster who found all Earthly life quite edible.

There was a blood-curdling yell from the *Thing* as IT leaped forward. Starved, exhausted, defeated, Dracula sank to the ground—and his doom. No sustenance for his tired old veins here, for even he was aware that the Thing was an intelligent *vegetable* from Outer Space. And even if it looks half-way human, neither man nor vampire *can get blood from a turnip-people or carrot-creature!*

The Far-Out Philosopher of Science Fiction

by FJA

"*L*AST AND FIRST MEN*" made a lasting reputation as an intellectual science fiction giant for William Olaf Stapledon, M.A., Ph.D., generally known as simply Olaf Stapledon.

What you are about to read appeared, in essence, on the back cover of the dust jacket for his book Worlds of Wonder, American publication of which I arranged in 1949. It consisted of his 3 shorter works, "The Flames", "Death Into Life" & "Old Man in New World".

Stapledon is well worthy of coverage of Moskowitzian proportions; this brief candle to his memory is included merely to whet your interest in him or refresh your thoughts if already acquainted with him. This pocketbook will be sent to a number of motion picture producers and I want to take this opportunity to try to influence the right one. My message is: READ "SIRIUS". A few years ago it would have been sheer insanity to (resisting the pun) seriously suggest that SIRIUS could be filmed. But after the death of Sister George, the serving of CANDY along with popcorn, the filming on location of THE TROPIC OF CAPRICORN . . . I feel the world is ready for SIRIUS. Not that there's anything salacious about it—far from it. At the time of its original publication, Time gave it a very respectable review. It's offbeat—but so was, for instance, ROSEMARY'S BABY. Incidentally, Mia Farrow would be excellent for the part of Plaxy, who loves Sirius.

Sirius is a superdog who can write and, as I recall, his vocal cords having been altered, after a fashion speak. He has canine feelings—and human. It is an incredible sensitive science fiction love story.

DR. STAPLEDON, BESIDES being the author of such science fiction classics as *Odd John* (purchased for filming by Geo. Pal), *Last Men in London* (a monumental sequel to the better known title) and *Star Maker*, produced a number of important non-fiction works concerning man, mentality, morality, the major issues of today & tomorrow, and the fundamentals of human existence.

At the end of his life in 1951, at age 64, he could look back on such contributions to the study of Darkness and the Light (indeed the title of one of his outstanding s.f. works was just that, *Darkness and the Light*)—such contributions as *A Modern Theory of Ethics*, *Waking World*, *Saints and Revolutionaries* and *Beyond The 'Isms*.

Educated at Oxford and Liverpool Universities, this brilliant thinker, who knew Wells, often lectured on English Literature, industrial history, psychology and philosophy. His lecture in '48 on "Interplanetary Man," given before the British Interplanetary Society, was the subject of a lengthy report in *Time*, portions of the speech being reprinted in *Science Fiction Digest*.

Dr. Stapledon was the only Englishman granted a visa to attend the Cultural & Scientific Conference for World Peace, held in New York in '48 or '49. While in New York he was interviewed over the radio by the noted commentator, Arthur Gaeth.

His last novel, *A Man Divided*, has newly interested a Hollywood motion picture producer. He married a cousin and I visited her, his widow Zelda, in their home near Wales in 1951 shortly after the death of the great man. Mrs. Stapledon had left his study exactly as it was the day he died. Stapledon wrote all his works—the original title for *Odd John*, I learned, was *John Alive*—in a thin spidery handwriting like Lovecraft, on sheets of paper approximately the size of those in his books. All his holoscripts were contained in a shoebox. It was a unique experience to hold the original of such treasured work in my two hands.

Mankind has been much poorer since Stapledon left this planet.

Laugh, Clone, Laugh

by FJA with A. E. Van Vogt

*L*ITTLE DID I dream (principally because he was keeping me awake nights) that when I was reading AE van Vogt's SLAN in serial installments in Astounding 29 years ago, I would one day be up half the night collaborating on a story with the friend I have come to regard as the Master Mind of Science Fiction.

Ever since I thrilled to the core to William F. Temple's masterful definitive classic FOUR-SIDED TRIANGLE (the book developed from the short story of the same name), I have been intrigued by the notion of doubling oneself. The prospect, once fanciful, far out and with little likelihood of realization at the time Temple wrote his masterpiece (during World War II), now, with the newborn science of clonology, takes on a more realistic aspect. Perfected sooner, we could have perpetuated Wells, Gernsback, Paul; the new Tony Boucher could, haply, be 2 years old by now; and we could look forward to John and/or Bobby Kennedy as Presidents in the early decades of the 21st century. (Unless, always extrapolating, we have something better than presidents by 2000+.)

Carry the concept far enough and, via clonics (not to be confused with the elementary canal) Adam & Eve could still be doing their thing (the original apple-knockers) in the Garden of Evil. (It fig hers.) Altho personally I think I'd opt for Lilith. (She had all the best lines.)

I fear I may have unintentionally created a quasi-New Wave story here—at least I can't understand it—and I have got to admit that was a quasi thing to do. Who do I apologize to: Fred Pohl or Harlan Spinrad? All I can say is, if anyone groks this story, please enderdorf it to me.

Formulating in the Realm of Unthought Things, now, are great stories of clones ready to be told. Imagine, for instance, a tale of telepathiclones: Psi Clones!

Yes, many fascinating stories of human duplicates are yet to come.

Unfortunately (thru no fault of van Vogt's) this is not one of them.

> Now men may wither, age and go,
> Yet live anew, twinned Blueprint Men,

> *When doppelgangers in*
> *The Phoenix Gardens grow*
> > —Chon Graystark,
> > First Poet of the Clone Age

A MIRACLE HAD happened with his birth.

The impossible.

The xillion-to-one deviation.

Incredibly, into the royal family a Good Guy at last had been born.

This was the secret that had burgeoned now within—

Himself.

Juniko, sole son of Erstava, Tator of Phrenophalia.

He had such humane thoughts, such ennobling aspirations, so many plans for the betterment of the world. He found it almost unbelievable that someone like himself, so close to the throne, should have a predictable chance of eventually being in a position to bestow and dispense and achieve so many many perfections.

Unlikelihood of near infinite order—yet there was no doubt: here he stood, self-realized, the only son, one step from the pinnacle.

The universe of man quivered and waited, a throbbing heartbeat away from its ultimate destiny.

FROM VERY EARLY in his youth Juniko had a plan based on a scientific development whose real implications had never seemed to occur to his father: the discovery of perfect cloning.

Take a few cells from a man and re-grow his whole body. Create a total twin of the original. It could even be with the same thoughts and attitudes: *duplicata exactica*. Altho it didn't have to be. Already subtle methods which did not interfere with the basic abilities of the individual in any way had produced successful modifications.

His father's plan was to project a clone of himself endlessly into the future. The Tator had a narrow view of cloning and intended to limit its benefits to himself and as a reward for loyal service to his person. Cloning was costly, he emphasized. Obviously, the great mass of the people could never afford its price. Accordingly, since it was automatically limited in application, it followed that other necessary limitations could be applied, on the principle that law and order must be served.

Juniko shrugged and smiled to himself whenever he heard his father expound on the price and realities of politics. Who cared about cost? Such problems could be worked out. Juniko felt even more scathing of the shortsighted biologists who were enthralled by the restricting concept of cloning future Shakespeares and other geniuses, which the Tator said he was willing to have done in all instances where it would serve the public interest.

"Naturally, *that,* also," Juniko thought to himself, smiling with scorn.

But *his* goodness, his ideal, transcended all such miniscule imaginations.

Let there come an end to sorrow!—to needless suffering, deprivation of body, mutilation of mind, starvation of soul.

Let sad things cease!—and in their place, a smile upon each human face!

And so, to begin—subtly, cautiously—the change must come in circles around the throne, spiraling downward thru the nobility to the fringe group and finally, systematically, to the great mass of The People themselves.

The heart beat—his father's—that stands between the slave Now world and the brave New world to come must not be allowed to clone endlessly into the future. One day that heart will falter and when it does the Tator will call for his eldest son, for he trusts no one to perform the cloning act but his smiling, loyal Juniko.

AN ASSASSIN'S RAY! The heat sears the flesh of the Tator from the waist up, scorches the hair from his head, evaporates one eye. More dead than alive, Juniko's writhing father screams for his son and is rushed to the secret laboratory. The Tator dies with a smile on what is left of his crisped and contorted face as his last conscious feeling is of the knife slice that will preserve the necessary portion of his flesh to insure his rebirth. He will be back!

But black, eternal oblivion is his fate. Smiling sorrowfully, royal Juniko feeds the fatal piece of his father's flesh to the Palace piranhas . . .

THE NEW REGIME BEGINS.

Curiously, some people actually resent cloning, resist self-duplication, not realizing it will be beneficial for them. They go so far—too far!—as to try to escape from Phrenophalia, to flee to Zarnocopia to the west or seek asylum in Megatropolis to the east.

(Of course to go north or south would be unthinkable.)

The robopo always bring them back, of course: "The Metal Police always get their man." Or woman.

And "afterwards," all clones admitted how wrong they had been and how right Juniko.

FROM THE BEGINNING Juniko had one personal thought, one small concession to ego: there should be a tiny differentiation between the created and the creator. Not much, nothing overtly egotistical—Phroide forbid!—but . . . instead of laughing like all the rest, he would . . . smile. Simply—smile.

Thus, the ever-laughing people would be able to recognize their benefactor. And, recognizing, love him.

Since, from birth, he had always been a smiler; had smiled perhaps with a little fear, perhaps even propitiatingly when his father stormed; had smiled with secret joy over his great plans and had smiled with pleasure as those deific dreams came to fruition—accordingly, there was no need for a Juniko clone. Juniklone—and he added one more smile to his life total as the portmanteau crossed his mind for the firstime.

After his father's death and his ascendancy to Tatorship, he bit by bit came to realize a strange phenomenon: there were a few *natural* laugh-prones around the Palace, people who always had, they confessed to him, had an innate desire to laugh and laugh all day long but had restrained themselves because of his father. Juniko was glad to spare such individuals the expense of cloning. He even felt better because such natural rictal stock existed. Natural born laughers were the automatic answer to any criticism from pre-clones who otherwise might dare to cavil at the idea that everybody but Juniko needed a clone.

In fact, thank God for the naturals! He welcomed them all with his warm heart; treated them like personal cloneys.

It was beautiful. Juniko even had to laugh to himself occasionally. There he would be among a group of happy laughers and all of a sudden his own perpetual smile would break and rictivate, elevate to laughter, and he would laugh uncontrollably along with the rest.

Phrenophalia became a funderful world of laughing people—until one day the Secretary of Offense (soldiers now laughed all the way to the wars) was laughingly telling something to Juniko and Juniko caught a strange look in the man's eyes.

The face was laughing. The eyes were not.

A fantastic, shattering reality struck Juniko: *he's not laughing with me, he's laughing at me!*

Juniko fought off a bad feeling, the feeling of, *shek!*—people are really no damn good after all.

Juniko, Tator of Phrenophalia, continued to smile before his people, of course but it was a Pagliacci smile for inside him now grew a grief ineffable, a sadness beyond name. And an awareness that he had actually noticed the phenomenon from the beginning but had valiantly forced himself to blindness, mentally blotting out the fact that the human race was really rotten.

As he thought these dark thoughts, he walked like a zombie along a corridor of the Palace. As everywhere else, it was bedecked with a multiplicity of mirrors. Reflected in one of these he saw that his smile had taken on some of the old fixed quality that had been there so often when his father was alive.

The silent, internal conflict ended in what he finally decided had to be a win for the world. It was necessary, he realized, to learn to distinguish between the people who were laughing for the joy of it and those whose laughter was ill-meant. Juniko was not immediately able to decide what should be done with those evil subjects who their abuse of laughter had despoiled his idyll. And that was his fatal mistake, for his paranoia began to become evident to those close to him, who remembered the example of Caligula, the Roman emperor who married his sister and performed an enormous number of crimes. Nobody wanted another Caligula, except perhaps Caligula's sister; but the problem was not complicated as Juniko did not have a female sibling.

All admitted that Juniko the Original did have some good points so his joint executioners agreed to reincarnate him via clonage and, opting for a non-paranoid Juniko the Second, a part of him was preserved and regrown after his assisted demise.

The world held it breath; watched and waited and wondered.

HERE, IN THE 22nd Century, Phrenophalia of course is no longer on the map. Some of our senior citizens remember when it was laughed right off it. That was the firstime Juniko-two had a re-birthday party with all his little happy joyous laughing friends, all hollers and horns and serpentine and games and goodies and funny hats and candy and cake and ice cream and—

Suddenly! Inexplicably!

Juniko-two was not laughing, was not even smiling, was not even crying. Juniko Jr. was—

Screaming!

It would have been comical if it hadn't been tragical.

You intuit what had happened, of course.

He was the first *I Scream Clone!*

THE END (of a shaggy clone story)

When Frighthood Was in Flower

And Monsters Were A Boy's Best Friend

by FJA

*T*HIS IS TRULY a case where the piece must speak for itself. There is very little I can say about it.

It was commissioned over the phone by PLAYBOY and I wrote it with the euphoric feeling that every time I typed two words I was earning $1!

But into each Dystopia much gall must fall and in this worst of all possible worlds (the evidence is mounting hourly) I was beat out by Bradbury after I mussed the custard instead of cutting the mustard. PLAYBOY paid me handsomely (tho not at the delirious 50¢-a-word rate) to bury my brainchild and turned to Mr Nostalgia himself. For a contrast of success with failure, you will find Ray Bradbury's version—"Death Warmed Over"—in the Jan '68 issue.

AE van Vogt is a very patient man and I sometimes wonder what I have done to deserve him. After "Frighthood" was rejected and I was feeling dejected, Van volunteered to look the manuscript over to see if he could pinpoint for me where it failed. He put in a lot of gratuitous work, cutting it apart (literally: with scissors) and pasting it back together again. Very little was lost in the transitions—all of my own words were still there, it was just that they had been re-arranged for conformity to a certain formula which, if followed, "virtually guarantees the sale of an article."

But a conformist I ain't. For bread & butter I'll conform (case in question: writing to the publisher's policy for FAMOUS MONSTERS) but for cake I make my own rules. Much as I appreciated Van's efforts to salvage "Frighthood" so that it could be sold professionally, I preferred to keep it off the market rather than, shall we say, tamper with things (Acker) man was meant to leave alone. In the case of this article, I want to be appreciated on my own terms or not at all.

Burroughs buffs will tumble to the fact that I have structured this article after the maestro's method of swinging back & forth between one action and another. What may be vine & dandy in a Tarzan novel possibly may be too novel for an article of this nature. I leave you to judge. All I can say is that this is the standard of writing I wish it had been possible for me to put out for the past 10 years in a *parallel world where* FAMOUS MONSTERS *was published as* WONDERAMA *and I could cater to high-Q teenagers and nostalgia-oriented adults.*

A PHANTOM TERRORIZED the opera in Paris and a Hunchback held Notre Dame in thrall.

A Cat played with a Canary and from the Cabinet of Dr. Caligari a sinister somnambulist clad from head to toe in black was commanded forth by an evil hypnotist in the dead of night to *kill! kill! kill!*

Lazarus lived again as dead bodies were stolen by a demented dwarf from freshly filled graves and secretly assembled by an iconoclastic scientist into a man-made monster who would turn on his maker and became a household word for Horror.

And in the ghetto of ancient Prague, Rabbi Judah Low invoked dark supramundane powers to cabalize a figure of clay into a simulacrum of life: Born to slay, the Golem, avenging Juggernaut of eight foot fury—the Jewish Frankenstein.

Warning Shadows were cast on the steps of the Devil's dais as a trembling mortal climbed Seven Footprints to (A. Merritt's) Satan.

From Bagdad a Thief set forth in the bronzed athletic form of superstar Douglas Fairbanks to do derring-do with giant undersea spiders and cavern-dwelling fire-breathing dragons; and in the Rhineland a blue-eyed blond-haired bare-chested Aryan *volk*-hero, *Siegfried,* clutching his trusty pre-Wilkinson sword-by-Mime in his sinewy right hand, rode out to conquer the ancient German version of the flame-throwing tank, Fafnir the Magic Drachen.

Professor Challenger (Wallace Beery as Conan Doyle's daring explorer) met his greatest challenge when he discovered a LOST WORLD of 49 different dinosaurs and one of these amphibious behemoths (a brontosaurus) raised havoc and razed London; then eight years later intrepid cameraman Carl Denham (Robert Armstrong) set sail for Skull Island with "the bravest girl the world has ever known," Ann Darrow (Fay Wray), to capture KONG—the 8th Wonder of the World.

Yes, there were giants in those days; actors, directors, cameramen, special effects artists who have become legends, some still living to enjoy their fame, others dead. Karl Freund, approaching 80, in February of this year in Holly-wood was honored at a banquet of the Count Dracula Society where he was among the winners of the 5th Annual Ann Radcliffe Awards in a retrospective tribute as cameraman and/or director for his contributions to such "Gothics" as THE GOLEM of 1920, SATANAS, DRACULA, THE MUMMY, METROPOLIS, HANDS OF ORLAC, MURDERS IN THE RUE MORGUE and Peter Lorre's first American picture, MAD LOVE.

A dead giant, Conrad Veidt, "the Lon Chaney of Germany," died of a stroke at the age of 50 in 1943 while playing golf on the course across from 20th Century-Fox Studios. Veidt was a one-man horror show. Bluebeard flowed in his veins (those fascinating veins that always pulsed in his forehead like unborn *medusae*) as he lived the roles of Gwynplaine, THE MAN WHO LAUGHS; Cesare, the claustrophobic occupant of THE CABINET OF DR. CALIGARI; Ivan the Terrible, WAXWORKS; THE STUDENT OF PRAGUE; ILLUSION; DER JANUSKOPF; SATANAS (1920); the pianist possessed by the murdering HANDS OF ORLAC; and Death in FUNF UNHEIMLICHE GECHICHTEN (*Five Weird Stories* or *Five Uncanny Tales* by Poe, Stevenson and Anselma Heine).

HORRORS of the Silver Scream.
What's it all about?

Lon Chaney Sr. shall not die.
Lugosi lives eternal.
Lorre lives in glory.
Boris Karloff is King.
And Christopher Lee is the Crown Prince of Darkness.

THIS IS THE message I was destined to convey ONE GLORIOUS DAY in 1922 when I, age six, saw a fantastic film of the same name, and cinematic sense-of-wonder seeds sprouted in my little sprout's brain.

Years later, when I had forgotten the title of the picture; or, rather, by then I had become convinced it was called *Eck*; I began asking cinemabuffs if they remembered ever seeing such a film. (To complicate matters, besides the wrong title I had firmly got it planted in my head that the role of Eck was played by that mass of freckles masquerading as a boy, Wesley Barry. I believe it was The Answer Man from the old *Photoplay* magazine who finally set me straight on the title, and Gray Daniels, the actor, who provided me just late last year with a review of the picture *and* several rare stills.) I had long known that Will Rogers was the star but—come out! come out! wherever you are—a *John Fox* turned out to be the ectoplasmic rascal called, according to information on the cast, not Eck but Ek.

Eeek!

Forty-five years after the fact it suddenly becomes transparently apparent to me that Ek was short for ectoplasm!

ONE GLORIOUS DAY was not strictly a horror or monster film but it did stress a strong element of whimsical fantasy and is worth rescuing from limbo.

Certainly Ek was a supernatural being, a kind of adolescent poltergeist half-materialized in quasi-human form. My childhood memory of Ek is that he was an astral imp who got heaved out of Heaven for being too mischievous; and at the beginning of the picture he came barreling down a spiral slide on his backside, shooting through a rooftop in wraith-like form and winding up in Will Rogers' living-room, thereafter bedeviling his reluctant host like an invisible ghost. Invisible to Will, Ek was translucently apparent to the audience.

FOLKS, I BARNUM you not: There was a Golden Age of fantastic films, half silent, half sound, and this period extended from approximately 1923 through 1936—thirteen magic Gothic years of quality shadowplays of the macabre, of men and women deformed in body and spirit, of werewolves, ghosts, ghouls, vampires, zombies, of monsters prehistoric and historic.

Quasimodo! Erik! Ygor! Frankenstein! Dracula! Renfield! Im-ho-tep! Mr. Hyde! Kong! Names that light up the marquee-de-Sade and throng Fright Films Hall of Fame, the stellar attractions of the "Ghoulden" Age.

What was the *first* horror or monster film? I've been asked this pregnant question a multiplicity of times during the couple of lustrums that I've been editing filmonster magazines. I doubt that anyone knows the birth date, name and place for certain; to this day I have no positive answer.

For a brief period, upon the discovery of a 1902 title, FRANKENSTEIN'S TRESTLE, it was believed that this was the first monster film. The misinformation was perpetuated as late as mid-1966 by a book, *Imagen y Ciencia Ficción*, emanating from Spain; but the disappointing fact is that when researcher Walter W. Lee Jr. checked out the American Mutoscope & Biograph production he found that Frankenstein was just a small American town which had existed around the turn of the century and the picture's plot simply revolved around the local railroad.

Incidentally, in 1963 I discovered a town of Frankenstein right here in the USA! Too small to justify a postmark of its own—its population at the time was a scarcely explosive 26!—it happened to be celebrating its 100th anniversary of founding at the time I found it, and a Mother Superior there, who had some community records in her files, produced for me a mimeographed *History of Frankenstein!* "I have heard the story of the Monster," she told me, adding with a twinkle in her eye, "and I believe some of the children in our school are descended from the original creature!"

The first known version of FRANKENSTEIN adapted for the screen from Mary Wollstonecraft Shelley's 1818 novel was the 1910 production from the studio of Thomas Alva Edison. A review of the time revealed— (But first we pause for the commercial.)

NOSTALGIA.

Actress Valerie Hobson has perhaps two claims to fame: She had the misfortune to find herself married, several years ago when his fortunes toppled, to one of the top figures in the Profumo scandal; and . . . I once frightened her half to death.

In the original FRANKENSTEIN, Mae (grapefruit-in-the-mug-from-Cagney) Clarke had played the bride of Dr. Frankenstein. For reason unknown to me then and now, Mae was replaced in the sequel (THE BRIDE OF FRANKENSTEIN) by Valerie Hobson. The year was 1935, and the same year valiant Val was also menaced (in THE WEREWOLF OF LONDON) by the lycanthropic Henry Hull, a Hull of a good wolfman and in fact my all-time favorite *loup garou*.

So Val's nerves were understandably unsteady. One night in late '35, I was in the old Filmarte Theater in Hollywood (the site, about 30 years later on, of the telecasts of Steve Allen's shows), and with the lights up for intermission I was walking up the aisle.

Suddenly, I recognized Valerie Hobson, seated toward the back of the theater, about halfway in from the aisle.

In my teens a pestiferous autograph bug, I immediately whipped out a blank card always carried for the occasion, and a ballpoint pen (a neat feat which only a time-traveling scientifictionist could accomplish, considering—small technical detail—that the ballpoint had not yet been invented, but still rested in a niche in Ray Cummings' Realm of Unthought Things).

The row behind Miss Hobson was empty so I sidled into it. Arriving behind Miss Hobson, I bent over her (interesting bosom) and, in all innocence of frightening intent, proferred her the card and pen (the latter have metamorphosed into the old-fashioned wet ink type in the meantime) and asked,

"Would you sign this for me, please?"

Had her shriek been recorded, she could still be collecting royalties on it for its subsequent dubbing in horror films of the succeeding 30 years.

BACK to the historical part, the Edison *Frankenstein* of 1910 and a review of the time: "The formation of the monster in the cauldron of blazing chemicals is a piece of photographic work which will rank with the best of its kind. The entire film is one that will create a new impression that the possibilities of the motion picture in reproducing these stories are scarcely realized."

The monster itself, by modern standards, looks ludicrous: Mack Swain (?) with a Phyllis Diller hair-do.

But "the scene in the laboratory in which the monster seems gradually to assume human semblance is probably the most remarkable ever committed to a film," reported another critic. The photo that survives shows a barrel-chested, possibly hunchbacked creature in rags who looks like he's suffering from delirium tremens, with wild staring deeply darkened eyes, broken twisted mouth, hands that might belong to a mummified Nosferatu, wild mass of hair on a massive head, matted chest to match a wolfman's.

Catch your breath.

Now . . . are you ready for this?

There are not one but *two* (count 'em) Forgotten Frankensteins!

Forgotten for 50 years.

Unrecorded in *any* film history of which I am aware (and I have studied more than my share). [Feb 69: In the meantime Carlos Clarens came out with his very fine *Illustrated History of Horror Films* and beat me into print with the following scoop.]

Unknown even in the pages of specialist monster magazines, a mystery to the experts, *Playboy* [Powell Sci-Fi] now astounds and scoops the weird, weird world of monstrophiles by the amazing revelation of—

LIFE WITHOUT SOUL

But first—the commercial. For Instant Nostalgia (just add years).

NOW fear this.

His outraged visage was horror incarnate: Bulging, bloodshot eyes fatigued with violet semicircles beneath them; the grotesquely exaggerated mounds of the cheekbones; the hooked-up, flaring, porcine nostrils; the rotted, jagged teeth, like the rim of an enameled tin can top opened with a ragged knife; the scraggly strands of dead gray hair hanging like soggy serpentine from the incredible pyramid of a head.

The description could only fit The Man Of A Thousand Faces and his greatest face, the face that launched a thousand shrieks—THE PHANTOM OF THE OPERA.

When Mary Philbin couldn't control her feminine curiosity and crept up behind Erik at his haunted organ and unmasked him, she opened a Pandora's box that was monster movies' finest horror.

The next time you meet a man or woman over 50 who is gray, ask them if they got that way gradually or it happened overnight from a dose of overfright in 1925. Long known to but an esoteric few, a closely guarded secret by the hair dye manufacturers, an entire generation's hair turned white at the sight of THE PHANTOM OF THE OPERA, and the fact was only carefully concealed by dint of tint.

You yourself may remember being a white-haired boy in the 8th grade.

Unless you were a white-haired girl.

Beyond that I wouldn't care to speculate. But if you're too young, ask your grandfather, he'll tell you. I asked mine—Robert (Psycho) Bloch—and he told me, "When I saw Lon Chaney's masterpiece, I gazed upon the face of naked fear. Within the past year I attended a revival of the same film. And despite the flickering flaws of this dated melodrama, the scene where Chaney is unmasked exerted the same monstrous magic upon a modern audience."

And Bob should know, he's seen them all.

Written some of the best.

We're the same age, which I won't reveal as there are "some things Man was meant to leave alone," although Bob has always been quick to point out to me that girls are not one of them.

No, I won't say how old we are, but there is a recurrent rumor among film historians that Robert Bloch played a midwife in THE BIRTH OF A NATION. I personally tend to discount this theory as I could never see Bob in drag but I have always been suspicious of one of those kluckers in the white sheets . . .

MEANWHILE, BACK AT Frankenstein's laboratory where there was being created LIFE WITHOUT SOUL.

The year—1915—dates this version of FRANKENSTEIN as a companion of HOMUNCULUS (the android) and the original GOLEM, the unholy three of the period 1914-1916.

LIFE WITHOUT SOUL was not just a Frankenstein-*like* picture but was actually based on the immortal melodrama of that teenage swinger, Mary Shelley. Acting on an exciting tip from a pseudonymous Good Samaritan known to me only through the mail as "Roman Soldier" (whom I wish to take this opportunity to thank publicly), I and two of my researchers spent a total of 24 man hours in the archives of the Academy of Motion Picture Arts & Sciences tracking down this information from the dusty past:

LIFE WITHOUT SOUL was a five-reel drama starring one of the five Standing brothers, the late Percy Darrell, whose "embodiment of the man without a soul adequately conveys the author's intent. He is awe-inspiring but never grotesque, and indicates the gradual unfolding of the creature's senses and understanding with convincing skill," wrote Edward Weitzel at the time.

While one Peter Milne reported of this Ocean Film Corp. production, "The producers have done well in introducing a prologue and epilogue which alleviates the gruesomeness of the action as it shows one of the characters of the play proper reading the book, and so after the brute man is through with his murdering it is pleasing to see that all the characters are still alive in the epilogue." Before the framework conclusion, however, we see "a medical student create a near-human body, in the shape of a big brute man who is blessed with the ordinary senses of a human being but who has few brains and not the slightest vestige of a human soul. The student suffers terribly for his invention. The brute man thoughtlessly murders his sister, murders his best friend, murders his wife, and so exhausts his creator that he expires."

Monster movies' oldest moral:

He meddled faith things Man was meant to leave alone!

He tampered in God's domain!

And the Other Frankenstein?

It was created during the 20s.

Overseas.

In Europe.

I don't have the title for it (unless it was plain FRANKENSTEIN) but I am assured by My Man in Milan, Luigi Cozzi, that there was a Man-Made Monster—Italian Style!

WHITE ZOMBIE . . . from Darkest Hollywood.

In his non-fiction book *Magic Island*, William Seabrook had set the stage for interest in the witchcraft and voodoo practices of Haiti. Garnett Weston whomped up a script for the Halperins (brothers, as I recall), who produced and directed this horror quickie of the undead. I believe WHITE ZOMBIE was about the last appearance of Madge Bellamy, who had been a favorite in the silent era, although Madge Bellamy Fan No. 1 will undoubtedly write in to set the record straight and list for me the fourteen further films Madge made: And when you do, dear Sir or Madam, please enlighten me as to whether she was any relation to Ralph. (I already know that Ralph Bellamy is some distant kin of Edward, the famed author of *Looking Backward*, the Utopian novel of the 21st century that caused such a political flurry at the end of the 19th.)

The main thing I have to tell you about WHITE ZOMBIE (which I remember as a dismal disappointment at the time but with the passage of the years and its star now eleven years dead, it's acquired a mellowing patina of nostalgia)—the main thing about WHITE ZOMBIE is this little anecdote about Bela Lugosi.

I met the old maestro of the macabre in 1953, three years before the final curtain on his life, the last act of which was tragic. "In the last year of his life," his fifth and final wife, Hope Lugosi, told me, "Bela and I were riding down Hollywood Boulevard, and as we motored past Grauman's Chinese theater, Bela noted the inevitable tourists gathered there in the forecourt, gaping at the cement squares with the stars' handprints, footprints and autographs. Bela leaned out of the window of the car and called, 'Hey, you people! You want to see a star? Look at me!'"

All flowers love the sun. Even a wilted "flower of evil," like Lugosi.

In his 70s, my friend Bela several times sang the blues to me—in his thick Hungarian accent—of how he bitterly regretted having accepted a flat fee of $800 (!) to star in WHITE ZOMBIE . . . and had lived to see it make about $8 million for its producers!

IF EVER A monster made a man, it was the FRANKENSTEIN of 1931. This classic, of course, established Boris Karloff as the successor to Lon Chaney Sr.

Born William Henry Pratt, Karloff had played the menace in many an earlier film (THE DEADLIER SEX, 1920; Kosmik Films' 15 episode serial of 1921, THE HOPE DIAMOND MYSTERY; Ahmed Khan in WITHOUT BEN-EFIT OF CLERGY; an African bandit in CHEATED HEARTS; an evil half-breed in THE CAVE GIRL; the ruthless ruler of Menang island in THE INFIDEL, 1922; PARISIAN NIGHTS of 1925 with B.K. as a sadistic Parisian apache); MAD GENIUS with John Barrymore; and in fact had given quite a Caligari-like characterization to his role of the mesmerist in THE BELLS (1926, with Lionel Barrymore and, though you may be too young to believe this, Gustav von *Seyffertitz*); but under the inspired direction of James Whale, FRAN-KENSTEIN was brought to life as an eerie masterpiece for the ages. (I am personally convinced that colonists of Mars, not yet born, will thrill in the 21st century to telecasts of FRANKENSTEIN from the Mother World. And, thanks to cryogenics, I expect to be around in 2031 to catch the 100th anniversary of the film's release!)

Colin Clive, the consummate English actor (who died, dammit, of consumption—the term for tuberculosis in 1937), was the perfect choice for Henry (in the book, Victor) Frankenstein, dedicated to the pursuit of unorthodox experiments in the reversal of eschatology.

Kenneth Strickfaden ("Elec-Strick") pulled out every trick in the book of special fx to bring to the screen the greatest mad lab since Rotwang's paraphernaliaful pad in METROPOLIS.

Dwight Frye was tops in the supporting role of the hunchbacked assistant, Fritz, the friendly neighborhood sadist.

And venerable Edward Van Sloan was never better than as Dr. Waldman, the mentor of the tormented Dr. Frankenstein.

"Dr. Waldman—" said Colin Clive in the threnodic tones of a man hag-ridden by a neurotic destiny, "I learned a great deal from you at the University, about the violet ray . . . the ultraviolet ray . . . which you said was the highest color in the spectrum.

"You were wrong."

"Here in this machinery I have gone beyond that: *I have discovered the great ray that first brought life into the world!*"

Dr. Waldman expresses skepticism that his pupil can bring life to the dead.

"That body has never lived!" corrects Clive. "*I created it, with my own hands, from the bodies I took from graves, the gallows—anywhere.*"

And, as Clive concludes "Quite a good scene, isn't it? One man *crazy*, three very sane spectators!", the electrical storm reaches its thundering heights, the fatal lever is knifed, the electrodes spark, the machineries of life hum, the snakes-of-fire spiral up the Jacob's ladder.

Decibels of macrophony assault the ear!

A paroxysm of pyrotechnics attacks the eye! And loud heartbeats later Clive is grasping the stitched hand of his creation and exulting, "It's moving! it's alive! it's moving! it's alive! it's alive! it's *alive!* it's ALIVE!"

And then he utters a blasphemy (?) which got by the Hays Office in the less sophisticated days of 1931 before God was reported to have died, but somewhere along the line got blurred over for home 16-millimeter projection and TV. Listen extra hard the nextime you see FRANKENSTEIN and you may just catch dampened undertones of "In the name of God, now I know what it feels like to be God—!"

Late last year, in his 79th, year, King Boris the Benign recorded a Decca longplay album (in scaryophonic sound) titled *An Evening with Boris Karloff and His Friends*. In the course of his reminiscences about his role as the misshapen humanoid with the accidentally criminal brain, he speaks of receiving letters from all over the world expressing sympathy for the monster, "and this pleased me no end, because it was exactly what I wanted to convey."

Shades of LIFE WITHOUT SOUL, sixteen years earlier, and the critic who observed of it, "At times Standing actually awakes sympathy for the monster's condition—cut off, as he is, from all human companionship."

Reviewing the new Karloff album in the Boston *Sunday Herald*, critic George Forsythe enthuses: "It brought back memories of Saturday afternoon shows where you watched the picture through your hand and the countless sleepless nights. Hearing the Frankenstein bit reminded me of having first seen the movie. My older brother took me with him to see it against orders and after bruising me with clutches of his fears (I had plenty of my own) defied me to tell our secret. My mother wondered why I wanted to sleep in a chair with the lights on and a baseball bat at my side!"

More about FRANKENSTEIN after this slight detour down mummery Lane . . .

***

"When Frighthood Was In Flower" was only a beginning. Come back next book, buffs, and I'll give you a sequel, "And The Tree of Terror Blossomed."

The Record

FJA . . . with an assist by?

*T*HOMAS ALVA EDISON *saved the world in a science fiction novel published around the turn of the century—"Edison's Conquest of Space"—in fact I am busy editing it for early publication by Powell Sci-Fi.*

Someone rather more unlikely saves the world in this story, which I first wrote in 1929. (To save you the bother of calculating, I was 13 at the time.) Forty years ago! When I sat here looking at the ms., trying to figure out when it was originally conceived, it was like a detective puzzle. I was thrown off the track by the section on paleontology, which was pure college course stuff (and only known use to which I put that one year at the University of Badwordly, I mean Berkeley, Calif., '33-'34: 150 words in a story never professionally published till now!)—the paleo paragraphs indicated to me authorship when I was 17, till I realized that portion had been added later.

Actually what pins down the chronology of the story is the last 2 words, which I won't tell you here and spoil it all, but as those 2 words only became famous late in '28—and hopefully still convey meaning to the majority of my readers today!—the story couldn't have been written much earlier than '29.

So basically it was composed when I was 13, "polished", I suppose, when I was 17, then published in a certain fanzine 3 years later by an editor 4 years my junior.

I wanted my teenhood collaborator's name on the story—and particularly on the cover—for a very obvious reason: his name would sell copies 10 times faster than mine.

But my friend didn't go for the gimmick. He once burned 2 million words of "youthful indiscretion" he was professionally dissatisfied with. I don't have that much pride—or that many words to spare: if I burned 2 million words I guess there wouldn't be anything left. (The next one who applauds gets it in the kisser.)

Half of you now know who I'm talking about.

The rest—

I've italicized the portion that my friend wrote into my story when he was typing the stencil for his mimeographed fanzine, futuria fantasia.

He said in my introduction to the story I could mention the circumstances surrounding his "collaboration" with me but he didn't want it played up big. Consider it played up little.

You'll find the name of the masked mystery manuscripter at the end of the story.

THE RECORD
by
FORREST J ACKERMAN

FOR 20 YEARS—for 20 long, horror-filled, war-laden years the Earth had not known peace.

Hovering over the metropolises of the world came long, lean battle projectiles, glinting silver in the sunlight or coming like gaunt mirages of gray out of the midnight sky to blast man's civilization from its cultural foundations. Man against man, ship against ship—a ceaseless and useless orgy of slaughter. Men, at their battle stations in the ships, pressed buttons, releasing radio bombs that blistered space and lifted whole cities up in shattered pieces and flung them down, grim ruins, reminders of man's ignorant hatreds and suspicions.

And gas—thick black clouds of it—billowing over the cities, seeking every possible egress, pushed forward by colossal Wind machines. But even when Victory came for the one side, often Nature, in one of her vengeful moments, would send the black gas flowing back to annihilate its senders.

Rays cut the air! Power bombs incessantly exploded! Evaporays robbed the Earth of its water—shot it up into the atmosphere and made of it a fog that condensed only after many months. *And heat rays made deserts out of fertile terrain.*

Rays that hypnotized, caused even the strong-minded to commit suicide or reveal military secrets. *Rays that affected the optical nerves swept cities and left the population groping and blind, unable to find food.*

It was a war that destroyed almost all of humanity. And why were they fighting? For pleasure and amusement!

***

IN THE MIDDLE of the 22d century, every nation had a standard defense. The weapons of war of each were equal—not in proportion to size, but actually, since man-power no longer counted high. *Pacifism had done its best but the World was armed to the hilt.* And now—though illogically—it felt safe—for every nation meant the same as if all had nothing.

Another thing—there was no work to be done. Robots did it. And there seemed nothing left to discover, invent or enjoy. Art was at its perfection, poetry was mathematically correct and unutterably beautiful—worked out by the Esthetic machines. Sculpturing had been given the effect complete, artists' hands guided by wonderful pieces of machinery. Huge museums were crammed with art put out synthetically.

And thus it was with the many Arts and their creators who grew stagnant in their perfection. And it was that way with the many sciences also . . .

Paleontologists had found, and articulated, and cataloged every fossil. The ancestor of the Eohippus, the little 4-toed Dawn Horse, was discovered; the direct line between man and ape established in skeletal remains; the seat of *life* itself definitely proved Holarctica.

And great bio-chemists, skilled in the science of vital processes, had created synthetic tissues and muscles and flesh, built upon the frames that had been recovered bodies with skillful modeling . . . even supplied them with blood and given them the spark of LIFE . . . so that Paleobotanists recreated the flora of a prehistoric era.

Again the ponderous amphibious brontosaur pushed thru marshes. Fish emerged upon the land, and the first bird archaeopteryx tried his imperfect wings for flight. In the regulated climates of long dead ages, fish, amphibians, reptiles, birds and mammals lived again for the edification of those interested in the very ancient—or who were amused with queer animals.

But that was only paleontologically speaking. There were the heavens to be considered. They had been: the stars and planets weighted and measured, their composition noted, courses plotted with super-accuracy. Every feature had been mapped—every climactic condition recorded. Life had been: the stars and planets weighed and graphed. And these were but first considerations. Actually, what wasn't known about the Solar System had not occurred as yet. But that would probably be remedied by a machine to view the future.

There was physics, biology, anthropology, zoology, bacteriology, botany— and 'ologies and 'otonies and 'onomies such as ran into figures which only machines could calculate.

A book could indeed have been written of the accomplishments of the super race. But this is of the WAR itself, and how it came about, and how it all ended.

***

STATED SIMPLY, IN 2150 the point of diminishing utility had been reached.

To the hungry man, the first course of dinner is wonderfully delicious, the second good, the third satisfying. Thru the ages people have hungered after luxury and leisure—but when he finds his food, a lot of it, MAN finds suddenly that it no longer appeals to him. In fact, too much is bound to make him sick and often disagreeable. He looks around for something else.

So did the people of the 22d century. They had all of the pleasurable amusements they wanted but it was all so intellectual. Everything was culture. They had surfeited with it.

And suddenly they wanted to forget it. All play and no work made MAN a discontented citizen. A reaction set in. Man was not completely civilized as yet—

THE WAR!

Twenty-one years the war raged. And scarcely a million survived. Bit by bit this million was whittled clown by the weapons of destruction to ragged handfuls of things that once had been cultured. Finally only one hundred humans remained alive—*and they kept fighting blindly, none of them realizing how close to oblivion they were crowding themselves and the future of humanity*—and they went on killing, killing, killing!

It is doubtless but what the entire human race would have vanished, leaving the world to the more competent, *though half-ignorant,* hands of the beasts, who fought and killed one another for self-preservation and for food—not because of madness...and who did not have books and talk and have *culture.* The human race would have gone, had it not been for the record.

***

THE FIGHTERS OF war's end, *leaving their machines and countries to congregate for personal combat,* were engaging in hand-to-hand attacks in the ruins of what once had been a tall and powerful city in the 20th century *but now lay crumbling, its proud buildings falling to the ground, sticking out iron-rusted skeletons to the sky*—and the city was LOS ANGELES.

HEDRICK HUDSON was fighting with phosphorized fists—hands enclosed in chemically treated gloves that burned as they struck the antagonist, insulated on the interior for the wearer—when suddenly the two of them were caught by a spreader. The other man died instantly but Hedrick got it in the side and *was whirled about sickeningly,* and survived.

He was lying painfully on something when he came to but felt too dizzy and sick to move. At last, when his head had cleared a bit, he rolled over into a sitting position and reached out his arms to grasp—a phonograph!

Big things came in small packages in the days of 2171 and a portable phonograph might well be taken for a weapon of some sort—which was exactly what Hedrick thought! And you can hardly blame him because no one in that generation had ever seen one of the things.

There was a curious story connected with the dying of music, concerning the days of 2050 when there was a movement to stamp out all symphonies and songs and things even slightly sentimental.

—But back to Hedrick!

***

HEDRICK FOUND the crank that wound the portable, turned it, reasoning that perhaps it gave power—and then—holding it away from him—he waited for rays to spurt out or something to explode.

Hedrick was disappointed. *After an agony of perspiration and puzzlement* he finally accidentally placed the needled arm onto the disk. The disk, he noticed, was black and filled with little undulations. The disk was like a wheel; so, Hedrick thought, it should revolve like one, shouldn't it? He pushed the starter thoughtfully and was more than surprised when the disk started spinning.

From the phonograph came music—music and singing! The lost Art had returned! *The Art banished under compulsion had made a comeback.*

Some man was singing on the record—in a queerly interesting and familiar tongue, the ancient English. The singer seemed sad, almost crying. And Hedrick was thrilled as he played it over and over again, drinking in the new experience like wine on the lips of a connoisseur. The voice rose, fell, lingered.

And Hedrick suddenly didn't feel like fighting anymore!

The music floated out over the tumbled ruins, descended to the ears of the other people.

AND THE FIGHTING CEASED!

They were transformed. They came running to crowd about the machine.

And there in that aged music shop they stood enthralled—music filled their souls. It was exactly what they had needed and wanted for many years. And it had been denied them. Music was the balancing force . . . the force that would help them struggle ahead, rebuilding the world. And next time they would be saner, they knew; the lesson of luxury had been learned and learned well. Never again would they leave all of the work to the machines. Now they would work and sing and play.

It would be work—hard work—for some time to come. But they had found music again *and that would anchor them to sanity.*

And thus was mankind saved thru a record—*SONNY BOY!*

279 teenage words contributed by Ray Bradbury.

The Man Who Was Thirsty

by FJA

YOU ALL KNOW *those couple of famous lines in science fiction: "The last man on earth sat alone in his room. There was a knock at the door."*

The brain blanches at the shuddersome thought: if he is Homo Finis, what can be knocking at his door?

Someone—I think it may have been Fred Brown in one of his super shorts— came up with a perfectly credible, non-frightening Who-not-What answer that was right there under everyone's nose all the time, only Fred's was longer because long noses run in Fred's family.

No, that doesn't sound quite right. Makes him out to be a blowhard.

Only trying to give credit where credit's due. (That way you avoid spending a lot of cash.) What Fred said was, that the knocker at the door was the last woman on earth.

The knocker—?

Sorry about that, Mr. Comstock.

Then—or so it seems to me at this late and lassitudinous hour—someone else came along with "The Story One Word Shorter Than the Shortest Horror Story on Earth." I am trying desperately to remember what the gimmick was. It seems to me they simply left one word out of the original, which completely and cleverly changed its meaning. I've tried leaving every word out, but—nothing. And you can't call Donovan's Brain for information at 2 o'clock in the morning. So, as the vampire said when he took a blood test for anemia, "I'm stuck."

Incidentally, I think this story holds some kind of world record: I once submitted it to Tony Boucher via Western Union in TELEGRAM form!

THE LAST MAN on earth, Szet, alone in his room. A shock at the door: a shaggy, slavering, bestial creature, half human, half lupine—a canine caricature of a man.

The monster—matted hairy gruesome imitation of humankind—attacks the last man in the world with fang and claw. An agonized shriek abruptly replaced by a liquid burbling as the man's jugular vein is ripped and his warm life's blood, red as the rays of the dying sun at world's end, slakes the crimson thirst of a Thing that might once have been his brother.

See Szet now: grub-pale shell of a man, white discarded skin-glove of a sapient homo, drained bone dry of the last ounce of human blood on the planet Earth.

Hollow laughter for a hollow man, a Halloween man, a juiceless, useless albino scarecrow.

The Man in the Moon shudders as the attacker, the bristly man-thing, blood of werewolves coursing in its veins, rises from its fallen prey, bays in the lunar face, lopes into limbo. The hirsute horror has knocked on the last door that can give it sustenance.

As its famine-distended belly digests its crimson contents, the man-creature takes human shape for the last time. Fuller is he than his maned and pelted cohorts of the crepuscular, corpuscular cannibalism.

He licks his bearded lips.

The last, fuller, brush man.

The House in the Twilight Zone

by FJA

S EVERAL YEARS AGO, *around Xmas time,* Esquire *magazine phoned me with a thrilling proposition: they wanted to pay me lots of money to give the world a word picture of my physical world of collected fantasy and my mental world of novacious eurons. I think it was 10¢ a word for 3000 words; title theirs—rest of it up to me.*

Their title: "A Few Words About This House". (The Ackermansion, that is.)

The most do-nothing, go-nowhere title I could imagine! Prosaic, lackadaisic—lousy. Not "The House That Sci-Fi Built" or "Is This the Strangest House on Earth?" or something dramatic and eye-tractive. No. "A Few Words About This House".

Oh, well—what's in a name? as Bill Schwartspeare said to me the other day.

They had some deadline of year's end so before, during and after Xmas I worked my tail to the coccyx for them, getting the completed article in under the wire. It was to be featured in an all-s.f. issue.

As you'll read in a minute, I also put up with hours of asinine photography, about which I complained bitterly to the editor, as I was not interested, even for their cash, in being made out to be an ass. A 2-page letter of reassurance came back! I would be treated with deserved dignity.

In the end I wasn't treated with anything but a Dear Odd John letter about how sorry they were that the project just didn't work out.

Just as commissioned by Esquire, *here is an Ack's-ray view of the House on the Borderland...*

A FEW WORDS About the Author:

Forrest J Ackerman is a 49-year-old native son of Southern California, Los Angeles born, who for 40 of those years has been a reader and collector of, primarily, science fiction and, secondarily, literature of the weird. Significantly, he edits 13 issues a year, plus an annual pocketbook, of movie magazines devoted to monsters; has won the science fiction convention's highest annual award, the Hugo, and (twice, once in tandem with Boris Karloff) the Ann Radcliffe

Award for top achievement in the Gothic genre; has appeared on radio, TV (*You Asked For It, Down Memory Lane*) and recently in 2 movies, THE TIME TRAVELERS and QUEEN OF BLOOD; and has reminisced 32 hours on tape for the University of California's Oral History Project. He lives in a 2-story home in a modern section of LA on the verge of Beverly Hills, a 13-room structure with triple garage...a house which Robert Bloch has described as "the only home in the world with floor-to-ceiling science fiction." It has been said of the garage (which bears the tongue-in-cheek sign Garage Mahal—*Son of Taj*) that "one could not park a pogo stick in it" because it too is packed solid with...science fiction.

***

THE EDITORS OF *Esquire*, having become interested in the interior aspects of the "Ackermansion," how it came into being, the rationale for its existence, where it is going, etc., have graciously granted me 3000 words to acquaint the mundane world with the facts of this fanciful establishment.

But first, the Commercial.

Please indulge me 300 words *a la* Alfred Hitchcock.

I want to emphasize that the owner of what science fiction film producer George Pal has called "the most interesting house in the world" (thank you) is not:

A freak.

A fanatic.

Some kind of nut.

A California crackpot.

Or a campy kinky Cloud Cookooland kook.

My greatest deviation from the norm may be said to be that I neither drink nor smoke.

I have never vacationed on Venus via flying saucer.

In other words I wish to go on record as not now being nor ever having been a member of the lunatic fringe. I feel this prefatory declaration advisable in view of the photo study of me which was made to accompany this article and for which I fear the worst. Explanation:

Esquire's lensman came to the house with an impressive array of photographic equipment and fascinating anecdotes of photographing stellar quality feminine epidermis. Any man who has shot Brigitte Bardot *au naturel* and held his camera steady, and induced Marlene Dietrich to reassume her classic seductive chair-straddling BLUE ANGEL pose, has not only my respect but my green-eyed envy. So I put myself completely in his hands.

But 1200 pictures later, when he left, and I mentally reviewed the *type* of poses he had concentrated on, I was shaken and unsure. In order to entertain 175 friends last Thanksgiving I gave 4 parties one night after the other (including one matinee) with such guests as Ray Bradbury, Philip José Farmer, Yma Sumac, A.E. van Vogt, Bert I. Gordon, Hulbert (son of Edgar Rice) Burroughs, Florence Marly, Ib (son of Lauritz) Melchior, Harlan Ellison, Ray Russell, Leigh Brackett, Alex Gordon, Carroll Borland and Robert Bloch and I have 175 witnesses to the fact that I did *not* greet them wearing a green mask with a 3rd eye. This is not to say that I lack a sense of humor, showmanship, etc., but I *definitely* *don't* lounge around in my living room in an heirloom in which Abraham Lincoln was daguerreotyped a little over 100 years ago, clad in a futuristic uniform (me, not Lincoln), toying with a couple of Buck Roger pistols! I don't even *like* guns except as inoperative museum pieces.

For science fiction fans it has been a long painful process emerging from the Ghetto of Ridicule into the light, even the Limelight of Respectability, and "crazy Buck Rogers stuff" are our unfavorite 4-word letters. So before proceeding to lay bare my soul I wish to make it crystal clear that the pictures were posed to the photographer's specifications and, depending on which are published, may not necessarily represent the true image of the owner of the house whose contents and *raison d'etre* are about to be described.

A FEW WORDS ABOUT THIS HOUSE

THIS IS THE house that Science Fiction built. In October 1926, when I was 9 years old, I purchased the then current issue of (still published) *Amazing Stories*, world's first periodical of what was then known by the portmanteau expression "scientifiction," coined by editor Hugo Gernsback from scientific + fiction. From that day to this I have never passed by a "sci-fi" publication—with the somewhat dramatic result that startles even me. When I was about 13 my mother beckoned me down into my basement den one day and said, "Son, do you realize how many of these magazines you've accumulated?" I said, "No." She said, "Well, I've just counted them...and you have *forty*!" The figure sounded pretty frightening, the way she said it. "Do you intend to keep all these and go on adding to them till you're a grown man?" she asked. "I guess so," I said. She gasped, "But do you realize how many you'd have by then?" I didn't, she didn't, I couldn't extrapolate at that time that at one time in the future an atomic bomb would burst and in the wake of its radioactive cloud would come a fallout of about 45 new science fiction magazines!

Anyway, my mother recently celebrated her 82nd birthday in my home and now we both know the consequence of 40 years of nonstop collecting of science fiction. I'm forced to eat all my meals out (fortunately I live within walking distance of what's known as Restaurant Row) because just last year I finally sacrificed the breakfast nook to another book room, filling its floor-to-ceiling shelving with the pocketbooks. And of course you mustn't expect to find food in the refrigerator: the frigid temperature there is ideal for storing film. I collect 16mm trailers from movies. Science fiction movies, of course; what else?

The dinette that became a pocketbook den has one unique feature that caught the *Esquire* editor's fancy when he visited me. He particularly wanted me to mention it. Alright: when I was a skinny introverted type I took a quixotic liking to sliding panels, hidden bookshelves, that sort of thing, as featured in such mysterioso movies as THE CAT AND THE CANARY, THE LAST WARNING, THE PHANTOM OF THE OPERA, THE BAT, etc. I always had a secret hankering for a hidden room. When the dinette was converted to book space, the carpenter, an imaginative chap, pointed out the possibility of creating an enclosed cubicle about the size of the Cabinet of Dr. Caligari by mounting one section of a swing-away bookshelf on hinges and rollers. I could not have more delighted been. I now invite unsuspecting victims into my ex-dinette and glow with ghoulish glee when they see a whole panel of paperbacks roll aside revealing on the other side—a life-size full color (blood red) lithograph of...the original Batman, Count Dracula! And *I* get a shock when I look at the contents of the cubicle: a 10' high Leaning Tower of Pisa of unanswered correspondence, unfiled clippings, unsorted stills and Jupiter only knows what else, which I laughingly refer to as "last week's work."

But now let's go about this tour of the Ackermansion in an orderly fashion.

You will know "this must be the place" when you see the fluorescent sign on the lawn with the emerald-eyed metallic black cat peeping over it. You know you are on Sherbourne Drive—but the sign on the lawn somehow has metamorphosed into *Space*bourne. You make a mental note to have your contact lenses reground at your earliest op.

As you walk up the pathway to the door, out of the corner of your eye you spot a homemade scooter out of the Ark, a contraption built from an apple box, 2-by-4, skate wheels and a sawed-off broomstick. In futuristic black lettering on the front is painted the now ancient legend: *Spirit of 1940*. Like Citizen Kane, this is sort of my "Rosebud" (remember Orson's sled?)—but that is a story too long to go into here. Suffice it to say the original model was created in about 1930 when 1940 seemed a century away.

You come now to the front door—and this is already half a day's project, just to read the various notices attached thereto. The largest and by far most foreboding sign (hand-lettered by a professional) proclaims: "WARNING! If you do not have an appointment, do not ring the bell—*if you value your life!*"

This is not meant to dissuade legitimate adult visitors from calling on me unannounced but it *is* necessary to discourage the subteen set from whom I would otherwise get no respite. Incidentally, youngsters don't realize that behind that carved wooden mask hanging to the left of the door is a live mike. It is not meant for eavesdropping on front door conversations (as I sit in the back of the house, working) but is merely a time-saving intercom system. However, it aided me in aborting a break-in one time, when I had the unique experience of sitting in my home listening to 3 youngsters plot how (convinced I wasn't home when I played "dead" to the doorbell) they were going to get into the house!

The house, incidentally, and sad to say, has been broken into 3 or 4 times. Not by professional burglars—any thief interested in cash or negotiable valuables would be out of his mind to burgle my place! Or, if he weren't out of his mind to attempt it, he would be after he got inside and got a look around! What I've collected might be worth a million dollars to posterity—but if you jacked up the whole *house* and spirited it away during my absence, the question is: who would you fence it to? It would be like stealing the Eiffel Tower or the Empire State Bldg.—where would you hide them or what could you do with them? My collection is quite safe from any except souvenir hunters who pocket a Big Little Flash Gordon book or something of that sort any time (a sick statistic) about 25 strangers are in the house simultaneously.

Are you ready to open the door and walk into the Twilight Zone? Alright, then fasten your antigravity belts and—No Smoking, Please! (Help Prevent A Forrest Fire.)

As you leave the world of reality behind and step into the phantasmagoria of Futurama Unlimited, you suddenly shrink in size. It *must* be that you have shrunken—it is the only explanation you can find for finding yourself suddenly inside a kaleidoscope! You have held those magic tubes to your eyes at some time in your life, turned them about and marveled at their riot of twisting colors. Now you find yourself inside such a 'scope. (When Worlds Kaleid!)

As you adjust to the first eye-dazzling burst of color, things begin to take on their proper perspective. You perceive that you are in a room about 14'x24' and that it is not a crazy quilt decorating the wall directly before you but a repository of a trillion words, enough books to stock a small town library—about 90% of the volumes still preserved in their original colorful dust wrappers. Drawn toward them, you discover the most easily accessible titles to be anthologies from A to Z. Then, if you are familiar with the top authors in the field—Isaac Asimov, Robert Heinlein, AE van Vogt, Arthur C. Clarke, Ray Bradbury—you note their complete works on the next most handy shelves. Beyond that the books fan out thru the whole spectrum of writers, mainly arranged alphabetically, with a few personal idiosyncrasy groupings such as Early

Utopian, Ancient Classics, Vanity Press Oddities, Numerical Titles (from *One by Karp* to *264 Trillion Miles in An Aeroplane*), Sci-Fi Femmes (*The Magnetic Girl, The Master Girl, The Immortal Girl, Girl Everlasting*, etc.) and—the shelf of Hugo Winners plus some very great personal favorites: *The World Below, Four-Sided Triangle, Summer in 3000, Childhood's End, Forever.*

In the front room there are also: numerous record albums such as *Aniara*, the Swedish opera of Epic Spaceflight in 2038; Orson Welles' panicking broadcast of *The War of the Worlds*; an Italian adaptation of Bradbury's *Martian Chronicles*; etc. There are many non-fictional books about the burgeoning Space Age and technical astronomical volumes. Mementoes and models from scientifilms: the spaceship from 20 MILLION MILES TO EARTH, a Don Post duplicate of Bud Westmore's head of the Metaluna Mutant from THIS ISLAND EARTH, a made-to-order model of the subterranean city's Warning Alarm from the 21st Century METROPOLIS. There are weird gadgets such as my "rhodomagnetic perpetual explosion machine," a rubegoldbergian hand-size device whose miniature light tubes flash intermittently on some kind of randometry principle. There are strange books with titles like *???* by Jean Doutreligne and *! ! !* (son of *???—?*) by Geo. H. Hepworth and rare books like *Some Women of the University* (100 copies), *Mars Mountain* (50 copies) and *Dawn of Flame* (5 copies only of my particular edition.) And there are toy robots, rockets, rayguns—gifts from sci-fi oriented friends who often visit *with their children.*

There are approximately 40 original scientifictional paintings on the walls, many of them used as covers on s.f. magazines. One day an additional 36 will be aerially displayed by ingenious utilization of 3 rods now decorating the subceiling space between the walls.

And the prize of the room, to me, is the priceless irreplaceable painting made during the last year of his life by the original maestro of s.f. art and the greatest s.f. artist who ever lived my opinion: Frank Rudolph Paul. Artist Paul's painting on the Oct. 1926 cover of *Amazing Stories* I credit as directly responsible for attracting me to science fiction in the first place, and the greatest favor I ever did myself was to commission the artist himself, about 35 years later, to repaint the cover for me—with several small but significant changes. The date became October 2026, the price, extrapolating from the trend of an ever-inflating economy, $2.50 for an average magazine. The original figure in the painting, confronted by a bugeyed monster, was replaced by a likeness of myself in futuristicostume. Instead of the original blurb about stories by H.G. Wells, etc., the legend reads: *This is Your Life Forrest J Ackerman.*

To step to the "dining room" you pass a small alcove in which are housed, alphabetically, hundreds of "one-sheets," those large colorful posters seen outside motion picture houses luring you in to see THE TIME MACHINE, KING KONG, THE INVISIBLE MAN, FRANKENSTEIN, FANTASTIC VOYAGE, etc. (Lacking and wanting: one-sheets for METROPOLIS, WOMAN IN THE MOON, HIGH TREASON, JUST IMAGINE and silents LOST WORLD, PHANTOM OF THE OPERA, LONDON AFTER MIDNIGHT, MYSTERIOUS ISLAND. I still don't have *quite* everything along these lines!)

In the "dining room" (quotes because no one really ever dines there) is a wall devoted to my favorite film, METROPOLIS: a montage of stills from the picture, displayed pressbooks, book versions, autographs of director Fritz Lang and cameraman Karl Freund, an original painting of star Brigitte Helm, etc. In this room is a model by master animator Ray Harryhausen of the *ymir* from Venus. There is one entire section devoted to the sci-fi published for teenagers, from *Tom Swift & His Electric Hiccups* to the public libraries' pets: the Heinlein juvenovels and Andre Norton's works. A corner containing the dark side of the coin of science fiction: the books about ghosts, demons, vampires, ghouls, werewolves, zombies, black magic and all the weird, mysterious evil occult horrifying aspects of fantasy. Paintings?—50. Another 50 could go on the walls if there were space to display them. As soon as I can afford it this situation will be rectified by the addition of something I've discovered called a Wingmaster.

Special display in dining room: *Frankenstein* vs. *Dracula*. The book versions. In the constant competition, *Dracula* is ahead at the present time by 5 copies: I have 40 of it (in French, German, Dutch, Japanese, in addition to English) to 35 of *Frankenstein*. But *Frankenstein* must, I feel, inevitably exceed *Dracula* in quantity for it was published approximately 80 years earlier and presumably exists in far more editions. Most amusing edition of *Dracula* to date the Japanese, known as *Devil Man Dorakyura* by Buramu Sutoka...better known to the Western world as Bram Stoker.

Thru a small room to my office. In the small room: the futuristicostume I wore on the sidewalks of New York and one day at the World Fair of 1939 when I went to the First World Science Fiction Convention. Draped on a mannequin, the quarter century old outfit is now embellished by a variety of spaceguns, topped by a macrocephalonic head of one of the Martians from INVASION OF THE SAUCER-MEN (one of a number—dare I admit it?—of stories I've agented to Hollywood.) More paintings, of course. And all the books I've been able to gather which have been broadcast, televised, staged or filmed.

The office. Neutronium could scarcely be more compactly packed. Where once stood a flower garden now blooms virtually every science fiction periodical ever known to have been published on the 3rd planet from the sun-star called Sol. Behind a sliding glass panel 200 Vol. 1 No. 1's of imaginative magazines since the first *Weird Tales* in 1923. Magazines from Germany, France,

Mexico, Japan, Sweden, Holland, Greece, Italy, South America, Finland—and in the artificial language Esperanto. (*Moderna edukata honao tre facile legas, skribas, parolas, komprenas la sciencfikcian internaeian lingvon, Esperanto.*)

Here, in the office, are 16 deep cabinet drawers jammed with uncounted thousands of alphabetized stills from the fantasci films of the past 65 years, from AELITA to ZEX. And a dramatic display of life masks of Boris (Frankenstein) Karloff, Bela (Ygor) Lugosi, Charles (Dr. Moreau) Laughton, Vincent (Robur the Conqueror) Price, Peter (20,000 LEAGUES UNDER THE SEA) Lorre, etc.

Backtracking to the—kitchen? Like Nature, I abhor a vacuum, so: all cupboards and wall space decorated with posters from science fiction and fantasy films. All cupboards filled with "fanzines" (amateur publications by buffs of sci-fi.) A onetime dinette now completely given over to paperbacks reaching back to the turn of the century.

Backporch? More posters, fanzines. We'll go out the door and to the garages eventually but at the moment: back to another downstairs area. Thru a narrow corridor lined with...posters, original artwork, plaques I have been honored with thru the years. As we pass the bathroom, an "in" joke: it's labeled "Odd John." The late Dr. W. Olaf Stapledon created a fictional superman with an I.Q. of 10,000 named Odd John, and producer Geo. Pal has announced his intention to bring John's autobiography to the screen (starring David McCallum.) In the bathroom, nothing much—yet. A photo of Boris Karloff facing the john, Karloff as the 3700-year-old living mummy Im-ho-tep, with an inhibiting red dimotaped message emanating from his mouth reading: BIG PHARAOH IS WATCHING YOU!

But all this tramping about the house must be tiring. Tell you what I'm gonna do: we'll reserve the rest of the trip till nextime. All x? That way, you can trip out twice—with this book and its coming companion, SON OF SCI-FI WORLDS.

The
Radclyffe Effect

by FJA

*N*OW IT CAN be told.
I am Philip José Farmer!
(And his wife Bette is pretty upset about it.)

I hope you realize that Acker-man breaks down in its meaning to acre-man, a man of the acres, in other words a Farmer.

So far we've got Forrest J. Farmer.

The initial "J" in my name has, of course, been a mystery for years.

Yes: José.

I could have stopped there, simply been José Farmer. But it seemed to need a little something extra.

So I added a fillip.

In a parallel world, I could have been Philip José Farmer. He made his sex-in-sci-fi pulp breakthru in '52 with "The Lovers". I could have beat him to a pulp if only an editor had had more nerve 5 years earlier.

In 1947 the editor of Thrilling Wonder Stories and Startling Stories *sent me as gratifying, if frustrating, a rejection as one could ask for. In returning "The Radclyffe Effect", known at that time as "World of Loneliness" (suggested by "Well of Loneliness") and later on "For Women Only", he said, and while I can't find the actual letter at this time, it is indelibly etched on my brain: "I would give a limb to be able to publish this unusual story but alas it would be too shocking for our middle-of-the-road readers." The roads must* roll! *Forward! And ever faster! That rejection simply meant I had acceptance by one of my peers (editor Sam Mines, bless his perception!) but that I was ahead of my time. Hell, that was nothing new; I had been since I was 9, and always hope to be.*

I'll let you in on a secret: I wrote "The Radclyffe Effect" for exactly one reason and that was that I wanted to be the first science fiction author to write a story revolving around lesbianism (a hobby of mine for many years: I collect lesbians. Flowers, anyone?). Perhaps I was the first, altho I wasn't the first into print, so my claim to fame in sci-Sapphiction is nil. I saw it coming; it came, but not with my name leading all the rest, chronologically.

I did & I didn't make it first on the s.f.-cum-lesbianism theme. "The Radclyffe Effect" was published on 8 July 1948 as "Mundo de Soledad" in the Spanish language in the Mexican science fiction biweekly Los Cuentos Fantasticos. *The thing that interested me most about the translation was to see what the word "lesbian" looked like in Spanish. To my horror: the most pregnant (you should forgive the anti-lesbian expression) sentence in the whole story had been changed to read: "Aquel hombre era un eunuco—!" Even without knowing Spanish I could tell that my lesbian had metamorphosed south of the border into a . . . eunuch! Actually it gives the plot the same effect—but it fractured me into tiny shards of tinsel. All I'm worth now in Sci-Fi History is an asterisk: He wrote the first science fiction story about a eunuch!*

My final version is neither about a lesbian nor a eunuch but an even more rara avis . . . so I guess the asterisk will be even smaller and the type will be microtype.

Anyway (if you're over 18) I hope you enjoy the story.

I shouldn't have stressed the age limit—it ain't all that sexy. Sophisticated, I would say. And there aren't any Anglo-Sexy words.

So—enjoy.

THE END OF the world came in a fantastic fashion. It never was satisfactorily explained. But then, to many, neither was its beginning.

The good earth abided, but what good was it, women asked themselves, when they were alone on it? Terra ceased being firma the black night it lost that all-important element necessary for man-woman bio-chemistry: the *masculine* element. Yes, without warning, on February 19, 197—, every male in the world suddenly disappeared from the face of the earth.

Including Steve McQueen, Richard Burton, Sidney Poitier, Elvis Presley, Rock Hudson, Ray Bradbury, Marcello Mastroianni, James Warren, Kirk Douglas, Hugh Hefner, Frank Sinatra, and the Beatles; from tycoons to truckdrivers, stars to bartenders, baseball players, boxers, businessmen and just plain bums; every mother's son, every boyfriend, husband, lover . . .

If you think you've heard or read somewhere before something somewhat like this, perhaps you have: Philip Wylie fantasied such an unlikely event in a unique novel which movie producer George Pal optioned, *The Disappearance*.

But being a prophet with honor didn't help Wylie out any when all the men in Miami disappeared; the Wry One disappeared right along with the rest. Presto. Poof. No special dispensation because of his IQ or auctorial Nostradamity. Nothing remained of that stalwart gray defender of Mom and distaffism but the cigarette that fell from his non-existent lips onto the scuffed floor of the lecture platform of the Florida Philosophers Club. A pale spiral of smoke rose unnoticed from the stub.

THE LIFE SHE knew came to a particularly shattering end for Cherilyn Munroe, the Cheese-Tease Girl. To the sex-moan of the sax the honey-haired beauty had undulated her way out of a silken sequined gown that was a second skin. To the primitive beat of the tom-tom she had bumped her bosomy, bottomy way—and her way was tops—out of her bra and bikini. Her moment was almost upon her, the climax when she would give her audience her all and feel like a jungle queen as the animal worship reached up to her and laved her receptive body with waves of applause.

The blue light fanned down from the balcony baby-arc and clothed Cherie's naked immodesty with the moribund censor's diffused hue of chastity. In the nocturnal shadow-light Cherie's cherries protruded like ripe purple grapes, ready for the heady wine of squeezing. "Miss" Munroe (married when she was 16, divorced at 19, currently balling with the show's juvenile lead) strained erect on one toe in the left wing of the skinerama palace and made suggestive motions in the vicinity of the figleaf bequeathed her not by Mother Eve but Madame Grundy.

The band crescendoed to the conclusion of *Sophisticated Lady* and Cherie, perspiring (pure perfume, according to her imaginative minded press agent), waited for her accustomed applause and approving wolf-whistles.

Her acclaim never came.

Instead, a terrific smash-bang insulted and unnerved her as the trombones, saxes, drumsticks and ensemble of orchestral instruments clattered unceremoniously to the floor of the pit. Fell to the pit's floor because the music makers who had been holding them a moment before—were no more.

And the applause from the audience was missing because the predominantly male patrons suddenly volatized, leaving only a flustered handful of females.

That must be taken back. It seemed that one lone man was a little later discovered among the women.

But the immediate reaction was: the ecdysiast emporium was thrown into pandemonium. Backstage, the stage manager, the stage hands, the comedians, the crooner, a *Life* lensman, a feature writer from *Help!* and a couple of stagdoor Johnnies simultaneously ceased to exist.

ALL PHENOMENON AND panic were by no means localized; they were world-wide and on a sanity-shaking scale. In a trillion streets, the same in Place Pigalle as outside Pinsky's Girlesque, unmanned cars crashed into female pedestrians, the fronts of buildings and other autos. Unmanned airplanes, trains and all manner of vehicles everywhere ran wild, wreaked havoc.

At Sing Sing the executioner's hand that knifed the death-switch vanished at the same time the killer tensed to resist the glory jolt. The rapist beat the rap by involuntary disintegration; the empty Chair sizzled and short-circuited. The sole woman reporter, "Ice-Gut" Gertie, a better man than Gunga Din and an unblanching veteran of war and gore, fainted dead away.

In San Francisco, as she pulled the trigger, a jealous wife's contact lenses popped off her corneas in amazement as she saw her philandering spouse *phffft* before her myopic eyes.

In Farnum Bros. circus a tragedy under the big top transfixed thousands when the belle of the trapeze reached out confidently to grasp her partner's wrists at the moment Eagle Man, King of the Air, ceased to be. She plummeted 300 feet to the soprano accompaniment of exclusively female shrieks and screams.

Ironically, Earth's first manned Mars rocket within moments of touchdown on the Martian surface, lost its astronauts to the universal mystery.

The incidence of hysteria was highest in the love nests of the world where, whether inhabited by white- or dark-skinned females, kimono-clad geishas or negligibly negligeed nymphs, every woman popped out of her Maidenform bra when her lover disappeared at an impossible moment. Hotels and motels became maelstroms of sex-madness. Bedrooms became bedlam.

Frightening things beyond counting happened when all the men in the world went suddenly somewhere out of it, as though they had simultaneously read, then reacted to Wylie's *Disappearance*; every man, every boy and un-born son vanishing in one fantastic, ultimately frustrating second.

BUT WAIT A second—you recall, perhaps, that *one* man was observed un-accountably to remain in the striptease show? Well, don't think the ladies in the theater were slow to notice him either.

He stuck out like the last man on earth!

True to their intuitive natures, the women had an intensified, mass presen-timent. Somehow they knew—without investigation or confirmation—what in-credible thing had happened. They felt it in their fluttering hearts that they would never again be

loved or lusted after
wooed or worried
charmed or harmed
or warmed
or alarmed by a

MAN.

No more babies!

Unless—

The crowd began closing in on Him like a black widow stalking her mate. The Last Man hastily executed a one-arm vault over the back of his seat and stumbled pellmell up the aisle. One aggressive matron caught hold of his sport coat, one desperate spinster grabbed from behind for his trousers.

The four-fifths empty theater took on the appearance of Bargain Day at Macy's, echoing to shrill cries of "He's mine!" "Don't let him get away!" "Stop him!" "Come back!" as the struggling male figure made a frantic dash for freedom.

Cherie sped down the runway fleet like the wind, fleeter than the rest by virtue—if it could be characterized as that—of her unencumbered figure. It was a credit to the manufacturer of her world-famous "z-string" that it did not slip or break, but he, alas, no longer existed to appreciate this moving testimonial to the sturdiness of his product.

The stripper scooped up the fleeing figure, ripping off his jacket in the process. Hugging him to her unfalsified double features, she tried to drag him to her undressing room, with the intention of restraining him there for "future reference"; but a dozen pairs of protesting hot hands grasped at his shirt and pants.

There was a monumental rip, a shocking tear. The shirt was shredded like wheat, the trousers torn as though by tigers' talons.

They let him go, after that.

In stunned silence.

As it turned out, it really was the end of the world.

You see: no Adam he. He wasn't the man we all thought he was. "He" was an ex-female, a make-believe male courtesy of a Danish doctor specializing in surgical remodeling, Jorgensen jobs in reverse, Christine-into-Chris operations. Chris-cross double-cross!

No superman, savior of the human race, but a pseudo-man who might as well have been sterile or a eunuch. He was a *she* where it really hurt: posterity.

Well of loneliness, hell of loneliness. A smorgasbord for the sisters of Sappho and daughters of Bilitis, a Shangri-La while it lasts for the gay girls from the isle of Lesbos.

But sooner or later womankind must follow mankind into limbo, and then it will truly be

THE END

Letter
to an Angel

by FJA

*E*ND OF JULY or beginning of August, 1954, I read the 18 words which were the genesis of this 3700 word story. The date is neither significant nor interesting per se; it just happens to be the only contribution in this collection whose origin I can peg down with such precision, and so I mention it.

Jerome (Twilight Zone's "It's A Good Life") Bixby was in a very literal sense the God-father of this story and I told him at the time if I ever sold it he was in for a commission. Technically, I never sold it; I have bought it myself; but don't worry about Bixby's commission—it's his.

However, I would never, I suspect, have composed a letter to an angel if, in addition to the "God"-given impetus of Bixby there hadn't been the added divine inspiration of Bradbury.

You might call it the Holy Goose.

On the other hand, you might not, because you might be religious, which I am not. I don't flaunt this fact, I simply state it. I don't think God is dead, I just don't think he ever lived. So, on my own terms, I'm not being blasphemous.

Oddly enough (if you are still with me) you are about to read a religious story. Therefore I must paraphrase Arthur C. Clarke's famous disavowal at the beginning of his classic Childhood's End—"The opinions expressed in this book are not those of the author"—and state that the author takes no credit for the God described in this story, which was the original fiction of some person or persons unknown to himself.

Shortly after reading Bixby's biographical notes in connection with a story he had in Imagination, I attended a lecture given by Ray Bradbury to a writers group whose leading light was the late Mark Clifton (a dear man.) Ray told that night, perhaps for the firsttime, of the incident from which he had developed his story "The Picasso Summer" (now a motion picture.) Ray was doing his thing long before, of course, people did their thing—and do you have the same trouble I do remembering what we all used to do before we did our thing?), which is to say he was catalyzing creativity, turning people on. I hadn't written a story in some time and I don't know if anyone else at that lecture ever wrote anything, or any-

thing that sold, as a consequence of Ray's unquenchable enthusiasm for express-
ing oneself on paper; but, from me, "Letter to An Angel" was the direct result. I
believe I went home, wrote it in one sitting, probably retyped it once, changing a
word here, a phrase there, as I went; and as far as I recall, I have not touched it
since.

I can't believe it but am suddenly caught up short to realize that 15 years
have fled since I wrote "Letter to An Angel". Oh, with what enthusiasm I wrote it,
how confident I was that it would immediately sell—and well! No mere pulp
market. It couldn't fail because it had a plus-factor built in: next year, in 1955, it
would be the 25th anniversary of Lon Chaney's passing. Magazines were sure to
recall; there would be a spate of features about him. When my story was laid on
an editor's desk, together with a variety of stills of Lon Chaney in his famous
disguises—well, this would be my first slick sale, a turning point in my literary
career.

My cup ranneth over when it was announced that Universal Studios would
film the life of Lon Chaney as an Anniversary offering. Now the story couldn't fail
to sell.

It did.

Despite the following fine quotes, which years later, on one more frustrating
attempt to find a market for "Letter", I offered to a short-lived companion to
Fantasy & Science Fiction magazine, a periodical whose brief existence resembled
the fruit fly, which came & went so fast that I must confess at this critical moment
I can't for the life of me remember its title. Had "Letter" been published in the
latter, it might have been prefaced as follows:

FORREST ACKERMAN was born in Celluloid City and saw his first Lon
Chaney film when he was an impressionable child of 7.

In his 40th year as a fantasy fan, Ackerman has created an impressive record
of over 500 stories and articles sold in the field of imaginative fiction. Nostalgia
for the Man of a Thousand Faces pours out of every Ackerman pore in this
period piece. With the aid of an eidetic memory for the Golden Age of the
Silver Screen, the man a million fans now call "Mr. Filmonster" has compacted
a lifetime of yearning for the good old movie days into this unique short story.
We believe you will find it Bradburian in its power to reincarnate the past, to
evoke again the matrix of yesteryear.

LETTER TO AN ANGEL is a love letter to the most beloved Phantom who
haunts the 20s' Hall of Fame.

In rejecting the story, Edward L. Ferman, Managing Editor of the publication
(not Encore, not Nostalgia, not Yesteryear, still can't think what its title was) said:

"Thanks so much for thinking of us with this story—it is a charming piece and it was a pleasure to read. The trouble is, that we're not publishing fiction as such in the new magazine. If we do decide to go ahead with fiction in the future, I'll certainly keep this story in mind."

And here were the principal other reactions it garnered:

Ray Bradbury: *"Fascinating idea. Some very nice sensual images. Appealing ending."*

"Quite gentle, sympathetic."—Gwen Cowley, *Fiction Editor,* Toronto Star Weekly.

Charles Beaumont: *"Honest, occasionally charming, and even more frequently touching."*

"A very tender, very touching story and the warmth and kindliness of its char-acters make it obviously written from the heart."—Curtis W. Casewit, *book critic and writer.*

John Drew Barrymore, son of John: *"The same day I saw Lon Chaney's film biography, I read 'Letter to An Angel'. The latter left me with a lump in my throat."*

Jim Warren said he loved it but considered it too mature for our (FAMOUS MONSTERS) audience of mainly minors. He said if he ever knew we were put-ting out the last issue, he'd publish it. (Under the title of "Monster in the Sky", of course.)

Well, I guess that's all I can tell you about the "legendary" Lon Chaney story. I don't believe a word of it, as far as the metaphysical aspects go; but I've always said if an orthodox Jew could play Hitler with hellish conviction, he'd be per-forming as a first-class actor. A first-class writer is something I don't recall having been called yet, and perhaps I never will be; but if my ability as an author of fiction is going to be judged on anything, I have called your attention to the handicap under which "Letter to An Angel" was written—personal disbelief in a fundamental factor in the story—and if you're looking to judge the best that FJA feels he can do, this is it.

P.S. The name of that nostalgia magazine was—P.S.!

THE DAY LON CHANEY DIED it came to Mrs. Roberta O'Toole like a banshee that this actor's death was to influence her life in some fateful fashion. Lon Chaney was not merely a movie star but more like a living member of her family. He was Timmy O'Toole's idol, just as young Tim was the shamrock of his Mother's eye.

All the time she was undressing Timmy for bed, worry-thoughts niggled and naggled in Mother's mind. How should she break the bad news to him? He was sure to be shocked. It was worse than the Christmas when you finally nerved yourself to confess to your youngster that . . . there is no Santa Claus.

Would her Mother's instinct tell her the right moment? Or could she skill-fully maneuver it some way? It would be cruel to leave him to learn about it at school tomorrow, from one of the members of his Monster Club.

The solution offered itself quite naturally. Timmy, the pajama fly neatly buttoned up over his plump little bottom, knelt by his pillow and said his good night prayers. After the family names and the President, he concluded: "And God bless Douglas Fairbanks, and Mary Pickford, and most of all God bless Lon Chaney." Then he turned and kissed his Mommy, and clambered into bed.

"Tell me a ghost story," he said. "With Lon Chaney in it."

Mother hesitated.

"Timmy—" she began. Her voice held a strange sound in it, moist and minory, like the time his little puppy, Clover King, had been run over. Sensing some tragedy about to enter his life, Timmy hugged his cloth-and-stuffings replace-ment of Clover.

"Timmy—Mommy has something to tell you. About Mr. Chaney. You know, people don't live forever. Especially people who work very hard. And Mr. Chaney—he died today. He—"

She said no more but helplessly regarded in mute horror what she had done to her little son. With all the love and best intentions in the world she had not been able to protect him from this moment. His china-blue eyes had gone saucer-wide. His naturally pale face had visibly whitened. Unconsciously he clutched Clover around his muzzle. His nose wrinkled, his face squeegeed up, and his breath escaped irregularly, as though he had the start of a sniffly cold.

"Lon Chaney . . . died? He *died*?" Disbelief, soul-deep, clogged Timmy's throat.

"Yes, dear. In the newspaper it said . . ."

"Show me!" His voice held the tone of Doubting Thomas, insisting to touch the wound in the side of his risen Master.

Mother moved into the front room, grateful for a momentary escape from her grim ordeal. "Jerome, have you got the paper handy?" Father handed the paper to Mother.

"How's he taking it?"

"Hard—worse than we thought."

Mother returned to the bedroom. Timmy sat up straight in bed, like a mar-tyr about to lose his eyesight. "Show me!" he said. "Show me where it says!"

Mother pointed to the headlines. The type was very large. WORLD MOURNS CHANEY. There was a montage covering half the front page: Chaney as Quasimodo, as THE PHANTOM OF THE OPERA, as the slant-eyed Oriental MR. WU, as the Pagliacci of HE WHO GETS SLAPPED, as the contorted cripple of THE MIRACLE MAN. August 26th, 1930, and Lon Chaney, the master of make-up, "the man of a thousand faces," was dead of cancer in a Hollywood hospital.

Timmy held the paper in his hands a long, long time. It trembled slightly. Mother said nothing. She saw tears forming in his eyes. She sat helplessly by, not knowing what to say in this crisis, what gesture of comfort or understanding to offer.

Then she saw something else forming in Timmy's eyes: resolution. He threw off the bed covers. "Timmy! Whatever are you doing?"

"I have to get dressed, Mom."

"Dressed? At this time of night? It's nearly quarter of nine, dear. Whatever for?" "Something."

"Well—" Mother hesitated. An appeal to authority: "I don't know what your Daddy will say. Perhaps I'd better go ask him."

Mother left the room in indecision. Timmy was busy shrugging back into his coveralls. Mother went directly to Father. Father put down his pipe. "Timmy is acting funny," she said.

"In what way'?"

"He's getting dressed. I can't think whatever for."

"Dressed? Let's see."

Mother trailed Father to Timmy's room. Timmy was sitting at his writing desk. He had torn a page from his Big Five notebook. He was laboriously printing something, nervously licking the pencil lead from time to time. When he was finished, he volunteered to show what he had written to Mother and Father.

Dear Lon Chaney. Don't be lonely tonight. I am praying for you, and missing you. I will never forget you. Please answer this if you can. Your Greatest Fan. Timothy O'Toole, 5327 Citrus Avenue, Los Angeles, California.

"Now I need an envelope. And a stamp. An airmail stamp."

Wordlessly, with a look of incomprehension to Father, Mother fetched Timmy his envelope and stamp. Timmy folded the note neatly twice, inserted it in the envelope, licked the flap, sealed it and printed on the cover: LON CHANEY, HEAVEN. Then he affixed the big red-and-blue five-center.

Again he found use for his parents. "Dad, have you a flashlight?"

"Why, what for, son?"

"I want to find my kite."

"At *this* time of night?" asked Mrs. O'Toole.

"Please—it's very important, Mother,"

"What do you want with your kite tonight, Timmy?"

"I need to send this message, Dad."

"To Lon Chaney? With your kite?"

"Yes. "

Mother turned away to stifle a sob.

"Don't you think it's a little late, son?"

"Gosh, it's already after 9 o'clock. Dad, what time do angels go to bed?"

"Why—I really don't know."

"I guess grown angels stay up pretty late," suggested Mother.

"Then I have to go."

Mother went to the closet and brought back Timmy's warm green pull-over. "I want you to put this on if you're going out into the chilly night air," she said. Gently she pulled the sweater over Timmy's head, and down over his little humped back.

IN THE DARK garage Daddy chased eerie shadows away with the pale beam from the Ten Cent Store searchlight. The amber ray fell on Timmy's home-made goblin mask with its hollow cucumber nose protruding like a tapir's snout and its mass of excelsior hair dyed blood red with Rit. The light touched his penny-a-day lending library of a baker's dozen of *Ghost Stories* magazine with their spooky covers.

Outside a chorus of crickets stridulated their nightsong: *crikadee . . . crikadee . . . crikadee.* Illuminated in turn were Timmy's "genuine" aborigine boomer-ang, procured from the catalog of the mail-order novelty house in Kansas; his precious personally scissored and pasted scrapbook of Lon Chaney pictures; the gunpowdery smelling shells of burned-out fireworks, still saved from the Fourth as fine mementoes of an exhilarating evening of pyrotechnics; and, at last, hung up on a ten-penny nail, his dusty kite. The bad tear in it would need repair before it could take to the sky again. Mother's brown stickum paper could take care of that.

A big Daddy Longlegs, his nocturnal affairs disturbed by this unusual activity in his demesne and sensing danger, hastily began to descend from the web he had industriously spun over the kite.

Don't step on it—it may be Lon Chaney!

If every kid in the country took the publicists as seriously as Timmy, no flack artist need ever worry about his promotion being successful. Yes, Timmy was convinced, a man who could make his legs disappear, who could grow a hump on his back *and take it off again* (that was a trick Timmy hoped to accom-plish when he grew up,) who could look like he was blind, who could throw real sharp knives with his toes and hit the bull'seye, who could slide down a tight wire on his head—who was to deny that such a god-like man might not also make himself look like a gorilla or a scarecrow . . . or even a spider?

Timmy, his own shadow wavering like some supernatural spectre, reached with a finger and cautiously picked Mr. Longlegs' web-strand out of the air. Gently he let the old grandfather down onto the oily gravel, watched him scuttle away to safety behind an empty orange crate. Then Daddy lifted down the Hi-Flyer.

They took the kite into the house. Mother insisted on taking it back to the backporch and dusting it off. Its rent was patched. Then Timmy took a safety pin and attached his envelope to the tattered tail of the kite—a couple of Father's Day ties that had seen better days.

Son and Father set out hand in hand for the ball park. Mother was agitated but Dad had nodded his browfurrowed quick short "don't interfere" nod, so she bided her counsel and contented herself with calling after them, "Try not to be too long, Daddy. Timmy isn't used to the night air and it's long past his bed time."

"Alright, dear."

"And *don't* let him overexert himself. The doctor . . ."

IT WAS HARD work to get the kite into the air; there was very little breeze stirring that night. Dad stood on tiptoes and held the kite way high as he could but every time Timmy would run off with it, it would abruptly nosedive to the ground, threatening to crack its wooden skeleton.

"Hadn't you better let me try, son?" Dad offered after Timmy had made half a dozen unsuccessful trial runs; but, no, Timmy had to launch it himself. It was his message and he was responsible for getting it delivered.

At last a vagrant breeze caught the kite and the ball of string unwound in Timmy's hands as the Hi-Flyer took to its medium and chased toward the clouds. Finally the string came to its end and only the stick was left.

The kite bobbed about in the vault above like a high flying phantom and Daddy thought he saw something flutter from its tail but he couldn't be sure. Little Timmy was panting from exertion, the freckled forehead of his flushed face spattered with perspiration. Mother wouldn't approve; in fact, Daddy wasn't too pleased with the situation himself. After about half an hour of the kite flying Jerome O'Toole tentatively suggested, "Don't you think it's about time to reel it in now, son?"

"Just 10 minutes more," Timmy said. "The message has a long way to go."

Moonlight made a white shield of the kite. Minutes passed in silence til, "He was a wonderful man," Timmy said. "He could do anything. I'll bet not even Dunninger or Thurston or *Houdini* ever could do Lon Chaney's tricks—like making a hump disappear."

"Yes," said Jerome O'Toole, avoiding to look at his son's forever-crooked back, "he was a great man."

When they reeled the kite in a few minutes later, the message was gone.

ON THE WAY home they passed Dorschkind's Drugstore, which was still open, and Dad said, "How about a double-decker cornucopia?" But Timmy replied, "I'm not very hungry tonight.

MOTHER TUCKED AN exhausted boy into bed a second time that night. "Do you think he got my message, Mama?" Earnest eyes looked searchingly to Mama for confirmation. Mama, her own eyes shiny bright with unshed moisture, bent and kissed her son on his sweet little mouth. "I'm sure of it, darling. Now, go to sleep—and pleasant dreams."

"Goodnight, Mommy. And God bless Lon Chaney . . ."

LONG AFTER TIMMY had been taken by the sandman Mother sat by his bedside and peered inwardly at the cinema of her own mind. She saw again his 7th birthday, when LONDON AFTER MIDNIGHT had been playing at the neighborhood theater and he had preferred treating all his friends to the show to having a party at home with games and prizes and all the trimmings. She had given him a dollar bill and he had proudly stepped up to the box-office window and pushed it through the wicket to the cashier. "*Ten* tickets, please!" Then he ushered his little pals and girlfriends into the lobby, down the aisle single file, and as near the front as he could possibly get. It gave Mother a headache to sit that near but she endured. She shuddered at the memory of the bone-white face Chaney effected as the London monster, with his eyes popping like olive pits out of hard-boiled eggs, and the scary teeth that sent shivers up her spine in retrospect. The man always frightened her but Timmy couldn't get enough of him. Cora and Fifi, the next door twins, however, were paralyzed with fear, and Mrs. O'Toole had to take them home before many reels had unwound.

She would never cease feeling jittery at the memory of that living death's-head that Chaney had somehow created in THE PHANTOM OF THE OPERA. She had actually shrieked right out loud in the theater and buried her head ashamedly on Father's chest when Mary Philbin slipped the mask off Chaney as he sat playing the organ. His outraged visage had been horror incarnate: bulging, bloodshot eyes fatigued with violet semicircles beneath them; the grotesquely exaggerated mounds of the cheekbones; the hooked-up, flaring, porcine nostrils; the rotted, jagged teeth, like the rim of an enameled tincan top opened with a ragged knife; the scraggly strands of dead gray hair hanging like soggy serpentine from the incredible pyramid of a head . . . But little Tim had screamed in pure delight and clapped his hands—and insisted on returning for the Saturday matinee. He was there Sunday too, sitting through two complete showings, fortified only by a bag of jujubees and an Abazaba. That Timmy! That precious little tyke!

Mother shook herself from reminiscing. She patted Timmy's tousled head, pressed a kiss to his soft young cheek, then went to the adjoining room and bed with Father.

TIMMY HAD A sore throat and running nose the next morning, which was a drizzly day anyway, so Mother decided to keep him home from school. He sat impatiently looking out the front window at the porch, waiting for the mailman. When he saw the rubber raincoated figure coming up the street, letter bag under arms, he ran and stood anxiously waiting by the door.

"Have you anything for me, Mr. Post-Toastie Man?" Timmy inquired expectantly.

"Why, no, 'fraid I haven't, young fella. Just for your Pop. How come you aren't in school?"

"Timmy has a cold coming on, I'm afraid," said Mother, arriving at the door to receive the mail. Pressing Timmy to her side she managed to suggest, "Maybe there'll be a letter for you tomorrow, dear."

"Who's he expecting to hear from? Little early for Christmas," said the Post-Toastie Man as he departed.

"An angel!" Timmy called after him.

The carrier halted momentarily in his tracks, looked back, chuckled, then continued along his route.

TIMMY PASSED THE rest of the day thumbing through his scrapbook for the thousandth time. Here was a bald Lon Chaney, confined to a wheelchair, in WEST OF ZANZIBAR (where the delicious Abazabas with their peanut butter centers came from)—yet here he had regained use of his legs and in fact was throwing knives with his feet!

This picture always made Timmy laugh: Lon made up like a *woman!* Imagine, a kind whitehaired old lady, old enough to be his own Gra' Maureen! That was a real funny one—Lon Chaney pretending like he was a lady. That was about the only thing Timmy *wouldn't* want to be.

Now look at those fingernails, so long they looked like those icicly things they called skalactites or something. Their length meant he was a very rich Mandarin and didn't have to work, so he could let his fingernails grow. Sometimes, and for the same reason, Timmy wished he were a Mandarin.

But most of all Timmy wished he knew Lon Chaney's secrets; how, from a hunchback just like him he could turn himself from Quasimodo into a wonderful clown with a back as straight as a school ruler.

THAT NIGHT MOTHER and Dad had a serious talk about their Timmy lad. Mr. O'Toole was of the opinion the boy would forget about his tragic loss and the letter in a couple of days and everything would return to normal. Mother wasn't so optimistic. "What would you think of writing an answer to Timmy?" Mother put forward the suggestion timidly.

"What! Me? Pretend to be Lon Chaney?"

"You could just say `Thank you for your kind wishes,' or something like that," Mother persisted.

During the night Timmy developed pneumonia. He tossed and turned and it hurt Mother and Dad to the heart to watch their son roll restlessly back and forth on his curved back.

In the morning the doctor thought Timmy might have to go to the hospital. The youngster insisted he would *have* to stay home and wait for the mail. Lon Chaney might want to hear from him again. Now that he was dead, he might even reveal his secrets—at least to his greatest admirer.

Timmy's spirits declined visibly when the mail came that day and there was no letter for him. Mother called Dad home from work at noon time and they had a hurried conference, as a result of which Dad agreed that he would write a letter from Lon Chaney that evening. That it was delivered the next day was too much for the brokenhearted O'Tooles to bear, because--

Timmy O'Toole died in his sleep shortly before midnight.

THE MIGHTIEST AND most majestic of all clocks, which tolls the time in Heaven, has a bell of supernal perfection fashioned of purest gold with tongue of solid silver. As it pealed forth the hour of 12 throughout the Kingdom, Timmy O'Toole approached the Pearly Gates. He did not even notice as St. Peter swung them wide for him: his gaze was intent on the angels, and he was seeking one in particular as the harps played promises of Paradise and the Heavenly Choir sang "Hallelujah!" to welcome this big-hearted little soul into the Father's Mansion.

Then Timmy's heart leapt right into his throat. *Timmy recognized HIM.* His beloved idol sat on a magnificent throne and he wore the most impressive make-up of all. He was giant tall; and a tremendous beard, white as the sun at noon, flowed from his infinitely kind face to the floor of polished ivory. And an astonishing circle of light shone over his head—a thrilling effect that Timmy had never seen in any movie.

"Come here, my boy," *he* bade him, and he spoke with the resonant volume of the organ that always accompanied his pictures.

"Lon Chaney!" Timmy cried with a cry of ineffable joy and sprang forward and leaped into his lap.

And the Good Lord's eyes were bright with understanding as He laid His arm 'round Timmy's shoulders. And Timmy's back miraculously straightened and his hated hump disappeared as God touched him but Timmy did not even notice he was free of his deformity.

His face was turned upward in adoration. "Lon Chaney!" he breathed.

And God smiled.

READERS OF THE WORLDS, WRITE!

The anthologist of this volume is anxious to hear from YOU!

How did you enjoy the overall contents?

What few stories did you like the most?

What few stories did you like the least?

Would you like to see a collection of FJA's own approximately 50 stories? (Starting in 1929!)

Would you like to see an Ackermanthology of a selection of Mr. Science Fiction's favorite sci-fi stories of the past 75 years? Favorite Fantasy?

Any requests for the anthologist?

Forrest J Ackerman may be contacted directly at:

> 2495 Glendower Avenue
> Hollywood, CA 90027-1110
> FAX: 323-664-5612

 # SENSE OF WONDER PRESS

Ackermanthology: Millennium Edition

From Dennis Palumbo's three page tale of truly diabolical revenge to Jill Taggart's one page epiphany on leadership and victory, the original *Ackermanthology* will arouse your sense of wonder! Stories by Ray Bradbury, Isaac Asimov, and H. G. Wells are nestled comfortably among lesser known authors such as Oliver Saari, David A. Kyle, Anne Orhelein and others. Foreword by John Landis.

6x9, Paper, 306 pp., $14.95, ISBN 0-9187360-25-0, *Available Now*

Rainbow Fantasia, 35 Spectrumatic Tales of Wonder

A huge and colorful collection of classic tales (many from sci-fi's pulp tradition) including stories by Mary Elizabeth Counselman, Ray Cummings, Donald Wandrei, Gustav Meyrink, A. E. van Vogt, Frank Gruber, Nat Schachner, Eli Coulter, Nictzin Dyalhis, Robert W. Chambers and Brad Linaweaver.

6x9, Paper, 576 pp., $23.95, ISBN: 0-9187360-36-6, *Available Now*

CLAIMED by Francis Stevens

You'll never feel the same about the beach or the sea again! An eerie classic, chosen by FJA. Gertrude Barrows Bennett, the mysterious woman who wrote under the pen name "Francis Stevens" has been hailed as the greatest female fantasy writer between Mary Shelly and C.L. Moore!

6x9, Paper, 192 pp., $14.95, ISBN: 0-918736-37-4, *Available Now*

Famous Forry Fotos

Kodakerman Memories! Famous Forry Fotos, from birth to 2000—over 70 years of photos from Forry at the Ackermansion, and before: photos of science fiction, fantasy and horror writers, film greats and more, with Mr. Sci-Fi as your guide! Friends, family, monsters, some great "Con" memories and much more!

8½x11, Paper, 117pp., Illustrated, $14.95, ISBN: 0-918736-32-3, *Available Now*

Metropolis: 75th Anniversary Edition

Lavishly "Stillustrated" with fotos from Fritz Lang's film and Forrest J Ackerman's 75 years of Metropolis memorabilia. Hardcover limited to 500 copies, signed & numbered.

8½x11, HC, 242 pp., Illus., Limited Ed., $45.00/prepub, $??.00 after
   ISBN: 0-918736-34-X, **Available Now**
8½x11, Paper, 242 pp., Illus., $16.95, ISBN: 0-918736-35-8, **Available Now**

LON OF 1000 FACES

Forrest J Ackerman's long out-of-print classic on silent film great Lon Chaney, Sr. Contains 100's of stills, as well as many tributes, biographical sketches and appreciations by Robert Bloch, Ray Bradbury, Vincent Price and many others.

8½x11, Paper, 296 pp., Illustrated, ISBN 0-918736-39-0, $21.95, **Available Now**

Sci-Fi WOMANthology

Classic stories by pioneering women writers in the genre edited and with introductions by Forrest J Ackerman and Pamela Keesey. Includes an extensive checklist of the editors' favorite genre contributions by women writers.

6x9, Paper, Illustrated, ISBN 0-918736-33-1, $14.95, Spring/Summer 2002

Dr. Acula's Thrilling Tales of the Uncanny

"Brush your hair with epoxy resin before reading this creepy collection, otherwise you're liable to lose it when your hair stands on end."—Dr. Acula. With a preface by Pamela Keesey.

6x9, Paper, ISBN 0-918736-30-7 $14.95, Summer 2002

Please check our website (below) for a complete listing of stories/authors in our anthologies.

SENSE OF WONDER PRESS BOOKS ARE DISTRIBUTED IN THE U.S. BY INGRAM DISTRIBUTORS

Sense of Wonder Press

BROWSE, ORDER, RESERVE, HANGOUT

http:\\www.senseofwonderpress.com

Find a complete listing of stories for all our "Ackermanthologies," updates on title availability and payment information. Or write to us at:

    Sense of Wonder Press
    113 N. Washington Street, Box 347
    Rockville, Maryland 20850

email: info@senseofwonderpress.com

www.ingramcontent.com/pod-product-compliance
Lightning Source LLC
Chambersburg PA
CBHW020416180626
46812CB00003B/1004